D0459677

Previous Books by Stanley Elkin

Pieces of Soap: Essays
The MacGuffin
The Magic Kingdom
George Mills
Criers and Kibitzers, Kibitzers and Criers
The Rabbi of Lud
The Six-Year-Old Man
The Living End
Early Elkin
The Franchiser
Searches and Seizures: Three Novellas
Boswell
A Bad Man
The Dick Gibson Show
The Coffee Room

Van Gogh's Room at Arles

For Molly

Van Gogh's Room at Arles

Three Novellas

Stanley Elkin

Hyperion • New York

Book design by Margaret M. Wagner

Library of Congress Cataloging-in-Publication Data
Elkin, Stanley
Van Gogh's room at Arles : three novellas /
by Stanley Elkin.
p.   cm.
Contents: Her sense of timing—Town crier exclusive,
confessions of a Princess manqué—Van Gogh's room at
Arles.
I. Title.
PS3555.L47V36   1993
813'.54—dc20   93-24802
                                                              CIP

FIRST EDITION

10   9   8   7   6   5   4   3   2   1

Contents

Her Sense of Timing

"All I can say," Schiff told Claire, "is you've got a hell of a sense of timing, a *hell* of a sense of timing. You've got a sense of timing on you like last year's calendar."

"Timing, Jack? Timing? Timing has nothing to do with it. Time maybe, that it's run out. This has been coming for years."

"You might have told a fella."

"Oh, please," Claire said.

"Oh yes, you might have prepared a chap."

"I just did."

"Given *fair* warning I mean. Not waited till the last minute."

"Two weeks' notice?"

"Ain't that the law?"

"For the help."

"You *were* the help, Claire."

"Not anymore."

"I can't afford to be single."

"Tough," she said.

"Tough," Schiff said. "Tough, yeah, that should do me."

"All you ever think you have to do is throw yourself on the mercy of the court."

"Well, ain't mercy of the court the law too?"

"For juveniles and first offenders. You're close to sixty."

"So are you."

"I don't talk about 'fair.' "

"Very refined, very grown-up. Come on, Claire, put down the suitcases."

"No. The others are all packed. I'll send UPS for them when I'm settled."

"I won't let the bastards in. The door to this house is barred to the sons of bitches."

"Oh, Jack," Claire said, "the things you

say. Stand up to delivery people? You? Painters and repair-
men? But you're such a coward. The man who comes to
read the meter terrifies you. Tradesmen do, the kid who
brings the pizza."

"Why are they blue collar? This is America, Claire."

"Is that my cab?" She looked down out their bedroom
window and waved.

"This is really going to happen?"

"It's happened," she said, leaned over the bed to kiss her
husband on the cheek, and just upped and walked out the
door on their thirty-six-year marriage.

"Wait, hey wait," Schiff called after her, taking up his
walker and moving toward the window. By the time he got
around the bed Claire was already handing the driver two
big valises. Schiff, bracing his hands on the sill, stood before
the window in his shorty pajamas. "Excuse me," he called
to the man. "Sir? Excuse me?" The fellow shaded his eyes
and looked up. "Where are you taking her?"

The driver, a young man in his twenties, looked at Claire,
who shook her head. "Sorry," he said, "destinations between a fare and her cabbie are privileged information."

Schiff held up his walker. "But I'm a cripple, I'm handicapped," he said. "I'm close to sixty."

"Sorry," the man said, shut the trunk in which he'd put
Claire's suitcases, and got into his cab.

"That," Schiff called after the taxi, "was no fare, that was
my wife."

And thought, Her sense of timing, her wonderful, world-
class, championship sense of timing. Leaving me like that.
Just like that. Just get up and go. Just got up and gone. Don't
tell *me* she forgot tomorrow's the party.

Schiff's annual party for his graduate students, though by
no means a tradition—Schiff, who was a professor of Political Geography, had started it up only two or three years
ago when, during a fit like some cocktail made of equal
parts of sentimentality and pique, he realized that though it
was barely a few years until retirement he had had only a
stunningly scant handful of students who ever wrote him

once they were done with their studies, let alone any who might regard him as a friend—had become, at least in Schiff's diminishing circles, one of the hottest tickets in town. Admittedly, it was not like Creer's annual anti-Thanksgiving Day bash, or one of Beverly Yaeger's famous feminist dos in honor of the defeat anywhere of a piece of anti-abortion legislation, but unlike the old manitou he could not claim Indian blood or, unlike Ms. Yaeger, even the menstrual stuff. Unlike any of his fabulous colleagues he was axless, out of it, their long loop of rage, degrees below the kindling point of their engagement. Outside all the beltways of attention and the committed heart. In point of fact so *un*committed that one of the next things he would do, once he struggled back to bed, would be to call his guests and explain that his wife had left him suddenly, the party was off.

They'd understand. He did none of the work for it himself, never had—my handicap, my handicap and footicap, he liked to say—and would simply set forth for them the now impossible logistics, freely giving Claire the credit for the splendid spread they put out—— not one but *three* roasts, rare through dark medium, turkey, sliced cheeses like slivery glints of precious metals, pâtés riddled with gemmy olives and crumbs of spice, breads and pastries, cakes and ale. Put out and gave away, in doggy bags and Care packages, Schiff—who addressed them in class as "Mister," as "Miss"—avuncularizing at them and propped up in the doorway forcing the uneaten food on his departing, liquored-up guests like some hearty, generous Fezziwig. Schiff's all-worked-and-played-out Bob Cratchits, his pretty young Xmas Carols. It was a strain. It was more. Not just another side but a complete counterfeit of his character and, while he generally enjoyed the masquerade, he couldn't help but wonder what his students made of his impersonation. Many sent thank-you notes, of course—a form Schiff regarded as condescending—but few ever actually mentioned the parties to him because the only other times they saw each other were in class, where it was business as usual, where the smoking lamp was never lit, and it was Mister and Miss all over again.

What he feared for was his dignity, protecting that like some old-timey maiden her virginity. The annual party, to Schiff's way of thinking, was pure ceremony, obligatory as hair let down for Mardi Gras, candy and trinkets tossed from the float, insignificant gelt on the anything-goes occasions. But only, they would surely see, *voluntarily* obligatory, obligatory for as long as his mood was up for it. This was what the great advantage of his age came down to. Added to the other great advantage of his disenabling condition, Schiff practically had it made. A cheerful, outgoing older man might have genuinely enjoyed it. Bargains struck with the Indians for Manhattan, a kind of openhanded heartiness done strictly on spec. Even—he's thinking about his rough bluff brusqueness with them—the flirting—the men as well as the women—— Schiff's sandpapery humours. (Well, it was in the nature of the profession to flirt, all profs engaged in some almost military hearts-and-minds thing.) Schiff *would* have enjoyed it. He *had* enjoyed it. In the days before he'd been struck down, when even at twenty-five, when even at forty and for a few years afterward, all this curmudgeon business had been merely a dodge, style posturing as temperament and all, he suspected (almost remembered) the customary mishmash of mush skin-deep beneath it. Because, again, the only thing that stood between him and his complete capitulation—he could not revert to what he had not really come from in the first place—to type, was that brittle dignity he had practically lain down his life for. Pretty ironic, he'd say, even in as ironic a world as this one, to have had stripped from him (and by mere pathology) the physical bulwark of his great protective formality and fastidiousness. (Completely toilet trained, according to family legend, at nine months.)

And now he has a choice to make: whether to wiggle-waggle on the walker (with no one in the house to help him should he fall) the thirty or so steps to the bathroom, or to scoot crabwise up along the side of his bed toward the nightstand, where he keeps his urinal, Credé his bladder by pressing up on it with his good hand, priming piss like water from a pump till it flowed, not in anything like a stream but in nickel-and-dime dribs and petty drabs from his stunted, retracted penis (now more like a stuck elevator button than a shaft). They tell him he must use his legs or lose them, but it's his nickel, his dime—— his, he means, energy, and he sidesaddles the bed, bouncing his fists and ass on the mattress in some awkward, primitive locomotion somewhere between riding a horse and potato-racing. Vaguely he feels like a fellow in a folk song, a sort of John Henry, or as if he is somehow driving actual stitches into the bedding and thinks, and not for the first time, that he ought to be an event in the Olympics.

His head within striking distance of the head of the bed, Jack Schiff laid into gravity and fell back on the pillow, then, with his palms under his left thigh, he pulled his almost useless leg up after him. The right one still had some strength and he kicked it aboard, leaned over to open the door to the nightstand, and took out the green plastic basin and thin urinal, angled, tipped at its neck (always reminding Schiff somehow of a sort of shellfish, indeed actually smelling like one, of the shore, its filthy musks and salts and iodines, its mixed and complex seas gone off like sour soup). It's into this, once he's snapped back its plastic lid, Schiff must thread his penis, hold it in place, pushing up on the bottom of his abdomen, jabbing and jabbing with his thumb until he feels the burn. (Taking pleasure not just in the release of his water but in the muted, rain-on-the-roof sound it makes once it begins to come.) Only recently has he noticed the bruise on the skin of his lower stomach where he's been punching himself silly. He examines it now, reading the yellowish black and blue like a fortune-teller. What, thought Schiff, a piece of work is man, and blotted at his pee with a Kleenex. Then he measured his output in cubic centimeters on the bas relief plastic numerals outside the urinal. His secret wish was to piss a liter, but the most he's ever done was six hundred cubic centimeters. This time it's

under two hundred. Not even average, but he's relieved because the fact is Schiff can't stand even 75 cc of discomfort,
not even fifty. For a man as generally incapacitated and uncomfortable as Schiff is he's a sort of snob, but pissing is
something he can do something about. Schiff is very conscientious about pissing.

And only now does his new situation have his full attention.

For the truth is Schiff has always been very organized.
Even before he was a cripple he was organized. (Schiff believes in a sort of cripple's code—— that one must never do
anything twice. It's a conservation-of-energy thing, an anti-
entropy thing, scientific, almost Newtonian, and now, in an
age of raised environmental consciousness, recycling, of
substitution and cut corners, the golden age, he supposes,
of the stitch in time, of taken pains and being careful in the
streets, he finds—for a cripple—he's not only, given his
gait, in step with his times but practically a metaphor for
them. It's a conservation-of-energy thing and a nine-
months-of-toilet-training thing.)

Of course—he's thinking of his new situation, he's thinking of the carefully trained guns of his full attention, he's
thinking of the inescapable fallout of the world, he's thinking of synergy, of the unavoidable garbage created not only
out of every problem but out of each new solution—the
pisser—he knew this going in, he couldn't help himself, by
nature he was a list maker—will have to be emptied, especially this particular pisser with its almost caramel-colored
urine. (Schiff prefers a clearish urine, something in a dry
white wine, and what, he wonders, is the liquid equivalent
of anal retentive?) This had been—even with the handle of
the urinal attached to the walker's wide aluminum crossrail
his wild limp would not have permitted him to take five
steps without setting up the dancing waters, a rough churn
of spilled piss—Claire's job, and though he doesn't really
blame Claire for leaving him—had their roles been reversed,
take *away* his nine-month toilet training and his incremental,
almost exponential squeamishness, he'd have bugged out on

her long ago—he understands that, should this thing stick, in the future he will have to think twice, three times, more, before using the urinal. (Or maybe, thinks the list maker, he can arrange for a *case* of urinals, keep them in the night-stand, turn it into a kind of wine cellar. Nah, he's kidding. Well he is and he isn't. It's something to think about, another thing he'll have to run past the cripple's code, the garbage potential latent in all solutions.)

But he set all that aside for the moment and took up the phone to see if he could get some idea where he stood.

The dispatcher at the cab company—Schiff had made a mental note of the number on Claire's taxi—said he'd like to help but the computer was down. (Schiff, who didn't believe him, wondered what the fallout would come to from such solutions.) He checked with the airlines, but since he couldn't give them Claire's destination, let alone times or flight numbers, they couldn't help him. (Couldn't or wouldn't. He insisted that even without the specifics they ought to be able to punch up her name on their computers. Claire Schiff, he said to one agent, how many Claire Schiffs could there be riding on their airplanes? She was his wife, for God's sake, and he didn't know of another Claire Schiff in all of America. Suppose this had been a *real* emergency. A *real* emergency? "Sure. If the plane went down, God forbid. If there'd been a hijacking." "If the plane went down, if there's been a hijacking?" the agent said slyly. "God forbid," said Schiff. "She's your wife," another agent said, "and you don't even have a destination for her?" "Well, my girl." "Oh, now she's your 'girl.' " "My daughter," he said, "we think she's run off." "Your daughter, is she?" the agent said. "Listen, you," Schiff, getting defensive, said aggressively, "I happen to be a Frequent Flyer on this airline. I have your platinum card, more than a hundred thousand uncashed miles and enough bonus points to practically charter my own goddamn plane. Either look up Claire Schiff for me or let me speak to your supervisor." The son of a bitch hung up on him. They'd whipped him. "I have to find her," he told the very last agent he spoke to, "I'm disabled and we're giving a party.") He probably spent thirty or forty dollars on long-distance fishing expeditions. Their friends, proclaiming no knowledge of her plans, went on fishing expeditions of their own. "No," he'd say, putting them off, "no trouble. As for myself, my condition's pretty much unchanged, but I think Claire may be getting a little spooked. Well," he said, still fairly truthfully, "we're both getting on. Hell," he said, "I'm close to sixty. So's Claire, for that matter. Maybe she thinks she won't be able to lift me much longer." But finally as cavalier with the truth as he'd been with the airline son of a bitch who'd hung up on him. "She's been depressed," he said. "I've got her meeting with a psychiatrist three, sometimes four times a week. We're starting to think about institutions. We're starting to think, now they've got a lot of the kinks worked out, about electroshock therapy. Life's a bitch, ain't it? Yeah, well, if you should happen to hear anything, anything at all, you have my number, give me a ring. Dr. Greif and I want to get this thing settled as soon as we can. Tell Marge hi for me."

No longer bothering to pick up the litter he left after these flights of fancy, no longer even thinking about it. Just working his new situation. And was still working his new situation when the idea came to him to call Harry Ald in Portland. Once he thought of it he didn't screw around.

"Harry, it's Jack. Is Claire with you?"

"With me? Why would she be with me?"

He recognized the tone in Harry's voice. It could have been the tone in his own voice when he was handing out his God forbids to the airline agents and transforming his wife's identity into his girlfriend's and then declining that one into some daughter's.

"Why? Well, for starters, I think she may still have a thing for you, you big lug."

"That was years ago, Jack. Christ, man, I'm sixty years old. We ain't high school kids any longer."

"Is she with you, Harry?"

"Jack, I swear on my life she isn't."

"Yeah, all right, it's a four-hour plane ride to Portland. Is she on her way?"

"Honor bright, Jack, I'm telling you that as of this minute I have absolutely no idea where she is."

So, Schiff thought, she's run off to play out her life with her old sweetheart.

"Okay, Harry. Hang tough. Stonewall me. Just you remember. I'm a helpless old cripple with a degenerative neurological disease who has to be strapped into the chair when he goes down the stairs on his Stair-Glide."

"Oh, Jack," Harry said.

"Oh, Harry," said Jack, and hung up.

It wasn't that satisfactory but at least now he knew where he stood. (Well, he thought, *stood*.) What he'd told his wife had been true. He *couldn't* afford to be single. Not at the rate his exacerbations had been coming. Only a little over a year ago he'd still been able to manage on a cane, he'd still been able to drive. He'd owned a walker—a gift from the Society—but hadn't even taken it out of its box. Now they had to tote him around in a wheelchair he hadn't enough strength in his left arm to propel by himself. Now he had to go up and down stairs in contraptions on tracks—— Schiff's little choo-choo. Now he couldn't stand in the shower, there were grab bars on the sides of his handicap toilet, a bath bench in his tub, he had to sit to pee, and couldn't always pull the beltless, elastic-waistband pants he wore all the way up his hips and over his ass. (Now, for the same reason, he didn't even wear underwear.) There were ramps at both the front and rear of the house. And every other month now there was some elaborate new piece of home health equipment in the house. Indeed, where once it had been a sort of soft entertainment for him to go into the malls and department stores, now it had become a treat to drop into one of the health supply shops and scope the prosthetics. On his wish list was the sort of motorized wheelchair you'd see paraplegics tear around in, a van with a hydraulic lift in which to put it, and one of those big easy chairs that raised you to a standing position. Also, although in his case it was still a little premature to think about just yet, he had his eye on this swell new electronic hospital bed. He found himself following ads for used hospital beds in the Society's newsletter. ("Don't kid yourself," he told colleagues, "it takes dough to be crippled and still have a lifestyle.")

You could be crippled or you could be single. Schiff, though he made a pretty good living at the university— Check, he reminded himself, the savings and money-market accounts, see if she cleaned you out before she split— didn't know anyone who could afford to be both. Oh, maybe if you went into a *home* maybe, but unless you had only three or four years to live that was prohibitive, too. (Wasn't everything up front? Didn't you have to sign your life savings over to those guys? He should have known this stuff, but give him a break, until this morning he hadn't even known his wife would be running out on him.) And, though he'd never actually been in one, he didn't think he'd like the way it would smell in the corridors.

So he was checking his options. Still working his new situation, he meant, still, he meant, thinking about the blows he would be taking in his comfort, he found his mind drifting back to that wish list. He found himself idly thinking about the skeepskin whoosies crips draped over the furniture and across their wheelchairs and sheets to help prevent lesions and bedsores. It was astonishing what one of those babies could go for in a wicked world. (It varied actually. They came in different grades, like wool rugs, fur coats, or diamonds. Lambskin was the most expensive, then ewes, then adult males, but it wasn't that simple. There were categories within even these categories, and certain kinds of sheep—castrated fully-grown males were an example—could sometimes be more expensive than even the finest virgin lambskin. Once you really got into it, it was a waste, a waste and a shame, thought Schiff, to be crippled-up in such an interesting place as the world.) Oh well, he thought, if he really needed them he could afford all the sheepskins he wanted. Sheepskin deprival wasn't his problem. His wish list wasn't. He *had* been drifting, he *had* been thinking idly. With Claire gone his problem was the real and present danger he was in, his problem was singleness and emergency.

He picked up his cordless phone and called Information. (Another thing he didn't understand about his wife. Since his disease had been first diagnosed, even, that is, when he was relatively asymptomatic, he'd asked the telephone company, and with a supporting letter from his neurologist received, for its free Unlimited Information Privilege. For years now he hadn't cracked a phone book. Claire had telephone numbers written down in a small, worn black spiral notebook she kept in a drawer in the kitchen. When she wanted the number of a plumber, say, or the man who serviced their air conditioners, she'd go all the way downstairs for it rather than call Information. Recently, it was the cause of some of their biggest fights. "Ask Information," Schiff offered expansively, almost like a host pressing food or drink on a guest. "The number's in my book," she'd say. "Why not ask Information? It's free." "I've got the number downstairs. Information has better things to do." "It's their *job*, for Christ's sake. What do you think the hell else they have to do?" "That's all right, I don't mind." "*I* mind," Schiff would say, and he'd be shouting now. "*Why?*" he'd yell after her. "*This is some passive-aggressive thing, isn't it? Sure,*" he'd shout, "*this is some lousy passive-aggressive thing on your part. Just your way of showing me who the cripple is in this outfit!*" Sometimes, out of spite and with Claire as witness, checking what was playing at all the movie houses, when the feature was scheduled to begin, he'd rack up a dozen or so calls to Information at a time. Or patiently explain to her, "You know, Claire, the Information operators don't actually look anything up. It isn't as if they were ruining their eyes over the tiny print in the telephone directory. It's all computers nowadays. They just punch in an approximate spelling and the number comes up on the screen." "It's wasteful," Claire might say. "It's free." "It's a drain on the electricity, it's wasteful." "You clip goddamn coupons for shampoos and breakfast cereals and shit we

Stanley Elkin

wouldn't even eat unless you got fifteen or twenty cents off the price of the goddamn box! *That's* wasteful! Do you know what they charge for a call to Information? *Forty-five cents, that's what! Forty-five cents!* They're ripping you off. I'll tell you the truth, Claire, I feel sorry for people who aren't handicapped today, I really do. I probably save us a dollar eighty cents a day. You know what that comes to over the course of a year? Practically six hundred fifty dollars a year! Go buy yourself a designer dress, Claire, go get yourself a nice warm coat." *"Big man!" "Big fucking passive aggressive!"*)

"S.O.S. Corporation," a woman said when the number rang through. "How may we help you?"

"I've seen your ads on TV and I'd like to speak to one of your sales representatives," Schiff said.

"Bill isn't busy just now. I'll put you through to Bill."

"I'm disabled," Schiff told Bill. "My wife of thirty-six years skipped out on me today to be with an old boyfriend in the Pacific Northwest and left me high and dry and all alone in the house, pretty much a prisoner in it, in fact. Claire left me the car, and I have my handicap plates—my 'vanity plates,' I call them, with their stick-figure, big-wheeler wheelchairs like a kid's toy—but I haven't driven in over a year and don't even know whether I still can."

The salesman started to explain his company's services but Schiff interrupted him. "Yes," he said, "I've seen your ads on TV," and continued, teaching Bill his life and current situation. Then the good political geographer went on to explain what he called "choke points" in his home, fault lines along which he could be expected most likely to fall, how close these were to the various telephones in the house. When he was done, the fellow, if he'd been paying attention at all, could have passed, and might even have aced, any pop quiz on the material that Schiff cared to give him.

"Yes sir," Bill said, "that's pretty clear. I think we'll be able to serve you just fine."

"I think so," Schiff said, "I've seen your ads on TV, I've heard them on the radio."

"Pretty effective spots," Bill said.

1 4

"Long-time listener, first-time caller," said Schiff.

"Hey," said the salesman, "you can rest easy. We could get the equipment over to you and set you up today."

"Well, I do have *some* questions."

"Oh," Bill said, disappointed, realizing things had gone too smoothly, sensing the catch, "sure. What's that?"

Schiff wanted to know if he could wear the thing in the shower, whether there was any chance he would be electrocuted. The shower was one of the major choke points; if he was going to be electrocuted the deal was off.

"No chance at all," Bill, who'd actually often been asked this same question, said brightly. "The emergency call button works on the same principle as the waterproof watch. Besides, everything in it, the case, the working parts, are all made of high-grade, bonded, heavy-duty plastic. The only metal part is the copper wire that carries the signal, and that's locked in bonded, heavy-duty, high-grade plastic insulation."

Schiff said that that was good, that people his age had been known to recover from broken hips, but that he couldn't think of anyone who'd ever come back from an electrocution. Bill chuckled and, feeling his oats, wanted to know if Professor Schiff had any other questions. Well, yes, as a matter of fact, he had. If he wasn't near a regular phone would it work on a cordless? The salesman was ready for him. He slammed this one right out of the park. "Yes, absolutely. So long as it's in the On mode. Then of course, since the battery tends to drain down in that position, it's your responsibility to see to it that you keep your phone charged."

"I could do that, I'm not completely helpless, you know," said Schiff, who, from the salesman's quick answer to what Schiff thought a cleanly unique question, suddenly had a sad sense of himself as a thoroughly categorized man.

"Of course not," Bill said. "Anything else?"

There was the question of price. Bill preferred to wait until he had a chance to meet Schiff in person before going into this stuff—there were various options—— if a doctor accompanied the paramedic on a call, whether Schiff would be using some of the other services the company offered, various options—but the professor was adamant. He reminded Bill of all he had yet to do if he was going to call off that party for his graduate students. He wouldn't budge on this one. The salesman would either have to tell him what it cost right then and there or lose the sale. Bill gave him the basic monthly rates, installation fees, what it would cost Schiff if they had to put in additional phones. He broke down the costs to him of the various options and offered a price on specific package deals. It was like buying a good used car.

It was expensive. Schiff said as much.

"Is it?" Bill said. "Do you have a burglar-alarm system in your house there, Professor?"

"No."

"Sure," Bill said, "and if that's what you have to pay to see to it your hi-fi ain't stolen or they don't clear out your spoons, isn't your very life worth a few dollars more to you than just making sure they don't get your tablecloth?"

"I said I *don't* have a burglar-alarm system," Schiff said.

"Whether you do or you don't," the salesman said. "It's the same principle."

On condition that all of it could be put in that day he ended up picking one of the S.O.S. Corporation's most all-inclusive plans. He got a bit of a break on the package.

"You won't be sorry," Bill told him sincerely. "They dealt you a rotten hand. In my business I see it all the time, and I agree, it's a little expensive, but you'll see, it's worth it. Even if you never have to use us, and I hope you don't, it's worth it. The sense of security alone. It's worth it all right. Oh, while I still have you on the phone, is there something else you want to ask, can you think of anything you'd like to know?"

Schiff figured the man was talking about credit arrangements, but he didn't care about credit arrangements. It was expensive, more expensive than Schiff would ever have thought, but not *that* expensive. If the bitch hadn't cleaned out his accounts—something he'd have to check—he could afford it. But there *was* something else. Schiff brought it up reluctantly.

"Would I have to shout?" he asked. "On the TV, that lady who falls down shouts."

"Well, you take a nasty spill like that you could just as well be screaming as actually shouting."

"I think she's shouting," Schiff said. "She's pretty far from the phone, all the way across the room. It sounds to me like she's shouting."

"Well," Bill said gently, "shouting, screaming. That's just an example of truth in advertising." And Schiff knew what Bill was going to tell him next. He braced himself for it. And then the salesman said just exactly what Schiff thought he was going to say. "Maybe," he said, "her phones aren't sensitive enough, maybe they're not wired for their fullest range. That's one of the reasons I want to be on the site, why I don't like to quote a customer a price over the telephone."

He has me, thought the political geographer, they dealt me a rotten hand—he's in the business, he knows—and he has me.

If it wasn't one thing it was another. Or no, Schiff, remembering his theory of consequences, fallout, the proliferation of litter, corrected. First it was one thing, *then* it was another. Once you put the ball into play there was nothing for it but to chase it. He had to find out about his funds, whether there were enough left to take care of it if S.O.S. insisted on payment for their service up front. (Claire paid the bills, he hadn't written a check in years. Except for a couple of loose dollars—it was awkward for him to get to his billfold, finger credit cards from a wallet or handle money—for a coffee and sweet roll when he went to school, he didn't even carry cash anymore. Even in restaurants Claire paid the check, figured the tip, signed the credit-card slip. His disease had turned him into some sort of helpless, old-timey widow, some nice, pre-lib, immigrant lady.) He knew the names of the three banks with which they dealt, but wasn't entirely certain which one they used for checking, which handled their trust fund, which was the one they kept their money-market account. (There was even a small teacher's credit-union account they'd had to open when the interest rates were so high on certificates of deposit a few years back and they took a loan out on an automobile Claire didn't think they should pay for outright.)

Information gave him the bank's number, but the bank— they might have been suspicious of his vagueness when he couldn't tell them what kind of account he was asking about—wouldn't tell him a thing without an account number.

"Jesus," he said, "I'm disabled, I'd have to go downstairs for that. My wife usually takes care of the money. Normally I wouldn't even be bothering you with something like this, but she walked out on me today. Just left me flat."

"I don't like it," the bank said, "when people take the name of the Lord in vain."

He knew where to find the stuff, in the top drawer of a high, narrow cabinet in the front hall—for reasons neither could remember they called it "the tchtchk"—the closest thing they had in the house to an antique, and except for the fact that two of its elaborate brass handles were missing it might have been valuable. The only thing was, getting there would not be half the fun. Even with the Stair-Glide Claire had to help him. Always she had to swivel and lock the seat, folded upright like a seat in a movie theater, into position for him at the top of the stairs. On days he was weak she had to lift Schiff's feet onto the little ledge—less long than his shoes—and pull down its movable arms held high in the air like a victim's in a stickup. Even on days he was strong she had to fold and carry his aluminum walker down the stairs for him. The logistics seemed overwhelming. He'd really have to think about this one.

He was in bed. He was lying down. Lying down, sitting, he was any man's equal. He didn't know his own strength. Literally. He had no sense of weakness, his disease. He could be in remission. Unless he tried to turn on his side, or raise himself into a sitting position, he felt fit as a fiddle. At rest, even his fingers seemed normal. He could have counted out money or arranged playing cards. Really, the logistics seemed overwhelming. He was as reluctant to move as a man in a mine field. Inertia had become almost a part of his disease, almost a part of his character. His character, Schiff thought, had become almost a part of his disease. A man's gotta do what a man's gotta do, he thought, and heaved himself upright. So far, so good. Not bad, he thought, and pushed himself up off the bed and, preparing to move, leaned into his walker. Not bad, he thought again, pleased with the relative crispness of his steps, but soon his energy began to flag. By the time he'd taken the thirteen or so steps to the Stair-Glide (the twenty-six or so steps, actually, since his movement on the walker could be broken down—to keep his mind occupied, he really *did* break it down—this way: push, step, pull; push, step, pull, each forward step with his right leg accompanied by dragging the left one up alongside it, *almost* alongside it. He felt like someone with a gaping hole in his hull). Push, step, rest, pull, he was going now; then push, rest, step, rest, *pull. Rest!* He lived in slow motion, like someone bathed in strobe light or time-lapse photography. He could have been the subject of time-motion studies.

In repose, folded out of the way against the wall, the Stair-Glide looked like a torso on a target on a rifle range. Gasping, Schiff fumbled with the lever that swiveled it into position and, almost losing his balance as he took a hand off the walker, had practically to swipe at its shallow little theater seat to get it down. With difficulty he managed to lower the chair's arms and wrap them about himself—there was a sort of elbow on each arm that loosely encircled his body and was supposed to keep him from falling too far forward—and lower the tiny footrest. (They design this shit for kids, Schiff thought. They think of us as a bunch of Tiny Tims.) He didn't know what to do, whether to pull his feet up on the footrest and then try to collapse the walker, or to collapse the walker and then worry about getting his feet up. (They're right, he thought. We *are* kids. We need nurse-maids. Or wives. Boy, he thought angrily, her sense of tim-ing. Her world-class, son-of-a-bitch sense of timing. Briefly, it occurred to him that he might be better off home-less, find himself a nutso, broken-down bag lady with whom he could bond and who would take care of him, or, if it was still too soon for him to make a commitment, get involved, or even too early for him to start dating again, some streetsmart, knowledgeable old wino with a feel for the soup kitchens, the ground-floor, handicap-friendly shel-ters. He had money. Surely she'd left *something* for him, though even if she hadn't there was the house. He could sell it, split the proceeds with her, and have enough left over to pay the wino or bag lady for their trouble. What could it cost him—— ten bucks a day, fifteen? Hell, if he didn't save almost that much on the calls he made to Information, he saved almost *almost* that much. I was already crippled, Schiff thought, now I'm crazy, too.) It was a dilemma, a whad-dayacallit, Hobson's choice. This ain't going to happen, he told himself. If I bring my feet up and fold the walker, my feet will slide off the footrest and I'll never get them back on it again. If I fold the walker and hold it I won't have the use of my hands to lift up my feet. Then, out of the blue, it came to him. He raised his feet onto the footrest and moved the chair into its glide mode. He leaned over and picked up the still uncollapsed walker. He didn't even *try* to fold it. With his arms on the armrests and the heel of his hand pressed against the button that made the Stair-Glide go, he raised the lightweight aluminum walker around his body and up about level with the top of his head and, to all intents and purposes, proceeded to *wear* it downstairs!

By the time he'd made it the eight steps to the landing—his hand kept slipping off the button and stopping the chair—a second walker—one he could keep permanently set up at the bottom of the stairs—had gone on his wish list. When the Stair-Glide slowly started its turn into the second flight—he'd timed it once, it took exactly one minute to do the trip—the telephone began to ring. He knew it would stop ringing before he could get to it. I'm in farce, he thought. I take to farce the way ducks take to water. But, even in farce, Schiff was a hopeful man—a man, that is, obsessed with solutions, even though he tried always to live by the cripple's code with all its concomitant notions about the exponentiality of litter and his grand ideas about every solved problem creating a new one. Now, for example, he had still more items for his wish list. He could leave cordless phones all over the house, in every out-of-the-way place he was likely to be when a phone started to ring, by the shelf where the toilet paper was kept, along the tops of tables, between the cushions of the sofa, in the gap between his pants pocket and the side of a chair, beside potted plants on windowsills—— in each inconvenient closet, pantry, alcove, and cuddy, adjunct to all the complicated, nesty network of random space.

The minute was up. He was at the bottom of the stairs. He disrobed himself of the walker and set it down, aware at once (by the relief he felt, that suffused him like a kind of pleasure) of how rough it could be, how heavy it became if one wasn't up to the burdens of aluminum. The burdens of aluminum. And, still seated in the Stair-Glide, already accustomed to his relief, no longer surprised by the return of his off-again, on-again energies, restored—so long as he remained seated—to health, which after the ordeal of the stairs he intended to savor a while longer, not even tempted by the telephone which he suddenly realized had never stopped ringing. It's Claire, he thought. Only Claire knew he was alone in the house, how long it took him to get to a phone. Then he thought, No, that's not true, plenty of people know, Claire's driver, even the dispatcher at the taxicab company, the agents at the airlines, the woman at the bank, friends to whom he'd spilled the beans, Harry in Portland, Bill at S.O.S. Even, when it came right down, Information. God, he hoped it wasn't Information. Then he realized he was wrong about that one too. He hoped it *was* Information. They could be checking up on him to see if he was still crippled. He wanted Information on his side and decided

not to pick up. The phone stopped ringing. Though, actually, Schiff thought once it had stopped, it *could* have been
anyone. Thieves checking to see if the house was empty so
they could come out and strip it, take what they wanted. If
it was thieves, Schiff thought, it was probably a good thing
he hadn't yet had time to do anything about his wish
list—— that second walker, the dozen or so extra cordless
telephones he'd thought he might buy. And suddenly
scratched the cordless telephones and had another, less expensive, even better item for the wish list—— an answering
machine. They didn't have an answering machine—Schiff
felt clumsy speaking to them and didn't like to impose on
others what he hated to do himself— but he had to admit,
in his new circumstances, under his novel, new dispensation, an answering machine could be just the ticket. It might
just fill the bill. The problem with an answering machine as
Schiff saw it was the message one left on it to tell callers you
couldn't come to the phone. If the device caught important
calls you didn't want to miss, it was also an open invitation
to the very vandals and thieves he was concerned to scare
off. "I can't come to the phone just now, but if you'll
just . . ." was too ambiguous. It wouldn't keep the tiger
from your gates. A good thief would see right through the
jesuiticals of a message like that and interpret it any way he
wanted. Schiff wouldn't take it off the wish list but he'd first
have to compose an airtight message for the machine before
he ever actually purchased one. An idle mind is *too* the
devil's workshop, Schiff thought, and rose from the chair,
plowed—he often thought of his walker as a plow, of his
floors and carpets as fields in which he cut stiff furrows—
his way to the tchtchk and, quite to his astonishment, found
almost at once statements from the banks with their account
numbers on them. These he put into his mouth, but he
couldn't go up just yet, couldn't yet face the struggle with
the walker on the Stair-Glide; he had to rest, build strength,
and decided to go into the living room for a while and sit
down.

Where he collected his strength and doodled messages in his head for the answering machine.

Hi, he thought, this is Jack Schiff. Sorry to have missed your call, but I've stepped out for five minutes to run out to the store for some milk for my coffee. Just leave your et cetera, et cetera, and I'll get right back to you.

That wasn't bad, Schiff thought, but what would people who knew him make of it, of his "stepped out" and "run out" locutions? Of the swiftness and fluency of movement—so unlike him—he implied in that "get right back to you" trope? Unless they read it as the code that it was, they would think they'd reached some other Jack Schiff. Also, what if the thieves waited five minutes and called back? Or ten? Or fifteen? Or a whole hour and then heard the same damn message? After they robbed him they'd probably trash the place, maybe even torch it.

Hi, et cetera, et cetera, he revised, but—— WOULD YOU CUT THAT OUT, PLEASE? DOWN, DAMN IT DOWN! Sorry, my pit bull's acting up again. Look, just leave your name at the sound of the—— oh, my God, BEEEEP!

Well, Schiff thought, pleased with the new composition and his invention of the pit bull. But there was a problem of verisimilitude. Wouldn't there have to be growls, the sound of snarls and vicious barking? Probably he could manage a fairly convincing growl, or even a snarl, particularly over a telephone with its gift of enhanced, electronic sibilance, but he was an academic not an actor, he'd never be able to handle the rough barking. (A pit bull went on the wish list. Then, thinking of the effort it would be to care for, came right back off again.)

Et cetera, et cetera, he began over, I'm too depressed to come to the phone right now. Thieves cleaned me out. I called the cops. They tell me it looks like the work of professionals. Like that's supposed to be a comfort? Leave your name, if I ever cheer up I'll try to get back to you.

There were people at his front door. From where he sat on the sofa he could see the S.O.S. van through the French windows. Well, thought Schiff, thank God for small favors.

It was good he was downstairs. If he'd gone up—he had the wrong temperament for someone with his disease; really, he thought, he wasn't laidback enough; not trying to get to the phone earlier before it stopped ringing was the exception not the rule—he could have had an accident in an effort to rush down to them before his visitors gave up and left. Even now, knowing what he knew about himself, and no more than twenty feet from the door, he scampered to it. The bank statements were still in his mouth.

"No no," Bill, who was in the business, who knew a rotten hand when he saw one, who'd told him as much, said, waving off the hand Schiff extended, "let's wait, why don't we, until you sit down before we try to shake hands?"

In the living room Bill introduced him to the technician he'd brought with him, a woman. For a fellow with a quiet libido, it was astonishing to Schiff how much at ease women could put him, even women like this one, got up in gray coveralls like a repairman's, moving man's, or delivery man's jumpsuit, a person's who worked basements. It was generally true what Claire had said. Workmen tended to frighten him. At something like the ambassadorial level Claire handled the workmen, though Schiff began to wonder if he hadn't been missing something. After some initial small talk—"Have any trouble finding the place?" "Yes, it *is* a nice neighborhood, St. Louis's best-kept secret"—which he quite enjoyed but wouldn't have guessed he had in him, Bill presented him with some brochures about the equipment and service. Schiff accepted and started to read them before Bill interrupted. "Those are just to give you an idea of the colors that are available."

"Oh, I don't care about the color," Schiff said.

"Well, good for you," said Bill.

"The olive would have to be special-ordered anyway," Jenny Simmons said. "So would the teal."

"We don't have the teal?" Bill said.

"I don't think Indianapolis even makes it anymore. When was the last time you saw a teal?"

"Come to think of it," Bill admitted.

"I really *don't* care about the color," Schiff said.

"Most clients don't," Bill said.

"Hey," Schiff said, "I'm far gone, but I'm not *that* far gone. I still get a kick out of life. It's not *all* monochromatic. All I meant was, it ticks me off when a company tries to make a profit off the paint it splashes over its products. I can remember when the Princess telephone first came out and Ma Bell charged you extra for any piece of equipment that wasn't black."

"That's what I thought you meant," Bill said. "Wasn't it Henry Ford who said you could get the Model T in any color you wanted so long as it was black? Some clients are a little fussy is all. It actually matters to them whether the unit they wear around their neck and that could save their life is green or gray. Though don't get me wrong. The S.O.S. Corporation isn't Ma Bell. We don't charge extra for the color."

"There's no scientific reason for it I can think of," Jenny Simmons said, "but it's been my experience that we have less trouble with a plain white unit than with any other color."

"Plain white it is for me," Schiff said.

"There you go," Bill said. "It's just we're required by law to show you what's available."

Schiff looked to Jenny, who seemed to be frowning. By law? Was he serious? Required by law? Schiff smiled at her. Jenny looked down. Then Schiff wondered if she knew about his situation. Sure, he thought, she had to. They'd come together in the van. They were partners. Like cops. The salesman would almost certainly have passed on all that Schiff had himself volunteered—— that he'd been married thirty-six years and that this was the day the Lord had made for his wife to just up and leave him, fled to her boyfriend in Oregon, spilling his life like a suicide. Also, she'd seen him with bank statements in his mouth. Now *Schiff* looked down. And only a few minutes earlier he'd been thinking of giving them tea, hard stuff even. (Schiff remembered when he was a kid, his parents offering "a shot" to men who came to do for them, carry their furniture up and down flights of stairs. Maybe that's why he was still afraid of them——their power and rough, blue-collar ways.) He felt a little betrayed. Even at that, though, he took a sort of comfort in their company, and if it wasn't for the fact that he had still to call the banks and check with them about his accounts he would have been content to spend the rest of the afternoon being sold to. There was something soothing about it, like watching a fishing show on TV that taught you to tie your own flies or showed you how to paint a picture. It was a little, he imagined, like a woman getting a free makeover in a department store. (Schiff, abandoned, on his own, was coming a little to terms with the domestic.)

"I took the liberty of making some notes during our earlier phone conversation." Bill said. "Whenever you're ready we can check out your floor plan. Jenny's the expert. I'd like her to walk us through it. Nothing's written in stone yet. There could still be some changes you might want to make."

"Of course, of course, but I don't think you really need me. While you're pacing if off I could be making some calls."

"Sure thing," Bill said, "we'll take care of it. Go make your calls."

"Well, that's just it," Schiff said. "I have this cordless phone? I may even have mentioned it to you."

"I remember you did."

"It's up on the bed in my room. I live by the cripple's code. That you must never do anything twice. Unfortunately, I do just about everything twice. Well," he said, "I'm crippled. I almost have to."

"You mustn't say that. You're hardly a cripple," the salesman said. "You know how to cope. I hope I cope half as well as you do if I'm ever handicapped."

"Well," said Schiff, "in any event. I wasn't able to bring it with me when I came down. If someone could just get it for me?"

"No problem," Bill said. "Your room is—— ?"

"First door on the left, top of the stairs."

Which left him alone in the living room with Jenny. She seemed shy for someone who worked with Bill. Stuck for something to say, she grinned at him goofily. It occurred to him she was embarrassed by everything she already knew about him. Bold cop, shy cop. Schiff poked around, looking for something he could say to put her at ease.

"I had you for a professor," Jenny told him.

Schiff felt himself flush, a stain of red discovery cross his features.

"I don't blame her," he blurted. "Not for a minute. She should have done it years ago. I would've. In her place *I* would've. No one owes anyone that kind of loyalty."

Before either of them could recover Bill was back with Schiff's phone. "There you go," he said.

"Thank you," Schiff said, "thanks."

"No problem. It was just where you said. You give very good directions."

Schiff waited impatiently while Bill explained what was going to happen, that he and Jenny were going to go over the house looking for the best spots to install their relays. He had his notes, he said, he just wanted to make sure they hadn't overlooked anything. "For example," Bill said, "I notice the house has a third floor."

"I'm never up there."

"Well, I know," Bill said, "but can't you conceive of a circumstance which might bring you up there?"

"There's no Stair-Glide. I couldn't get to the third floor if I wanted to."

"What about the basement, what if something went wrong in the basement? If the furnace went out, or, God forbid, your storm drains clogged and you had severe water damage?"

"Same thing," Schiff said, "no Stair-Glide."

"Well, sure," said Bill. "I'm not prying. That's just the sort of thing the corporation has to find out about if it's to render its services properly. Also, I'll tell you something, we have to cover our behind. If something happened to a client in an area of the house we overlooked or failed to warn him he was vulnerable we could be looking at a pretty good lawsuit."

"I consider myself warned," Schiff said, getting a little cranky now, the charm of being sold to having worn off, and oppressed by all he had yet to do.

Bill chuckled. "Well, I know," he said, "and I hope you don't mind putting your signature to that when we close the deal."

"I have to sign a consent form? Like you're my surgeon? Like you're operating on me?"

"It's for both our protections," Bill said in exactly the same tone of voice Schiff often used in class when he had to explain something. He turned to his partner. "What do you say, Jenny? We start down here?"

Shit, Schiff thought, fingering his bank statements, getting anxious now, feeling suddenly rushed, hurried, his oppression compounding into a sort of spiritual indigestion he could almost feel.

Now see, he told himself, that's exactly what I meant about farce. He was furious he had to call the bank while S.O.S. was there, more outraged than by his condition itself, than by Claire's leaving. It wasn't fair. It was none of the corporation's business that his wife might have plundered their accounts. It was that straw that breaks that camel's back. He waited for them to clear out of the living room, which they went over, deliberate as sappers. Maybe she'd been his student when he still taught undergraduates. But that was just what he meant, too. It wasn't just her odd garment that threw him off the scent. He simply didn't *know* these people. His students, he meant. It wasn't even only that they failed to keep in touch. They weren't in touch to begin with. Many of his colleagues' former students were like family. They had pictures of the people their students had married, of their kids. Also, it a little depressed Schiff to see one of his old students got up in coveralls, doing, he didn't care how much electronics she probably knew, a sort of manual labor. It was a long way from political geography, from the high ground of pure theory, the strictly hands-off of scholarship and the sheer delicious luxury of an arcane discipline. Schiff knew professors of painting whose students had pictures hanging in museums, business profs with kids who were CEOs. It diminished already diminished old Schiff that he couldn't think of a single one of his students who'd gone on in the field. He taught graduate students pursuing advanced degrees in history, in poli sci, and many of them had distinguished careers, but Schiff kept up, he knew the people in his field, hotshots in Washington think tanks many of them, high-ups in the CIA, consultants to or officials in the Census Bureau, advisers to Rand-McNally, the publishers of other important atlases, and couldn't think of anyone who'd been in one of his classes who was a practicing political geographer. They were probably waiters, he thought, drivers in the taxicab trade very likely, or, like Miss Simmons here, got up like people you see when your airplane has landed, signaling jets to the gate.

They left the living room and moved through the rest of the first floor, going into the dining room, Schiff's kitchen, his half bath, the small storage area at the rear of his house where the backdoor opened out onto the porch, the small in-ground pool.

Schiff waited until he heard their steps on the stairs. Then, cupping his hand over the speaker, he lowered his voice and asked Information for the bank's phone number. Even as was doing so he saw it, plain as the nose, right there on the statement. It would have been too much trouble to tell the operator that never mind, forget it, he'd found it (never mind, forget it, more farce), so he waited for the little mechanical recitation to come on and dutifully checked it against the phone number on the statement.

Now that he could give them their account number (sotto voce, as sotto as he could make it and still be heard, so sotto, in fact, that he sounded suspicious even to himself), the bank was nice as pie. Too nice, you asked him. He could have been anyone. He was upset with them that they'd just hand out information like that. He even thought he recognized the voice, that it belonged to the religious zealot he'd spoken to earlier. Now here it was again, giving out inside info on him like there was no tomorrow. Taking his substance in vain. Which, even in his pique, he was pleased to learn Claire had made no inroads on. He called their other banks, the one where they did their checking, the one used for the trust-fund account.

Which couldn't have been more cooperative, sir, pleased to provide him with that information, sir, yes sir, connected with an employee who might, Schiff felt, had he only asked for them, have called out the intimate weights and measures of anyone who'd ever done business with the bank, not only to the last penny but right down to the last overdraft, the last bounced check. Not only was money fungible, apparently an account number, *any* account number was too, or maybe just any five random digits, like figures on a Bingo card. He felt like a government agency. He felt like a car dealer, Jack Schiff Oldsmobile, say, calling for the lowdown on a would-be customer.

He probably wouldn't have felt this way (or felt anything more than a little surprised) if just at that moment, the very moment when the bank's teller, or clerk, or paid professional informer, was singing out Schiff's bottom lines, bright, clear, and brassy as a belter on Broadway stopping the show, someone somewhere in the house hadn't picked up an extension.

The cooperative teller asked if Schiff had gotten that and, before he could answer, broke down the sums for him again.

"Oh," said Miss Simmons, "is that you, Professor? I didn't know you were still making your calls."

"I got a wrong number," he said, and disengaged.

The three of them were downstairs.

"Yep," Bill was saying, rubbing his hands, "you got it right the first time. Turns out we didn't really have to check. We could almost go with the plan we specified on the telephone. Jenny found one or two places the signal may have to be reinforced, but you could do a voice level, she'll meter

you and, who knows, you might just be able to get away
without us having to change a thing in the original specs.
Even if we do have to make an adjustment it wouldn't run
you more than an additional two or three hundred dollars."

"I have to go upstairs?"

"No, no," Bill said, "she marked off the distances. You
can do the reading right down here, can't you, Jenny?"

"Sure," said his former student. She took something that
looked rather like a light meter from one of the deep pock-
ets in her coveralls and held it up. "Go ahead," she said,
"pretend you've fallen. Just speak into the air."

"What should I say?"

"Anything. I'm just getting a level."

"Calling all cars," Schiff said in a normal voice. "S.O.S.
S.O.S. Save our Schiff."

"What do you think, Jen?" Bill said.

His former student looked at her old professor whose
worth she knew—as a teacher, as a husband—she looked at
his weakened limbs, may even, when she was upstairs, have
seen his urinal—as a man.

"It's all right," she said.

"*Is* it?" said Bill, surprised. "How about that?" he said.
"You got it right the first time, but then that's your business, isn't it, Professor? Floor plans, knowing the territory."

In spite of himself, Schiff basked in what, in spite of himself, Schiff knew wasn't really a compliment. But he did, he
did know the territory.

"Yep," Bill said, "Jenny tells me you used to be some
kind of geography professor."

"I still am," Schiff said, "*I* still teach."

"Do you?" Bill said. "Well, good for *you*."

He knew the territory, all right. He should have thrown
the S.O.S. s.o.b. out of the house. He told himself it was
only because Claire had left him and he needed the service
that he didn't. But it was because of what Claire had said,
too. His fear of tradesmen, of almost anyone who didn't

teach at a university. At least a little it was. So he *knew* the territory.

"Well," said Bill, "all we have to do now is a little paperwork, fill out a few forms."

He was asked questions about his medical history, stuff out of left field. Not just about his neurology but about childhood diseases, allergies, even whether he'd ever had poison ivy. He listed his medications. It was for show, not for blow, but again, and still in spite of himself, he took a certain pleasure in this medical inventory. It was the first time in years anyone had taken such an interest in him, even a faked one. Bill was more thorough than any of his physicians, and Miss Simmons seemed to hang on his answers as much as the salesman.

"That should about do it," Bill said.

"Oh," said Schiff, a little let down.

"Well, except for a few housekeeping details the corporation has to have for its files. Nothing GMAC or any financial institution wouldn't need to know if you were applying for a loan on a car."

Schiff couldn't have said why he was so steamed. He'd expected it. Wasn't this the reason he'd been trying to get through to his banks? Wasn't it why he'd attempted to be so circumspect?

"Will you be paying by check?"

"Yes," Schiff said, thrown off, expecting some such, but not exactly this, question. "The corporation takes checks, doesn't it?"

"These systems are fairly big-ticket items. It takes cashier's checks."

"Well, that poses a problem, doesn't it?" Schiff said. "Me being crippled and all? My wife having lit out for the territory and leaving me up shit creek without a paddle with a car in the driveway to get to the bank but not quite enough strength in my legs to press down on the accelerator let alone the brake pedal?"

"Don't get so excited," Bill said. "We're flexible. We'll work with you. Hey," he said, "we're nothing if not flexible. If you can demonstrate you have enough money in your account to cover the check, we'll work with you."

"Ask Miss Simmons if I have enough money in my account to cover it," Schiff said.

"No offense, old man," the salesman said. "Hey," he said, "take it easy. No offense. Often, a spouse quits on a partner who's been dealt a bad hand she Hoovers out their joint accounts before she goes."

"This happens?" Schiff, oddly moved, said suddenly, in spite of himself, interested, narrowly studying the man, a sort of political geographer in his own right, a kind of bellwether, some sibyl of the vicissitudes.

"Well, a lot of resentment builds up," Bill explained. "I mean, put yourself in her place. At least *some* of the trouble between you had to have been physical, right?"

Schiff stared at him.

"Sure," Bill said, "and it's my guess that until you were struck down you two probably had it pretty good in bed together. Go ahead, write the check. It's the amount we agreed on. You're good for it."

"Am I?"

"Well, sure you are," Bill said. "She ever have to lift you up off the floor?"

"Yes," Schiff said stiffly.

"She ever have to carry you?"

"Once in a while," he said.

Bill clucked his tongue. "You enjoy that? You come to enjoy that?"

"Well," Schiff said evasively.

"Well, sure you did," Bill said.

"I didn't want her to hurt herself."

"Of course not," Bill said.

"She's pretty strong, but let's face it, she's no spring chicken."

"Let's face it," Bill said.

"I don't have my checkbook."

"Want me to go get it? Want Jen to?"

"I think it may be in one of the drawers in the tchtchk."

"Say what?"

"The cabinet in the hall. We call it the tchtchk."

"That's a new one on me. You ever hear that, Jen? The choo–choo? Heck, I can't even pronounce it. How do you say that again?"

"Tchtchk. It doesn't mean anything."

"Just a pet name, eh? From your salad days."

"I guess."

"Well, sure," Bill said. "It's just something you ought to bear in mind." Schiff didn't follow. "Well, that you *had* salad days," Bill said.

"Oh, right," Schiff said, who didn't need the lecture but wanted to placate the man just long enough to write the check and be rid of him.

"That's why the good Lord usually lets us hold on to our memories," Bill said. "So we can remember the times before our wives had to carry us around piggyback."

"She never carried me around piggyback," Schiff said.

"No? How'd she manage you?"

"She held me around my waist."

"Off the ground?"

"Thanks," Schiff told Jenny, "thank you." She's brought his checkbook. She could have brought him the one from the money-market account, even the tiny credit-union one. It was the account with money from the trust. "May I use your pen?" he asked coolly. It was hard to get a good grip on the pen with his weakened hand, difficult for him to write the check, almost impossible to form the numerals, some of which he had to trace two or three times and which were an illegible muddle when he finished. He didn't even bother to sign it but pulled the ruined check from the book and started another. Miss Simmons looked elsewhere. Bill watched Schiff closely, bearing down on him with a knowing stare. "My small motor movements are shot," Schiff explained. "I didn't forget how to make out a check."

"Of course not," Bill said. "It's like riding a bicycle."

"I forgot how to ride a bicycle," Schiff said.

"We have to keep our chin up," Bill said. "Hey," he said,

"I've got to get back to the office. Jenny still has to do the installations so I'll leave her here with you."

"Sure," Schiff said.

"Watch yourself now."

"I will."

"Don't fall."

"I won't."

"I don't know if Jenny could handle you," Bill said. Schiff didn't answer. "The service, though, the service is another story. Sometimes the service sends out women."

Schiff had enough. "What is this?" he demanded. "What are you getting at? Just what are you hinting? Do you talk this way to all your customers?"

"Why are you so excited? Do you think it's good for you to get so excited? I know your blood-pressure medications. I know what you have to put into your bloodstream to keep a lid on the stress. Do you think I'm against you? I'm not against you. Quite the contrary. I represent the service. Does the service stand to gain if its clients become upset with it? I know how highly you think of our advertising campaign but believe me, brother, what it finally boils down to is word-of-mouth. And, if you want to know, I wasn't 'hinting' or 'getting' at anything. All I was referencing was man's dependence on woman for her ability to nurture."

"All right," Schiff told him wearily.

"Sure," Bill said, "that's all there is to it. She helps him out with his motor movements. Large and small both."

"Okay."

"Ain't a mother's son of us don't want to float around in the pool in his mama's arms. Ain't a joey alive don't enjoy going for a ride in the mommy roo's pouch. Security is the name of the game."

Okeydokey already, Schiff thought.

"So I wasn't suggesting anything kinky. *Honi soit qui mal y pense,*" the salesman said, took up the check in Schiff's smashed handwriting, and left him in the house with Miss Simmons.

Who to this point, she told him, had only been seeing what had to be done, that now she could start to plant.

"To plant?"

"Your garden," she said. "Lay out your seeds and bulbs for you. It doesn't mean anything. It's a serviceman's term in the industry."

The professor nodded, surprised by the term "industry," though once he thought about it, maybe not so surprised. Increasingly, he'd been noticing those ads on TV. It was some crisis of the infirm and elderly thing, high tech's interim arrangement with the nursing-home interests, with Medicare, the aging demographics, the death-with-dignity folks. He explained this to Miss Simmons as she laid out her tools, set out the equipment she brought into Schiff's home from the van.

"Oh, now," Miss Simmons said.

"By which, thought Schiff, she meant to assuage him, ease him, allay his fears, cut him, he meant, from the herd of the infirm, aging and elderly, anyone struggling for a few last breaths of dignity. Because it was true what the salesman had said. Women *were* nurturers, even women like this one. Beneath her repair or maintenance man's gray union suit, this person who worked in the basement down with the pipes, boilers, and boards of circuit breakers, was probably just another bleeding-heart nurturer and enabler.

And my God, Schiff thought, I wasn't even fishing. Though maybe, he thought, all he ever did now was fish, his condition, his very appearance these days a fishing expedition, searching out reassurance like a guy on a treasure hunt. (Appalled by his letters of credit, his devastating carte blanche entrée like some terminal kid's on a trip to Disney World. Appalled, too, by what he must have done to Claire, who'd abandoned him, forcing her against *her* nature by the cumulative, oppressive weight of his need.) Shit, he thought, I am what I am, and asked a question that had been at least somewhere on his mind since she'd told him he'd been her professor.

"I've been trying to think," Schiff said, "was I still on a cane when you were my student?"

"A cane?" she said. "I don't think so. I don't remember any cane. No," she said, "you walked like everyone else."

"That had to be at least a dozen years ago."

"I graduated it'll be fifteen years this June."

"You knew me when," Schiff said.

"Oh, now," Miss Simmons said.

"I knew *you* when," he said.

Miss Simmons looked down at her wrenches and scissors and rolls of duct tape, at all the instruments he did not have names for. She appeared to blush, though women were clever, he thought. Blushing and downcast eyes could be a sort of nurturing, too. Outright flirting could. How could men trust a sex that lived so much by its inborns and instincts, that stood so firm by the agenda of its drives and temperament (anything for the cause), its goals and nature? Christ, he thought, they might just as well have been critters, low and furious on the biological scale as spawning salmon. (Giving another passing, glancing, bruising thought to what he must have done—his disease must have done—to his own wife's damaged intrinsics and basics.) And, quite suddenly suspecting she may have thought he was coming on, momentarily panicked.

"Oh, no," he said, finding his place again in the lecture she probably hadn't even recognized was one, "I'm all for it. I believe it's exactly the thing, quite the right way to go. I mean after the initial outlay it's rather economical. And Bill is right, a sense of security *is* the name of the game."

"Well," she said, gathering up some pieces of equipment and rising, "this is going to take at least a couple of hours. I'm afraid I have to tie up your phones; you won't be able to use them till I'm done. If there are any calls you have to make you ought to try to make them now. Otherwise . . ."

"What if someone was trying to reach *me*?"

"Well, they'd get a busy signal."

"At least two hours, you said. No one talks on a phone two hours. They'd think something was wrong, that I'd had an accident. Well," he said, "they could call the operator, I suppose, ask her to check to see if the line really *was* engaged."

"That's right," Miss Simmons said.

"I think of all the contingencies," Schiff somewhat apologetically said.

"I see you do."

"Occupational hazard," he said. "Plus it has something to do with my being a gimp."

"Oh, now."

"No, really," he said, "I could give you a whole song and dance about the cripple's code. But I'd bore you silly."

"Oh, now."

Schiff, who still had some character left, was becoming as tired of the game as Miss Simmons.

"Really," he said, "two hours?"

"If I get started right now."

"I take your point," he said, and gallantly moved his arm as if signaling her to pass, to play through.

She excused herself and disappeared from his living room.

Well, thought Schiff, reminded of sudden furious electrical storms when he was a boy on vacation with his parents in the summer bungalow they had in the country, of great howling winds and plummeting temperatures and of wide shadows that spread from horizon to horizon and came down over the bright, burning afternoon like dark paint, this is cozy. He meant it. His legs and his telephones useless, he felt stranded, shut off, closed down, all the abrupt, unexpected holiday of emergency, of every chore suspended. (He could have lived, he recalled thinking, like this forever, and remembered his disappointment when the storm passed and the world resumed.)

Miss Simmons had returned. She was screwing some tiny piece of equipment into the handset of the extension in the living room.

"I didn't mean to abandon you," she said.

"No, not at all," he said. "I think I may have dozed off."

It was a lie, but he did feel refreshed. He watched the efficient movement of Miss Simmons's fingers, her accom-
plished cybernetics. It would be like this in a home, he
thought. All the activity of the nurses, their aides, the physical and occupational therapists, the people who brought
you your trays, the nimbleness with which they stripped the
little lids from your jellies and butters and creamers, undid
the impossible knots of Saran Wrap from around your salads and sandwiches. He wondered if he could talk the university into letting him teach his classes from his room in a
home. He wondered if the laws protecting the disabled covered cases like that, if his entitlements extended to people to
mark his papers for him, deliver his lectures, lead his discussions. Because otherwise, Schiff thought, the deal was
off. If he had to lend anything to the process except his presence (his consciousness, he meant, his sheer witness) the
spell would be broken. Because that's what it was, all that
activity—Miss Simmons's, the nurses' and aides', the food
servers' and PTs' and OTs', as much as the sudden, explo-
sive summer storm—had been—— a spell, an enchantment,
and as quickly broken. And the lines had been down then,
too. (Perhaps that's what had put him in mind.)

"Oh," she said, "I forgot about your cordless. I'll have to
put an adapter in that, too."

He handed it over.

"These," said Miss Simmons, "are a son of a bitch."

"Oh, now," Schiff said.

She grinned. Schiff didn't remember her but thought she
must have been a good student.

"Is everything hooked up yet?" he asked when she gave
back his phone.

"Almost. Maybe another half hour."

Because of course there were calls he had to make. (As a
cripple, he lived like a bookie.) The listmaker had not forgotten his situation, the necessary stations of his crip's paced
cross. Had not forgotten the party for his students that had
still to be called off. Had not forgotten the probable roasts
and hams, turkeys and pâtés, and could easily imagine the

possible meaty haunches—goats', stags', and rams'—ticking their timed shelf life in Claire's party-stocked refrigerator even now; the spoiling berries, oxidizing melon balls, and splinters of crystallized ice creams forming even as he thought of them, as they went on his lists; the sweet, separating, stratified milks and creamy desserts turning, going off, the freezer-burned breads tanning cancerous in the kitchen. Because (now it occurred) it wasn't the banks he'd needed to call, it was all the little food boutiques, awning'd purveyors of powerhouse cheeses, of tinned smoked delicacies, oysters and *fruits de mer* (squid and tiny, fetal octopi, lavender as varicose veins), as if fed-up Claire, working their only recently annual party like a serial killer, had taken it into her angry old head that even getting even wasn't enough, that only vengeance and wrath would serve.

"*Jesus!*" oathed Schiff, sniffing violently, taking rapid, shallow gusts of air into his hyperventilate nostrils, slapping his head, clipping it with the heel of his hand like a self-inflicted personal foul. "*Jesus! Jesus! Jesus!*"

"What," Miss Simmons asked, "what is it? What's wrong?"

And, believe it or not, it was suddenly revealed to Schiff that it was no mere accident that Jenny Simmons had been a former student of his, that she'd been—yes, he knew how he sounded, he knew *just* how he sounded—— like Creer, like Beverly Yeager, bowed beneath the weight of their mad, customized agendas—sent like the closing couplet in some fabulous poetic justice to save them. Jenny d'Arc. If all that "Oh, now" had been genuine nurturing and not just conventional courtesy, let her nurture him now or forever hold her peace.

"I was thinking," he said. "I haven't had anything in my stomach all day. I'm so hungry I could eat a horse."

"Really?" she said. "You haven't eaten all day?"

"It puts me off my feed," Schiff said, "when my wife walks out on me."

"You've got to eat."

"I know," Schiff said.

"Shall I make you a sandwich?"

"Jeez," Schiff said, "that'd be putting you to a lot of trouble, wouldn't it? I'm going to have to get connected up with one of those Meals-on-Wheels deals or something."

"Well, but I could make you a sandwich."

"I *am* hungry," admitted Schiff.

"I'll just make you a sandwich. What would you like?"

"Gosh, anything. I think Claire may have left some stuff in the refrigerator."

"Coming right up," she said.

"And if anything suits *your* fancy . . ." Schiff said, breaking off.

She was back within minutes. There, on a plate on a tray, was a peanut butter and jelly sandwich, the bread perfectly toasted, its crusts almost surgically removed. There was a tall glass of innocent-seeming milk.

"Peanut butter and jelly?" Schiff said.

"Don't you like peanut butter and jelly? I thought everyone did. You haven't eatten all day and it's easy to digest."

"No no," Schiff said, "this is fine. It's just I had this craving for some of that gourmet shit my wife left in the freezer for this party we're giving. We're giving. She stocked up, I thought she left stuff in the refrigerator. I was going to cancel out anyway, I just didn't want it all to go to waste."

"There's nothing in the refrigerator."

"In the freezer part."

"I looked in the freezer part. There's nothing in the refrigerator."

"That's impossible," Schiff said. "The party's tomorrow night. We give it every year for my students."

"Well, maybe," Miss Simmons said, "she planned to leave you. If she was planning to leave you, why would she take the trouble of going to specialty shops and charcuteries to stock up on exotic foods she knew were never going to be eaten in the first place? That stuff isn't cheap. Why would she waste the money?"

Planning to leave him, planning to leave him? Schiff couldn't quite take it all in, but if she was *planning* to leave him—he'd announced the party to his class three weeks ago, Claire knew that—that somehow put everything into an altogether different light. A poorer light, a darker light. Could this have been up her sleeve for three weeks now? Had she been setting him up for three weeks? More? At the *inside* three weeks? Had she been setting him up all term? Longer? From the beginning of the school year? Boy oh boy, thought Schiff, who understood he was no prize, who for years now, even when he'd been on the cane, even when he'd still wielded it with some authority, when it had been simple ancillary to his balance, pure latency, say, like peroxide, analgesics, tapes, and bandages in a first-aid kit, had begun to notice something long in the tooth about himself in mirrors and photographs—*particularly* photographs—something faintly sour and beginning to go off in his posture and features like all those imaginary delicacies in his refrigerator, must *she* have had it in for *me!* So *planning, planning* to leave him? Planning, that is, to set him up, planning to wait until the day before their annual party before she stepped out on him. (Who knew how important these parties had become to him!) What did it mean, wondered the old geographer. Would she have already notified his students, the party called on account of divorce, or at least an upcoming separation down the road she knew of and let his students in on but that the old geographer himself hadn't heard about yet? What did it mean? What did it mean, eh?

On the principle that it takes a thief, et cetera, et cetera, these were the questions he put to that other old nurturer, his former student, Miss Simmons.

"What do you mean do I think she called them up to tell them her plans?" she said. "What do you mean do I think she didn't call anyone up and that she left that for you? What do you mean when they show up at the door she hopes you'll be so humiliated you won't know what to do?"

"Yes," he said. "That's just what I mean."

"Well, *I* don't know. How would *I* know?"

"How did you know about the empty refrigerator? All

right," he said, "that's a bad example. But you knew about her planning to leave me."

"I never said she planned to leave you. I suggested it was a possibility."

"You knew she left me. Bill must have told you in the van. You can't deny that."

"I *don't* deny it," she said. "People gossip about people. It's human nature."

"You knew to the penny what we have in the trust-fund account. When you were up in my room, when you were up in my room, you probably saw my urinal. You're practically my confidante. You took pity on me and gave old Bill the high sign that enough was enough, that he needn't pad the equipment, you told him my credit was good. If all that doesn't make you my confidante, I don't know what does."

"What's more likely," she said, "is that it makes me old Bill's confidante."

"Oh," said Schiff, "oh."

"Hey," Miss Simmons said, "hey now."

"That's all right."

"You bet," she said. "Because if that's what you're driving at, you can just forget it, you can just put it out of your mind."

"What," asked the helpless cripple with the useless legs, "what?"

"You know what," she said. "I'm not standing in as your hostess. It's been at least fifteen years since you were my professor, at *least* fifteen years."

"That's right," he said, astonished, amazed. "At *least* fifteen years. That's right. So don't tell *me* you're not my confidante. Now that Claire's gone that makes you one of maybe only half a dozen people in this town who knew me when."

"I'm here on a job," she said, all business.

"Of course."

"Another few minutes I'm through. I'm almost through now. Here," she said, "I need you to put this on for me."

She handed him a sort of necklace with, for pendant, a

button and light on a little plastic box like a switch on a heating pad or electric blanket. He recognized it from the S.O.S. commercial on TV. "Just put the chain over your head," she said. "It should fit. If it doesn't there's a way of adjusting it." Now the moment of truth had arrived Schiff felt some qualms about actually wearing such jewelry. It was another giant step toward his invalidism, like having the Stair-Glide put in or going into a wheelchair. Miss Simmons, misreading his reluctance for mechanical uncertainty as to how the equipment operated, took it back from him and fastened the collar about his neck like a kind of electronic bib. "There," she said, "is that comfortable?"

"Is it ever," Schiff said miserably.

"Why don't we test it to see if it's working?"

And see, he thought, he was right, his identity already subsumed in plural baby talk.

"Test it out," she said again. "Press the button. That dials the service for you. Wait six or seven seconds, then just speak into the air. If everything's been connected properly, they should be able to pick you up at the service." Schiff pressed the button and spoke into the air. Miss Simmons took the little console out of his hand and hit the button a second time. The light went off. "You didn't give it time to dial. You have to wait a few seconds before you start talking. By depressing the button a second time I aborted your call."

"Whoa," Schiff said. "This thing's a lot tougher than it seems."

"You're not used to it yet, that's all. You'll get used to it."

"Shall I try again?"

"Sure. Just give it a chance to dial the phone before you speak."

He pressed the button. He waited half a dozen seconds. He glanced up at Miss Simmons. She nodded. "Help," Schiff said quietly into the air. "Help me, I've fallen and I can't get up." It was the message he'd heard the old woman deliver on television. The only difference was Schiff's bloomers weren't up around his ears.

"What," someone shouted back at him down at S.O.S, "what's that? Speak up, I can't hear you."

"Is that you, Charley?" Miss Simmons called out. "Charley, it's Jenny Simmons. I'm at 727-4312, 225 Westgate, in the Parkview area—— Jack Schiff's residence. Dr. Schiff's new on the service and I'm walking him through the procedures."

(Well, Schiff thought, *walking*.)

"Hi, Jenny. Hi, Dr. Schiff."

"Hi, Charley," Schiff said.

"You're coming in fine now, sir. You don't have to shout, though. Just speak up, that'll do it."

"I'm sorry," Schiff shouted.

"That's all right, you'll get used to it."

Everyone kept telling him he'd get used to it. A good sign and a bad sign both. He didn't need all that accident in his life, but it was comforting to think S.O.S. would pick him up each time he fell down. This is what it comes to, he thought. If you just hung on and managed to live long enough you turn into a bowling pin.

Now he knew he was expected to do a fair share of falling he was reluctant to be left alone. It was Schiff's suggestion they go through the rest of the house, check out each of the base stations Miss Simmons had rigged. She had to push him in his wheelchair, help lift his feet onto the little platform of his Stair-Glide, help raise his pants up (he wore only pants with elastic waistbands these days, shirts whose buttons, except for the top button and the one beneath that, had been already buttoned so that all he had to do was slip it on over his head, his shoes were fastened with Velcro tabs, and he dressed not so much for comfort—when was the last time he'd been comfortable?—as for sitting down on toilet seats and getting up from them again, so he wore no underwear, and tended, the elastic waistband reconfiguring itself about his body each time he moved, casually to moon the world each time he stood) for him again as he got out of it and leaned into his walker. It took another forty minutes for them to do the rounds of the second floor and he was satisfied that all systems were go. Each area was a little different from the others and required, as if he were reciting from the stages of separate theaters, a slightly different projection of his voice. By the time they were finished, however, Charley was complimenting him on his levels. He sounded, Charley said, like someone who'd been doing pratfalls for years.

There was nothing left for her to do. He could stall her no longer, he'd have to let her go.

"Oh," she said, "I forgot to get your key from you."

"My key?"

"For the house. The service will need it if it has to get in."

"Gee," Schiff said, "my key, I don't know."

"We take an impression, we duplicate it on our premises and get it back to you."

"No," Schiff said, "I mean I don't know. Where it even is. I can't remember the last time I used it."

"Maybe it's in the tchtchk," Jenny Simmons said.

"Gosh," he said, "you pronounced that perfectly."

She seemed to blush. Which would make it once for him and twice for her. Were the two of them falling in love?

"I'll look and see," she said, and left him in his bedroom, sitting on his bed.

"That's just where it was," she called up in a couple of minutes. "I've already checked to see if it's the right one. This is it, all right. It unlocked your front door straight off."

"That's terrific," he called. "It was clever of you to think of the tchtchk."

"People have patterns," she called back up the stairs. "It's human nature."

"You're right," he said from where he sat on his bed, projecting perfectly now from all the practice he'd had on their dry run through the base stations, "it *is* human nature."

"Goodbye," she called. "I'll have this duplicated ASAP. I'll see to it someone gets it back to you. Oh, and Professor?"

"Yes?"

"You mustn't worry about any of this. It's like health, or fire, or automobile insurance. It's for your peace of mind. You hope you never have to use it. You just know it's there for you if you ever do." It was exactly what Bill would have said. He heard the front door close behind her.

So much, Schiff thought, for love.

Well, thought dignified old Schiff, *that* was a close one. Because for a few minutes there he'd begun to rethink his decision to call off the party. He was going to invite Miss Simmons. If she'd come upstairs to say goodbye properly he would have. It wasn't crazy. He could have asked without embarrassing either of them. It was perfectly natural. She'd been his student, too, once. Of course, she seemed put off when he mentioned the party, but that was because she thought he was trying to get her to stand in for Claire. She'd seen there was nothing in the fridge, that the cupboard was bare. She may have thought he wanted her to do his shopping for him. She was a busy woman, he knew that. A dozen or so phone calls, he could have taken care of it himself. What did Miss Simmons know of his arrangements with Information?

Well, he thought, there's no fool like an old fool. Hold it right there, old fool, he told himself. Because where, really, was the foolishness in all this? Hadn't she recognized him? It had been fifteen years. At *least* fifteen years. She could have been a sophomore when she'd taken his class. Even, with permission of the instructor, a freshman. So at least fifteen years, probably sixteen, but possibly seventeen or eighteen. If she wanted to get her distribution requirement in political science out of the way.

But *say* fifteen years. She knew him when, he'd said. She'd known him when. He didn't kid himself. He knew well enough what he looked like these days, his frail, shot, worn-out, emeritus looks and cripple's diminished, broken bearing. Yet she'd recognized him through all the schmutz of disability, through all the scaffolding of his wheelchairs, Stair-Glides and walkers, the heavy disguise of his ruined body. So where was the old foolishness? Where exactly? He was a geographer, show him on a map. And if it had been fifteen years since she'd graduated, that made her, what, thirty-seven? (At least thirty-seven.) Which would have made him about forty-four—she knew him when—when she knew him. Or, depending on those distribution requirements, that permission of the instructor, conceivably only forty-one. Looked at in this light, not so much *sub specie aeternitatis* as in the enchanted, almost charming relativity of love and other such matters, that made them practically contemporaries. So where, *where* was the foolishness? Where was there even such a big-deal age difference? Because didn't young women often develop crushes—he used the lightest, most flattering term for such things—on their professors? Didn't they fall in outright love with them? Develop grand passions for them that ended up not just in some motel room but frequently in actual officially sanctioned, ceremonially blessed marriage beds? He could name at least half a dozen such arrangements right here on this campus. Sure. Happens all the time. (And, frequently, with happier, longer-lasting outcomes than his and Claire's.) Or maybe she *didn't* care for him in that way (or it could be she knew all too well what was happening and had simply been too shy to come up), but how did no-fool-like-an-old-fool apply? He could have as easily said—this was *love* he was talking about, *that* grand enchantment, *that* charming relativity that smashed time's tenses—that he'd been thinking like a high school kid, and what did *he* see in *her*, a woman at *least* thirty-seven?

All right, that was stretching things. But he at least wanted it on the record that he was taking back all his disclaimers. He was ruling nothing in, he was ruling nothing out. And if this *was* some May and December thing, okay, all right, but at least it was some *late* May, *early* December thing!

And besides, Schiff thought, he was alone in the house, he was in enough trouble as it was. He had to think about something that would keep his spirits up.

And not only alone in the house, *left* alone in the house. Left like some kid babysitting himself for the first time. Face it, he was spooked. Not by ghosts and not by darkness. But by all the hobgoblins of contingency, what Charley called pratfall, a comic term that didn't fool him for a minute, that he knew all along masked a broken hip. Or worse. Help, Schiff rehearsed over and over in his head, help me, I've fallen and I can't get up.

When he woke he figured from the fullness of his bladder he must have slept for at least two hours. He reached into the nightstand where he'd stashed the basin and pisser and peed into it without even having to Credé himself. Added to what was already there, there's now about seven hundred cc in the urinal. Jesus, he thinks, and prays that next time it will be his ordinary dribs and drabs again. Ultimately, of course, he would have to risk walking into the bathroom, but he doesn't think he feels up to it tonight. He's still spooked, wants to get this first night left alone in the house behind him before he tries anything brave. And *Damn*, he thinks, feeling hunger pangs, and maybe even a little thirst there at the back of his throat, that son of a bitch. Meaning Claire. Who'd abandoned him to his bare necessities, his basic needs and what to do with his wastes and grimes. That no-good whoreheart! *Damn her and all who sail in her!*

He takes up the remote control for his television set and turns the power on, not because he wants to watch television but because he needs to see the yellow date and time stretched across the top of the screen like a banner headline. Ten thirty-nine. Figures, he figures. (He's not particularly superstitious, but he doesn't like it when numerals add up to thirteen.)

Well, he wonders, knocked back on his own devices, what to do, what to do?

Idly at first, his head and heart not only not really in it but not even aware that that's what they're doing, he begins to make up another of his messages for the answering machine he does not yet even own. Please leave a message at the beep, he composes, then, inspired, takes out the

"please." Leave a message at the beep. Yes! he thinks. That's
it! No frills. No chinks in the sheer insurmountability in so
imposing a cliff face. What could be simpler, yet pack more
powerhouse ambiguity? Thieves, even those professionals
cops so loved to brag on and seemed to respect (if not flat-
out admire, as if they were so many Sherlock Holmeses con-
fronting so many Professors Moriarity), thugs worthy of
them, thugs with mettle, thugs with brains, would be put
off. Or would they? Is this guy for real, they might wonder.
Who does he think he's fooling with this bluff? Surely, if
they were truly worthy of the professionalism the cops
claimed to respect them for, they'd recognize the Mayday
appeal in such a communiqué. Oh, oh, the looseness of
cripples, mourned buffeted, crippled Schiff, who, on second thought had seen that *real* professionals, *genuine* gang-
sters, or even only revved kids hopped-up on drugs, could
read the vulnerable, terrified wimp factors right through
such ploys. It was practically an open invitation practically.
Why not just come out and say just come out and get it?

Good Christ, Schiff thought, taking another reading off
the television screen, it was already eleven twenty-nine
(again thirteen). Almost an hour had passed since the last
time he'd checked. Was it too late to call his students to tell
them the party had been scrubbed? Well, they were graduate
students, accustomed, he would have thought, to burning
the not-yet-but-almost midnight oil, hitting the books or,
sunk in the creases of their own complicated lives, their various affairs and dramatized politicals, even their own ardent
lonelinesses (drinking or partying or doing their thing in
their stricken privacies), so he was pretty certain he
wouldn't be waking them, ripping their sleep like the torn
fabrics over the furniture in their secondhand rooms.
Rather, it was still a question of his dignity-meister's
guarded dignity. Full professors didn't telephone graduate
students. Not at this hour. Not at high noon. He couldn't
conceive of a message that would not wait. That's what
campus mail was for, stairways, restrooms, and corridors
where you could bump into each other, office hours, those

three or four minutes before class started up, the choreo-
graphed minute or so afterward when one hefted garments
and maneuvered briefcases or bookbags into the fast-closing
stream of things at the door. ("A word with you, Bumas,
please, when you have a chance.") It was bad enough when
the student called the professor up. Oh, Schiff didn't mind
the kid's preliminary feint and shuffle, his nerves and courtesy like a bout of flu, was even a little grateful for the tribute of all those deferential, stammered reluctancies. ("I hope
I'm not calling you at a bad time, Professor, that I'm not
interrupting your and Mrs. Schiff's dinner or anything. I
hate bothering you at home like this, sir.") But bad enough
anyway. Because you had to be on your toes when the
phone rang. You had to see to it that the TV was inaudible,
had to fumble for the Mute button on the remote control,
or turn down the volume on the radio, make certain the
silence the kid heard at his end of the line was the pure,
unadulterated noise of interruption, the sound of difficult,
significant books being read, the quiet of a busted, damaged
concentration.

Of course Schiff's being crippled excused him from a lot
of that crap. He didn't get to campus often enough to use
campus mail, he no longer kept regular office hours, people
tended to steer clear of him in the corridors, he never went
near a stairway, and no longer did choreography in the fast-
closing stream of things at the door, don't ask him. So he
could have called. Technically. It was the message that would
have compromised his dignity. Announcing at damn near
midnight that their—well, *his*, his now that Claire had
blown him off—party would have to be canceled. And not
only damn near midnight, but, by the time he'd reached all
of them, damn near one o'clock, too, later, the very A.M. of
the very P.M. of the party in question. Still, he could have
called. Technically. Even, technically, his message notwithstanding. Though then the embarrassment would be on the
other foot. He'd be the one breaking the peace, breaking *into*
the peace, calling at a bad time and interrupting God-knew-
what, bothering their lovemaking perhaps, disturbing their

youth. His own stammered hesitations and uneasiness barely audible over the unturned-down volume of hi-fi and boom box. ("Professor Schiff here. Schiff. SCHIFF!")

What time was it now? Twelve one-niner. (Again thirteen? This was beyond high odds. This was into fate.)

Still protective of his dignity, he thought, fuck it, picked up the phone and asked Information for the telephone number of Molly Kohm.

Miss Kohm (though this was unclear, she could well have been married; older than his other students, in, he judged, her early forties, and got up always in the costumes, the cloaks, boots, skirts, and dresses of ladies, he imagined, on symphony, museum, and various other arts boards; and something too dramatic, even a little hysterical, about her dark makeup, its etched or engraved character, almost as if it were not makeup at all but a sort of tattoo, a kind of stenciled quality to her enduring tan, something about Miss—or Mrs.—Kohm that suggested, well, weekends spent elsewhere, her passport in her purse as surely as her car keys, coins for tolls; something—he admitted this though she was not his type—vaguely exciting about her, her intelligence grounded—if that was the word—in intimacy and some mysticism of the far, as though—he had no other way of putting this—Schiff was the geographer but she was the traveler) picked up on the very first ring. And, when he identified himself (hemming and hawing, beating about the bush, shuffling with the best of them), pretending—he assumed pretending—she'd been expecting his call.

"Oh," she said, "you poor man, I was going to call *you*."

"You were?"

"Well, when I heard what your not-so-better-half had *done* to you . . . And on the eve of your *party!* Outrageous! People ought to know that some of the most significant damage one can do to others is to force them to change their plans at the last minute. Too too rude, I think. To treat other persons' lives as though they were subject to alterations like something off-the-rack. Barbaric!"

"Then why didn't you?"

"Why didn't I—?"

"Call me," he asked her.

"I thought Dickerson would take care of it. Dickerson was *supposed* to take care of it. That's what we arranged at any rate."

"We? You and Dickerson? Arranged?

"We, the members of the Political Geographers Party Committee."

"There is such a thing?"

"Well, now there is. The people in your seminar threw it together as soon as we heard."

"Heard? Heard what?"

"Why, what Mrs. Professor S. did to Mr. Professor S., of course."

"What's none of your business is none of my business, I suppose, but I'd like to know—" Schiff said formally, and with as much dignity as the thought would allow, "this just happened—who put the word out? How did you know? Is it some jungle telegraph thing?" Then, risking the inside joke, "Or are you folks connected to Information, too?" Chilled to the bone when Miss or Mrs. Kohm gave her immense and raucous board member's society laugh.

"We take care of our own, dear," is what she said.

"The Political Geographers Party Committee," Schiff said. "Is that like a fan club or something?"

"Would you like a fan club?"

"I'd like," said Schiff, sorry as soon as he permitted the words to escape, "for my life to go into remission."

"Well," she said, "there's nothing the seminar can do about that one, of course, but it can and will rally round its annual party."

"The party," Schiff said, "the party is off."

"Of course the party's not off. As far as the party's concerned, well, damn the torpedoes, full-speed ahead."

"It's off," Schiff said.

"Why? Give me one good reason."

"I've nothing to serve."

"Eats," she said, "the subcommittee on eats is taking care of that."

"There's a subcommittee on eats?"

"There's a subcommittee on booze, there's a subcommittee on party decorations."

"Who organized all this? Did you?"

"Oh, that isn't important," Ms. Kohm—it was how he neutrally addressed her in class, too—dismissed. "You won't have to lift a finger."

"I can't lift a finger."

"You won't have to."

"Look," Schiff said, "it's late. There are other people in the seminar I still have to get in touch with."

"But I *told* you, there's nothing for you to do. Dickerson will take care of it."

"Dickerson," Schiff said. "Dickerson didn't even call me."

"Possibly he was nervous about catching you at a bad time, or that he was interrupting your dinner, or that he hates bothering you at home. In any event," Ms. Kohm said, "there's no reason for you to call the scholars. Everything really has been taken care of. The PGPC is on top of it."

"The Political Geographers Party Committee," Schiff said, exactly like a moderator of a news show identifying a reference for the audience.

"Exactly," Ms. Kohm said, exactly like a panelist.

"Listen," Schiff said, "what you and the others in the seminar have done is very kind. Really," he said, "*very* kind. And I appreciate it, I *do,* but to tell the truth, I don't believe I could even handle a party just now. Be a guest at one, I mean, never mind its host. I don't much enjoy playing hearts and flowers, Ms. Kohm, but it's been a pretty rough day, I've a lot on my mind, and the last thing in the world I'm up to right now is a celebration."

"Jack, let me give you some advice: the worst thing someone like you can do at a time like this is to feel sorry for himself."

Jack? Jack?

"Negative energy, particularly for someone in your condition, has devastating effects."

In *his* condition? In *his* condition?

"Let me tell you something, Ms. Kohm," Schiff said,
"unless they're referring to alternative fuels or to how
they're feeling, I'm always a little suspicious of, and embarrassed for, people who use terms like energy."

"Jack," she said, "I know you're upset, that you're just
sick with worry about Claire, and, incidentally, I shouldn't
think she's in Portland."

Claire? Claire?

Where did this woman get off? (Or would she stop at
nothing?) Was she drunk? She might be drunk. She looked
like a drinker, had, he meant, a drinker's dramatic, slightly
hysterical expression, and her makeup, fixed in place like
cosmetic surgery, might have been a drinker's makeup,
something planted on her face for emergency, like a name
sewn into her clothing.

Still, he didn't know which bothered him more, the dignity he'd leaked through his mean outburst about her use of
language, or the dignity he lost through her (and he could
only assume everyone's) general knowledge of his business,
how it was between him and Claire, how it was between
him and his condition.

"I know," she was saying, and Schiff, who'd tuned out
for a couple of moments, once for his indignation and once
again for the regret he felt for permitting himself to give in
to it, knew he'd missed something, perhaps even something
important (maybe she'd gone on to say what the thinking
was in political geography regarding Claire's whereabouts),
"things are pretty much up in the air just now, but, you'll
see, they'll come down, they'll settle. It isn't the end of the
world. Oh, I grant you, when these things happen, one always thinks it's the end of *one's* world, and, occasionally,
even frequently, one's often right about that. After all,
there's no arguing with a judgment call, but I wouldn't
count myself out just yet. The consensus now is that three

things may still happen. Your wife could come back. Two,
time heals all wounds. And, three, you could make an adjustment, discover not only that you don't really need her
but that, if you make the adjustment, become more independent, you might even be better off without her."

The consensus? The consensus?

"You're right that she could come back," he told her,
"but it's a long shot. Even about three—though it's iffy,
improbable, the odds are against it—that I might adjust. But
that, two, time heals all wounds, is out of the question."

"Time doesn't heal all wounds?"

"Only if there's time," he said.

"I'm sorry," she said, "I don't underst——— "

"Well," Schiff said, stinging her, hoping to anyhow,
hoping she'd take it back and pass it on to the consensus,
"aren't you forgetting my condition?"

"Oh," she said.

"Yes," he said, "you bet." Then, while he had her on the
ropes, following through. "But my real objection to a party
this year is that I couldn't possibly clean up afterward. My
'condition' militates against it." Forgetting about the PGPC
and realizing his mistake at once. And—perhaps something
to do with his hand eye coordination, his cripple's slowed
reaction times, just the merest piece of a beat off but a miss
as good as a mile and except in horseshoes close didn't count
for diddly—Ms. Kohm, losing no time, all over him.

"Did you forget what I told you? That you won't have to
lift a finger? That we wouldn't permit it even if you could?
Listen," she said, "this isn't even a committee thing. I mean
no one's been assigned to wash, no one's been assigned to
dry. No one's been named to empty the ashtrays or run the
vacuum over the rug in the living room. This is an area
where everyone pitches in. Should someone see anything
out of place, he or she straightens it up. This party will be
a strictly straighten-up-as-you-go party. Will that be all
right? Is that good enough for you?"

"Well," Schiff said.

"Will it?" she asked. "Is it?" she teased.

"Well," said Schiff. "Do I have your word? That no one leaves the house until it's neat and clean as when they came in?"

"Neater and cleaner," Ms. Kohm said.

"All right," Schiff said. "Look, I'm sorry I'm such a tightass, but really," he said, "unless everything's just the way you found it . . . I'm going to let you in on something. I try to live by the cripple's code."

"Yes?"

"One must never do anything twice."

"Oh, what a good rule! That's a good rule even for persons who aren't physically challenged."

"Actually it is," Schiff said.

"No, I mean it," Ms. Kohm said.

"Okay, all right. We'll try having the party."

"Do you know what time it is?"

"No. Is it late?"

"Twelve thirty-seven."

"Thirteen," Schiff said.

"What?"

"Nothing," Schiff said.

"Well," said Ms. Kohm, "it's been a long day. Tomorrow's the party. Tonight, actually. Better turn in."

"I will," said Schiff.

"Me, too," said Ms. Kohm. "Well," she said, "see you tomorrow night."

"Tonight, actually," he said, and both laughed and hung up, and Schiff, too tired to try to make it into the bathroom, took up the pisser and peed within a cc of his life.

He slept like a baby. He didn't dream. He didn't once wake up. And, in the morning, it was like being roused from a trance, awakened, like someone from the audience, on stage, in the middle of a hypnotist's act, come to life after a surgery in a room one can't remember. Even, in those first several blank-slate seconds, experiencing what was not joy, not hope, not peace or patience, curiosity or wonder or even pleasure, so much as a sort of passivity, even obedience, something almost theological, some deep trust, almost—

and here's Schiff's brain kicking in, and here's Schiff—he
supposes, like faith, like a perfect numb composure, Schiff
detached and poised as an angel, like one of those rare
dreams—and here's Schiff with the slow, ever-so-gradual
beginnings of self-consciousness—where he dreams himself
moving, walking, running, pleased with the smooth point-
to-point of his compliant synapses. And *here's* Schiff. Tumbled from grace like a man overboard. Alert, alive, aware of
the facts, passed sudden and roughly from one condition to
the next like a clumsily transferred baton. Here's Schiff. All
at once the phone is ringing, his bladder is bursting, virtually screaming, "Do something, do something, will you,
before I wet your pants all over you, your blankets, sheets,
and pillowcases, your carpets and furniture and upholstery,
before I take matters into my own hands and leave what
used to be your dick jumping around every which way,
loose and as out of control as a live wire spraying indiscriminate voltage like a hose in the street," and his bones and
body are stiff, filling up with pain in every cavity like air
stretching a balloon, and—here's Schiff, here's Schiff now—
he pulls himself up in bed to sit on its side and he reaches
for his pisser but the son of a bitch is filled to the top—the
job he did on it before retiring last night—and somehow he
has to get into the toilet without—there's no time to put
them on—his shoes with their footdrop braces standing up
in them like long shoehorns, and which permit him to put
his feet out in front of him without kicking a foot into the
carpet, smashing his practically hammertoes, tripping and
stumbling the length of his body headfirst into the floor.
So, here's Schiff landed back in Farce, his homeland practically, and he pictures himself falling arse over tip down the
stairs shoved tight against the aircraft and diving, face
down, nose to the tarmac, which he kisses as if he's finally
come home after a long exile.

He's up on his walker now, skedaddling to the john before he bursts, Schiff's version anyway, his *modified* skedad-
dle, distracting himself, thinking, Push, Step, Pull (on
"Push" pushing his walker out in front of him; on "Step"

stepping out with his right foot; on "Pull" pulling his left foot up almost even with it), though even as he thinks Push, Step, Pull, he's wondering if it wouldn't be better to change his mantra to Push, Step, Drag, because times change and a chap owes it to himself to keep up with his disease. (And because the effort is so great. He should, he thinks again, have been an event in the Olympics.) What, it occurs, are these tears in these eyes? Because suddenly he can't remember the last time he walked without having to resort to these diversionary tactics and gambits, when he didn't have to think of his walker as a plow, or his floors as fields, when he didn't have to break down his progress—progress, *hah!*—into tiny, divisible bits like so much sovereign acreage or, just to keep himself from going nuts—walking was so difficult now, required *such* concentration; this was how he concentrated on it—providing a running—running, *hah!*—commentary on it, like some kid muttering the play-by-play in his head as he throws a rubber ball against a stoop. The pressure on his bladder is driven by its own terrible, gathering momentum. Schiff, still pushing the walker, concentrating, but switching over to alternative modes even as he begins to feel a little, a little, not much, leakage—— *I think I can, I think I can!* Or "Schiff not out of the woods, yet, ladies and gentlemen, though even if he pees now, at least it won't be on the Berber. Because once that stuff gets on wool, it's *yech,* and watch out, it's time for the Home! Over to you in the crapper, Jim." "Thanks, Dave Wilson, but you've just about told the whole story. Schiff, as you say, had begun to feel a little moisture, but, fortunately, this was just about the time he was swinging his walker around, dropping his drawers, and already lowering himself onto the toilet seat. Maybe I can get him to give us a comment. Jack, Jack, it's Jim Johnson. You do much damage?" "No, Jim, I don't think so. There's a phrase in Ward Howe's 'Battle Hymn of the Republic' that best sums it up, I think. Something about the 'evening dews and damps.' I don't think anything actually got on the tile though there may be some small humidity in my pants, however. In any event, I'm chucking them into the laundry basket on my way out."

Which made him think about laundry. Which, Jesus, gave him a jolt. Because, really, with Claire gone, how was he ever going to handle that one? He didn't know if they even still did laundry service, couldn't recall the last time he'd seen a laundry truck. Claire, Schiff thought, you're the rat and I'm the sinking ship! And where, he wondered, had his mild hope for the day gone? Those few seconds or so of respite he felt when he'd first waked up? That perfect, numb composure?

On his walker again, returning to his room, so caught up in his analysis of where he was, letting his fans know—he's beaming his coordinates back to the PGPC—the long row he's yet to hoe—"Technically I'm still in the bathroom, though the wheels of the walker, and even its two hind legs, are over the threshold and out in the hall, heading south, my right foot on Steppp, my left, huff puff huff puff, on Draaaag. And I'm in the hall too, now, in the hall and making my adjustments, shifting my trajectory, handling the walker, raising it up off the carpet and swinging it east, bringing my body into alignment with the walker. All right. All right. Just about ready to move on. From here it's a fairly clean shot east to the bedroom, where I'll have to hang a north, then jockey from there northeast to the bed. You know something, folks? I'm not saying it's a blessing or promising rose gardens, merely mentioning in huff-puff passing that this disease could have done worse than chosen to be trapped in the body of a political geographer"—that he realizes the phone is still ringing only after he's back in bed, that probably it hasn't stopped since it first began eleven or twelve minutes ago. It has to be Claire, he thinks, it *has* to be Claire. Anyone else would have hung up after eight or nine rings, ten rings tops. When he realizes this he wonders if he should pick up at all. It's Saturday. She knows he has to be home, that except for Tuesdays and Thursdays when he teaches his classes, unless she's there to take him somewhere, he *has* to be home. Sure, he decides, let Claire ring the phone's ass off, let her ring and ring until she pictures him dead. *Then* she'll be sorry, *then* she will. I'm a grown fucking man, for Christ's sake. And he picks up the phone.

"Claire?"

"Harry Ald, buddy. Boy, you really *are* crippled up. I've been on the line fifteen minutes waiting for you to answer. I direct-dialed, for God's sake, but the long-distance broad broke in anyway, wanted to know if I 'wished' to place my call later. I told her no, let it ring, I had this stiff-in-the-joints pal took his own sweet damn time coming to the telephone. Breaks in *again* in five minutes, tells me, 'Sir, please place your call later, you're tying up the lines.' I say, 'How can I be tying up the lines, I'm not even connected.' Miss Priss offers it's some satellite thing, very technical. I go 'Oh yeah?' She's gonna disconnect me, she says, if I don't hang up, and I shoot back that that'd be a violation of the First Amendment, but I see where she's coming from and tell her, all right then, charge me for the goddamn call, you can count from the time I first began dialing. You know what she does, Schiff? You know what she tells me? She says to hang up and call person-to-person collect. I ask how that would change anything, I'd still be tying up the line, wouldn't I? 'Oh no,' she says, 'collect, person-to-person calls go through on a different circuit, that's why we have to charge the customer extra for them.' 'And all the time,' I tell her, 'I thought that had to do with greed and operator assistance, so-called,' which is when she starts giving me this you-can-talk-to-my-supervisor crapola. Well, do I have to tell you, there's nothing in the world worse, or more boring and futile, than talking to some telephone-company operator broad's supervisor. Fortunately, as it turns out, however, I didn't have to because that's just when you finally decide to pick up. So how are you? D'ja hear anything from Claire?"

He could be making this all up, Schiff thought. Claire could have put him up to it. He could be Claire's beard, or decoy, or special agent, or whatever. She could be sitting beside him (even lying beside him) right now, for goodness' sake, or listening in on an extension. It wasn't proof she still loved him or anything, but after as long as they'd been married she was vested. Well, they both were.

"Nothing," Schiff said, "not a word. Did you?"

"Me? God no, Jack. Anyway, you know what would happen if Claire ever did show up here?"

"What?" He felt like a straight man.

"We go back you and me, but we ain't seen each other in years. We probably wouldn't even recognize each other in the street."

"What are you saying to me, Harry?"

"I'm a different person, Jack. Just like you're a different person."

"I'm not a different person," Schiff said. "I'm the same person I always was."

"Jack, you used to do the hundred in split seconds, you used to go out for the long ones."

"Those are physical things," Schiff said.

"*Physical* things? *Physical* things?" Harry Ald said. "What the hell else is there? It took you fifteen minutes to answer the telephone. This doesn't do something to a man's soul? But all right, okay, you're still the same old Jack Schiff. The spitting image. But me, *I've* changed. I'm a roughneck. I've got tabs in bars. Sixty years old and I'm a regular in bars. Sixty years old and I've got, you know, girlfriends. I'm living right now with a squaw."

"A squaw? Really?"

"Well, a half-breed, really, but this is the Pacific Northwest. It ain't that big a deal with the braves, but the women take it very seriously. You know what they say about Catholic converts, how they're more Catholic than the pope? Well, that's what your half-breed squaw is like."

"More Catholic than the pope?"

"Ha ha," Ald said, "that's a good one on me all right."

"What?" Schiff asked. "What would happen?"

"If Claire showed up here? Oh, nothing. She'd get gut shot is all. Flowers of the Field would see to it personally."

"Flowers of the Field? This is your squaw's name?"

"It's a beautiful name."

"It *is* a beautiful name," Schiff said.

"You don't believe me? You want me to put her on? Wait, I'll put her on, she'll tell you herself. Hey, Flowers of the Field, put down the Maize Flakes a minute, come over here and tell my old friend what you'd do if all of a sudden his wife showed up and wanted to move in with me."

"I'd gut shoot the bitch," a woman said.

"Jesus," Schiff said.

"How do you like that?" Harry Ald, who'd taken the phone back, said. "And don't think for a minute this is some young bimbo we're talking about here, Jack. She's got almost a decade on *me*."

"She sounds like a pistol," Schiff admitted.

"She's a bow-and-arrow."

He told Harry Ald about his graduate students coming over that night. He explained about the PGPC. Harry thought it was wonderful, that it would do him a world of good. "Just don't let them mug you," he warned.

"Mug me? They're my students. Why would they mug me?"

"Sometimes," Harry Ald said, "graduate students see a helpless old professor in his house, they can't help themselves, they mug him, then they throw him down the stairs."

Schiff couldn't have explained it, but he thought he was feeling better. Sometimes a good laugh, of course, but he felt *stronger,* too. He got off the bed and, moving about his bedroom, tested himself on the walker. He actually *was* a little stronger, back to Push, Step, Pull, from Push, Step, Drag, down to the occasional huff puff from the occasional huff puff huff puff. This wasn't, he understood, mere fancy. He'd been to too many neurologists by this time, and knew that it was in such tiny incrementals and small diminishments that the state of his disease was tracked, his particular pathology relatively long-haul, even his death a matter more of yards than of inches. (He thought now might be a good time to fit the handle of the urinal over the walker's cross-bar, take it into the toilet, and flush its contents down the commode, but then he realized he'd have to rinse out the pisser in the bathroom sink, that, or sit with it on his shower bench and let water into it from the faucet in the tub, running over his feet, spilling on his legs.) But already his strength draining, settling, separating, retreating into its nooks, crannies, holes and corners—— all the ragged features and interiority of its customary itty-bitties. The phone ringing again and Schiff fading fast.

Sam Creer was on the line, the law school's Native American activist, its expert on Treaty Law, practically its inventor, in fact; world famous, in fact, who had turned down an offer from Harvard because, as he said, he'd be damned if he'd teach school in a place that had been hacked out of pure aboriginal real estate. Sam wanted to know if Jack happened to have heard from Claire yet. No, Schiff told him, and said that as long as he had Sam on the line, he wondered, had Creer ever run across a dame called Flowers of the Field?

"Flowers of the Field," Creer mused, "Flowers of the Field. Is she Penobscot?"

"There's no telling," Schiff said.

Others called wanting to know about Claire. Even folks with whom Schiff couldn't recall having ever brought up the subject.

"You know," he was saying to a colleague with whom he hardly ever had contact, "for a guy as protective of his dignity as I am, people seem to know a whole shitload about my affairs. Every Tom and Dick. Maybe I'm not half as dignified as I think I am."

"No," said the colleague, a man whose face Schiff couldn't conjure and even whose voice was unfamiliar, "I don't think that's it. Why, your wheelchair alone earns you a certain amount of dignity, say thirty to thirty-eight percent. Then, anyone who ever saw you struggle on your walker into a men's room or maneuver it into a stall would grant you at least another couple dozen dignity points.

That's, what, sixty-two? Dignity-wise, all you'd need for a gentleman's C would be another ten or so points."

"Just see to it my fly is shut when I come out of the stall, as it were."

"As it were," said the colleague.

He was in bed, absently fingering the S.O.S. collar about his throat and resting up for his assault on the shower, when the phone rang again.

"Hello?" Schiff said.

"Professor Schiff?"

Speak of the devil, it was S.O.S. itself. In the voice of Miss Simmons.

"Miss Simmons?"

"What happened? Are you all right? If it's anywhere near you, see if you can pull the blanket off the bed and cover yourself with it. Try to stay warm. Try to keep calm. Now tell me what happened. I'm not so concerned with the extraneous details as I am with your precise location. Where are you right now? Does anything hurt? What hurts? Do you know where your wounds are? Do you know if you're bleeding? If you're not in a position to tell, can you say if there's a sticky sensation that might *be* blood? Do you feel as if you're going to faint? Does my voice sound muffled, does it sound like it's coming from far away? On a scale of one to ten, mild to severe, what would you estimate the extent of your injuries to be? Do you have any chest pain, or pain radiating down your left arm? An ambulance has been dispatched to your house and should be arriving within seven minutes."

"Well, gee," said Schiff, "I think I may have the wrong number."

"The wrong number? You haven't fallen? You're not exhibiting the classic symptoms of heart-attack discomfort?"

"As a matter of fact," Schiff said, "for me, I'm feeling pretty darned relatively good."

"You turned in a false alarm. There's a two-hundred dollar fine for turning in a false alarm," Miss Simmons said.

"A false alarm? Hey, no," Schiff said.

"You were playing with your button, weren't you?"

"Not consciously I wasn't," Schiff said.

"Unconsciously is just as bad. S.O.S. has three teams on call. One's out on a job and the second's on its way to 225 Westgate. If the third's called away and we get a call and are left unprotected, do you know who's responsible if there's a disaster that results in a subsequent lawsuit?"

"Me, I bet you," Schiff said.

"That's right," said Miss Simmons.

"How can this be?"

"You're a consenting adult, you signed papers."

"Ah, papers," said Schiff.

"That's right."

"They aren't here yet, call them back."

"It's too late, I'm not allowed. You'll just have to absorb the two-hundred-dollar fine and pray there are no emergency complications."

"Help me," Schiff said. "I've fallen and I can't get up."

Then Schiff moved to the edge of the bed and, leaning over it as far as he could, as if he were stretching for something just beyond his reach, he put out his balled fists, sought reliable purchase on the rug, and maneuvered his stronger right hip, thigh, and leg scant inches out over the mattress, and dragged his left leg up with the right one, hovering there for a moment in a sort of crippled yoga levitation. Then, gently as he could, he lowered himself carefully down off the bed and onto the floor. Stretched out on the carpet, he turned on his back, pulled the blanket off the bed and covered himself. For good measure he reached up and managed to find a pillow, which he placed behind his head.

He was breathless, but he'd just saved himself two hundred dollars, more if you threw in lawsuits and emergencies.

"Professor Schiff?" Miss Simmons was saying. "Professor Schiff?"

He was on the floor in his bedroom, he explained, nothing hurt him, he didn't think he was bleeding, he didn't feel faint. She was coming in clear as a bell, and his heart, knock wood, felt sound as a dollar. He was no doctor, he told her, not that kind anyway, and couldn't estimate the extent of his injuries.

But they'd know soon enough, he said, he thought he heard the ambulance now.

And he did, a crazed, mechanical *Geschrei*, somewhere between the regulation alarms of police and fire and the amok pitch of a child's video game raised to its wildest power.

"I know what you're doing," Miss Simmons said. "Don't think I don't know what you're doing."

When the S.O.S. men let themselves in with their key they found Schiff on the floor.

"I see you've got a pillow," one of them said.

"Presence of mind," Schiff said offhandedly.

Then the other examined him before both lifted him back onto the bed.

"Thanks a lot," Schiff said.

"Hey," the guy said who'd noted his pillow, "no problem."

"I guess I was trying to do too much."

"Yeah, how's that?"

Schiff lowered his voice. "Well," he said, embarrassed, "I was just getting out of bed to try to empty that when I fell." He pointed to the nightstand.

"I'll take care of that for you," said the paramedic who'd examined him.

"Would you?" Schiff said.

"No problem."

When the man brought it back, empty and odorless, Schiff wondered if he should tip them, then thought of the fines they'd have demanded of him, of all the ways he'd opened himself up to the possibility of bankruptcy by signing their papers. Not one cent for tribute, he decided; then, as they were leaving, called after them. "If you see Bill," he said, "tell him hi for me."

"I know what you're doing," Miss Simmons said, startling him. He'd forgotten they were still linked up.

"Do you know what I forgot?" Schiff said, realizing he had to pee again and taking advantage of the empty urinal.

"What?"

"To ask for my key back."

"Gee," she said, "I had it duplicated. I forgot to get it back to you."

"That puts us about even then."

"Oh?"

"Sure," he said, "my playing with the button, your forgetting my key."

"I guess maybe it does," she said.

"Except for one thing," Schiff said.

"What's that?"

"My key," he said, "I need it, I have to have it back today."

"I'm sorry," she said, "I'm filling in on the switchboard today. I can hardly send out another ambulance. I suppose I could bring it by after I'm off, but that's not until six. Can you wait that long?"

"Hey," Schiff said, "no problem."

Checkmate! thought wily old Schiff. Gin! Name of the game! the crippled-up old political-geographer gentleman thought, planting his flags for Spain, for France. Well, he thought, for Farce, at least, Schiff's own true motherland with its slapstick lakes and Punch and Judy rivers, its burlesque deserts and vaudeville plains, with its minstrel peninsulas and cabaret hills, its music-hall mountains and its dumb-show shores, all its charade forests, all its low-comedy lowlands.

His body not only ravaged—well, he was sixty, or near enough, closing in on retirement, closing in on death, personal wear-and-tear coming with his jokey territory—but savaged now, too, effectively gut shot, brought low, lower than good taste permitted, a dispensated man, on Information's arm, on some general sufferance—there were federal laws now protecting him like some endangered species—his ass not only covered but sanctioned, like some loony or fool whose culture would not permit itself to raise a hand against him. These were the perks of Farce, the privileges of citizenship, like coins sprinkled to street mimes.

Not, thought Schiff, unearned or had cheap. For even before he'd so openly lived in Farce, even, he meant, when, like some dual-citizen'd child who could declare his allegiance in ripened time, Schiff had had his tendencies; marked by a weird boldness, some not fully thought-out bravery, blind, or anyway indifferent, to consequence, a very inversion of the cautious, look-before-you-leap models of whom he boasted, and whom, at least theoretically, on paperly, boosted, all those coded, once-burned-twice-shy gimps and wary worrywarts whose nine months of toilet training had, in spite of everything, been wasted on them, a crack in their anality and something let-loose and litterbug struck into their souls like a brand. You might as well hand him a pistol and put a single bullet into its chamber like the buck you slip into a gift wallet.

Luring Miss Simmons—Jenny—to the party without even *moving* the finger Ms. Kohm herself had promised him he'd never have to lift. Here's, he mentally toasted himself, to dangerous Jackie Schiff, the Have-It-Both-Ways Kid.

Hi! You've reached 727-4312, the home of Professor Jack Schiff. I'm sorry, caller, but I'm not in just now. Please wait for the beep and leave a message. This block is protected by armed vigilantes. I'm not saying it is, and I'm not saying it isn't, but the house just might be booby-trapped. Why take chances?

Because a certain part of him couldn't afford to admit thoughts toward the down side of things. And even as he thought this—maybe it was the word "afford" that triggered the idea—*this* occurred: that he'd been a damn fool to call those banks yesterday, that he'd wasted his time. (Oh, his *time*, thought the damn fool.) That having been married to him all those years, Claire was incapable of great train robberies, of major or minor larcenies, that walking out on him was one thing but stiffing him another. She was, finally, incapable of caper. She hadn't disturbed the money in their accounts because that's how she continued to think of them—— as "their" accounts, the fiduciary aspect of their relationship intact. Because, because—and this made him furious—they would both be working off the same accounts! Drawing down off the same funds like a couple of old-timey teenagers in the malt shop sipping their soda from the same glass through two separate straws. And why he was furious was that she'd turned over the accounting to him, that he was the one left behind to balance their checking. (All right, granted, her canceled checks would give him, if not her address, then at least some general idea of what she was up to and where she was up to it at.) So this was what his cripple's code came down to—— that he stay out of it; not just that he must avoid doing things twice, but that he must never do them even once if he could help it. Being disabled had made him lazy, his incentive shot, a sort of welfare drag. It was his fate, he saw, to depend—how he'd plaintively pointed out the pisser to the paramedic—on everyone's mercies. That it had become his job, duty, his life, like some old zayde worrying Torah in shul, to lie in his bed and worry his character. (*Flash!* he thought. *I'm disabled and can't come to the phone right now, I can't come to the phone, I can't come!*)

Enough! Enough and enough!

He moved off the bed, as demanding of himself as a physical therapist. Thinking: Tonight's the party. People are coming, students, maybe two or three spouses, Jenny Simmons is dropping off the key to the house. Thinking for the first time since God knew when: *Not* thinking, Push, Step, Pull, or *I think I can, I think I can*, or doing any of his other play-by-plays and routines. Merely hauling his ass like any other severely disabled human being; merely minding his business, his heart too full of its sorrows to pay much attention to anything *but* his business, to his problems and their solution. Hey, he thinks, this is serious; perhaps he should call it off, put his foot down, get back to Ms. Kohm, tell her he's made up his mind about it once and for all, *this* party's canceled, ask could she get word to the others, tell them he's sorry, hand them some blah blah about maybe later when he was feeling better, maybe once he knew where he stood, maybe, as it were, next year—— Or no, forget that, just tell them it's off. Besides, he sees through his window how dark it is out, how rotten it looks, how it's probably going to Sturm und Drang buckets, how he wouldn't want it on his conscience, couldn't stand it in fact, if a student of his, *any* young person, liquor- or weather-impaired, should be hurt in an accident in the rain, sideswiped dead in the slick, slippery streets on the way to or fro any party of his. How he'd never forgive himself, who'd been there and back, if he were even merely the glancing, proximate cause of—never *mind* actually killing him or her—putting a person in his educational charge into a cast or brace for so much as a week or even a day, an hour, even a minute. He was sorry, he'd tell her, it was just the way he was. I am what I am. He is what he is. And if that was the bedrock bottom line of why Mrs. Professor S. left Mr. Professor S., well then, so be it, the leopard couldn't change its spots or the doggie its growl. One was stuck with oneself. The world had too few competent political geographers as it was, he'd be darned if he helped contribute to the further diminution of talent in his field.

Somehow he showered.

Somehow, dispensing with the services of both wife and valet, he dressed.

Somehow, the cook run off to join the circus, the navy, see the world, take Europe by storm, he managed breakfast. Two handfuls of dry cereal, some grape jelly spooned into his mouth from a jar, a few sips of half-and-half from an open carton. Even preparing future meals for himself by holding a carton of eggs carefully in his lap and propelling himself across the smooth linoleum toward the gas stove by alternately hunkering his upper torso, then suddenly pressing himself hard against the back of the wheelchair so that he seemed to move by a kind of peristaltic action, rather like a gigantic inchworm. It was slow work, and exhausting, but when he reached the stove he laid down his dozen eggs gently as possible into a large, high pot a little less than half filled with water left there to soak a sort of rusty crust of

Claire's days-old tomato sauce from the pot's insides. He set the flame very low.

And somehow, awfully tired now and the butler nowhere in sight, he managed to get back to the second floor and, fully dressed, settle into his unmade bed. From which he would have put through his call to Ms. Kohm on the spot had not he first turned on the television and, quickly reviewing the thirty-or-so network and cable channels available in his city, taken up his remote-control wand and recorded the finals of the *Sports Illustrated* swimsuit competition on ESPN.

Schiff had long ago discovered the mildly erotic possibilities of the Pause button on his VCR, the flagrantly concupiscent ones inherent in slo-mo and super slo-mo. Certain music videos played back in the super slo-mo mode made Schiff, for all his physical deficits, ardent as something in rut, and caused him to participate in a sort of endless, extended foreplay, the images on the screen grainy as the thrown, close-up pouts and moues of received pornography, his own responses as real in their way as the perspiratory, steamy efforts of the actual. He did not so much play with as handle himself, fondle himself, his eyes on the television screen, on the practically time-lapse movements of the girls, muscles barely visible to the naked eye pronounced, vivid and fluid as avatars in dreams in the delicate, strobographic revelations before him, so that what he saw was a sort of palpable anatomical demonstration, some nudity beneath nudity, going on under the flesh, oily, somehow slow and forbidden as an exhibition of mandatory poses of female field slaves on an auction block.

But could not quite bring himself off, this all-but sixty-year-old man, only sensation available to him, love's mood music, his hand finally falling away from himself, satisfaction locked up tight inside him like a kind of sexual arthritis.

And might have called Ms. Kohm then and there had not something warned him not to be too precipitate (he knew what it was, that weird boldness and devil-may-care indifference to consequence of the cautious), not to cut off (whatever the hell he meant by that) his chances (maybe only to preserve for as long as he could the last faint, surviving buzz of sexual vibration lengthening in frequency in him like a neurologist's tuning fork held against the skin). Hanging on, he meant. Hoping, that is, to be saved by the bell.

Which, believe it or not, he literally was. His doorbell rang just as he was about to give in and call Ms. Kohm. Once he managed to get into the Stair-Glide, ride downstairs and open the door, it turned out that the PGPC's subcommittee on decorations was standing on his doorstep in all its rigged and prompted patience under the light rain, which just that moment had begun to fall.

"Come in, come in, you'll catch your deaths," Schiff welcomed, breezy as a man half his age and many times more healthy.

For presumedly bluff volunteers—Schiff thought of "neighbors" in films come to raise a barn or bring in a harvest—there was something rather hangdog and shamed in their bearing.

Schiff, a stiff and somewhat formal grown-up better than twice their age who called them "Miss," who called them "Mister," supposed them in on their professor's domestic secrets, supposed himself (one of those—he supposed they supposed—hotshot, crisis celebs, a consultant in times of national stress to movers and shakers with means at their disposal—their bombs and high-tech devices—quite literally to move and shake the very political geography that had hitherto been merest contingency, simple textbook, blackboard example, his finger—their professor's—on the planet's pulses, its variously scant or bumper crops, its stores of mineral, vegetable, animal, and marine wealth—currents where the advantageous fish hung—an advisor—he supposed they supposed—to presidents, kings, and others of the ilk, who could determine a vital interest simply by naming it, pronouncing it, pointing to it chalktalk fashion on a map, virtually talking the hotspots into being) fallen in their youthful, fickle estimation, emotional, skittish as a stock exchange. So no wonder they seemed so nervous around him. His wife had left him, he stood as exposed as a flasher. His wife had left him, and now they perceived Professor S. as one who evidently—and oh so feebly—pulled his pants up over his uncovered ass one damaged leg at a time; a man, in the absence of crisis, not only *like* any other—his wife had walked, had taxicabbed out on him—but maybe even more so. He was revealed to them here on his—the political geographer's and erstwhile hotshot, crisis celeb's—very turf as one more defective, pathetic, poor misbegotten schlepp.

Ms. Kohm must have turned them. Ms. Kohm must have been running them. Ms. Kohm, who, if he was the political geographer, must surely have been (with all the coordinates, inside info and morning line she put out on him) the political geographer's geographer. Who'd told Schiff they took care of their own, but really meant *she* did, and had organized committees and subcommittees like this one on a moment's notice. Apparently she had named him a sudden, inexplicable vital interest. Why? Had she set her cap for him? What was this all about anyway? How had he—the defective, misbegotten schlepp—managed to become a target of opportunity, anyone's eligible man?

Leaning on his walker and reciting at them like a moron, "Come in, come in, you'll catch your deaths. Let's have your coats." Which, had they given them to him, would surely have knocked him down.

"Will it be all right," Mary Moffett said, "if we put these up now? They're for the party tonight."

She held a shopping bag out for his inspection. In it, like wires, lights, tinsel, and Christmas-tree ornaments that could be used, put away, and used again the next year, were a variety of comic maps in assorted joke projections. (Their rendition of *The New Yorker*'s rendition of the United States.) Some, certain classic campaigns (the siege of Troy, the Norman Conquest, Custer's last stand at the Battle of the Little Bighorn), were offbeat versions of history, even of epochs (Schiff's St. Louis suburb at the time of the Ice Age), and many were as topical, or once were, as the monologues of talk-show hosts. All were cartoonish, satirical. There was, Schiff recognized (and had, the sad man, even before he'd become so sad), a kind of desperation in these efforts, almost as if his students were pretending to be like the campus's engineers and architects, who turned out prototypes of ingenious machines and interesting buildings that seemed to have sprung up overnight on celebratory weekends and occasions. There, tossed at his feet on the hall carpet like a sample of fabric, was this pleated string of construction-paper, accordion-fold maps, silly, insignificant as party favors.

He had to sit down or die, so scarcely had time to do more than acknowledge the presence of the course party's inherited, cumulative two- or three-year archive.

"Yes, yes," Schiff said, "very nice, very nice."

Fred Lipsey carried a sort of easel under one arm, a paper bundle of what could have been placards under the other. Joe Disch held a small stepladder, a Scotch-tape dispenser.

"That won't stick to the walls, will it?" Schiff said. "It won't pull the paint off with it?"

"No sir," Disch said.

"Because that's all I need, if the paint started chipping and peeling away from the walls."

"It's one of those low-grade adhesives."

"I mean because that's *all* I need," Schiff said, inexplicably close to tears, "this place turned into a *total* shithouse."

"No," Joe Disch said, "that won't happen. I use it to hang posters and prints in my apartment all the time. It comes away as easily as if you were turning the pages in a newspaper."

"Posters and prints," Schiff said. "You graduate students don't know how good you have it, do you? These are the best years of your life, you know that? You have any idea how happy you are? What you get away with at your age? I mean, for God's sake, just on the level of posters and prints. You can decorate a whole apartment with bullfight posters, airline ads for Bora Bora, Big Ben, the Great Wall. Low-slung canvas chairs, do they still have those? They were very popular when I was a graduate student. We thought them quite beautiful. Red light bulbs screwed into the lamps. The place looked like a fucking darkroom. The stub of an incense candle stuck into a Chianti bottle, wax on the colored glass and collected in the fishnet that wrapped it like a package. Then, you threw in a few boards over building blocks for your bookcase and you were all set. Remember hi-fis, LPs?

"Well," Schiff said, "listen to me, will you, running on at the mouth about the old days. I go back. Hell, I remember when Oldsmobile introduced Hydra-Matic transmission. We thought *that* was a miracle. Who'd have believed there'd ever be a system a cripple could install in his house, or *anyone* on their own, really, that if they fell all they had to do was press a button and practically in minutes have an entire hospital at their disposal? Well," he said, "I'm just going to sit down over here and let you do what you have to. Do the departments still have softball leagues? We were out every Saturday. I played first base."

And some of this, he couldn't have told you the exact percentage because he wasn't that sure himself, but probably, conservatively, oh, eighty or ninety percent, was for their benefit. Put on. Made up. They wanted fear and trembling, he'd give them fear and trembling. Hey, it was their party. ("Remember hi-fis?" the old first basemen had asked them.) He was his own comic projection, something funhouse-mirror to his reality, the same distorted representation on the flat surface of his curved personality as Greenland's. That was Schiff, all right. A joke like Greenland, sprawled across the top of the world like a continent.

And now sat down over here, just as he said. To let them gt on with it. Never letting them out of his sight. Never letting himself out of theirs.

At about three he sent out for pizzas. Two large with the works for his tiny crew. Plus Cokes in cans. Though he hated, he said, to buy them at the prices they charged for a Coke these days. He remembered when Coca-Cola was a nickel.

"A nickel?" said little Miss Moffett. "Really? A nickel?"

"Damn right," Professor Schiff said. "Twentieth part of a dollar. That's what the candy butchers at burlesque shows used to call nickels in the old days."

"I never knew Coca-Cola was a nickel."

"*Pepsi*-Cola was a nickel and you got twelve ounces! Automobiles were four hundred dollars. The Sunday paper cost two cents. You furnished a five-room house in a stable neighborhood for a hundred dollars."

"A hundred dollars? Really?"

"Tenth part of a thousand."

"Professor Schiff's jerking you around, Mary," Fred Lipsey said.

"A grand piano set you back ten bucks."

"My goodness," Mary Moffett said.

"Scalpers wanted fifty cents a pop for the hottest ticket in town. Kidnappers asked seventy-five simoleons if you ever wanted to see your kid alive again. Oh, yeah," Schiff said, "it was simpler times. A meal in a good restaurant was free, and a Picasso . . ." He didn't finish the sentence. What were these children doing in his house? He was sixty years old, why was he still throwing parties? Why had Claire left him? Did she think she could change her life? At *her* age? What would she change it to? Admitted, living with him couldn't have been any picnic. It was hard work. Granted. The hours were awful and the sex was lousy. They'd left life long ago. Ten years easy. Now they floated above it like folks in an out-of-body experience, or like people drugged. They had no children and couldn't even fall back on the surrogate joy of watching their kids succeed—— seeing them through school, finding partners, a career, having children of their own. Or on even the motions of going through a life—— taking up a hobby, going on vacations, celebrating holidays, even their own birthdays and anniversaries. He wasn't for a minute pessimistic on the world's account, only on his and Claire's. He didn't resent other people's happiness—he was that cut off—only his and Claire's misery. Nor did he question why they'd been singled out. They hadn't. It was

all luck of the draw. Everything. Luck of the draw. Nature
never screwed anyone. That's why disciplines like his were
invented. To explain the borders, to draw up new ones. To
make, in the best light of the best-case scenario, amends,
restitution, seeking, in that same good light, what there
could be, and when, and where, of order. It was like anything else. A political geographer who determined his own
political geography had a fool for a traveler. Which was why
he was more disappointed than angered by Claire. Had she
learned nothing from her years with him? She would change
her life? Yes? How? Tell him that, how? Oh, she could become a bag lady. Just as he could throw his lot in with the
homeless. (Hadn't he had this thought today? Yesterday? It
seemed to him he had, though he couldn't put his finger on
it, or in what context, which circumstances. Though if it
had occurred to him earlier, it just went to show that it was
on his mind, that he was *that* far from taking violent charge
of his life. Though he wouldn't have given you two cents
for his consistency: Help me. I've fallen and I can't get up.
This block is protected by armed vigilantes!)

Meanwhile the PGPC subcommittee on decorations was
directing a sort of traffic in his dining room, Mary Moffett
the traffic cop on duty, signaling Lipsey and Joe Disch
where to hang the maps, and reciting a sort of background
litany, which in other circumstances might almost have
been comforting: "A little to the left. A little more. No,
good. Now up on the right. Right there, hold it right there.
No, you went too far over. All right, good, that's got it,
though maybe the whole thing ought to be a little lower so
everyone can read it better. What do you think, Dr. Schiff?"

Dr. Schiff thought it astonishing he hadn't thrown them
out.

"Oh," he said, "you know, mi casa, su casa. I defer to
your judgment."

"No," she said, "really."

"My dear," said Schiff, suddenly finding himself trying
out a new role on them (who had played so many; who had
kept his studied, professional distance and who, even on the

occasion of his annual party when the barriers came down for a few hours, but only, he'd always been careful to assure himself, in the interest of preserving them, rather like those old-time, once-a-year, red-letter bashes of the aristocratic when the servants and rabble, and all the good people from the village, had the run of the grounds and great house, and stayed up late into the night, taking such liberties and doing such damage—damage encouraged and even willingly eaten by the squire, just part of the expense of doing business as a landowner, of having vast holdings—that they would hate themselves in the morning, ashamed, accepting, even embracing, their fate for another year), "have I forgotten to mention I've worked up the will to go homeless? That it's true what they say—— you can't live with them, you can't live without them. No no," said Schiff, holding his hand up as if to forestall an objection (and not knowing, really, where he was going, only that surely, really, this was too much: that she should have left him at *this* juncture, good *God,* what a sense of timing, because he knew she knew, he even remembered their having discussed it just this week, Claire herself suggesting that maybe they should open the party up to some of their colleagues, and Schiff considering it until Claire said no, on second thought it probably wasn't such a good idea, that it would dilute the point of the evening if they did that, and throwing in, too, that it could hardly be expected to put the students at their ease if they had to sit around at attention all evening with a bunch of old farts, and Schiff agreeing, saying, right, that was a good point, no old farts, and here he was, one of the oldest, throwing his tantrum, making his scene, going Christ-knew-where with their attention tucked under his arm like a football—— only that he had to keep on talking, like a drunk who knew he had to make himself presentable for important company, perhaps, and who was determined to walk off the toxins). "Well, isn't it always darkest before the dawn or somesuch? Political folk wisdom has it right, the word on the street. Contrast plays its role in life. Well, the element of surprise, for instance. Being what it is in both warfare and negotiation. Have you noticed how often they play down our expectations, then go off to the summit and come away with a treaty you wouldn't have guessed was in the cards for another twenty years?

"Listen," Schiff said, "I really appreciate your coming over. It's cost you your afternoon, putting out the party favors, throwing your lot in with the old prof like this. I only hope Ms. Kohm, God bless her, didn't do too much damage to your arms when she twisted them. No? Good. Because she means well, she really does. She means well by me, she means well by you. Heck darn it, it isn't too much, or telling tales out of school, to say she means well by the entire hemisphere and all the ships at sea. She's one of those women who abhors a vacuum. I mean, well, I spoke to her last night. I wanted to call this party on account of, hey, you name it—— I'm crippled, the place is a mess, there's nothing in the house to serve, my wife couldn't be here because she's running around on me. But Ms. Kohm wouldn't have any of it. She told me to hang tough, to wait till she showed up with the torch and touched the holy fire to the holy fire. I'm sorry the nuts and dip aren't out, the crackers and candy, but Ms. Kohm will be by soon with fruit, with melon in season. Smoke if you got 'em," Schiff said, eying his living room.

The tops of the pizza boxes had been torn from their bottoms, and everywhere, teetering on the arm of the sofa, on the coffee table, left on a seat cushion, on a stereo speaker, in the makeshift dishes, the smeared, greasy, bronzed mix-and-match of the cardboard china, lay pieces of cold, uneaten pizza like long slices of abstract painting, their fats congealing, fissures opening in their cooling yellow cheeses, burst bubbles of painterly cholesterol, chips of pepperoni raised on them like rusty scabs. Bits of green bell peppers, tiny facets of oily onion, bright hunks of tomato like semiprecious stones caught Schiff's eye, glinted up at him from the carpet. Crumpled paper napkins, like the soiled sheets of wet beds, soaked up spilled Coke. There was an aluminum rubble of crushed cans.

"The geopolitical reasons for Daylight Saving Time," Schiff said suddenly. "Mr. Disch?"

Mr. Disch, holding a beer, extended an arm, raised it toward Schiff in a sort of dippy, upward salute, body English for "Have one, Professor?"

His professor scowled narrowly, tersely shook his head, body English for "No thanks, where'd that come from, the sun ain't over the yardarm, take care you don't spill it!" (For he was, this clumsy, even, by disease-defaulted, sloppy-appearing man, almost compulsively neat, spic 'n' span in his arrangements, who'd have his own narrow area ordered as the universe. Which was maybe why he went into political geography in the first place, as though the planet, its seas and landmasses, its rivers and mountain ranges, its hemispheres and continents, its nations and borders and cities and towns, its houses, its rooms, was ultimately rather like a class of furniture, like closets, like dressers, like wardrobes, like cupboards and desks and chiffoniers, like cabinets and files and chests of drawers, language a furniture, too, finally, only a way of gathering and organizing all the far-flung *stuff* of Earth.) Schiff looked toward Mary Moffett and Fred Lipsey, hunkered down over Mary Moffett's shopping bag (meant to hold more, evidently, than the committee's joke maps and decorations), pulling cans of beer from it like dogs scrabbling at dirt. "If I'm not mistaken," Schiff said loftily, "there's a question on the floor."

"We're on break," said Miss Moffett.

Schiff, oddly unconcerned, thought, She's drunk, and wondered when that had happened, suspecting he'd dozed off, suspecting they'd heard him snore, greedily scoop great gobs of air into his nose, pass gas, probably giggling about their old political geography teacher (who'd turned out to have a behind, habits), not only crippled, but reduced, too, and was impatient for the party to begin, knew it had, and already yearned for the time when they'd all clear out and he could go back to bed. And realized (having taken this all in, his brief snooze, their surreptitious drinking and, glancing once more at the remains of lunch, at the beer cans scattered about the landfill starting up—which was a sort of furniture, too, wasn't it? perhaps some final furniture, some ultimate piece—in what was his hall, his dining and living rooms) the farce question about Daylight Saving's geopolitical reasons had been merely his failed, reflexive, face-saving opening salvo, like dropping the checkered flag, say, not only after the gentlemen had already started their engines but had already completed their first several laps. It was out of his hands. Officially or not, the annual class party had begun!

Changing his mind, accepting Joe Disch's beer, and abruptly all over them with a riff of gag questions. "Why have ocean currents been the casus belli of most civil wars?" "Explain how prevailing winds determine national borders." "Discuss the concept of the island. How is it a macrocosm of the tribe but a microcosm of the family?" "How do the animals indigenous to a nation determine the character of that nation's underlying political structure?" "What's the difference between a 'region' in a first-world country like Italy and a third-world country like Paraguay?" "How is it that the so-called 'hot-blooded' peoples have had fewer revolutions than their more northerly neighbors?" "Speculate on the reasons for the *inverse* ratio between the beauty of a nation's flag and its contributions to the fields of art, music, and poetry." "If individuality, rather than community, accounts for most of the world's great inventions and economic progress, why is it that countries with the greatest populations tend to be the most backward in their cultural and economic development?"

"Mr. Lipsey? Miss Moffett? Mr. Disch?

"Ms. Kohm? Mr. Hughes? Miss Simmons? Mr. Wilkins? Mr. Tysver? Miss Carter? Miss Freistadt? You, Dickerson? You, Bautz?"

Because these others (without, he noticed, their two or three spouses in tow—— was this, he wondered, out of deference to him, or were all marriages foundered on the rocks?) had begun to drift in while Schiff was still in the nervous throes of his rap. Because he missed Claire and hoped and, despite himself, almost believed she would relent, reverse herself and, using her incredible sense of timing for good, still show up to save him, and because on one, the most furious, level of his forced, inspired hospitality, he was playing (for all that he knew better) for time, for some impossible dispensation, as though, could he but keep coming up with his loopy diversionaries, he might never have to answer to the still (for him) more alarming demands of serious social obligation. Soon, he quite feared, he might be telling them everything, conducting his guests on the grand tour around the posted neighborhoods and dark, off-limits districts of his heart.

"Tell me would you if you will all the ways the counter-clockwise movements of water going down a drain in the southern hemisphere may account for the greater number of languages and dialects spoken below the equator."

They stared at him.

"Anyone?

"No? No one? Well, I should do some checking if I were you, you degree candidates, for that's a question that's almost certain to turn up on your prelims. Really, people, if you haven't got the basics down, I don't know how you hope to be political geographers. Do you think others in the political sciences are as unfamiliar with their areas of concentration as you seem to be—— the political biologists, the political chemists, the political comp. lit. majors?

"Well," Schiff said, apparently relenting, "let the wild rumpus begin. Miss Simmons," he told the somewhat surprised-looking woman who had separated herself from the graduate students and was approaching the wheelchair to which he had transferred and in which he was now sitting, "how *nice* to see you! How *good* of you to come!"

"I brought you your key back."

"Listen," he said, lowering his voice, "can you stay? We give this party for my students. I may have told you. I'm caught short here. Claire's left me. I'm caught short here, I could really use the buffer. You'd be doing me a favor. Really. Please don't go, please stay. It'd be swell if you would. You don't know how much more comfortable I'd feel."

"I came with your key. I haven't even been home yet. I'm not dressed for a party."

"Well, of course she'll stay. How do you do, dear? I'm Molly Kohm. I'm very pleased to meet you. How interesting our professor is, what astonishing resources he has! Practically a paraplegic and confined to a wheelchair (even a somewhat older paraplegic), yet here he is dispensing keys to his home as if there were no tomorrow and neither one of you had ever even heard of an actuarial table. My goodness, how fast one may get about in a wheelchair! I hadn't realized! Oh, and you mustn't even think of returning that key. Don't take it back, Professor. It was a misunderstanding. These things happen, they're worked out every day. And night."

"This is Jenny Simmons," Schiff said. "Miss Simmons was a student of mine."

"A student. Really, a student. Oh, now I *am* jealous, I quite actually *am!* Professor, you rascal, if only I'd known. I might have made a play for you myself. I might have," she told Miss Simmons. "And I wouldn't be threatening him with the return of his keys," she added huskily. She bent down in front of Schiff's chair and, resting her hand across the inside of his thigh, almost absent-mindedly, began stroking it. "Oh good," she said, "there's evidently still some feeling down there." Schiff caught slight gusts of conditioned, alcoholic essence coming from her, pleasant, agreeable (despite her obvious drunkenness) as the gentle drafts and enticing steams one smells outside a steakhouse. Also, he saw up past her crouching, silk-stocking'd knees and along her own flexed thighs high into the dark of her skirt where they joined like perspective in a painting.

Ms. Kohm suddenly seemed as oddly capable as a witch, an impression enhanced by her pitch, shiny hair, the bright, thin streaks of white silver that crackled through it like some personal storm of the head. A dramatic purple-and-black-checked cape hung about her shoulders and over a dark tank top. She wore no brassiere, and Schiff saw the hard points of her nipples rising from what he momentarily conceived of as rings of soft, purple, lava-like slabs, imagining their faintly brackish taste in his mouth like the flavor of struck matches.

Giving him a soft, dismissive pat on the knee, she rose effortless as a yogi from the deep squatting position she had held before him like some patronizing tribute. (As if he'd been a child, say, to whose level she'd lowered herself—— or the cripple he was. And Schiff, as though Ms. Kohm, come to him almost like some Dickensian specter, had an abrupt image of himself through women's eyes. Why, he was like somebody behind and over whose head life was conducted, arrangements made, a kid traveling alone, say, or someone handicapped—well, hell, he thought, I *am* someone handicapped—whose needs were negotiated indirectly, guided past metal detectors in airports for a hand-check as if he were absent, a party in the third person, as though his earlier impression of having left life were true as far as it went, only reversed, life floating about a foot or so above him. Schiff some doll-like object present less in spirit than in sheer, brutal deadweight, his feet there to be stockinged and shod, his arms to be helped into the sleeves of his jackets, whatever was left over, *say* his spirit, to be lulled and comforted, regarded, even loved, admired as a piece of art might be admired, something not responsible for itself, diligently plied into being, as anything worked on hard enough or worried over long enough had to be turned into an object worthy of the effort, like silverware polished down to its highlights. This was how women saw him. For it was only women—he had left life—who dealt with him these days. It was how Miss Simmons, who had gone out of her way to bring him his key, saw him, how Ms. Kohm, who single-handed had refused to let his party go into the record books with an asterisk this year, did. Finally, it was how Claire must have seen him up until the time she discovered that enough was enough and refused to take one more minute of him, and left him, on the day of her incredible sense of timing, on the eve of his party, to deal with the women who would deal with him. Well, you know what? Saving Claire's absence, he didn't much mind, was willing as ever to throw himself on their—on women's—mercies like a log on a fire.)

She turned around and made a signal to her helpers. (The rest of the students, he meant.) Without a word, Miss Carter appeared with a big galvanized pail. The pail was new, shiny, the sort of pail one associates with mops and wringers, with dark, greasy water.(Oh, shit, he thought, suddenly remembering the eggs, surely exploded by now, he'd dropped into the rusty water that morning.) It was filled to the brim with salad. With great leaves of lettuce, violently torn from what must have been eight or nine heads. There were long shards of cucumber and zucchini. There were whole rings of sweet onion like small quoits. There were jagged slices of tomato and, here and there, dollops of red, tomatoey pulp like a sort of jam. Sprinkled throughout were raisins like the droppings of rodents. Mr. Tysver carried an open butter tub of oil-and-vinegar dressing, already mixed, and Miss Freistadt and Mr. Wilkins each swung three or four large cartons of pasta like Chinese takeout from their thin metal handles like a sort of Jack and Jill. Bautz brought bread and Dickerson paper plates, white plastic cutlery, a box of salt, tins of colored seasonings, napkins. Each appeared before Ms. Kohm with his or her offering.

"Does this go in the kitchen, Molly?" asked Miss Carter of the galvanized pail.

"Put it down here. We'll be eating soon, why make two trips?" She was pointing at the carpet.

"Hey, wait a minute," objected Schiff from his wheelchair.

But she had already set down her burden on the living-room carpet.

"Hey," said Schiff. "Hey."

No one listened to him. Many seemed drunk. Schiff turned to Ms. Kohm. "Hey," he said, "hey."

An awful picnic of the awful graduate student food began to blossom on the carpet beneath him. Pieces of lettuce and cucumber and zucchini spilled over the pail or fell from heaps stacked too high on the paper plates and lay on Schiff's beige carpet as if they grew there in actual nature. Bright bits of tomato, red onion, and pasta spotted the carpet like flowers. They've turned the place into a damn garden, Schiff thought bitterly. You could dig for worms in here. Miss Simmons, bless her heart, seemed as appalled as Schiff, and made no move to leave. Between trips to the salad bar on his floor for refreshment, Disch, Lipsey, and Moffett spelled each other as bartenders, offered mixed drinks from the remarkable bag where they had set up shop. Schiff, who didn't think he saw that many takers, couldn't account for the astonishing level of intoxication in the room. This crowd was *high!* Either they were already three sheets to the wind when they came in, or something about being in his house had unsettled them, roused them he meant, sprung them he meant, from the general graduate-student monasticism and hole-and-corner roughhouse of their days. Something about being in their mid-to-late twenties and still under the vows of delayed gratification, their lives unbegun. It was the old story of the total shithouse Schiff had complained of earlier, of posters and prints, of canvas chairs and incense, cement-block bookcases and all the make-do improvisation of their lives. Sprung from that. Grown-up for a day! Not Ms. Kohm. He excepted Ms. Kohm. Ms. Kohm was their ringleader, their unmoved mover, something thwarted in Ms. Kohm, something about Ms. Kohm profoundly unchecked and envious, infiltrated and into deep cover.

Only then did he understand what he had noted earlier—— that there were no spouses here, not even his own. So sprung from spouses, too, from mewling babes, even from baby-sitters they couldn't afford to pay and so had— another improvisation—to trade off with, time-sharing each other's kids as if they lived in a commune. It was how Claire, high on a whiff of the other guy's air, must have felt.

Only God forbid that Claire was in some other old gent's place finger-painting with pasta on the rugs.

Whether they knew it or not, whether they meant to or not, they were looking for trouble. In some weird, incomprehensible way, understood neither by him nor themselves, they had entered into some odd conspiracy with him. Drawn, it could be (though pushed by Ms. Kohm) by his handicap, by his own low troubles.

Somebody came by and offered him a plate of food, of the handled salad drenched in dressing, of the cold, pasted, stuck-together pasta. Which he refused like someone gently shaking off a sign. As much out of his own stuck-together dignity as from any failure of hunger. Though he was hungry. Could have done right now with some of the terrific foods he and Claire used to put out—— the turkey and roasts, the pâtés and swell cheeses. (As much, perhaps, out of some need to wow them into respect as to satisfy the inner man.)

He accepted a poor plate of church supper from Miss Simmons, the plastic cutlery wrapped in what he now saw were cocktail napkins.

"Join me?" he said.

"Well," Miss Simmons said hesitantly.

"No really," he said, "make up a plate of rabbit food for yourself and rough it with me, why don't you?"

"Well," she said again.

"Afraid of ruining your appetite?"

It was difficult for him to eat in the wheelchair. He had lost considerable muscle mass in his hips, whatever it was that kept one upright, and he bobbed, weaved, swayed, lunged and lost his balance whenever he tried to fork food from the thin, fragile, wet paper plates and bring it to his mouth. He was spilling salad all over himself, on his lap, down the front of his shirt. There were salad-dressing stains on both shirt cuffs, high up his sleeves. "Can't tempt you, eh?" he said, and this struck him as very funny, starting what might have been an out-of-control, almost hysterical laugh, but quickly turned into a helpless series of snorts.

"No," he managed, "can't seem (snort) to (snort) tempt (snort, snort) *you!*" Long, extended snort. Snorting through. Snorting while his heart was breaking.

"No," he said when he was in control again, correcting himself, "not rabbit food. But look at the pail. Doesn't it remind you of something?"

"Of what?"

"No, you'll get it," he said, still the teacher. "What does it remind you of? Where have you seen pails like it before? All that chopped-up green shit?"

"Where?"

"At the *zoo!* In cages at the *zoo!* In the gorilla house. Where the elephant roams, and the skies are not cloudy all day."

"Oh yeah," she said, "right."

"Look at this place," he said.

"Oh, it'll be all right. No permanent damage has been done."

"Look at this place. Look what I've allowed to happen. My wife would kill me." He was quite sad. It was as if Claire were dead and his house were being reclaimed by nature.

To keep himself from falling forward again, or from slipping to the side, he hooked his left arm under the arm of the wheelchair and steadied himself, sitting in a sort of stolid, struggled balance. In this way, planted as somebody in a tug-of-war, he managed to feed himself some of the pasta and salad. But it was rigid work, he knew how stiff he looked.

It was as if she could read his mind.

"Would you like me to help you with that?" Miss Simmons volunteered.

Still hungry but pretending not to have heard her, Schiff set the plastic fork down on the paper plate. He took a cocktail napkin and tapped at the corners of his lips in mock satiety. Had he the ability to belch at will he might have fired off the better part of a twenty-one-gun salute in Miss Simmons's direction. He patted his stomach in a round, broad dumbshow of yum-yum satisfaction. Miming full holiday dinners, a kind of exhaustion, a vow not to eat again for a week, to forgo feasts forever. With his faked belly applause and silent, phony tongue-in-tooth, chewy exaggeration, it was almost as if he were congratulating himself. He was conscious that his forearm was still hooked under the arm of his wheelchair, that he might even have appeared defiant the way he held on to his balance for dear life, protecting himself from all comers like a kid playing king-of-the-hill. He might almost have seemed to have been challenging someone to break his hold, to see if they could tip him over. It seemed an odd thought for an old fellow with an S.O.S. amulet under his shirt, around his neck. "I know you wouldn't think it to look at me," he told Miss Simmons, "but I actually used to be fairly athletic I won't even say when I was a kid but back before I was stricken, while I was still a professor even, almost up until the time it might have begun to appear maybe a little unseemly for somebody my age to be scrambling around doing the run, jump, hit, and throw with fellows ten years younger than himself, almost as if he was trying to recapture his lost youth or something. That wasn't the way of it," he said. "I wasn't even particularly competitive. Except in table tennis. I was good at table tennis. Oh, I wasn't one of those guys who stand twenty feet back from the table, I'm not saying *that*, but I had a relatively exceptional slam. That's why I preferred sandpaper over rubber paddles. To my way of thinking, a rubber paddle was for putting spin and English on the ball, to *deceive* your opponent to death, to turn Ping-Pong into a game of chess. For me it was always a physical, aggressive sport. With sandpaper you could hear all the bang-bang and take-that that the game was designed for. Whenever my opponents took up a rubber paddle I pretty much knew what I was in for—— defense and stinking strategy. Some joker who'd just pretty much just stand there and let me wear myself out. I loved playing with the punchers and always pretty much resented the little judo and ju-jitsu guys who nickeled-and-dimed me and in the end usually beat my brains out. You think that's odd in a fellow trained in the art of political geography? It probably is, but probably it was my way of letting off steam, of that final, futile satisfaction one must feel after he's dropped the big one.

"It was pretty much the same when I played softball," Schiff said. "I was a fairly lousy first baseman, but not a bad hitter. Good hit, no field. Story of my life. And you'll have to take my word for this—— Hell, *I* have to take my word for it, because seeing how I am now it's pretty difficult to believe, but I was actually something of a diver back in high school. My specialty was a double somersault off the high board, though I have to admit I always lost a few points for my angle of entry when I hit the water. If you were anywhere near the pool you probably still feel the splash, and . . ."

Hearing himself, his flagrant boasting, Schiff quite suddenly paused, broke off. "Well," he said a few seconds later, "you get the idea. I knew him, Horatio. I'm sorry," he said, "I don't know why I take on like this. Possibly to keep you from noticing the salad dressing on my pants."

"Oh, those stains come right out. They're nothing to worry about," Miss Simmons said.

"No, I'm not worried," Schiff said.

"I'm like that, too," Miss Simmons said, "I think everyone is. It's a nuisance when you get all dressed up, then spill something on yourself."

"Good hit, no field."

"That's right," Jenny Simmons said.

Schiff was thanking his lucky stars he'd had enough sense not to loosen his grip on the arm of his chair, fall forward and kiss her—presence of mind, he thought, regarding the terrible disorder throughout his house, the joke decorations that had come undone and fallen, draped now in waves of construction paper over his sideboard, his dining-room table, over the Oriental rug in his entrance hall like a comic treasure map, casting an eye on the abandoned picnic table that was his living-room floor, the uneaten plates of food, the crushed cocktail napkins working their capillary action on the liquory dregs and stubbed, cold cigarettes at the bot-

toms of the plastic glasses of booze, abandoned, displaced
sofa cushions, on the carpet, against the living-room walls;
presence of mind when all about you are losing theirs—
when he became conscious of the buzz and grind of his
Stair-Glide. Unmistakably—from where he sat he could not
see this, merely heard their joyous squeals as they went up
his stairs—people were riding his chair, Ms. Kohm directing
them like someone working a ride in an amusement park,
the Ferris wheel, say, the carousel.

"All right, Bautz, you've had your turn. Get off and let
Miss Carter have a ride."

"Aw, come on, Molly, one more time. Please?"

"No, it's Carter's turn. Then Tysver, Miss Freistadt next,
then Wilkins, Dickerson, Lipsey, Miss Moffett, and
Disch."

"I don't see why *she* gets to have all the say-so."

"What are *you* complaining about? You're next. I don't
get to go until last."

"Disch, you're *such* a baby!"

"I'm not a baby. I was here putting up the decorations
hours before anyone else even showed up."

"Oh, yeah, *hours*," Dickerson said.

"Well, I was."

"Big fucking federal deal," Dickerson said.

"Yeah," Tysver said.

"If you want," Miss Freistadt said, "you can ride up with
me. You can sit on my lap."

"Really?"

"Would I tease a baby?"

"Hey!" Schiff called. "Hey!" He turned to Miss Simmons. "Are they really using my Stair-Glide, you think?"

"Gee, I don't know. Shall I go see?"

"Go see," Schiff said.

In seconds she was back. A trip that would have taken
him five minutes at least, he couldn't help thinking. *If* he
was even up to it.

"They are," she said.

"Hey," called Schiff. "Hey now."

There was hysterical squealing, shouting, a terrible clamor of drunken, almost falsetto rivalry. Schiff would recall crying out at them to cut the foofaraw, using this word which he'd not only never used before but which he couldn't remember having ever even heard. Remembering, moreover, that he called it out not once but three times. Like some magic cockcrow in legend. Angered now, crying, "Cut out that foofaraw! Knock off the foofaraw! Enough with this foofaraw!" Thrice denying them foofaraw, forbidding them foofaraw within his house, as if to say, not in *this* household you don't, or, take that outside where it belongs, or proclaiming that the neighborhood wasn't zoned for foofaraw. But overruled. At the very least ignored. Almost, so unmindful of him were they, cut.

Close to tears now he was, the rage of his helplessness. As if they didn't understand him or, worse yet, as if they did, some nice question of choice here, equating the hick, obsolete word with the hick, obsolete professor. Their continued laughter and cackle not merely an unmindfulness of his sovereignty here, but of his simple (simple, hah!), physical (physical, *hah!*) presence, an absolute refutation of his existence, an argument against his claims and rights as a landlord. The inmates were in control of the asylum. The students were calling the shots, making the assignments, handing out the grades. Now he was scared, beside himself.

"He *is,* he *is* on her lap!"

"How is that, Disch? You like that?"

"May I ride with Dickerson, Ms. Kohm?"

"Little Miss Moffett."

"Sat on Dickerson's tuffet."

Their voices were like noises made in free-fall, a glimpse of the abyss from the apogee at the lip of a thrill ride. Then, suddenly, abruptly, their brassy shrillness ceased—— all their odd, excited, asexual soprano. Displaced by a screech. Something mechanical. A sick, scraping sound. Something unoiled and harsh. To Schiff's ears, perfectly pitched for the noises of stuck, soiled machinery, stalled, soured works.

"Take me in there," he commanded Miss Simmons.

"Bring me, take me. Hurry, I have to see! My wheelchair. Damn," he said, "the brakes are locked. Wait, I'll unlock them. Shit," he said, "my feet aren't on the footrests. Wait, no, those swing into place. No, the whole whoosis swings over. Right. Yeah. Listen, can you lift up my legs? There. Thanks. There. Hey, thank you. Thanks. Push me into the hall.

"Hey," he called in the hall, "what's going on?" But he could see what was going on. His Stair-Glide was stuck, on the blink. Engaging the buttons on its arms, Dickerson could not get it to move. All ten of his students were arranged on the stairway. Frozen in his stare, they seemed like deer startled by headlights on the highway, like folks caught confused in a burning building, not knowing which way to turn in the fire, whether to try to make it to the top of the stairs where it wasn't yet burning, or to plunge through the fire toward the door. Indeed, some seemed headed in one direction, others in another. Ms. Kohm had somehow been stripped of her powers. Schiff, to judge from the way they looked at him, at least temporarily restored to his. Yet he wasn't sure he wasn't mistaken about this. Many of them could have been hiding their real attitudes toward him under what might have been smirks behind the hands they held in front of their mouths. Smirks, or fear, or outright laughter.

Clearly they were still under the influence, had not yet come down. Schiff couldn't understand the cause of their intoxication. He was certain they hadn't imbibed that much liquor. Unless, again, strangely, *he* was somehow the cause, his freedom about himself somehow contributing to their vandalism of him.

"What happens now," he demanded, "what happens now? Am I supposed to sleep on the couch, or what? Look what you've done. You've busted my Stair-Glide. How do I get upstairs? How do I get upstairs now?"

"That's nothing to worry about," Miss Carter explained. "There are ten of us here, eleven counting that one." She pointed to Miss Simmons. "If worse comes to worse, we could always carry you."

"That's right," a cry went up, "let's carry him."

"You get his feet, Lipsey," instructed Molly Kohm. "Tysver and Wilkins can hold him under the arms."

"No," said Miss Freistadt, "that won't work. This stairway's too narrow, the chair and the track are in the way. I'm smaller, I'll get one side. You look strong," she said to Miss Simmons, "can you take him under the other?"

"I guess," said Miss Simmons.

"No sweat then, Disch said. "Let's get him up out of his wheelchair."

Now they started down the stairs toward him.

"Wait!" Schift shouted. "Not so fast! What about all that food on my floor? No one leaves until it's all cleaned up. I don't have a wife now. I'm crippled. How do you expect me to get that crap up? I warned Ms. Kohm about this. I couldn't clean up after the party, I said. I *did,* didn't I? My condition, I said. I asked her what about afterwards, and she specifically said I wouldn't have to lift a finger, that she wouldn't even let me, that you'd empty the ashtrays, that you'd vacuum the rugs. It wasn't even a committee thing, she said, you'd all straighten up, everyone would pitch in, do their fair share. You promised, Ms. Kohm.

"Well, what about it, Ms. Kohm? Those ashtrays are full. Most places these days, they don't even *let* you smoke. It wasn't all that long ago the only place they might not permit you to light up was the main branch of the public library. You could puff away everywhere—— health-food stores, City Hall, any part of the cabin after the No Smoking sign was turned off. Even in your doctor's waiting room, for Christ's sake! Not now, not today. Most places are off-limits. Entire cities, complete countries. I gave you the whole house, and what do I see? Ashtrays spilling over!

"And as far as the carpet's concerned, incidentally, it would be swell if you vacuumed, but let's get real here. I'd be satisfied if you picked most of the salad up off the floor, the onions and cucumbers, the zucchini, the loose lettuce and tomatoes. If you got up some of the raisins. There's a broom in the closet off of the kitchen should God or good conscience lead you to see the light."

But they weren't listening. they seemed to be bickering, arguing amongst themselves on the stairway. Their voices were raised, some were actually shouting. Indeed, it seemed to Schiff to be the end of the PGPC as we know it. He was more than a little alarmed for his stairway, his rail and balusters. Ten people were on the eight steps.

"It's not an entrance to a museum," he explained to Miss Simmons. "It's only a fairly modest home in a nice, middle-class neighborhood. It's not the summer palace, that ain't the grand staircase."

"They'll calm down," Miss Simmons said.

"Is that banister swaying, you think?"

But they had calmed down, their argument, if that's what it was, now declined to a simple discussion. Schiff, his own rage building, could even make out what some of them were saying. Moffett, Dickerson, Carter, and Tysver knew of other parties that might still be going on. Wilkins and Bautz wanted to go dancing. It was six of one, half a dozen of the other to Disch and Freistadt, to Kohm and Lipsey. Whatever the rest of them decided, they said.

"Oh no," Schiff exploded, "oh no you don't!"

They looked down, startled.

"Nobody move! Stay right where you are!" he ordered.

They stared at him, taking in his outburst, it seemed to Schiff, with something of a mild, patronizing amusement. Oh, he thought, I tickle you, do I? Well, he thought, I may be down, but I ain't out. Who's the political geographer here, anyway? he thought. And, gathering himself where he sat in the wheelchair, sized up the situation on his jammed, peninsular stairway.

Four wanted to go to parties. But from what he could make out, they were different parties. At least two, possibly three. Counting his own, the party they were already at, there might conceivably be four. Bautz and Wilkins wanted to go dancing. Taking the most conservative view of it (four people choosing between two different parties, two individuals who preferred to go dancing) meant there were six people holding positions on three options. Disch, Freistadt, Kohm, and Lipsey were undecided, which meant that all that was needed to capture the swing vote was just two of these.

Schiff thought carefully.

Not fifteen minutes before, Ms. Kohm had been in clear, unchallenged charge. She'd assigned them turns on his Stair-Glide, had granted permission to various students to ride Schiff's chair while various other students sat on their laps. If she'd lost command, it was to the situation she'd surrendered it, the breakdown of Schiff's Stair-Glide. To the general panic and disarray that followed in the wake of that event, the terrifying, momentary, anarchic tableau they made on his stairway. No one had moved to take her place. Indeed, all that had happened was that various new alternatives had been proposed. It was entirely possible the group still didn't know it was leaderless.

Schiff, the crippled but wily political geographer, knew what he had to do.

He addressed Ms. Kohm as if it were status quo ante.

"I'm sorry, Molly," Schiff said calmly, choosing his words carefully, "but this is where I put my foot down. I have to pull rank on you, I'm afraid. First off, I don't trust that stairway. Second, you've broken my Stair-Glide." (*Molly*, he chose. *My* Stair-Glide. Two *I'm*s, three *I*s, he chose.)

"Come down from it now, please. One at a time. Calmly, calmly. No need to panic. That's right, that's right. As a matter of fact, you might even try to pick it up a little. All right," he said when most were down off the stairway and bunched about his wheelchair in the hall. "Well, Molly," he chose, "if you get your people to do the salad and pasta, I'd no longer have any reason to hold all your grades hostage to fortune," he chose.

Molly Kohm shrugged as if the game were up. Low man on the stairway, she came down a step and into Schiff's hall. "Come on you guys," she said to the other students as

Schiff turned his head and beamed up at Miss Simmons. The rest dutifully followed. They went with her into the living room. Without bothering about anyone else's, she found the paper plate she'd been eating off, leaned down, scooped it up, and walked with it past Schiff toward his kitchen. Apparently she hadn't noticed the cherry tomatoes that rolled off the plate when she stooped to scoop it up.

Meanwhile her classmates, only a litle more ambitious than their leader, stumbled through Schiff's living room, grabbing up handfuls of lettuce and clumps of pasta, picking over Schiff's rug like drunken field hands.

"Fuck this," Disch said, took his jacket, still wet from the rain, up off the dining-room table where he'd left it when he'd come in, shrugged into it, and walked out the door.

"Yeah," said Lipsey, "fuck this all right," and followed Disch out.

"Invited to a party," mumbled Miss Freistadt, "don't have to take this shit," and she left too.

He'd lost three of the undecideds.

"Hey, what about me," asked worried Schiff, trying to stanch the flow, "how am I supposed to get up those stairs?"

"Hold it!" Ms. Kohm boomed. "Hold it, he's right!" Schiff looked gratefully up at her. "Somebody get that pail!"

"The pail, the pail! It was as if her priorities lagged three or so beats behind Schiff's own. Or no. Had leapfrogged his priorities altogether. Hopscotched them. Or no. Were on an entirely different plane. Or no. Were not priorities any longer at all. Not priorities, not even choices. Neither picks nor preferences. Completely off any even platonic idea of a ballot and, now in the hands of his lone remaining undecided, catapulted into the range of fitful caprice. So she'd called for her bucket. Next it might be for her fiddlers three.

"I'll get it for you, Ms. Kohm," said Miss Carter.

"Push me, push me," he snapped in Miss Simmons's direction. Lazily, she wheeled his chair in and out of the first-floor rooms. "No no," he said, "after Miss Carter. She's gone into the kitchen."

She had. She was standing beside Ms. Kohm, to whom she had handed her pail, at the sink. Where she was emptying the remains of the salad. Pouring salad into the sink from the pail. Mindful of her fingers, pushing salad carefully into the sink, down into the rubberized maw of the garbage Disposall. Force-feeding the garbage Disposall. Taking leftover pasta and salad from the paper plates handed on to her in a sort of crazy bucket brigade by a chain of migrant student workers and adding these scraps into the now unwilling, refractory machine, grinding and grinding down, growling and choking, coughing up lettuce, spitting zucchini over mounds of red, regurgitant pasta.

"Please stop, it's breaking," requested Schiff. "Please?" he offered. "No, really," he said. "it's all right. You don't have to bother, I'll get it. She won't stop," Schiff complained to Miss Simmons.

"Those other guys were right," said Miss Simmons. "Fuck this," she said, and she walked out on him, too.

"All right," spoke Schiff from his now pusherless chair, hoping to catch someone's attention, "see what you've done? Miss Simmons is gone. The strong-looking one walked out. See what you've done? Who'll get me upstairs? How will I manage? What's going to happen to me?" he appealed to them. And where, he wondered, did his own intoxication come from? Why, from woe, he thought. Woe was its source, and he was as helpless to stanch it as he'd been to keep Lipsey and the others from leaving. Helplessly he continued to ask his rhetorical questions. "Why do bad things happen to good people? Or vice versa?" he asked. "If one knew going in that this was how a pretty fair country Ping-Pong player was going to end up, would one even have bothered? What are the odds, would you say, of my ever getting your respect back after putting you through an evening like this? All right," he said, addressing Ms. Kohm, "I've got one for you. If Claire's not in Seattle, where is she you think?"

But Ms. Kohm was still at her blind ablutions, bent over the kitchen sink, her arms plunged into the extaordinary pile of salad, lifting strands of it toward her face and examining them as if there were something inherent in the salad itself that prevented the Disposall from handling it. "Nope," she pronounced, "she won't go down. Say," she said, turning to Schiff, "what are we thinking of here anyway? This stuff is still fresh. You could live off it for a week. Let's get it into the fridge." No one but Schiff seemed to be listening to her, though, so she set an example. She took up an armful of the stuff and started with it toward the refrigerator. "Someone get that door for me, will you," she said, "my arms are full."

"No, really," Schiff said, "you don't have to bother. Not on my account. Tomorrow I'm making these arrangements with Meals-on-Wheels."

But by this time she'd managed to work the door open. Unceremoniously, she dumped her green burden onto a shelf in Schiff's refrigerator. "There," said Ms. Kohm, "it's on one of the lower shelves. See, I've made it handicap accessible for you."

"Right," said Schiff. "You're in compliance. Now I won't have to take you to court."

And idly wondered not only why he hadn't thrown them out of his house, but why he hadn't called the cops, why even now, abandoned in the dead center of his kitchen as the others began to drift back into his living and dining rooms, into his hall, back up onto his stairway, which they'd taken over, had gravitated toward like some playground for the able-bodied, in the wheelchair he hadn't strength enough to guide, or move by himself, so that he had begun to think of it as of a riderless horse on some sad state occasion, and of himself as a witness to his own lugubrious funeral, why even now, terrified as he was, as frightened (not of them, not of his students, who wouldn't harm him, who wouldn't throw him down the stairs, but had only meant to ride out the storm of his mad display, and who were still high, it could be, on sheer proximity, not, as he'd first thought, on something reprieved in him, in his life, on something, well, matriculate in the stepping-stone progression of his—*their*—curricula-loaded being, close, pledged as they were, to vocation, calling, some academic plane of the almost religious, some devoted, tenure-sustained existence of the pleasantly civilized, of books and ideas, redeemed from their monasticism and lifted into a realm of sheer pure reward and perk and blessing, the goodish furniture, the respectable house, the solid neighborhood, but to its opposite; knocked for more of a loop by the debit side of his ledger: his physical deficits, all the more visible in the privacy of that respectable house in the solid neighborhood on the goodish furniture, most of which he couldn't even use, than ever they were in mere public; by his not-only-absent, but positively run-off, whereabouts-unknown wife, fleeing him, could be, for all she was worth) of the long-term exigencies as he was of the short, tipsy on woe, fuddled on fear, why even now he couldn't bring himself to urge them to leave, signaling the end of the evening with all the politically correct semaphores available to an internationally wised-up guy like himself, all the recognized, honored peremptories, a stretch, a yawn, an extension of arms, of reversed, interlocked fingers. Though he *knew* why, of course, understood that it was because he did not want to be left alone, was willing to accept on behalf of his house all the risks that letting them stay in it for even a little while exposed it to. Those risks, he understood, which were only the cost of doing business. (Which was why, he supposed, cumulatively, belatedly, he felt so abandoned now that Lipsey, Freistadt, Simmons, and Disch had ditched him.) It was his funeral. Where was everybody?

"Hey? Hey? Hey?" he called, taking the roll. "*Hey!*" he yelled, calling the class to attention as they dribbled back in.

(*All, all* of them pie-eyed on woe's potent, astronomical proof, sozzled on the neat punch of grief.)

"Listen," Schiff said, "maybe you're right. Maybe it ain't such a hot idea to take me upstairs. What with the Stair-Glide out and all. I mean, suppose there's a fire? You people smoked up a storm. I mean, *look* at those ashtrays. God only knows what could still be burning, smoldering in there, what might even yet only be waiting on oxygen, drafts, sparks, the rain to subside, whatever it takes for conditions to ripen, ignition, combustion, the balloon to go up. Maybe if you just stretched me out down here on the couch. On the other hand, if there *were* a fire, why, down here's where it'd probably start, wouldn't it? Oh, *I* don't know, when you get to be my age, when you have to live the way I have to live, why, it's sixteen of one, thirty-seven of the other, isn't it?

"Well, just listen to me. Is this what I sound like? Do I always come on with all this self-pity? Talk about party poopers. And the irony is, it's my own party I'm pooping. I'm worn out and old. What do you expect? Hey, there I go again. Listen, I'm sorry. Maybe I'm overtired, maybe that's why I'm so cranky. Give me the benefit of the doubt, will you?

"*I* know," he said. "While we still have the numbers. Let's go back to plan A. Take me upstairs? Put me to bed?"

So a few of them gradually came forward. Little Miss Moffett. Tysver. Mr. Dickerson. Mr. Bautz. Only Kohm and Wilkins hung back.

But he didn't like the way they were handling him. They started to pull him from his wheelchair but, inexpert as friends enlisted to help move another friend into a new apartment, had no clear idea of what they were doing. They *jostled* his old ass. Miss Moffett, who held him under his left arm, was way too small. She was only getting in Mr. Tysver's way. No one was supporting him at the middle and, since they were too close to each other to begin with, part of his body tended to bump along the ground rather like a rolled-up carpet, say, new, tied-up and still in its paper, that was being carried from one point to another.

He was almost too alarmed to complain, but managed, despite a sort of vertiginous fright, to get out a warning. "No," he said, "this ain't going to happen."

"He's right," said Ms. Kohm, who had apparently been studying the situation. "Get him back into his wheelchair."

Which might not, he was thinking, be such a hot suggestion because it would involve a sort of customized fitting, a proper folding and, at the same time, working him into an upright position, rather, he supposed, like maneuvering one of those heavy dummies they use to test-crash automobiles, into the driver's seat. He shut his eyes. Perhaps they were better at erasing mistakes than at making them. In any event, he was back in the chair in no time at all.

"Now wheel him into the hallway," Ms. Kohm said. "What's the point of trying to carry him there? This is the kitchen. The stairs are in the hall. What could you have been thinking of?"

Was this a political geographer, Schiff thought, or was this a political geographer? Remind me, he thought, to give her an A in this course.

In the hall, Ms. Kohm took over.

She dismissed big Tysver, little Miss Moffett. "Too many cooks spoil the brew," she said. "All right," she said, "Kohm in for Moffett, Dickerson in for Tysver. Wilkins in for Bautz at the feet. Can you get out of that wheelchair by yourself?" she asked him.

"Sure," Schiff said. "If it's locked, if the footrests are out of the way, if I push myself up on its arms."

"Go on," she said, "do it. Dickerson and I will be at your side ready to grab you. Wilkins will take your feet."

He had his misgivings, of course, but then recalled Ms. Kohm's flexed thighs when he'd looked up her dress as she'd crouched before him that evening and, rising, gave himself over to the group like some kid with Outward Bound on a confidence course. And was correct in his instincts. Effortlessly, it seemed, they started to carry him up the stairs. Tysver followed with his walker. "I used to be quite athletic myself," he told them mindlessly. They didn't bother to answer. They had work to do, proceeding to do it with all the silent efficiency of kidnappers, bank robbers.

Then, to himself, chastised himself for what must surely

have seemed to them such a silly, pointless remark. And, flinching, cursed his life, his rotten fate, as they took him the rest of the way up the stairs.

Perhaps, he thought, this was the fate of a gasbag, a punishment for being an academic, for daring to undertake any analysis of the world, for not taking it, that is, for granted, but always to be looking for reasons behind the great gift horse that was life; though he didn't truly believe this, believed deep down that pain was reason enough, its own excuse for being, that anything complicated as the machinery of existence had already built into it the flaws of its own annihilation. There was something redundant about the routine responses to pain, something tchotchkying up disaster, rather like calling in all those FAA inspectors to start their investigations after some big jet had gone down, hundreds dead, dozens unaccounted for. Why, it was simple, really, when all you needed to understand in the first place was that it was an airplane.

It occurred to him that this might be a message worthy to leave on the answering machine he had put on his wish list. Though, really, he thought, he didn't have much of a wish list left. Just, he supposed, that his plane hadn't gone down.

They were in his bedroom.

They laid him down on his bed.

"Phew," said Miss Moffett, "what's that smell?" Schiff had forgotten about the nightstand, the carafe of his pee. He shut his smarting eyes. "Wherever can it be coming from?" she said. "Oh," she said.

Crazily, he was glad Miss Simmons wasn't here to witness this final humiliation. Even as he acknowledged the terrible casualties he'd sustained this evening, his tremendous loss, practically Oriental in its proportions, of face, he leaned on this frail, single plus—— that there was someone who'd been there that evening who'd probably never know the full extent of his tumbled circumstances. Disch, Lipsey, and Freistadt he wrote off. They would be filled in soon enough by the others. (He could just imagine their version, the portrait they would serve up of him. "He lives like a farm animal. Really. Like a farm animal. Like something you could wring cheeses from, or whose fats are industrially rendered, or that you raise for its by-products, its stinking, organic mulch, the ripe, rife salvage of its bones and grease, its hair and hooves, the crap that goes in the cold cuts. All right, he's a cripple. But not a very self-respecting one. Anyway, there are cripples and there are cripples. You should see where he lives. Or, no, where he keeps himself. Neither lair nor burrow, nor stall nor den, neither quite nest nor coop nor sty, though something of all of these. But off the beaten path, secret, out of the way, like those places beasts slink off to to die. Brr, it was creepy.") But Miss Simmons, a stranger to them, was outside the orbit of their gossip. It was amazing, Schiff thought, the fig leaves one could, in extremis, pull about oneself for warmth and modesty. Like drawing a curtain between two beds in a hospital room and emptying one's bowels into the bedpan, grunts, farts and all, separated not only from the party in the next bed, but from all his visitors as well. We live, he thought, by the frail myth of boundary.

And was sustained, however flimsily, by just this sense of things as Ms. Kohm and the others, good neighbors now rather than guests, went about straightening his room, offering to change his sheets, to crack a window a few inches to let in a bit of air. Even little Miss Moffett, who without a word, now that she knew the source of the at-once sharp yet faintly sour ammoniac odor in the room, could see its dark, caramel-yellow reasons beneath its loosed lid, took up the urinal and emptied it in the toilet, rinsed it under the tap, brought it back to the room and returned it (smelling fresh now, even lightly, pleasantly scented, as though she'd washed it out, scrubbed it with cleanser) to the nightstand by his bed. No more put off by his sick man's foul ways than she might have been by her own child's sullied diapers. But of course, Schiff thought, they lived in the age of Candy Stripers, nurse's aides, sponge bathers, administers of enemas, handlers of bedpans, masseuses of the comatose, vol-

unteers at just about anyone's bedside, heroines of vicious
diseases, broken in by AIDS patients, for whom the body
and its poisons were just more brittle frontier. Fallen flesh
meant nothing to them, nothing. (Just try to pinch one
though, or steal a kiss. Cops would be brought in. Calling
all cars, calling all cars.)

So they hovered, flitted about him, the alcoholic levels in
their blood probably no lower now than they'd been at the
height of their games on his stairway, or spreading out their
picnic on his living-room floor. Whistling, giggling while
they worked. Playing a sort of house with him now, a kind
of family, even Bautz and Tysver, even Wilkins and Dickerson, the special care they took of him maybe even a game
of deathbed, making sure as they fluffed up his pillows and
smoothed down his sheets to keep their voices low, addressing each other in exaggerated whispers, cautious high sign.
Two or three of them actually tiptoeing, so that, despite
himself, he found he could not keep his eyes open, was suc-
cumbing to the lullaby of their oddly soothing movements.

He must actually have dozed, for when he opened his eyes
again everyone but Ms. Kohm was gone from his room.
Only the lamp beside his bed was on.

Molly Kohm was sitting sidesaddle on his bed at about
the level of his chest, her hip just pressing comfortably
against his arm.

"Shh," she said, "hush," though he had uttered no
sound. "I just wanted to thank you for the lovely evening."

"You're welcome. No problem," Schiff said hoarsely.

"Shh," she said. "No, really," she said, "thanks *very*
much."

"Hey," Schiff said, wondering if he dare lift a finger, "I
didn't lift a finger. It was all the PGPC's doing."

"The PGPC is dissolved now," she said. "They say that
once the Macy's Day or Rose Bowl parade is over, the people who put it together are back at it again the very next
morning, preparing for next year. Don't you believe it."

"I don't," Schiff said. "I never did."

"Well," she said, "are you going to be all right?"

"Oh, sure," he said.

"Your wife never called?"

"No," he said.

"I don't know where she is. She *could* be in Seattle. She could be anywhere."

He was gathering courage, putting together a sort of schoolkid's nerve he hadn't used in years. All that stuff yesterday about Miss Simmons had been wishful thinking, pure pipe dream, idle fantasy. At no time had she perched on the edge of his bed, been this close to him, her haunch brushing his arm, mere inches from his hand, his cupped palm. Yes, Schiff thought, I'm going to touch her. I'm going to reach over and hold her.

And was just shifting his weight when he heard a great, joined barrage of laughter from downstairs. His students. He thought they'd left. Had even taken this into account before he'd decided to make his move. And not only that, but what's more, had even believed that their departure—he could picture them, their fingers at their lips, shushing each other, up on point, on tiptoe again, in exaggerate, conspired, sneak-thief pantomine—may even have been a sort of deliberate ante-upping, building the story, the Disch, Lipsey, Freistadt version, leaving Ms. Kohm alone with him on his bed as though making off with the metaphorical silver. So, already enlisted in the farce, caught up in it, he was doubly disappointed, once for his ruined moves, once more for the shortfall of legend.

He heard their wild laughter again, helpless as a fit of coughing.

"What's that?" he asked her. "What are they up to?"

"They're young," Ms. Kohm said, rising, "they're having fun. Weren't you ever young?"

"Sure," Schiff said. "I was young. I think I was young."

"Well there you are."

"They sound drunk. They sound out of control."

"What are you worried about?"

"Jesus," he said, "they already broke the damn Stair-Glide. There's every kind of pasta, oil-and-vinegar, spilled

wine, and lettuce stain you can think of on my carpets and
furniture. The Disposall's stopped up like a toilet, and you
tell me the PGPC is shut down for the duration. What do
you *mean* what am I worried about?"

"All right," said Ms. Kohm.

"All right? All right? My *Stair-Glide* is busted! Look
around you, this bedroom, the other rooms on this
floor—— these are my borders, lady, this is my political
geography!"

"Take it easy," she said. "Do you want to have a stroke?
That's just the way people bring them on. You don't want
to have a stroke, do you?"

"No," Schiff said, "I don't want to have a stroke."

"Because I didn't realize you were so upset. No. Say no
more about it. I can take a hit. All of us can. We'll just clear
out."

"You can take a hit?"

"What?"

"You said you can take a hit."

"No I didn't. Did I? I meant a hint. I can take a hint. Did
I really say hit? Well, no matter. Ta," she said. "Ta ta." She
blew her professor a kiss from the doorway.

He heard her going downstairs, heard her roust the rest
of the students. So they still had a leader, a spaced-out one,
but a leader.

He heard them leave, in a few moments heard their two
or three cars start up, heard them drive off.

What he *hadn't* heard, he suddenly realized, was the door
close behind them. And sure enough, in just about the time
it takes weather to travel from a door left open on the first
floor, up the stairs, and into a fellow's bedroom, he felt a
draft.

But it would be all right. He knew what he could do, and
reached inside his shirt and felt for his pendant, his magical
S.O.S. jewelry, found its special, emergency button, and
pressed it.

While he was waiting, it occurred to him that once they
got here he could offer them fifty dollars or so and ask if,

so long as they were already there, would they mind straightening up for him downstairs?

In the distance he heard a siren. It mightn't be for him, of course. It was a weekend night, there were plenty of emergencies to go around.

And then it came to him, the message he'd have put on that answering machine. "You have reached 727-4312," he would have said. "I can't come to the phone right now. I've fallen."

Town Crier Exclusive, Confessions of a Princess Manqué: "How Royals Found Me 'Unsuitable' to Marry Their Larry"

How We Met

I shouldn't have thought I'd have gone public like this. Well, to begin with, there's the question of our musty old laws, isn't there? Oh, solicitors have gone all over it with their fine-tooth combs to see that the paper's in the clear. I never referred to myself as "La Lulu," and neither did Lawrence, Crown Patriciate, Duke of Wilshire, nor any other of their royal lord and lady highnesses and mightinesses. Nor all the king's soldiers, nor all the king's men. There's no such person. That was chiefly an invention of the press; a legal fiction.

For a supposedly free country the press in this land is fair gagged and hobbled by all its Official Secrets Acts with their preemptive seditionaries and thorny libel laws like so many unexploded mines and bombs lying about the landscape. Self-serving, anti-blasphemy law's what it is, establishment gossip insurance. Hence, if you want to know, the reason so-called checkbook journalism got invented right here in Fleet Street. To cover, if one's a press lord, pardon me, one's derrière. Because no one believes this stuff. "For entertainment purposes only," as they say in the Horoscopes. It's my humble opinion a lot of the buggery fascination in this country comes right out of that tradition, the tradition, I mean, of being all caught up in this or that condition of contingency, laying out advance positions, fortifications. Larry himself told me not even the old Roman legions made more of a thing of putting out guards, that the Brits invented lookout men so-called, and that the principle of the alibi has its roots in English common law. What I'm saying is that your sodomy had its origins in simple sport and getting round the rules as much as ever it did in pleasure—— in seeing, I mean, just how much one can get away with. Oh yeah, it's all a game. I have my theories, and one of my humble own pet ones is that the very ideas of Monarchy and Blood and Class come right out of that same tradition.

But I can almost see Sir Sidney reading my copy over my shoulder and complaining to his editors about what in b-oody, infinite h-ll do I think they're paying me for, certainly not my theories, and why don't I get on with all the nasty bits? In due time, Sir Sid, in due time. I just want it understood that no matter what you or anyone else thinks, I'm not in this for the money. If the investigative reporters on the *Sunday Times* team wanted to write up my story they could have had it for nothing. But of course they wouldn't dare. It's the paper of record. People might believe it.

I'm *not* in it for the money. I'm not. I want it told is all. But because Larry is Larry—and I don't blame him, I really don't, I still believe he loves me, I really do—and the Royal Family is the Royal Family, there was just no way of getting it done unless I took *Town Crier*'s fifty thousand pounds sterling and did it myself.

And though I'd never acknowledge I owe the public a thing—what, after the way *I've* been depicted in the papers, on the telly and the oh-so-civilized BBC 3 even?—it may almost be my patriotic duty to let it know some of the real circumstances by which it is ruled. La Lulu, indeed!

"Oh yeah," you're saying, "for God and Country, for England and St. George." "Hell hath no fury," you're saying, "like a woman scorned." "Or tattood!" you're saying.

We met, as everyone knows, in Cape Henry, on the westermost of the Lothian Islands, fifty or so nautical miles from Santa Catalina Island and the village of Avalon, themselves about a thirty-minute ferry ride from Los Angeles and the southwest coast of California.

Whatever you might have read in the press to the contrary, I was not at that time in any way connected with the Ministry of Tourism; I did not sell coral or exotic flowers to day trippers from the States—ridiculous on the face of it since the United States government has strict rules preventing anyone from bringing any sort of flora or fauna into the country—or work behind the counter in the souvenir or duty-free shops at the airport. I did not sing with the band at the hotel. I had been made, like several of my countrymen at that time, redundant, and was sharing expenses and living the life of a sort of glorified beachcomber with two other girls in a discounted, low-season, already two-a-penny shelter more wicky-up than guest cottage or even hut with its rough, frond-covered frame, and dry, thick, still sharpish-edged grasses, which my cut hands too well knew to their sorrow and that sometimes in the mornings after a particularly issueless—even out there on the Pacific it was still just as much a drought as ever it was on the California mainland—but powerful blow of the previous night, we actually had to reweave back into the semblance of a wall. Often we'd pick up the odd fifty pence "sewing houses"—as we named our queer profession—for some of the older or less resourceful of our beachcomber colleagues, or shaking out mats, or sweeping up sand. Beachcombers, indeed.

"Oh, damn," I told Marjorie on the early morning of the day of Prince Larry's visit, "I've gone and cut my hands. I see I shall have to go into a different trade. Have you seen the aloe?"

"There is no aloe, Louise," Marjorie said.

"How can there not be aloe? Living as we do, where we do, there has to be aloe."

"We are quite out of aloe, Louise."

"Impossible. I saw it myself it can't have been but two days ago."

"You are not the only party who sews houses in this house, Louise. You are not the only one with stigmata."

"My fault, Louise, dear," said Jane. "I was down for the

aloe run. I'm afraid I forgot. If you wait, I'll go after I beachcomb myself some sandfruit for my breakfast."

"Sandfruit gives you the runs. Why do you eat it?"

"I quite enjoy the runs, Louise."

Now to this point the public knows nothing of this. My friends Jane and Marjorie swept aside by history, their own stories lost if not to time then to time's blatant disregard of a proper attention to detail, which I, as a public figure so-called, begin to suspect happens with the stories of most of history's cohorts, so apparently caught up and transfixed by the shine of celebrity and notoriety. But actually such trashing of individuals and their particulars is as much evasive action (like piling up sunblock on one's skin at the beach, say; just so much more posting of guards, just so many more lookouts, the fiddle of yeomanry our national sin) as ever it is the logic of a true humility. Well, it's never the logic of a *true* humility, and what I think, what I think, *really,* is that like sodomy, like buggery, our notion of subjectivity, of submitting—submitting? volunteering!—to be the subjects of kings and queens has to do with *wanting* to disappear, with building up heroes to draw the lightning. Limelight was ever a distraction to time's healthy, childlike fear of limelight. (This is fun, you know? Limelight has its compensations, hey, Sir Sid?)

So to this point, the public, for all the attention it's paid us, knows absolutely nothing. Jane and Marjorie not only out of the picture but never in it to begin with. (No, I'm not making this up. Not any of it. I'm English as the next bimbo. There's still all those official secrets acts and libel laws. Why would I stick my neck out? Yet I hardly flatter myself I think I've earned any of those fifty thousand pounds yet.)

That drought you read about? You don't know the half. (Is that to be my theme here?) It played California hell, put half the state out of work, and not just the agricultural illegals up out of Mexico. Trained dental technicians let go. What, you think not? All that water running all day, all that rinse and spit? Shipping clerks and gift wrappers in the best department stores laid off because of the water shortage or forced to quit because they couldn't work up enough moisture to lick one more label or stick on another fancy seal. Going on the dole for parched tongues and chapped lips. Or my own case.

I left England because of a tragic love affair (which since it has nothing to do with my involvement with Larry I'm under no obligation at this point to discuss with my public, so-called) and came to the States not to emigrate but in order to put some time and distance between my heart and its circumstances. It had been my intention to be gone no more than six months, but as the old saying has it, man proposes and God disposes and, in the half year I'd given to it, nothing had been resolved. Even back then, in the early days of the drought, it was still easy enough to find a job in Los Angeles. You know some of my background. You know that while I had something of an independent income it was never near big enough I could afford to live abroad indefinitely without finding means to supplement it. Also, it's good for people to be gainfully employed. It makes life that much more interesting.

So I went for an au pair girl. My English accent was all the character I ever needed. I offered to show my passport but they wouldn't even look. It didn't make any difference to these people. Almost every au pair in Beverly Hills was an American actress hoping to catch on at a studio. They could all walk the walk and talk the talk. A reason I wasn't found out when my photographs started to appear in the papers, I think, is that if they remembered me at all, the people of the house must have thought they recognized me from the industry. Besides, it didn't last all that long. For a great democratic show a lot of these people began to lay off their "nannies" and "au pairs" even before the drought started to bite. They gave us bonuses and apologized that they had to dismiss us because we'd become "just one more thirst that had to be quenched." And continued to quench the remaining household thirsts with the same bottled mineral water they'd been using all along. Restaurants were still hiring on, but it didn't need any Greenwich Mean Time celestial clock watchers to see that the hostesses they employed were just more actresses and that when the time came they'd let these go just as quick as all the rest of those other nanny-cum-film stars. (And the time came and they did. Even the less expensive restaurants were selling bottled water by the glass then. The difference was that very few people believed it wasn't tap water they were actually paying for. Oh, I know, I know. I really do. This sounds like satire and the States sound much like England and, in some ways, it is and they are. And I still can't even get the punctuation right. Can't or won't. Preferring much that's American to that which is British. Putting my full stops inside the quotes, for example. Choosing the Yankee *zed* in "civilization" to the *s* in its chiefly Brit VAR, as they say in *Webster's*. Dropping my *e* out of "judgement." Slipped between the cracks of two different worlds. And if that's one of the reasons the royals found me unsuitable to marry their Larry— and, in an odd way, it is—it's the least of them.) Suffice it to say, however, I didn't even bother to apply. And set up instead for an ordinary housekeeper's job making up beds in a hotel. What I never expected was the unwillingness of people from parts of the country unaffected by drought to endure even for one or two days whatever insignificant parch they might have been put through in the one two days it would have taken them to do their business. When the drought really became serious the girls with the English accents were the first ones to be cut.

It was all very well for me to be larky and thirsty while I still had a job. My employers were paying my health insurance, after all. But once I was without work I knew that I would have to find something for a—ha ha—rainy day.

I still had no reason to go home. Well, I'd fallen a. over t. for the climate, hadn't I? That was when I first thought of Cape Henry and the Lothian Islands. In England even the King is on the National Health, even the Queen.

(Still another aside: I can't shake the sense I have of Press Lord Sir Sidney reading over my shoulder as I write, and

I'm beginning to feel if not my obligations to the reader-
ship, then at least Sir Sid's sense of them for me, and I find
that compelling and, in small ways, oddly touching and
will, when there's time or it seems fitting, henceforth alert
my readers—or maybe only Sir Sidney himself—that
they—he—may skip over the asides until I take up my
"story" again, or "la Lulu's Account," or whatever they're
calling it these days on hoardings on the sides of buses.
Anyway, you know what seems strange to me? The general, disparate, all-purpose exile that moves over the world.
That piecemeal, bit-by-bit colonization of earth. People, for
whatever reason, coming together on all sorts of foreign
shores, washing up in the strangest places. The mysterious
working out of the great queer plot of the planet. Different
motives, mutual ends. Well, it finally accounts for the very
idea of empire, doesn't it?)

Whatever I may feel now it no longer seems unusual to
me I hadn't even known Jane or Marjorie back in Los Angeles. Indeed, when the three of us met at the beachcomber
estate agency where we let that wicky-up, and not three or
four days later one of us—I forget which—suggested we
might pick up the odd pound or so if we put our backs into
it and helped with the morning ablutions on other people's
shelters, I naturally assumed—as I later discovered we each
did—that my two new friends were just more actresses
marking time and waiting to be discovered. Which brings
me back to that missing aloe and the first time I saw the
Prince.

Well, it was those embargo, or quarantine, or meat-and-
potato prohibitions of course, the flora-and-fauna rules, all
the high-priority, low-level laws of jealous international
agreement and stickler decree by which nations claim they
not only protect themselves but insinuate the superiority of
their Nature over *your* Nature. Showing the flag, grandstand-
ing the public on the cheap—— all that subject population,
all those abiders. And getting, Prince Larry, grand photo
ops out of it, too, making the most of his signature gesture.
Though I swear to you, I'd forgotten all that, had been away

from England almost two years by then. Out of sight, out of mind. One forgets. Though I suppose the things one forgets are always perched somewhere near the tippy tip of one's head, because when I saw him there posed in the aloe shop, quit of his equerry and all his retainers, I remembered at once of course. This was the one who made a point of buying off the local economy all those ceremonial wreaths he's charged with laying on all those public buildings, natural monuments, and great men's graves. And maybe that's why those ordinances came into being in the first place—— because whoever made up kings figured it might come in handy one day, that someday *this* prince would come. Rome *wasn't* built in a day, and the ruling class is nothing if not clever.

And he was handsome. I remembered from my life in England that he was handsome, but now he was possessed of an almost surfeit of beauty, and of an age when he was at its (or he of its) very peak. Like special fruit that has come into its season. Don't mistake me, this is no mournful occasion, the sad affair of a moment, some here today, gone tomorrow mayfly condition. I'm not speaking of God's or humanity's fairy tales, the ephemeral, too delicate arrangements of nature and myth. Yet there was a kind of hapless nostalgia to him, some secret knowledge. I do not think I noticed this then. How could I have done, I was a different person then. So I didn't notice it; I only remember it. I don't even know if the Prince was aware of it. I believe rather not. As I say, I allow him what I allow myself. Some secret knowledge, the long-term profit of the heart. Yet something, something. Got up, it might have been, in his very swagger, the peculiar, put-everyone-at-ease pomp of his self-consciousness. He was at once breezy and shy with a crowd that, knowing his habits, had gathered early in the morning or stayed up all night (some of them) in Cape Henry's discrete shopping district on the westermost island of the long Lothian Islands chain. An anomaly, one of those freaks not so much of geography as of naming and settling. Those fifty or so nautical miles off Santa Catalina would be an example. The counterpart American village of Avalon hard by on California's southwest coast would. Just a thirty-minute ride as the ferry floats.

Sad as Spring's first perfection, the trees never so beautiful again as they were in the prime joyous days of their first being though they had weeks, months, seasons, even half a year yet to green. Nor ever so ripe as in those first close-cropped days of their initial blooming.

So I saw him but didn't recognize him, don't you know.

The prince waved at me. Not the elbow, elbow, wrist wrist wrist of majesty gone easy on itself, the accustomed, practiced pacing of what had already been a long reign, but something more awkward, more attractive than that——— a matter, a question of image. And, though I was surprised, I could hardly have been aware of my awareness. "Good god," I remember thinking, "was that a prince?" Not "Was that the Prince?" Caught short, clued-in finally only by the royal retainers pretending to try to keep up. If the Prince knew it was only some dog-and-pony show he didn't let on. Only later, in the town square (*and* mall *and* tourist trap) did I recognize him, don't you know.

Though I'd known he was coming of course. As did Jane, as did Marjorie. We'd even discussed our plans to go see him. Allegiant, interested, dutied, patriotic'd. (Curious, too. We forgot because we were new on the island and caught up in our individual rebeginnings.) In the square the Prince picked up his pace, as the retainers, seeming genuinely to try now, did theirs, though knowing in their accustomed souls they could never keep up but that somehow they had an obligation if not to the realm then at least to their corps, to some tradition of equerries, retainers, and handlers, knowing it would cost them nothing to be loyal, that this Prince would have his way with them no matter what they did, so that even if they did let up their merely shown-flag haste would lose out anyway to the real power of his insouciant, sincere deferentials and bluff, awkward bearing. The crowd not crowding him but fallen back as if he were some battle prince out of history, not boarding or clamoring him as if he were a rock-and-roll star, his fans not standing tiptoe, just standing back, behind the velvet ropes, not in retreat, fallen back even from me, so the Prince, seeing what was what, turned to one of us, to me in this instance, and spoke up. "Oh," he said, "I'm terribly sorry. How inexcusably rude of me. I was just going into this shop." "Go in, Your Highness," I said, and, courtly as could be, nice as pie, His Highness singals, "After you." Of course I defer. As does the Prince. As then do I. Until, in a kind of shock, the crowd signals, "Well, if it's what His Highness *wants* . . ." So I go in. And Larry turns to the people in the road and signals "After *all* of you." And passes them through like someone taking tickets. Like an usher. Like a cop directing traffic or a coach waving a runner in from third. And then goes through himself. Leaving the others behind like people lined up for the second show. Leaving the show-biz retinue behind too.

And this occurred—— that I might have been the only non-show-biz type left in the shop, my Prince's lone remaining bona fide witness, a fiddle if not of yeomanry then of just that much more hero-building effacement, more historic gull to the historic shill of all those drawers of the lightning; behind the elaborate lines and colorful smoke screen of all that cadre of lookouts and posted guards—— that this was just for my benefit, that I was as necessary a part of the process as the Prince himself; that all that was left in the aloe shop now were myself and the show-biz tourists got up in the lamb's cloth of what was merely that much more retinue—— that even the wreath-and-aloe saleslady was a show-biz wreath-and-aloe saleslady. (But conflicted, too, don't you know. Mindful that perhaps I'd been in the States too long. Where they take their drawers of the lightning even more seriously than we do in England, and almost every other person in the crowd—not counting the armed chaps on the roofs and in all the windows or the reporters who ask some of the toughest questions at the press conference—is Secret Service, SWAT, or CIA.) And, My, I'm thinking in the tropes of a paranoia turned inside out, all this attention. For little me? Why, thank you, kind sirs and mesdames, and thank *you*, kind Sir. Self-conscious as the recipient of a singing telegram, don't you know, or a guest of honor, or someone not used to it at her very first Command Performance.

I may have been blushing; I was probably blushing. Whereupon the most remarkable thing.

He dismissed them.

In that same efficient semaphore with which he'd passed them through. At the same time, seeing me with my banknotes in my hand, signaling me to remain behind, and freezing the show-biz wreath-and-aloe lady in her place. One look, one look did it, one all-inclusive gesture—— this complicated syntax of self-assured silence. So that when the shop had cleared and he finally spoke to her, I was the only one left to hear.

"I'm looking," says the Prince, "for a wreath. Do you *do* wreaths?"

"Oh yes, Your Highness, but we're such a *small* village. The resident population can't be but four or five thousand at most, though closer to four, I should think."

"Yes?" goes His Highness.

"Just enough commissionaires to open the doors at the taxi rank, just enough porters to handle the cobble and trim of the holiday makers, just enough publicans and innkeepers, barmaids, tapsters, and potboys. Just enough ostlers. Just enough chars. Just enough buskers to sink in the streets and play their guitars outside the cinema."

"So?" says the Successor.

"Just enough drivers to drive the red double-decker buses and just enough Pakis to collect your fare and hand you your change. Just enough unarmed bobbies to answer questions about directions and make sure the pubs close after last call. Just enough Tommies. Just enough of the King's Home Guard Cavalry to stand in the sentry boxes under their bearskin busbies and challenge the tourists to provoke reactions for snapshots. Just enough men to change the guard outside the Governor's Palace. And just enough people to pick up the post from the kiosks for day trippers to send home just for the sake of the canceled stamp."

"I don't make out . . ." says the Heir Apparent.

"Just enough cockney accents; just enough Liverpudlian, Yorkshire, Welsh. Just enough Scots, Sir; just enough Lincolnshire. (Though we both know, don't we, Sire, how clannish East Englanders are and how they pretty much keep to themselves.) Just enough C of E rectors to offer up mass and call out the number of the hymn from the Book of Common Prayer. Just enough choristers . . ."

". . . your meaning."

"Well, it's not as if we had a proper cemetery, is it, Highness?" says his subject-apparent.

"Madam?"

"Well, we're an outpost of Empire, aren't we, Prince? Closer to the States than Bermuda, we are. We drive on the left side of the road here, we do, and quainter we are than bowlers and bumbershoots. We're an enterprise, we are."

"I'm not sure . . ."

"You're not sure? You're sure."

"Is this the way, madam, you address your future King?"

"Well, you're not my King yet, you know. And really, M'lud, when push comes to shove you haven't any *real* power. You can't shut me up in the Tower or have me beheaded, can you? I mean, you're all symbolic-like aren't you?

"It's the bargains you come for. You came for a price on the flowers. It's your way and it's charming, and you're quite famous for it, but do you know what I give for a wreathing? The labor alone? The cost of all that coiling and twisting and interweaving? We're not, as I say, a big population—— three or four thousand at most, but closer to three, I should think. And no more graveyard to speak of than what fits in back of a church. And the artisans died out. And most of the personnel on this tight little fun fair of an island, this picturesque theme park of an empire—those not gone to bush—posted back to Britain before they're fifty. And it isn't as if we're equipped to lay out holiday makers, so I have to bring in extra hands, don't I? Navvies and erks and night porters. Factoti. So I'm dead sorry, Wilshire, my wreaths *have* to be pricey."

"I'm still looking," he says to me, "you go ahead."

"Some aloe, please," I tell the woman and give over my banknote while at the same time I try to hide my cut, chafed and burning hands.

"It's ready," she says, "but wasn't it Jane's turn, or Marjorie's?"

"Jane quite forgot, I'm afraid," I said.

"No, please," said the Prince. "Wait and I'll help you with that."

In the end he didn't bargain with her, he didn't even seem angry. He let her rude remarks pass like the great gentleman he was. "I'll take that one," he said, and pointed to a large, leafy wreath interlaced with long ropes of bright yellow flowers.

"Yes," said the awful woman, "it's the only one we have, isn't it?"

"If you know so much about my ways," said the Prince, "then you know I never carry money. Indeed, I hardly ever look at it. My personal equerry will take care of you." He turned to me. "Give me that," he said. Well, I was confused. The aloe plant was rather big, and he was already carrying his great heavy wreath. I half thought he meant to steal it from me.

His equerry was waiting outside. All the others had gone. Not even a bobby was to be seen in that queer, translated, odd English street. No cars were there, no red double-deck buses with their extraordinarily high route numbers—I already knew there were only two routes in that tiny town and that while they took you past different points of interest, both ended up discharging their passengers at the same spot—and now the place, except for the shops on the High Street—the greengrocers, the Boots, the W. H. Smith, the Marks and Spencer, and various others—the hire purchase and estate agents and removal companies and cafes and fish-and-chips, the offtrack betting, the theatre and the cinema, et cetera—seemed not so much deserted as abandoned, evacuated even. In the distance I could just make out a residential area—— a block of flats, an occasional thatched roof, one or two County Council–looking structures.

"It seems we must pay a hundred pence on the pound to the tick," he told the fellow. "Organise it for me, would you? There's a lad. Oh, and take this for me, Colin, I'm assisting the girl."

He handed the wreath over to his equerry.

He relieved me of the aloe plant and, exposing my raw, rubbed hands, said, "Oh, your poor hands." He broke off a leaf and squeezed out its white juices. Laying the plant down, he rubbed the stuff across my palms and the back of my hands. He spread it up and down my fingers. It was as sticky as sperm.

"You're not a tourist then," he said, chatting me up like any young man any young girl.

I saw what was up, I knew what was what. "This isn't some droit du seigneur thing, is it, Your Peerage?"

"I hate that," said the Prince.

"What do you hate?"

"All those awful 'Your This' and 'Your That' jokes. Calling me 'Highness,' calling me 'Wilshire.' 'M'lud.' Calling me 'Sire.' Calling me 'Peerage.' Having a prince on. She was right, though, that dreadful woman. I *am* 'symbolic-like,' I have no real power. It's almost the start of the next century. People have had it with Royals. They're starting to agitate for reforms. We can't say we blame them."

He suddenly seemed boyish, he suddenly seemed shy.

"Say, you're not one of those Let's-Trade-Places sort of princes, are you?"

"What if I were?"

"Well, I should be very sorry to know it, My Lord Grace," I said, teasing him.

(Flirting! I was actually flirting! Not only for the first time in years, but with someone whose power, symbolic or not, was as real to me, or to my outraged class-conscious blood, as it might have been not so many centuries before when he *could* have shut me up in the tower, or had me beheaded, or made me his strumpet. Am I getting warm, Sir Sid?)

"Lawrence! My name is Lawrence, and if someone doesn't call me by it soon, I shall go over the wall!"

" '*Up* the wall,' " I corrected.

"*Over* it, by God bl--dy f---ing he-l! *Over* it!"

"Oh, Prince," I said, by which I meant speak to me, make yourself clear, help me to understand.

"Well you would do," he said as if reading my mind, "if you spent any only three days filling the appointments on the Court Calendar. Any only three? Any only two. *One!*

"I'm young. Not yet thirty. It isn't that I'm bored— though I'm bored—so much as exhausted. And these tours are the worst. I put on a good show, I give them a run for their money. Well, *you* saw! It would kill a normal man, what I do. I'm like a trained athlete. But there's just so much even a trained athlete can take. During the Season I put in a half hour at a Ball, then rush on to the next. And the next. And the next. I mingle and mingle and mingle. And always with some aide-de-camp or plenipotentiary two decades older than myself at my car and whispering the names of those I must greet as if they were state secrets. What I need is someone at the other car giving me the names of all those plenipotentiaries and aides-de-camp. Well, *you* saw. I called him 'Colin.' My equerry. That wasn't Colin. Colin is heavier.

"But these tours are exhausting. They take it out of one.

"Hither'd in America forty miles in a motorcade to watch two innings of a ballgame, and yon'd to take one course at a banquet.

"And all the time working out our rehearsed idiosyncrasies. Well, you *saw*. One young prince was famous for trying to perfect a steam-powered perambulator most of his adult years. And there was another, this royal was owed a permanent crown for a back tooth. When she died the monarch who succeeded her insisted the work be completed by the dentist. I understand the poor man had to pry the dead queen's jaws open in order to replace the temporary with the permanent crown. He delayed his mother's burial for thirty-five hours until the dentist who'd been working on her could make good on the crown."

"How mean, how awful for the dentist."

"Not really. The fellow got a 'By Appointment to HBM' plaque out of it and the new king earned a reputation for being frugal.

"So you see. It isn't so easy being in my position."

"There's lots have it worse."

"Are there? Do they? Oh, I hope so!"

Sunday, January 19, 1992
How We Got Engaged

"Lord Mayor Miniver, My Lord and Lady Lewes. Anthony Fitz-Sunday, Right Honorable MP from the Lothian Chain. Miss Bristol, honored guests, loyal subjects, and welcome friends. We would be remiss if we did not take the opportunity today to tell you how very, _very_ glad it makes us feel to be home. Even though till this morning we had never set foot on your beautiful island, Cape Henry, or, indeed, as much as glimpsed the Lothians on the horizon like so many gray serpents at the bottom of a spyglass.

"We were 'too young' to accompany His Royal Highness, our father, when he visited these islands with Her Royal Highness, our mother, in the sixties, or to accompany them on their second tour when they returned in the seventies, by which time we were engaged in our training at the Royal Naval Colleges at Dartmouth and Greenwich. For the reason we did not come with them on His and Her Royal Highnesses' yacht on its famous round-the-world cruise in the sixties was not, as the story that was put out at the time had it, that we were 'too young,' but that, even at five, when most children that age have already become jaded by the roundabout and demand to be taken on thrill rides at Battersea Park that might put off men and women four and five times older, we had not yet found our sea legs. Now it will not do, of course, for a future King of England not to find his sea legs. After all, what is it they say—— 'Rule, Britannia! Britannia, rule the waves . . . '?

"But our theme is coming home, pride, gladness, the almost physical release one feels in finding oneself in the bosom of one's kind, within, as it were, all the warming fires of consanguine blood, all the . . .

"Pardon us. We are no metaphysical prince and the last thing on our mind today is speculation, let alone attempting to fit such speculation to a lofty rhetoric. Henceforth, we shall endeavor to banish from our speech that which as merely Prince we had only arrogated anyway—— the royal, we mean, pronoun, and address you properly, with 'I,' with 'me,' with 'my' . . ."

And I, though I was close enough to him to have heard his words—in a front-row seat, actually—even without benefit of the various microphones on the lectern before him that fed the words into the public-address and other equipment, one mike, I guessed, for radio, one for TV, another perhaps for the local archives, and still one more for the high-resolution Minicam machinery used by the crew that traveled with him in order to prepare a documentary on Lawrence for French TV—— all the time thinking: *Miss Bristol? Miss Bristol?*, and parsing the eloquent syntax of the name's placement between the Right Honorable MP from the Lothian chain and all those loyal subjects, honored guests, and welcome friends.

" . . . and because I do not feel symbolic here in what is neither protectorate nor commonwealth, republic nor state, hegemony nor league nor loose association. Not confederation or jurisdiction, not even this, well, *not Canada*, with— Their Majesty's faces on the money or no—all its pretensions to home rule, but only, quite simply, this honest-to-God *home*, a place which actually has its own MP—— this vestige and outpost, this geographical quirk, like an outbuilding, say, as accessory as Northern Ireland or Wales. . . ."

Thinking, *Miss Bristol, Miss Bristol?*

" . . . where I am not just passive witness, watching the ritual dances, accepting the flowers, the grayish leis of rotting bones and teeth, hearing the tuneless, gibberish chants to the arrhythmic, asyndeton claps on human skin and heads like the pat-down hand search of someone suspicious picked out of a line filing through Customs. But home, at home, taking my ease, *feeling* at ease, and laying this wreath at the tomb of Captain Spears-Henry out of ordinary common courtesy, not ceremoniously, but rather like a guest bringing a bottle of table wine to his hostess at a dinner party."

Thinking, wondering, trying to translate the priorities—— after the Lord Mayor and nobs and hons, but before
the gentry, all those captains of all that cottage industry
which was the reason the town existed at all; before the
spouses; before the Anglophiles over from California and up
from Mexico for the day. Miss Bristol? Miss Bristol?

"Yet I would not have you think Cape Henry is just another stopover on my voyage. Indeed not. For me it will
forever have its associations, even its historic associations,
even—dare I express it?—its romantic ones. For it is here, in
this lovely place, that I have the pleasure and honor of announcing my engagement and of introducing my fiancée to
you.

"Miss Bristol? Louise, darling, would you please join me
on the rostrum? Our friends so very much want to meet
you."

For a moment nothing happened at all. Then there was
this pure reflex noise of reaction, almost, I should imagine,
like the sound on a battlefield when flashes of light are followed by the pop of shells—— some inside-out physics of
sound and light. One could hear the motor-driven cameras,
this buzz of photography as everyone in the crowd turned
and snapped pictures of everyone else, clicking off random,
indiscriminate images, shaving their odds, wasting their
film, hoping that if they just took enough pictures the
chance of taking the right one and of catching the pleased
Louise, whoever she might be, would be just that much
more enhanced. Even the French camera crew wheeled,
recklessly aiming their Minicams. It was the din of farce.

The press could not buy up *all* of them. There must still
be, in private collections, at least fifty photographs and a
dozen videos of my at-first-startled, then bewildered, and
finally annoyed, face.

Louise was not in the least pleased.

"Come up, come up," commanded the Prince and, when
I did not move, actually started to clap his hands, leading
the applause, exactly as if he were an entertainer in a club

trying to embarrass a member of the audience into coming up on stage with him.

I was not pleased, I was not embarrassed. If anything, it was out of some vestigial patriotism I joined him. I swear to you, loyalty was what first got me into this fix.

I let him take my hand. I let him hold me. I let him kiss me in public. I kissed him back. I swear to you, it was out of duty I did it, this old atavistic, juvenile echo of my first impressions of the Crown, of God and Country.

In the same fashion I stood passively by as he explained to our countrymen the history of crossover blood, of kings and commoners. In the same fashion still, I held my tongue while the s-- of a b---- went on about what a boon it was for the imperial stock to indulge such marriages. I think I was visibly shaken only when he announced that he had obtained his parents' prior consent to make this engagement.

(All right, Sid, he'd comforted me. Are you satisfied? Those spermy juices of my aloe plant on my palms and fingers. What, did you think I was stone? I'm not stone, I wasn't stone. Are *you* stone, are your readers? Why, then, do they turn these pages? So I'm not stone. Nor any pedestaled female woven of ivory by some Pygmalion. You men. Though I'll say this for him—— he comforted me. H--l, even if he wasn't Pygmalion, he could have been some perfect prince of massage!

(Why did you give me that check? No one's perfect. My failed and tragic love affair, remember? That sent me packing from England off to the States to put some distance between my heart and its circumstances? For what I thought would be only six months, but which in the event . . .?

(All right, Sid, we'd d--- the ---d! W-'- done the deed, I say. There, are you satisfied?

(But it didn't have to be fifty thousand pounds now, did it? It didn't even have to be the Prince. All it had to be was a woman, any woman. Any woman owning up. Any woman owning up to what she put there and then what he put *there*. Whatever it was that sent me packing in the first place.

Whoever it was. Or whatever it was I did with whoever it was I did it with during my hiatus, or exile, or expatriation, or whatever you want to call it, in the States. Because I'm not stone. You don't pay a stone fifty thousand pounds just to know who's thrown what where. I'm telling you. You men!)

Fortunately, I'd dressed for the occasion (even though I didn't know what the occasion was going to be, even though I didn't know I was the occasion I was dressing for), and had on a flowery silk print dress, with a stylish but oh-so-proper hemline, with matching high-heeled shoes and a large, wide-brimmed straw hat. I fancy I *seemed* rather like a prince's fiancée and would have looked at home at Ascot, under a tent at Henley for the boat race, or at any royal garden party, but was as overdressed for this lot—because outpost or not, home or not, even England or not, it was still the provinces—of tourists, day trippers, and holiday makers, in their blue jeans, sportswear, and bathing costumes, as the Prince himself in his bespoke suits, custom ties, and handkerchiefs, and all his never-to-be-broken-in, throwaway shoes, might have seemed before a band of Fiji Islanders performing their ceremonial fire dances, or rain-making, or sacrificial bloodlettings or somesuch, and that he'd been at such rhetorical pains to distinguish them from just moments before. (And I'll tell you this, Sir Sid; one of the downsides of being a prince, or his fiancée either, is that you're never quite comfortable in the clothes you wear. And between the fittings and all those public appearances one's always making, you hardly have time to breathe, or—pardon my French—find a spare moment to go to the W.C. Larry was quite right when he complained about his boredom and exhaustion. He was quite right when he said that about his being like a trained athlete. These people must shower three and four times a day. In all their untried, first-time-out boots, waders, and brand-spanking-new fishing gear, cunningly worked creels and the packed seaweed that lines them as if for fresh fish flown in daily to world-class restaurants. Athletes indeed. Like artists' models or film stars trained in the arts of standing still, posing, their muscles as glib as bird dogs', hounds'. Speaking for myself, I know I became this like trained—pardon my French—bladder athlete during my reign as his Princess manqué. Pardon my French.)

All right, Sid. I know. I still haven't earned it. A tuppence of toilet humor don't make a dent in fifty thousand pounds.

We went back to the wicky-up.

"Now I know what all that aloe is for. You weave wicky-ups, don't you?"

"How would you know about something like that?"

"Oh, I've been around," he said.

"You?"

"I bivouacked in plenty of places like this when I set up for a sailor. It wasn't all Dartmouth and Greenwich at Dartmouth and Greenwich. The Royal Navy was never any respecter of persons. The British Empire depends on its Fleet even if it ain't the British Empire anymore. I may as well have been a cabin boy as a prince for all the difference it made to my warrant officers. So, sure, I've woven plenty of walls from these sharp, saw-toothed fronds. We called it 'sewing houses.' "

"That's what *we* call it!"

"We?"

"My roommates and me. Jane and Marjorie. I think they're actresses."

"So, certainly. I've swept up many a peck of sand in my time, and taken what comfort I could from what aloe I could get whenever I could get it. Of course," he said, "it isn't supposed to be as important for a man to have smooth, creamy hands as it is for a woman, Louise."

He took both my hands and held them in one big, smooth palm.

"Yech," he said.

"I beg your pardon?"

"Nothing," he said, "I was just thinking about all the times I beachcombed sandfruit for breakfast, and how it gave me the runs."

I withdrew my hands.

"What?" he said. "What?"

"It gives Jane the runs, too," I told him coolly.

"Look," said the Prince, "didn't you just ask whether I was one of those Let's-Trade-Places sort of princes? Well, I am, Louise."

"A commoner in every port, is it?"

"No," he said, taking back my hands and pressing them to his lips. "What, are you kidding me, Louise," he muttered his demurrers, looking up, "you know me better than that." He took me in his athlete's arms. It was thrilling, Sid, thrilling. Well, he was handsome. And all those months in the States living one's life like a more-or-less nun. And him with all his dark good looks. I tell you I felt like a nurse in a novel.

So, what with this and what with that, we were soon enough rolling round down on the sandy floor of the wicky-up enjoying a bit of the old leg-over, so given up to passion I didn't realize what happened when we crashed into the hotel bellman's cart Jane and Marjorie and I used to hang up our clothes and was all we had for wardrobe or even for furniture in that tiny hut, spilling the clothes, tumbling the coats and shifts and dresses and gowns down from where they hung on the rack, Prince Lawrence so excited and lusty I could almost believe his earnest demurrers of just three or four minutes before.

(Was I naïve, Sid? Who's to say? Anyway, I don't think so, for what was the morning line on this prince while his two younger brothers and two younger sisters were off sowing their wild oats and getting their names in the papers, making it into the gossip columns with their famous scrapes and muddles that had always the faint air about them of throwbacks to different, gayer times—— like ne'er-do-wells running with a fast crowd, and fortunes lost gambling; careless Sloane Rangers sent down from Cambridge or Oxford, or come away with dubious seconds and thirds; his siblings excused or explained away or even written off by their place in the birth order? Only that, baby-boomer prince or no baby-boomer prince, in the curious reign of the peculiarly marked incumbency of these particular sovereigns he was conscientious, notable for the advantage he took of photo ops—and why not with his beauty?—and for his solicitous gestures, his polished idiosyncrasies and special relationships with all his inferiors—well, I was an example, wasn't I?—and that he might be too good to be true, right down to the impression he gave of having just stepped out of a trailer on locale somewhere, of being this, well, film star got *up* as a prince, not a hair out of place, all perfected and rested while a stand-in stood on his mark taking the heat for him while the crew got ready, setting the lights, fussing the sound, till they sent a gofer to the trailer to fetch him— "Five minutes please, Prince"—and he stepped out, majestic and grand as you please, his jacket and tie and collar as perfectly in place as they'd be on some little girl's cutout of a jacket and tie and collar that she tabs on a doll that she's punched from a book.)

So excited and lusty that at the moment of truth he neither called on God nor made the customary noises and growls and oh! oh! oh!s of satisfaction but shouted out: "IT WAS THAT ALOE THAT BROUGHT IT ALL BACK!" And from somewhere deep within his seafaring engrams and naval neurals actually began to sing—— "On the road to Mandalay,/Where the flyin'-fishes play,/An' the dawn comes up like thunder outer China 'crost the Bay!"

"Good Lord," he said checking his new watch and jumping up to gather his new things when we had done, "just look at the time, will you! They'll be waiting for me! Hurry, Louise, but don't rush. I've reserved a seat for you!"

So as least I didn't make a complete fool of myself, and either luck was with me or I'd had the unconscious foresight to be dressed for the occasion when Larry called me up to stand beside him on the reviewing stand. Even though I was still uncomfortable. And I'm not only referring to my state of mind when I say that—though, as I've said, it was out of vestigial patriotism that I was up there at all—but literally, too. Physically uncomfortable. Well, there was sand in my high-heeled shoes, in my stockings and in the dress I was wearing. And though it doesn't come through well on the videos (thanks to that flower print I had on), not even on that special high-resolution tape the Frenchmen were using for their documentary about Larry, if you know where to look you can almost just see the aloe stains and vague patches of chlorophyll on my dress from when the Prince and I were rolling around in abandon on the frond-strewn clothing-carpeted floor of the unwinding wicky-up.

(Sid, "I've reserved a seat for you!" not "I'll reserve a seat for you." Sid?)

There was a press conference of sorts, ad hoc, shouted out, summary as an encounter with prime ministers or presidents on the way to their helicopters. The Prince's unexpected announcement of his engagement was the proximate cause, but it was only my appearance with him on that provisional reviewing stand, or rostrum, or stage, or, considering the occasion, pulpit or hustings even, that the reporters started to call out their questions.

It was to me, not Larry, they called.

"Miss Bristol! Miss Bristol!"

"Miss Bristol?"

"Miss Bristol, over here. Over here, Miss Bristol."

"Louise? Oh, I say, Louise."

The Prince squeezed my hand, but thinking he must know me, I'd already acknowledged whoever it was that used my Christian name.

"Yes?" I said. "You, the one standing. Off to the side."

"The Prince says he obtained the King's and Queen's prior consent. Have you met their Royal Highnesses then? And I have a follow-up."

Out of the corner of my eye I could see how troubled Larry was, but he needn't have been. I've already said that about duty and loyalty. It's what they say about heroism, too. That you don't even think about it. That it comes second nature or not at all. That you fall on the grenade or jump in front of the oncoming car to push the child away without thought to the consequences. I was already answering the man's question.

"Not actually *met* them," I said, "but I've heard so much about them. What is your follow-up?"

"Would you show us your engagement ring?"

I extended a finger with a loud, fussy-looking costume-jewelry ring on it.

"That's it?" said a female reporter crouched in the front. "That bauble? That's what he gave you?"

Smiling, I looked over at the Prince. Who seemed discomfited. To put the best face on it. To say the least.

"Yes," I said, "hardly the Crown Jewels, but isn't it sweet? It has incredible sentimental value."

"Oh, I *do* love you, Louise!" the Prince curling me to his side whispered in my ear. Then he spoke into the microphones.

"When we get back to London we'll run up to the Tower and Miss Bristol can have her pick of a proper jewel," he volunteered shyly.

"Sir? Oh, Sir?"

"Over here please, Sir."

"Yes, then," he said, "last question."

"Sir, Miss Bristol referred to the ring's sentimental value. Could you describe for us, Sir, what were some of the circumstances under which such meaning come to accrue about a ring what is so obviously a piece of cheap jewelry?"

There was this long, complicated, almost squeezed look of helpless discomfort in the Prince's eyes. "I won it for her at the fair?"

Because I think I was starting to love him then. Well, not actually love him of course. Not yet. Not so soon. But certainly the beginning of some such feeling.

I stepped forward.

"He's so modest," I told them. "Do you remember when the Prince was in New Guinea?" I was speaking directly to the chap who had put the question. Vaguely, he nodded. "It was a gift from a Cargo Cult there. Who had it, according to the beliefs of its members—— from God. Hence, as you see, its sentimental value."

"Thank you, ladies and gentlemen, thank you so very much for coming," said the Prince.

(A lot of this is in the public record. I know that. I haven't even begun to budge those fifty thousand pounds yet, have I, Sid? I'm giving you my side. If you think that doesn't count for much, wait, be a little patient please.)

Then, suddenly, his retinue reappeared—— that magic, show-biz retinue of royal retainers, equerries, and handlers, that sworn corps obliged not just to the Realm but to each other as well, so professional you didn't even see them coming. One moment they weren't there (or you weren't conscious of them), the next moment they were. Not even noticeably swelling the crowd but almost like actors in some cleverly staged play who merely by taking up a prop or altering their position somehow manage to change not only their character but their actual roles. I even spotted Colin— or, no, not Colin, Colin was heavier, but Colin's stand-in— the one who'd gone into the shop earlier and paid for the fateful wreath while the prince carried the fateful aloe.

Because I couldn't see Jane, because I couldn't see Marjorie. And me musing along: Why, he was ripe! ("I've reserved a seat for you!") *Not* not just any woman, any woman owning up, any woman owning up to what she put there and then what he put *there*. And not just any prince but this shy, diffident, earnest one. That explains it. It could as well have been Jane, it could as well have been Marjorie. That explains it. All the biff-bam of our encounter. Explains his fire, explains his lust and abandon on the frond-strewn clothing-carpeted floor of our unwinding wicky-up. *This* prince, this shy, diffident, earnest, and virgin prince. It was only a question of being in the right place at the right time, a serendipity, some upside-down, inside-out For-Want-Of-A-Nail thing. He was the conscientious one, the one with the character. That's why I say fateful. That's why I say it could have been Jane, it could have been Marjorie.

On shipboard or boatboard, or whatever it's called when

it's the Royal Yacht and the distinctions still aren't clear in a working girl's head, he asked how I knew he'd been to New Guinea and that he'd actually seen a Cargo Cult.

"Why, I thought you'd been everywhere, Sir."

"I have been everywhere."

"Oh, my," I said, "this isn't to be another of those Poor-Little-Rich-Prince conversations, is it? Filled with languor and acedia and lots of lecturing about how one mustn't judge until one's plunked down one's behind on another man's throne."

"*Louise!*" shocked the Prince.

"You're not going to make me play How-Heavy-Hangs-the-Head again, I trust."

"I'm sorry if I bore you."

"Bore me? You don't bore me. How could you bore me? When you suddenly up and announce I'll be Princess of England one day, and that when you succeed to your succession I'm entitled to walk a neat two or three steps behind you. You lead, I follow. Why, we'll look like one of those silly, overdressed couples that show up on the telly during the International Ballroom Dance Competitions. I think the only thing you left out is who gets to wear the number on the back. So, no, you don't bore me."

"You didn't turn me down, Louise. You spoke up to those reporters."

"Yes. Well. There you have me, Prince. Suddenly I thought you needed defending. It was like doing my National Service. My British passport was practically burning a hole in my purse."

"You don't love me?"

"Excuse me, Sir. I figure you can easily enough get yourself out of whatever it is you think you've gotten yourself into. That whole business this afternoon could have been something you made up on the spot to detract attention from coming late to your own ceremonial. It certainly wasn't to make an honest woman out of me."

"What if it were?"

"Well, it would have been too late, woul'n't it? You can just drop me off anywhere you think it's convenient."

Was I fishing? Haven't I already said I was starting to feel something for him?

"Louise," he said, "we've been intimate!"

"I was right," I said, "you were a virgin!"

"*Where would I have found the time?*" he demanded. Yes, Sid, demanded. He was angry now. His face was red and he wasn't blushing. He might almost have been that battle prince out of history he'd seemed to me that morning. (That morning. My God, was it still the same day?) For all I knew he could have thought it convenient to throw me overboard then and there. I think I may have flinched. I saw him make a deliberate effort to calm down. "Where would I?" he asked again, softly. "These sailors are some of the same people you saw with me on shore this morning. They were at the proceedings this afternoon." He lowered his voice still more, speaking in a register so deep it could have been amorous. "Your eyes were shut," he said.

"What?"

"I'm under a sort of constant surveillance. Well, not surveillance exactly. No one actually spies on me. It's just my nature, Louise. Even in public shool at the Royal Naval Academy when the other boys had no trouble doing number two in front of each other in the open stalls I had trouble doing even number one." He looked away. Abashed, he gazed down at the deck. "I'd wait until they were asleep and then I'd get up in the middle of the night . . . I was always costive," he admitted. Then, his resentment apparently not leveled at me this time, he altered his tone again. "Well I'm going to be their King one day, aren't I? It isn't seemly. A king oughtn't to be seen in his throes. It isn't seemly. Noblesse oblige. Kings must set an example. Forgive me, Louise, I know it must sound mad to anyone not in my position but if it ever got out that kings f--t and p--ss and shi- like other people it could destroy their reigns. That they vomit or mas---bate or have fantasies about women g--ng d--n on them, or are sometimes too ravenous at their food, could go bad with them. I know it must seem mad."

"Too right."

"So how could I?" he said as if he hadn't heard me. "Because except for the odd birthday party when I was a child and ran about doing naughty things to my cousins at the bottom of the garden, messing their frocks and playing silly games with them, playing Harley Street, playing Spin the Jar, playing Postbox, where *would* I have found the time? And I'm always so tired, and—— "

"So you do mean to tell me your troubles."

"We can talk about anything you want, Louise."

"Why did you say we were engaged? Why did you tell everyone you'd obtained Their Majesties' prior consent to the engagement?"

"Not just their consent. Their encouragement."

"They don't even know me," I said.

"Well, I was ripe," he said, echoing the term I had used to describe him to myself only that astonishing afternoon.

(And I'll tell you something, Sir Sid. For the first time I began to regard it as a possibility. Not only the engagement, but the possibility of the Royal Wedding, too. For the first time began to think it might not be a bad trade-off—— a life with a mad Prince and then another with a mad king. To be Princess of All the Englands. And he was handsome. Possessed, as I say, of almost a surfeit of beauty. And I would be one of the world's richest women. And, too, I was starting to have these feelings for him. Tell me, my dear press lord, was he the only game in town or was he the only game in town?)

"Ripe?" I said.

"They too," he said. "All of us."

"Meaning?"

"They signaled their eagerness to abdicate. They're ready to step down. It came in over the wireless. 'Sparks' passed on the message."

"What are they like, your family?"

"Well, you know about my cousins."

"Not your cousins. Your mum and your dad."

"The sibs get their names in the papers."

"You get your name in the papers."

"The columns," he said disapprovingly. "But you know that of course."

"I've been in the States two years. They have their own distractions and preoccupations in the States."

"Oh right," he said. (You see, Sir Sidney? How our affair was proceeding? How at once whirlwind and old hat it must have seemed to the both of us? It didn't seem possible to me it was still the same day. Larry had probably already forgotten those two years in the States I had told him about. We were like some old married couple. We couldn't remember each other's sizes.) "I love them. It's not that," he said. "It's not even that they're bad. They're lively, they've very good hearts. But I'll tell you the truth, Louise, they're not fit children for the sons and daughters of royalty. I blame the parents."

"You blame the parents?"

"Our crowd has a saying: 'It starts in the castle.' "

He had me jumping. I couldn't read him clearly. Now some girls will tell you the first thing they look for in a man is a nice smile, or a sense of humor; or they look at his hands, his teeth—— if he keeps them clean. His nails, his hair. Or see can they tell if he's vulnerable, say. Something physical, something spiritual, six of one, half dozen of the other. But the very first thing that catches my attention about a man is whether or not I can read him clearly. If he's mysterious, inscrutable. Well, it's in the tradition. In my tradition. He had me jumping. I felt like a nurse again, Sid.

"They're irresponsible, Louise. If we weren't merely symbolic, what I'm saying would be treasonous."

"They signaled they're ready to abdicate, you said. Step down, let you take over. You're the conscientious one."

"Make me Regent before my time, you mean."

"You're twenty-nine."

"Damn it, Louise, it's not even their fault."

"What's not? Whose fault? I don't follow. I'm not reading you clearly."

"Alec's, Robin's, Mary's, Denise's. It's not their fault. It's George's, our father's fault. It's Charlotte's, our mother's. Who introduced them? Who taught them to run with a fast crowd, rattle about in all that loose company? Who do you think leaked their names to the columns? Who lazied them down from University? Who coaxed them away with those dubious seconds and thirds? Two years ago? They weren't like that two years ago. How could you know?"

How I Was Received

Of course we were expected. They knew we were coming.
They must have been waiting. They must have prepared the
whole thing.

They looked like sovereigns out of Noël Coward. *He*
might have been the actor/manager of his own touring theatrical troupe, *she* his principal player—— sixty if she was
a day, yet still called on to do ingenue parts, sophisticated
ladies.

Because it's amazing how much can be kept from the
public, how there's spin on the spin control, these now-you-
see-it, now-you-don't arrangements.

There Their Majesties were, two conflagrant figures,
Himself in a red silk dressing gown and seated on an honest-
to-god throne with a yellow ring of gleamless crown
perched light and rakish on the top of his head like the wavy
concatenations on a suspension bridge or the points on the
crown of some picture-card king; Herself in a gilt chair a
few feet off to her husband's side and chugalugging smoke
through a long silver cigarette holder.

He didn't even look like the King. Because this was the
stuff that didn't get into the papers. I was certain I was the
only one not of their inner circle ever to see such a sight.
There were what seemed like ancient props from the reper-
toire lying about—— scepters and orbs out of Shakespear-
ean history plays. Indeed, it looked more like the
greenroom of a theater in the provinces than like a room in
a proper palace.

"*M'boy!*" the King said, pushing down from his throne,
spry for a man his age, embracing his son. "Welcome! *Welcome!*

"And is this your young lady? And welcome to *you*,
m'dear! I must say I admire your taste," he told the boy as
he deftly let go his arms around Lawrence, placed one hand
on my shoulder, touched my rear end with the other and,

shielding us from the Prince's view, pinched me. Alarmed, I said nothing, merely, in a nervous attempt to brush it off, curtsied in His Majesty's direction where I was met by his palm cunningly there to catch my curtsy and which he pressed smartly against my breast. "Ah," said the King, hamming it up, projecting, stopping the show. "You're worldly! She's worldly, Lawrence. Excellent choice, lad, *excellent!* Good! I don't much care for priggishness in a man, and quite despise it in a gel!"

"Do let go of her for a moment, George," said his wife, "so I may give her a whiskey. Have we such a thing as ice? Make yourself helpful, my darling, just would you? The poor thing has come all the way from the States and is almost certainly in need of ice."

"There is no ice," the King pronounced solemnly.

"My husband informs me that there is no ice. We were all a bit nervous that the ice would have gone off so of course it seems that it has. I do apologize. I am so very ashamed. But please don't think too ill of our people, there are some quite civilized patches here and there in the Kingdom. Larry, you shall have to show your young friend—Louise, isn't it?— that she's not to judge by us, that not everyone does these blue, druidy things at the solstice. Of course you don't have to drink that if it's too despicable, dear. Should you not rather have one of those sweet, poofy drinks that don't absolutely require ice—— Louise, isn't it?"

"I'm fine, Ma'm. Yes, Ma'am, Louise."

"Charlotte, dear, or as it seems you're to be my daughter-in-law, Mother, or Mummy either if that's more comfortable for you. We don't stand on ceremonies here. Larry will have told you that, I expect. Ceremonies are such a bore, finally. They so throw one off one's fun. But Americans would know that, wouldn't they?"

"I'm not American, Ma'am, I'm British."

"Charlotte," she drawled, "or Mother, or Mummy." Then, glancing pointedly toward the King but without skipping a beat, went on. "Well, I'm happy to hear it," she said. "In that case, nothing that's happened this evening and nothing that happens shall leave the premises." Though she was talking to me her eyes never broke contact with the King's which, incredibly, seemed to dodge and to dart, to shy and startle and evade, but which despite all he could do to escape her accusing examination had locked onto his own nervous squinny as effectively as some deadly, heat-seeking missile fixing an enemy in its laserly sights. King George tugged at his ascot, ran a finger about an apparently tight collar. It was, on both their parts, the hammy King's, the sophisticated lady's, the most remarkable acting I'd seen that evening.

"Speaking of which," she said.

"Which?" I asked in all innocence.

(Because the minds of these people don't ever bother with transition. It isn't anything owing to contempt, Sid, for others or even for ordinary sequitur, some lack of respect for logic and all the connected dots of aligned synapse—— the half hour at one Ball, the fifteen minutes at the next. The single course that's taken at this banquet and cup of coffee and bite of dessert that's taken at the next. The two innings' worth of witness at a ballgame, say. The rush of all that nextness, I mean, all that press of a Royal's business Lawrence spoke of before seducing me. Because their minds are always racing, Sid, always jumping ahead of themselves, from one thing to the other, not only their power symbolic but their presence, too—— their here-today-gone-today, spread-too-thin essence.)

"Which?" I asked.

"Why, of fun, dear. I should have thought Lawrence would have told you."

"Aye," said the King, rubbing his hands together, his sham discomfort at having been found out already forgotten. "Tell the children about the party you've arranged in their honor, Charlotte. Have you et?" he asked enthusiastically.

"Well, Prince Alec will be here," she said, "and I think Princess Denise blah blah blah and, oh yes, I've invited the

sweetest assortment of jolly incumbents in some of the most
arcane of our traditional offices to meet you."

"Invited, Charlotte?"

"Well, commanded. Did I say invited? I thought I'd said
commanded."

(I tell you, Sid, it doesn't get out. You'd never recognize
them in the streets for all that their portraits are on the
stamps and the money, couldn't guess at their improbable
behavior, or at any of the broad farce of our slapstick Royals. I swear to you, Sid, all they care for is to be off by
themselves—— more ethnic than Africans, more tribal than
cousins.)

Odd as it may seem, that sweet assortment of jolly incumbents Charlotte referred to, and who I implied consti-
tuted their inner circle, weren't necessarily blooded, though
all, at least in some political or vaguely gangsterly sense,
were connected. Most of them held public office. Don't
mistake me. Not one of them could pick up a telephone and
have someone killed. If Their Majesties' powers were symbolic, their own were less real. Whereas monarchical power
hadn't always been so ceremonial—though even today, this
late in history's game, there are absolute monarchs who
don't have to trouble to pick up a phone, they can kill you
themselves—theirs had always been ceremonial and smelled
of basic, blatant ineffectuality, of the merely traditional and
picturesque, like Swiss Guards standing outside the Vatican
at an uptight attention posing for tourists and protecting, in
a time of car-bombing, plastique-throwing terrorists and
kamikazes, some other age's pope in only their fourteenth-
century caps, billowy shirts, and silly pantaloons, with only
their pike staffs.

(Am I a keen observer of the passing parade, or am I a
keen observer of the passing parade? I can almost hear you
taking on about those fifty thousand pounds again. "Get on
with it, get on with it," you're saying. But I throw the
op-ed stuff in gratis. You didn't bargain for that when I
signed on, did you, Sid, that true confessions has its themes
too?)

Yet even at that, even on the most traditional and ineffec-
tual level, what almost all these offices had in common was
death's oblique symbolism.

There was the London Royal Intentioner, whose duty it
was to greet every parade of warriors returning to the city
from the front, glorious and victorious—and abject, too,
what with all those riderless horses and muffled drums and
black, mournful, crepe-draped artillery pieces and other
death-decked-out matériel—to discover their intentions,
whether they were peaceful toward the Crown. I have it by
report that he simply took the commander's word for it, on
the principle that he would not have been a commander if
he had not first been a gentleman. I say I have it by report
because I didn't get to ask the Royal Intentioner himself. He
canceled at the last minute. He told the King he was too
busy to come to the party. It gave both Their Majesties a
laugh.

Which seemed, really, to be the point of the party.

"They're court jesters, aren't they?" I asked the Prince.
"I mean, that's what this is all about, isn't it? They're court
jesters."

"Ask someone else," the Prince said coolly.

"All right, I will."

And did. I was a little tight. George was feeding me
drinks now, volunteering to refill my glass every time I took
three or four swallows from it or set it down for a minute.

"There's a good girl," said the King as if I were a child
sick in nursery and he was holding out a spoon of my medicine.

"Goodness me," I said, "you're plying me with drink,
aren't you, Dad?"

"Call me, George, sweet thing," said His Royal Highness.

I admit it, it's a turn-on to be plied by a king. As Lord
Acton might have said, "Power seduces and absolute power
seduces absolutely."

(Well, you know my track record, don't you, Sid? C.f.
All that about the Prince and his beauty.)

Though I acknowledge he never touched me. He didn't even pinch me again. Our Sovereign was on his most sovereignly behavior. The kingdom was in good hands, if its Princess manqué wasn't. Perhaps it was Charlotte's presence, or the Prince's sour mien, or it could be the King no longer found me attractive tipsy, or maybe he was bored with causing scenes, though that's a bit hard to credit.

"These people are like court jesters, aren't they, George?"

"Ask someone else," the King said, breaking off, and then, practically phoning in his performance, flatly, "Ah you're worldly. She's worldly, Lawrence. Excellent choice lad. Excellent good."

And did. Still tipsy and even a little turned on by the room itself, by my situation (the former Louise Bristol, recently exiled to America with just enough to live on for about six months but beginning to feel the pinch as the time wore on and then, later, this au pair girl in her late twenties and, further on down the road, a maker of beds in the Housekeeping Department of a Los Angeles hotel and, later still, a down-on-her-luck, pushing-thirty beachcomber and sewer-of-houses and sandsweepstress, but currently fianceé to Lawrence Mayfair of the House of Mayfair and, not then knowing myself manqué, future Princess of England), sat down beside a stocky, almost preternaturally rosy-cheeked, jolly-seeming man of about fifty or so.

"Are you a court jester too?" I said, prepared by now to be told to ask someone else.

I would like my readers to know I know I was rude, brazen even, and that it will not do to dismiss this, to write it off to the fact that I was drunk. Ignorance of the—— Well, you know. Nor do I plead my low tolerance for alcohol or put down to drought and holes in the ozone layers the extent of my thirst. Not much that brought on my troubles in this account was of my own doing but I openly acknowledge that which was.

As sometimes occurs in narrative what happens next is not always what is expected. The somewhat cherubic, rosy-cheeked, jolly-seeming man did not send me away. If he had, chances are I wouldn't have left. His very avuncularity intensified my feelings of euphoria. I was not only brazen now but mildly randy, flirtatious, teasing, lightly touching his arm, deliberately brushing against him where we sat together on a sofa, my voice raised but not hysteric; acting out, strutting my stuff with the rest of the players in the room. I do not put it down to drink, I do not. I was tipsy as a gambler on a roll, mood-swung, high on luck, the boost in my fortunes.

"I am Selector of Ropes," he answered simply, and it was as if he'd chastised me, so struck was I by the depth of his underacting. "Henry VIII was not an unfeeling man. He invented the position."

"I never heard of your office," I mentioned conversationally. "What is it you do?"

"I am not your straight man," he said.

"Truly," I told him. "I don't know. I'm only asking."

"We look at hemp."

"Yes?" I said.

"We look for finer and finer rope. Softer silk."

"Why?"

"Henry was not unfeeling. He had no stomach for beheading his women."

"Why did he do it then?"

He looked toward King George.

"Go on," the King said softly. "Tell her, Selector." The room was already quiet. Now it was still. You could hear a pin drop.

(Mark this, Sir Sidney. Mark your marked manqué.)

"He'd already broken with one tradition when he withdrew from Rome," the man said, still restrained but rushing now, doing with rapid pacing what before he had done with calm, "why would he want to break with another one?"

Then, suddenly, he pulled another technique from his quiver, assumed yet another style, closer to what the King's had been when the Prince and I first came in, gesticulating wildly, playing for laughs.

"He was ahead of his time, don't you know. *Oh* yes.

Didn't 'alf 'old with axes, 'e didn't. Not 'im. Not 'enry. Haxes was sharp and wulgar. All that spilled blood? That were *Royal* blood!" And stage whispered, " 'e anticipated hinterregnums, rewolutions—— 'e hanticipated 'angings!

"Oh yes, one of my predecessors introduced the Windsor knot to make it a *bit* more comfortable around the royal neck of one of them Tudors or Stuarts or Windsors or Mayfairs. Just in the *event*, don't you know!" he said, the last sentence delivered as if it were some famous, uproarious tag line. And sure enough the King was red-faced, almost hacking up his laughter. Even Charlotte was grinning.

There were other jolly incumbents. One came up to me, bubbling with inside information, tricks of the trade.

"You know those royal orders monarchs sometimes wear? Those broad, colorful bands of cloth that pass down diagonally over a king's or queen's right shoulder like the supporting straps on Sam Browne belts? Well, if the color scheme isn't carefully coordinated or the order clashes too severely with the rest of the costume, it could throw off the entire occasion. That's why our kings and queens have always had art directors."

"You're the royal art director?"

"No, I'm in a related field. Monarchical medallions can be very heavy. Well, they aren't shields made out of tin, are they? Often they're heavy enough to tear a fabric apart, so the fabric has to be reinforced to support patches to fix to the cloth of ceremonial gear—your designer dresses, your gowns and robes and uniforms—to support the weight of those medallions. That's what I do, I'm Royal Fashion Engineer."

And another who said he was Royal Taster and credited his astonishing slimness to the fact that he had to keep his palate clear in order to distinguish among the flavors of the various poisons that had, over the years, been used in attempted regicides. He felt, he said, he owed it to his sovereign to partake, at most, of one or two spoonfuls of royal soup, a bite of meat, a sip of wine, a nibble of bread. I was reminded of Lawrence working his symbolic presence during the Season's Balls and dinners and, now I noticed it, of Their Majesties' own trim, fit figures.

"Ahh," I said, "that explains it. They owe them to their diminished dinners."

Royal Taster smiled. "Just so," he said, exactly as if he knew to what I referred.

Royal Peerager spoke to me. He told me, rather too pointedly, I thought, that it was his job to watch out for pretenders. The Mayfairs, he said, could be traced back to Lear and Macbeth.

He would have gone on—I was interested enough despite a fear of the silly starting to take hold in me—but just then some new personage, burdened by several parcels, burst upon the scene.

"*There* you are!" King George said.

"And high time, I would have thought," Charlotte scolded. "You knew I especially wanted you to meet your brother's new fianceé."

"As if ever he had an old one, Mother dear," said Princess Denise.

(For that's who it was, another ingenue for what might turn out to be—I hadn't met Princess Mary yet—an entire company of ingenues. She'd changed in the two years or better since I'd last been in England. I suppose her picture had been in the papers plenty of times but the truth is I had enough on my mind in those days not to have noticed. Well, not actually the truth, Sid. What the truth actually is is that I consciously tried to avoid what was going on at home, to the point that I wouldn't even go to an English film or watch *Masterpiece Theater* on the telly—which I'd started to call TV—and had stopped drinking tea. So the last thing I needed was to keep up with the British fascination with the prurient goings-on of its more hereditary characters, pushing aside as much as I could of the silly gossip that surrounds one—surrounds? embraces—in both countries like climate. Maybe America was the wrong place to go. Perhaps I should have chosen somewhere less civilized, some hot, plague-ridden African place, where I might have comforted dying children and futilely brushed away flies from their faces that the children themselves were too weak to brush off and probably didn't even notice for all that the flies crawled across the huge, swollen surfaces of the very eyes they didn't even seem capable of shutting. So why would I? What did I need it, Sir Sid?)

I hardly recognized her, though how much could a seventeen-year-old girl, now a twenty-year-old young woman, have changed in two years? There was something slightly askew and off-plumb about her appearance, and as soon as she burst into speech as she'd burst into the room (as one is said to "burst into song," from a standing position as it were—— like some instantaneous, transitionless transformation or sea change or jump cut in the pictures), I thought I knew what it was. It was as if she'd undergone some powerful, personal Damascene rearrangement—— a persona inversion of the seventeen-year-old, almost womanly creature I vaguely remembered from photographs I'd seen in the papers over two years before into the twentyish, pretty, oh-so-girlish young thing before me—before me? practically all over me—now.

Although she was got up as a sort of latter-day flapper— fringe swayed at the bottom of her too-short skirt like the fringed, beaded dividers that separated backrooms in the décor of thirites-era movies, or plays set somewhere in the Orient, from the low taverns and bars on the ground floors of whorehouses, places where sailors are shanghai'd or slipped Mickey Finns—with dark, wide eyes immensely open and sketched in with eyebrow pencil, and her red, fire-engine mouth had been painted into a pout at once as cynical and cute as someone about to cry, this flapper-cum-ingenue seemed hyperactive as a kid at a slumber party.

"Why, Larry, she's *adorable*! You're adorable, Louise! *Isn't* she adorable, Father? Isn't she adorable, Mother? You'll make just the most brilliant Princess, Louise. No wonder even an old pooh like Larry lost his heart. Well, I should think *so*. Here, sweetheart, here are some things I bought

you. (That's why I was late, Charlotte dear. So there!) I just
guessed at your sizes, but don't fret if nothing fits. We won't
even bother to return it, we'll just give the stuff away to our
servants or those absolutely smashing Mounted Horse
Guards in Whitehall to offer to Oxfam. Then we can go
shopping for all *new* things!"

As she spoke she produced one exotic garment after another from her various boxes and bundles. I recognized the
names of boutiques all along the Kings Road, some so chic
I'd supposed they'd shut up shop years ago. I couldn't have
told you the function of some of this garb or, had the Princess not held a few of the pieces against me, have identified
more than the general area of the body they were supposed
to cover. Of the material of which they were made I could
have told you nothing, only that much of it must have been
experimental.

"Oh, Louise," she said, "you look quite fabulous in
that!"

She was enjoying herself and, to be frank, I was too. Despite the public character of our performance, I felt comfortable, somnolent, spoiled and at ease as a teen having a
makeover.

In the end, however, she discarded almost all of it, dropping stuff on the floor, kicking it away, a bit disappointed
in both of us because we'd both failed to live up to some
vague, preconceived image she had of me which her gifts
represented, but pleased, too, because now we could go
shopping for new things, just, as she put it, "us two girls."

She paused a moment, then retrieving a sort of turban,
held it out toward my head. "Never mind," she said. Carelessly, she dropped it again. "Of course," she said, "we
won't *really* know until we do something about that hair."

She began to bat at my hair rather as if it were on fire.

When I continued to flinch Charlotte at last intervened.
"Oh do stop, Denise, you're alarming her."

"I'm only trying to *help, Mother*! I'm only seeing if it can
be fixed. If you'd only stand *still*, Louise! So I know what

to tell the hairdresser before us two girls go shopping again."

"For goodness' sake, Denise," said Prince Lawrence, "stop carrying on about 'us two girls,' why don't you? It's 'us two girls' this and 'us two girls' that. 'Us two girls,' indeed. How can you speak so? You're a Princess of England."

"I was putting *her* at ease."

"Oh please," the Prince said. "Louise is my fianceé. One day she'll outrank you."

"Oh, Lawrence," said the Princess, "we're all of us only these accidents of birth, so why must you be so stuffy all the time? It really is too boring. Anyway, it isn't even true. Dear, adorable, brilliant, fabulous, and absolutely stunnin', charmin', smashin', and perfect for you as she quite so most obviously is, *I* am the daughter of royalty, after all, and darlin' Louise here is only a common commoner. So what do you mean she'll outrank me? She never will, will she, Royal Peerager?"

"Scissors cuts paper, paper covers rock, rock smashes scissors," the Royal Peerager said.

"What do you mean?" Charlotte said. "I never understand what you mean when you say that."

"Me t' know . . . you t' fin' out," he muttered, sulking.

"Really, George," Charlotte objected, "listen how he speaks to me. Do I have to put up with that? A proper king wouldn't stand for it. I daresay a proper husband wouldn't."

"It was a joke, Your Royal Highness," the Peerager said. He turned to my mother-in-law manqué. "It's a joke, Your Highness."

King George sighed. "Well," he said, "I suppose she *is* dear and adorable and brilliant and all the bloody darlin' rest of it. I only wish Their Royal Caterers and all the Holy British Empire's Florists and Band Leaders would just get on with it so we could have the damned wedding and retire. If she's all right with you, she's all right with us. Your friend passes muster, Prince," he said as though I really didn't.

"Where's Alec?" the Princess broke in. "I thought Alec

was coming. He promised he would. He should have been here by now."

"I told him to come, I spoke with him just this morning. Oh my," Charlotte said, as if remembering something she'd forgotten. Troubled, flesh-is-heir-to things played across her features, plain, ordinary as a sneeze, and, quite suddenly, she ceased to look regal, bereft of even those vestiges of bearing left to her in even only her theatrical ways. "Oh my," she said again, worriedly. "Today's the seventeenth."

"That's right," Denise put in, "tomorrow's the time trials."

And now Charlotte was possessed of a flustered, lashing, unfocused anger, her rage oddly, ineptly maternal, like the helpless, confused rage of a woman just back from hospital with her first child. Even before I understood the reference of her anger I understood the reference of her anger. "He collected his new Quantra today!" she cried. "He's off testing his damned limits, isn't he, George! He's off pushing his damned envelope!"

"He's a perfectly capable young man, Charlotte. You mustn't coddle him. The boy knows what he's doing."

"Oh, George," she said, "if only he did. I *wish* he did."

"It's just an automobile. He's been driving a car since his eighth birthday."

"Too right," she said, "the day he swerved to hit the gillie to avoid hitting the gillie's dog."

"That was an accident, Charlotte."

"The man will never walk again, George."

The King nodded. "I know," he said, and for the first time that evening neglected his posture. "Look here, Ropes," he said. "Look here, London Intentioner, Royal Peerager. Look here, Royal Taster, look here all. I'm sorry," he said. "I am so really very sorry, but the Queen, worried as she is regarding our Alec, is a bit out of sorts this evening. Now our revels all are ended, thank you very much for coming."

I started to move off with the rest but Prince Lawrence

motioned me to stay. Princess Denise, patting the broad piano bench on which she was seated, indicated I should join her.

"He's crashed the car," Queen Charlotte said. "I know it, he's crashed the car." Unexpectedly, she turned to address me. Denise, very softly, was picking out a tune on the piano, providing a sort of quiet background music behind her mother's speech. She was very good. "He's probably had one too many. He's fond of surprising people in their local, Prince Alec is. He loves it when they fall all over themselves to buy him drinks. And him a prince," she said, giggling, taking up another role. "Not once has he ever volunteered to return the favor, Louise. He brags on this as if the most wonderful service he can render them as a Prince of the Realm is to let them stand him drinks."

"It is," the King said wistfully.

"He's *so* charming," Charlotte said.

"Very charming," said his sister, never breaking the rhythm of her sad, bluesy tune.

"But too much of a drinker," his mother said. "George dearest, what's the horsepower on the new Quantra?"

"It has a Rolls-Royce engine," my Larry said, "I heard it can be pushed up to a thousand horses."

"A thousand horses. A veritable cavalry," the King said, interrupting his own husky, hummed accompaniment to Denise's accompaniment.

"Should he be driving it through the streets?" wondered the Queen.

(Did you know, Sid, they may not be brought up on charges? I didn't know that. I don't think most people know. I daresay you yourself don't absolutely know. Oh we've all heard rumors from time to time, and many of us have known of someone of whom it is said that once she'd known someone who was supposed to have known someone else who had had it on good authority from a friend with a pal who had connections with a person who used to be in a position of authority, but all of it is just so much blown smoke or, rather, smoke wrapped in time, or mist.

Smoke wrapped in mists wrapped in time lost in legend, like the identity of Robin Hood, say, or who Christ's cousins were.

(It isn't even a question of influence. Of course they have influence. Everyone has influence. *I* have influence. And for darn damn sure it certainly isn't written down anywhere. I mean, you could search in all the books and charters, pamphlets and whatnot in the British Museum and never come across it, and of all the controversial things I've set down here—the King's Pinch, how Larry was a virgin when he done me, how Royals behave at home when they let down their hair—surely this is the most controversial. That they can't be brought up on charges, that that gillie who was sacrificed to his own dog and was run over when Alec was eight and out on a joyride and who'll never walk again while Alec, eight-year-old or no eight-year-old, but simply because he was a Royal and not only couldn't be hauled into court but wasn't even grounded, for God's sake, and who to this day drives a souped-up thousand hp Quantra capable of whipping down the narrowest, twistiest country lane in all of England, never mind powering about Trafalgar Square or Piccadilly Circus pressing the pedal to the metal!

(This isn't rage, Sid, so don't mistake me. It isn't rage but merely the gentlest indication to my gentle readers to let them know how badly I feel to have lost out on so much, because if only a pipsqueak younger brother at a two or three times remove from the throne can have so much freedom and latitude, then how much more free and how much more wide would the latitude be for the bona fide royal-wedding-related bride of the out-and-out King! Sid, I mean, they're not even *licensed*! All that hocus-pocus and rigmarole and long, winding trail and trial by blood descent they have to go through just in order to get to be considered to be in the just royal aristocratic running, and then they're permitted to skip and finesse entirely the simple red tape of filling out a form to apply for a driver's license! I mean, once in a while you can depose them, or maybe actually even kill them, but you can't sue them for damages if you slip and fall on their walk if they haven't shoveled their snow or they blindside you for life on the clearest day in the world when they drive home drunk from the pub where you've bought all their drinks!)

Denise, sighing, said, "Please, Mother. Mother, please don't," and shut the lid over the piano keys as if she'd finished the evening's last set. "No use to fret, darling," she said, and took up the Queen's hands in her own. "Mustn't be anxious. Alec's all right. You'll see. He's much too fond of his life to give it up stupidly. There," she said, "that's better. You look so much better. Doesn't she look so much better, Father?"

"A dainty dish to set before the King," the King said.

"Oh," she said, "you two!" And she might have been some cosseted Midlands farm wife dismissing a compliment and not the sophisticated lady of an hour or so earlier. She'd been smoking all evening but her long silver cigarette holder was nowhere to be seen. Denise for that matter had ceased to appear girlish, had as effectively suppressed that side of her personality as she had seemed to make the piano disappear by closing its lid. Only the King remained in character, and it occurred to me to wonder whether that wasn't what differentiated him finally, that what made a king a king was the power of his concentration, that what may, as Denise put it, have started as an accident of birth wasn't maintained by some absolute act of the will. How else account for the staying power of a reign, our image of kings—and queens too—as persons, whatever their age, continuing in their primes, long enough at any rate to put their stamp upon an era?

(I don't want my readers to think I was that objective, already this journalist of a princess manqué taking notes, recording her impressions. Not a bit of it! I was swept up, I was plenty swept up. So swept up, in fact, I never took Lawrence up on his offer to run off to the Tower with him to have for engagement ring the Crown Jewel of my choice, but kept instead the fussy costume-jewelry ring I had bought for myself on the ground floor of a Los Angeles

department store and had shown to the reporters back in
Cape Henry. So I was swept up all right, plenty shook by
these people, as much taken by them as any who pay their
good money to read this stuff. Still, a girl will have her instincts, won't she, Sir Sidney?)

Having pumped Charlotte up with her reassurances,
Denise now made an effort to reinforce her original entrance, displaying her earlier, larkier pedigree. Turning back
the clock, she mimed an excited, jumpy applause, impaling
herself, whatever her reasons, on some sort of dismal, faked
enthusiasm.

She seized on me as if I were someone from the audience
pressed into service to assist her.

"Never mind, dear," she assured me, "rudeness is just
Alec's way. It isn't as if he means anything by it. It's only
his way of getting attention without actually having to try
to kill anyone. His bark is way worse than his bite, though,
once you get to know him, that is. It's really too devastating
he's not here though. I shall never forgive him. No. I shall
never forgive him. We'd planned to take you round
Knightsbridge to show you to all our mates. Have you your
card with you? Not to worry, we can have one made up in
the morning. Did you know, incidentally, it was Alec's idea
to reintroduce the calling card back into society? If there's
nothing to do, sometimes we'll both take up a bunch of
them and drive out in my Jag to Croyden or Putney or Wil-
lesden Green and pop them through the postal slots of some
of the ratepayers. Can you imagine the looks on their faces?
Such fun!

"*I* know," she said, "we can call on some of the cousins.
We can call on Cousin Nancy, we can call on cousins Heide
and Jeanne and Alice and Anne—— Cousin Anne is in town,
isn't she, Lawrence? I say, Lawrence—oh look, he's blushing—is Cousin Anne in town?"

"Leave off, will you, Denise!" my intended yelled at her.

"Pa," she appealed, "make him stop. Show him who's
King."

"The both of you stop."

"Oh all right," she said, "I won't show you Nanc—— I mean Anne."

"*Denise!*"

"Anyway," the Princess confided, "often—well, sometimes—Alec and I—— Oh, speak of the devil."

And, suddenly, someone who could, in accordance with all his advance notices, only have been Alec, blustered into the room. He was bloody, muddy, bruised, and drunk. His clothes were torn. Alec the Rude, glancing once about him, at Charlotte and George, at his sister Denise, at his brother Lawrence, the King-in-waiting who'd been off working the world and whom he couldn't have seen in at least two months, looked in my direction, came toward me, bowed deeply, and kissed my hand loud as you please, quite solidly, and dead center on its costume-jewelry ring finger.

Sunday, February 2, 1992

How He Courted Me

It wasn't jealousy as you and I know it. Well, it wasn't jealousy at all, really. No matter what you've read in the press, the truth is I was never attracted to Alec. I don't *really* think he was attracted to me. I'm not telling any tales out of school if I remind the public that Prince Alec is not highly sexed, only heavily hormoned. His skin, if you look closely, is actually rather fair and only appears swarthy because of the dense stubble of five-o'clock shadow that covers it. I don't know why he doesn't grow a beard. Unless of course the vaguely tough-guy look on his handsome, somewhat disheveled face is something he deliberately cultivates. Like the dust-up (rather than car crash) it turns out he provoked on the evening of my first visit to the palace. Which is why, really, I was never attracted to Alec.

Well, put yourself in my place. Knowing, I mean, what I knew. About, I mean, that business of their never being brought up on charges. Mere Figureheads? Symbolic power? I should think not. No, they *can't* take us into foreign wars and don't even have all that much say-so in domestic matters. They couldn't, I daresay, fix a ticket for anyone below the rank of a marquess. But forget about not being allowed to make laws or fix tickets. But not ever having to answer to anyone? Symbolic power? Power like theirs, the power, I mean, to run amok with impunity, is the most seductive and dangerous power there is. So so much, I say, for the pretty myth of their Figureheadhood!

Yet there's no denying it. It is seductive. All that force, all that dash and fire, all that vim and verve. To wink at precept and live in some perpetual state of willful disregard the indulged, insouciant life is a temptation indeed. I was not tempted.

I am, I think at least as much a woman as Prince Alec is a man. Where he is testostcronagenous and aggressive, I am largely progesterogenic and nurturing. And I never forgot that Alec is a bully—is this libelous? let them go prove it— and that too much of his bravura is vouchsafed by his princely immunities. If he was bloody, muddy, bruised, and drunk, if his clothes were torn, what had he to lose in a dust-up? He's on the National Health, his clothing allowance is seventy-five thousand pounds a year. You should see the other guy.

To his credit, Lawrence was not jealous. To mine, I never gave him reason to be.

(Sid, let them bring *me* up on charges. Let them just try! In this La Lulu-Tells-All enterprise we're supposed to be engaged in here, let me remind them that I *haven't* done, I haven't told all, not yet I haven't. Only what relates to me. And this isn't blackmail. I haven't asked for a penny of their money. I wouldn't, I won't. And if they try to put me under a gag order, I'll just take my story somewhere else. I'll get in with the Yanks and give it away free to the paper with the highest circulation!)

So.

On then to my whirlwind courtship, my introduction to the British press, my background, who my people are, what I did for love, et cetera, et cetera.

The public's up to here with most of this anyway, so I'll simply synopsize what they already know, or think they know, throwing in where warranted one or two of my theories.

Of course it really isn't enough for me to state that Alec and I were not attracted to each other. Who would believe me? In light of all that photographic evidence? It's only natural the public would want some proof to counter the claims that we were up to something. In a civilization like ours, where each new dawn brings with it a fresh breath of scandal, in our Where-There's-Smoke-There's-Fire world, in this brave new age of nolo contendere and out-of-court settlements, the tendency is to believe in the failure of human character. Well. Unfortunately I can offer no proof. However, I think I can supply the reader with a context, what proper journalists call a backgrounder.

Consider England's circumstances, the sociology of our times. Despite anything I may have said, or, rather, *because* everything I've said about the deeply cynical nature of the zeitgeist is true, our sudden appearance in the social sky was welcomed, even applauded. It is simply in the nature of things when they are at their worst to hope for the best. What better time to hope for the best? Very well then, I come along, or Prince Lawrence does and I come along with him. It's announced we're engaged, that your future King has chosen his future Consort. We are both an item and a distraction, something like a hopeful leitmotif in an otherwise dreary composition. We not only know we're a field day for the press, we positively count on it. Because it's true, all the world does too love a lover. They size me up, they eye my breasts, they look at my legs.

I am, quite literally, presented at Court. We have become, the two of us, a Season unto ourselves. It's middle to latish summer, just after Wimbledon, about. A time of hampers and picnics in people's private deer parks. We go round to meet the peerage in their stately homes—— dukes and marquesses and earls and viscounts and lowly barons. I meet the Lawrence's grandparents. (Sid, I *haven't* told all. Only what relates to me. This *isn't* blackmail!) I meet some of those famous cousins of Larry's, and am surprised at how plain they are—— astonished at this one's buck teeth and that one's incipient hump. And am seized by a sudden shyness when they look too knowingly at me.

The paparazzi are having a field day. They are meant to, of course. This exercise is as much for them as it is for us. They are to be my conduit into the homes of my prospective subjects. (La, will you just listen to me with my count-my-chickens? Pride goeth before a fall.) Butlers and gillies and that magic show-biz retinue of Larry's that I hadn't been conscious of since we got off the yacht have been given instructions to let them be as we make our way through the daily round. They are not to be disturbed so long as they stay in the trees or hide in the bushes with their long lenses and special equipment. At certain houses they are even given sandwiches and offered tall, cool glasses of milk.

As our tour continued during those three or four weeks of visits in that spectacular English summer when the conditions for photography, that smashing, perfect balance of light and shade, were so ripe that the dullest of that gang of paparazzi would have had to forget to load their cameras or remove their lens covers to fail to get perfect pictures, the family affair became a family affair. I mean we were joined by Larry's sisters and brothers.

I mean—— enter Alec.

The man had an absolute instinct for when a picture was about to be taken. Oh, how that horser-arounder could horse around! It was uncanny. Quicker than an f-stop or the setting of the shutter speed, he could reach across a field of vision and thrust himself into a photograph without leaving even the faintest trace of a blur. He was, that is, a scene stealer par excellence, and probably inherited his natural gifts for mugging, timing, and blocking from the innate theatricality of his parents. (Because Darwin was right, Sid. I'm just a simple celebrity, just this year's flash in the pan, but even I can see that when, over the years, the necessity for monarchs to be the stalwarts of eras and policies dropped away, they must have oh so gradually adapted and become instead these figures for pageantry, this little, highly specialized race of creatures who are at their best set off in golden coaches, as fashioned for tableau vivant as if they'd been invented by tailors and jewelers.) At any rate, Alec was a sort of genius of displacement. He could so dispose imself—by a look, by a gesture—that it often appeared in these photographs as if I were looking at him admiringly, even though my attention may actually have been engaged by some particularly astonishing effect in one of the fabulous gardens on one of the fabulous estates we happened to be visiting that weekend. Conversely, he could somehow intuit when my face was about to assume what, for lack of a better term, I can only call a compromising expression, and then flash some last-minute smile of yearning and longing in my direction. Or, magically, he might appear next to me in certain photographs where I cannot even recall his being part of the group. In these pictures our eyes seem to be holding hands.

"Look here, Alec," I told him one day, "this will have to stop."

"Whatever are you talking about?"

"You know what I'm talking about. Those photographs of us that appear in the papers and magazines."

"It's not *my* fault there's freedom of the press in this country. *Areopagitica*, don't you know."

"Just stop it that's all. Columnists are beginning to suggest things."

"I wonder why," Alec said. "I have no interest in you."

He was telling the truth. I think it was out of simple mischief he did these things. Alec was rather like one of those irrepressibles, a best man, say, who might thrust his finger up behind the groom's head in the formal wedding portrait.

In the event, Larry was never jealous and, if he ever harbored even the least suspicion about either of us he gave no hint. It was Princess Denise to whom it occurred that something might be fishy. In my own, Lawrence's, and Their Majesties' presence she brought it up herself, and in almost the same abrupt words I had used.

"Ho hum ho hum hum ho," replied Alec.

"He's your *brother*," Denise said.

"Yes, I know. Lawrence the Steady."

"Good lord, Alec, sometimes you can make me so cross!"

"I love all my children equally," Charlotte put in.

"I love all my *children* equally," King George said, giving the line a different reading.

Prince Lawrence barely looked up from the charts he was preparing for our honeymoon voyage.

Well. Alec didn't bother to stop pulling his faces even after Denise and I called his attention to those potentially damaging photographs. You will recall, I'm sure, what he said the single time he was directly challenged about any of

this by a member of the press. "You may say," he said without blinking an eye, "that Louise and I are just good
friends."

Whatever the public's speculations about Alec's and my
behavior, I was too caught up in the genuinely hard work—
harder work, oh *much* harder, than when I was in California
running the vacuum, cleaning washrooms, scouring toilets,
turning mattresses, making up beds; harder even than the
hours I put in out in the Pacific rubbing my hands raw, raising blood, and doing without the benefit of appliances to
entire wicky-ups what I'd been obliged to do to only a
handful of guest rooms in the Los Angeles hotel—of our
official engagement and ceremonial but backbreaking
courtship to take all that much notice of what I knew to be
vicious, baseless rumor, no matter what I, or Denise either,
may have said to Alec when we confronted him. Perhaps
Lawrence's own phlegmatic response lulled me into an un-
realistic appraisal of my danger. (Or perhaps—do you
gather my meaning, Lord Sidney?—I had not yet come to
appreciate the subtler, almost chemical properties, ex-
changes, and reactions of families.) So, much was lost on
me. Though I'll be frank, I didn't blame myself then and
don't blame myself now.

Who would in my position? New to fame? I mean *fame*,
my friends. And if, today, I can write myself off as a simple
celebrity, in those days—I hadn't realized until I put down
that last phrase how very long ago they now seem though it
can't have been more than four or five months back that all
this took place—I was an historical figure, a matrix for
monarchy, the potential breeder of queens and kings. It's no
wonder I was under such close, if misdirected, scrutiny.

As I was saying.

New to fame. New, though at twenty-eight I was perhaps
a few years past the right age for it, to a whirlwind tour—
indeed, there were times when I actually thought of myself
as living in a kind of montage—of social geography I'd seen
depicted in films—bars of crayon light spelling the names of
nightclubs in flashing pulses of neon like a kind of urban

code; wheels spinning on roulette tables with colored chips on special numbers like canted stacks of denomination; dice on green baize; corks popping out of champagne bottles; dance halls and dance bands, the musicians sitting primly on chairs behind music stands whose vaguely scrolled shapes were like the fronts of sleighs; couples barely moving to slow, easy music from some universal time zone of romance; sleek cars on streets still shiny from recent rain—— all the world that did *too* love a lover wrapped in creamy layers of early A.M. cliché—but never really believed existed.

Oddly, it was at these times I most had Larry to myself. It was as if the paparazzi had been bought off, or as if we'd somehow managed to give the Prince's family the slip. Maybe this was only a professional courtesy—another tradition—paid to princes during certain of the more tender phases of their courtships. And odd, too, how strangely returned to myself I felt, and to a time when I was not yet the toast of Western and Mediterranean Europe, shy, almost defensive.

There was, for example, the incident at The Springfield, one of Britain's, indeed the Continent's, most important but—because of its relative inaccessibility and the steepness of the stakes risked there—least frequented gambling casinos. The Springfield is in Llanelli, an unattractive borough and port town of under twenty-five thousand in County Dyfed, South Wales. Lawrence, who wasn't much of a gambler—"More Denise's, Mary's, and Alec's line of country," he'd said both times we'd been to London clubs, quickly adding that craps, cards, roulette, and offtrack betting were some of the nation's principal industries and, as such, required his attention during our engagement, as, once we were married, our presence would be expected at foundries, coal mines, and shipyards; it was good, he said, for tourism—drove us down as much, or so I was told, to see his old boyhood chum, Macreed Dressel, the casino's owner, as to show the flag.

In London, no matter I was no more gambler than Lawrence, I rather enjoyed the glamorous ambience of these places, enjoyed the exotic liquors they passed round, enjoyed the au courant fashions of the women, the striking black-tie presence of the men, was enchanted by the sourceless background of classical chamber music played by live, but hidden, musicians, so at odds with the ostensible activities in the big rooms, but so fitting, too, suggesting as it did an earlier age, some fastidious buck-and-wing of cotillions and quadrilles, of silk breeches and linen petticoats, great fortunes won and lost, love tragedies and suicides and young men killed in duels.

The Springfield, however, was a different story.

For one thing, after what Larry had told me about the club, about its being a kind of Lourdes or Mecca for people of serious fortunes, a place so remote it was almost as convenient to approach by ship as by rail or airplane, I had imagined a sort of Monte Carlo for the rich, even picturing those freaky, out-of-the-way palm trees you sometimes get in Great Britain here and there along this or that ocean current, my mind actually conjuring a ruined castle (brilliantly restored, of course), the chamber musicians of the London clubs augmented by a full-fledged orchestra, gaming tables like an incredible furniture, fine Oriental scrim displacing the ordinary baize beneath the dice, gracious suites where guests refreshed themselves after an evening's play, magical fountains and gardens where wild animals, odorless, disported, their killing teeth and dangerous claws removed. . . .

In the event, of course, The Springfield was as plain as its name.

And stranger, too, than anything I had yet conceived under the spell of my touched, teched, chosen, prenuptial fairytale life.

It was as drab as anything else in that drab port town and, in lieu of the safe lions, gardens, and tigers of my overheated imagination, hadn't even the advantage of a view of the sea. And rather than the cunningly restored castle I'd imagined, the structure itself was nothing more stately than both sides of an ordinary semidetached. Nor was there anywhere to be seen the extravagant, requisite fashions of the London clubs.

Here, the men's suits and ladies' dresses could have been seen between five and seven P.M. on the station platforms, or staked out along the steep ascending and descending escalators, and in every car on the London Underground.

Here the unadorned men and prosaically clothed women—many more men than women—not only hadn't arrived as couples but, one understood, if they recognized each other at all it was only what they had observed of one another's habits at the gaming tables. One understood—and this was *not* my overheated imagination rekindled—that one was in the presence if not of disease then at least of obsession. The Springfield, like some sanitarium-in-reverse, was given over to the practice of gaming as sanitariums were once given over to a cure for tuberculosis, or, nowadays, to losing weight, say, or weaning people off drugs.

Macreed Dressel, Larry's old pal (though it was never clear to me how Larry had met him, he proved so entirely strange I never pressed the Prince on the subject), was standing in the doorway when we arrived. Unlike anyone else I was to see there that evening, Mr. Dressel was got up, in a sort of costume like Rick's in *Casablanca,* as if the white dinner jacket and the carnation in his lapel were meant to identify him as the owner/manager of the place.

"Larry!" he shouted as we stepped out of the car.

"How are you, Macreed?"

"Is this she? Oh, it is! It is indeed, but take my advice, my dear," Dressel said while we were still several yards off, "what those photographers have done to you is actionable! Were I your solicitor I'd advise you to haul them up on charges! The most beautiful woman in Europe and they shoot you as if you were some common starlet!"

"What's an old poof like you know about beauty in women?" Larry said.

"Oh nothing, nothing at all. You've quite found me out, yes you have."

"Have you seen my brothers and sisters?" Larry asked.

"What do you take me for?" said Macreed Dressel as if he'd been insulted.

"Have you?"

"No, of course not! Certainly not! I should say not! Not in ages!"

"You're quite certain?"

"Quite certain! Absolutely! I'd take my oath on it! You have my word!"

(Oh, I *should* have been a queen, I really *should*. I have the temperament, I mean, certain passive instincts. I am, I mean, occasionally visited, as women are supposed to be, by great illuminating flashes of knowledge, received as Sinai conviction. Because I knew what this was all about. The Prince, who *was* no gambler, in exchange for Macreed's promise never to admit his siblings into the casino—that fast crowd, those ne'er-do-wells, the fortunes they owed in gambling debts—had undertaken to come to Llanelli in their place, volunteering to dip into his own Royal-Duke-of-Wilshire-Heir-Apparent's funds rather than have them, though more experienced in these matters than he, venture from their smaller reserves and diminished reputations one solitary pound. I asked myself, Louise, say what you will about him, is not this Lawrence the Steady one hell of an honorable man? Then thought to myself—— Whoops, Louise, whoops there, what about Alec and Denise and company, aren't they not only the fastest runners in that pack of ne'er-do-wells and compulsive gamblers, but Princes and Princesses of the Realm in their own right as much as Lawrence himself? What's to prevent a three-star bully and photo hog like Prince Alec who doesn't lack for the temerity to enter any low pub in the kingdom to demand of the locals that they stand him drinks, or to provoke dust-ups with no thought to his victims' safety and well-being, no matter what he may have for his own, and then come away, barreling his Quantra at one hundred, one hundred twenty-five and one hundred seventy mph with a souped-up, one thousand hp Rolls-Royce engine under its bonnet through the narrowest passageways in Bond Street, from going into any damn gambling den he thinks to take it in his head to go into and not only playing *for,* but actually determining *what* the table stakes will be? And, Sid, because it's you I'm talking to in case you didn't catch on, I knew the answer to that one, too. It was because, even though they were Princes and Princesses in their own right, they were *never* as much so as Lawrence. Who was Heir Apparent, practically as good as King already. By virtue of which, at least to pledged professionals like Mary and Robin and Alec and Denise, oathed to primogeniture, to the simple principles of fealty and liegeship and obligation, were servants to Order, to some pure, attainable ideal of Succession, wouldn't their brother have loyalty and compliance, if not actual out-and-out faith, practically coming to him? An Heir Apparent who stood above those mere Heirs Presumptive as confidently as Alec, who not only felt at ease in those low pubs and on those only just civic lanes and roads and motorways, and who, the Heir Apparent, were he of a mind to, could have commanded of the younger brother that he stand him to the same stout that the younger brother had just expropriated from the day laborer in the low pub. So that all he ever had to say to any of them was, "Steer clear, no little romps at the gaming tables for you kids, but, *whatever* you do, stay the hell away from The Springfield!")

"Will you be purchasing any chips this evening?" Macreed Dressel asked me after we'd freshened up.

"I'm not much of a gambler."

"Oh," said Macreed, "but it's so *boring* to stand by watching someone else hazard. I don't care how much in love two people are, it makes for a damned tedious evening. No, surely you ought to put yourself at some risk."

"No, really, thank you, I'm fine. I'll try to bring Larry some luck."

"I can't sell you a few chips? Two or three thousand pounds?"

"Louise?" said Larry, turning to me.

Well, I'm not much of a gambler, and Dressel was right, it is tedious to watch other people make bets. When I was in America, I noticed that every local television news program would run the winning lottery numbers across the screen. What could have been of interest to no one except the three or four people out of the several hundred thousand who'd purchased tickets seemed to take up an immense amount of time as the numbers went by. Then they'd put the numbers up a second time. (I have the same reaction watching the weather report or listening to the scores of games.) Actually, when the only thing at stake is money and depends on chance—oh, I know there's a certain skill, and even bits and pieces of character involved in understanding house odds, in knowing when to risk and when to stand pat—I have trouble developing a rooting interest. I'd have to know all the gambler's circumstances before I could get involved. The kick I got in those London clubs had more to do with watching how people behaved, what winning or losing meant to them and, well, quite frankly, the clichés about English character are quite accurate. We're too stiff-upper-lip to give much away.

But this is what I meant before when I said that at these times—when the Prince and I were off on our own and, well, dating—I felt most returned to myself. Because the truth was, I hadn't any money. Denise had taken me shopping. What I wore in Llanelli Denise had put on my back. Even my shoes and undergarments had been billed to the Princess's wardrobe allowance. I took my meals at one palace or stately home or another, or dined in England's finest restaurants and it hadn't cost me a cent. (Indeed, I never even once saw a bill presented.) I slept each night in a spectacular room between gloriously smooth sheets on wonderfully stuffed pillows in beautifully embroidered pillow slips on a marvelous turned-down bed, and not only was everything free but I never even thought to bring my hosts a gift.

Only when Macreed Dressel had offered to sell me chips, and only when Larry had turned to me and spoken my name, "Louise?" did it occur to me that I had no money. That it's all right to accept every hospitality—even the hospitality of the gift of the clothes on one's back—except the hospitality of money. And, as I had no money, and would take none from Larry—even though it would have been disguised as Macreed Dressel's chips—I did, I felt returned to myself.

"Let's get on with it then, shall we?" Lawrence said, and Mr. Dressel opened an ordinary door and led us through it and into his graceless, charmless gambling parlor, which would, had not the common wall in the ordinary semidetached been knocked through, have been two quite ordinary lounges.

Lawrence is a steady and responsible man but not a stern one, and his tone, when he indicated it was time to begin the ordeal, was more pleasant than stoic or neutral. And though there was nothing inflated in his voice when he told his old friend he was ready to get on with it, no more blame or censure coming from him than if he'd been pulled up short by a kink in his muscle on a walk in the woods, just this perfectly agreeable signal that whatever it was that might happen to either of them on the rest of their ramble, for his money, rambles were a crapshoot anyway, no one was responsible, not him, not his old pal, all three of us knew where Macreed Dressel stood. These were the inflections of some accustomed, charming dominion, so maybe I wouldn't have made such a hotshot Royal after all. I was too old to learn the language, I would speak it with an accent for the rest of my life.

At first, I didn't even recognize that this was where the gambling happened. It looked as if gambling were still illegal in England and that Dressel had a tip that The Springfield was about to be raided by coppers from the flying squad. True, there were card tables, but these were all lightweight, the kind whose legs fold and that you put back in the closet when your company has left. There was a tiny toy roulette wheel on an upright piano pushed against the dark, flowered wallpaper, its keys uncovered as if the piano player had had to leave in a hurry. Indeed, it was as if almost everyone had left in a hurry. I knew better, of course. The seven not in our party, the five almost shabby men and two dowdy women, I took to be some of the highest rollers in Europe, though perhaps this was only my imagination, ready for awe, kicking in again, were seated around a couple of card tables, the two dealers (not, as it happens, the "house"; Dressel was the house) as quiet as the people to whom they dealt, not bothering to keep up any chatter about the value and implications of the face cards, a music I'd particularly enjoyed at the two clubs we'd visited in London. They didn't, for that matter, even bother to look up when the future King of England came into the room. And, for my part, it was the first time in months, the first time since that funny little stutter step the Prince and I did outside the aloe shop in Cape Henry, *I* hadn't been stared at. I was a little disappointed.

I've said I understood I was in the presence of obsession, that the plain clothes they wore were signs of their indifference to everything but the compulsive gambling they were engaged in inside the featureless, institutional-looking Springfield. In an odd way they could have been, caught up in their furious concentration on each other's cards, a kind of support group. I was wrong though, as Larry later told me, to think that great fortunes were won and lost there. The truth was much scarier. These people were so rich that, while they gambled, just the interest compounding on their money in secret São Paulo, Seoul, Luxembourg, and Cape Town accounts, in banks in Spain and Peru, more than covered their losses. It was like that old premise in one of those films where characters have to get rid of great amounts of money within a specified time or forfeit their claim on even greater amounts of money. That would almost explain why the dealers dropped their customary running commentaries, all their clipped, kibitzless silences.

"Well," Macreed Dressel said to the Prince, "what's your pleasure then, sir?" Except for his white dinner jacket he might have been a publican asking a customer for his order.

"What's that one?" asked the Prince.

"Bless me, Larry, your high rank hasn't spoiled you not one whit, you've still your not inconsiderable instincts for the fun of a thing! That one, why that one's bezique, those ladies are enjoying a friendly game of bezique! There's aces, kings, queens, jacks, tens, and nines in bezique. You score your points by melding particular combinations of cards or taking tricks. Meld a queen of spades and a jack of diamonds and you win even extra points. It's quite like pinochle. The difference is you play with sixty-four cards ins—— "

"All right," Larry said, "I'll do the bezique one. How much?"

"Well," Dressel said, "let's see, I believe the ladies are playing for ten quid a point. Six or seven thousand quid should do you just grand for a few hands of bezique."

"I'm new at this. I'm not much of a gambler. I'll take ten thousand pounds."

He didn't watch as the women played out their hand. He didn't sort his cards when he was dealt them. I don't think he even looked at them. He was behind three hundred points at the end of two hands and, when it was his turn to deal, he wondered if the ladies minded if he raised the stakes to twenty pounds a point. It was up to them, he said, and they quickly agreed to the new arrangement.

"You're both of you too good for me," he told them after another two hands. "I'm quite out of chips, I'm afraid. How much more do I owe? Is it four hundred thirty pounds? Yes, I see it is. Macreed?"

He paid Dressel for an additional four hundred thirty pounds' worth of chips and graciously thanked the women for permitting him to sit in on their game. He had, he said, to excuse himself now because he wanted to get back to London at a reasonably decent hour and he saw there were still some more games he needed to learn.

"What's that other one?" the Prince asked his host.

"Well, that one," Dressel said, "is chemin de fer."

"All right," Larry said.

"In chemin de fer two hands are dealt. The players bet against the dealer. See, Mr. Collganardo is dealing now. The winning hand is the one that comes closest to, but doesn't go over, the count of nine on—— "

"All right."

"—two or three cards. It resembles baccarat."

"All right."

"You put up fifteen thousand pounds to start."

Larry gave him the money. It took him only half an hour to lose seventeen thousand pounds over and above his original fifteen-thousand-pound investment. When it was his turn, one of the players told him it was dealer's choice and that he could change the game if he wanted.

"Euchre, what's euchre?" Larry said.

"Euchre is cards," Macreed Dressel told him. "A player is dealt five cards and makes trump by taking three tricks to win a hand."

"Only five cards but he has to take three tricks to win? I don't know, it sounds to me that euchre can be pretty slow going. I like it when there's a bit more action. What's whist? I've heard of whist."

"Whist is even slower than euchre."

Larry let out a sigh. "If you gentlemen will excuse me," he said apologetically, rose, and gave up his place at the table. "What's the fastest?" he inquired of Dressel.

"Well," Macreed said, "for your purposes I'd have to say that roulette is the fastest. Roulette lasts for only so long as it takes the wheel to slow down enough for the little steel ball to settle in one of the thirty-six little compartments."

"And I bet on the number it will come to rest in? Is that about it?"

"That's about it," Macreed Dressel said. "You can always, what we call, 'hedge your bets,' " he added. "You do that by putting your chips down on more than one number."

"It doesn't sound as exciting if I hedge my bets."

"Well, no, it isn't as exciting." Macreed Dressel went over to the upright piano and took the toy roulette wheel down off its top and placed it on the piano bench. This was to be the venue for the game. "A moment, Prince," he said. "I'll fetch you a chair."

"No no, don't bother, I can stand. It will be more exciting if I stand."

"As you wish."

"How much?" Larry asked.

"I don't know," Dressel said quietly. "Whatever you want. I'm at your service."

"Could you tell me," said the Prince, "could you tell me how you make your money?"

"I take twenty percent of what a player gives for chips. If I sell you a hundred pounds, you get eighty pounds in chips. Between fifteen and twenty percent is pretty much the rate in private clubs."

"Ah, fifteen percent."

"Twenty percent at the upscale clubs. I don't impose a limit, I don't employ dealers."

"I see."

"In roulette I'm the house. I pay if you win and collect if you lose."

"I wonder, could you tell me," said Larry, "in roulette, in roulette, do I purchase chips at the upscale rate? Is that about it?"

"Yes," Dressel said, reddening.

"Let's get on with it, shall we?"

The others had laid down their cards and were watching the Prince. It was very moving. My fiancé put all his chips on number twenty. Macreed spun the wheel. The steel ball settled in number five. It was very moving.

"You beat me?" the Prince said.

"Yes," Dressel said, "it seems I have. Yes."

"Good show, Macreed!" said the Prince. "Well played, old friend!"

All seven gamblers stared at him.

"We'll be going back now," Lawrence said, and took a check from his pocket, which I'd seen him make out earlier. He stuffed it into Macreed Dressel's white dinner jacket. "Here," he said, "for your trouble."

It was very moving.

I'd never felt closer to him. He never said a word to Dressel about his brothers and sisters.

It's been said that the life of a member of the Royal Family is as different from the life of a member of even the upper middle class as the life of a member of the upper middle class is from the life of a caveman.

I eat, I have clothes to wear, even in Cape Henry there was a place for me to go to sleep every night. But I have no *money*. Certainly they pamper me, they give me these clothes, they see to it I'm fed. They even seem fond of me. Still, the fact remains, I have no money. It would be unseemly of them to offer me any, it would be unseemly of me to take it, even walking-around money, even chump change. I have no money. By that measure alone—I'd never felt closer to him—we were separated by the greatest distances, the widest ways. So I did, I felt returned to myself. Can you understand what I'm trying to say?

Even two or three weeks after our visit to the club in Llanelli in Wales, it was still the montage, that blur, I mean, of love and courtship like a kind of tour. We felt (or I did) surrounded, protected by romance like some cloak of delighted (real or not, present or not), unseen onlookers—the forgiving interested, call them—whose psychic stand-ins Larry and I were, almost their representatives in some parliament of hearts, as emboldened by youth and looks and luck to get away with the outrageous, the murder of the daily, as someone genuinely funny, say, or as a pair of attractive, tired tipsies—— dressed-up, black-tie, wee-small-hours types in the back of someone's milk truck, clippety-clop, clippety-clop—— so many of love's and wooing's vouchsafed antigens around us it seemed as if, though (the paparazzi called off, Larry's parents, brother and sisters and cousins and all the peeraged rest of their high-placed pals on all their great stately estates given the slip) I had him to myself now, we were on some honeymoon *before* the honeymoon—but that's what romance is, isn't it?—a high holiday of mutual regard. It would have been impossible even to imagine a lovers' quarrel. We'd have had to have drummed one up—— one of us take offense at the color of the other's clothes, or argue whether this or that restaurant deserved a third star.

We went to the theater and never told them in advance we

were coming. We didn't ask for the royal box, or even dress circle (Larry wore off-the-rack clothes for the first time in his life), but chose the upper circle or took out-of-the-way seats deep in the Gods where we could hold hands. When we were recognized in restaurants—it was surprising how seldom we were—we refused the best tables and Larry tipped the maître d' to find us something toward the back, near where the staff took its cigarette breaks, or waitresses traded their shifts with one another because they had dates, or their kids were sick, or blokes were coming to have a look at the spare room. Or sought out third- and fourth-world restaurants, restaurants from countries that hadn't been completely charted yet, and sampled exotic meats killed in the Amazon rain forest, and exchanged spoonfuls of each other's soups made from rare Indonesian and African birds, or puzzled how deeply into the rinds of seals and sea otters it was wise to eat and tried to figure out what to do with the beautiful phosphorescent skins and soft bones of tropical fish. And went to motion-picture houses where we stood on line with everyone else when the show was changing and, once inside, stared at ourselves in the newsreels as if we were other people, or laughed about Alec's genius for omnipresence. And, if the feature was a romantic comedy, we watched it, completely absorbed, as forgiving of the slap-dash principals as if we were those unseen onlookers, the forgiving interested, and the characters we forgave were ourselves.

It was like dating. Well, it *was* dating. It was dating exactly. The Prince confessed he'd never had so much fun and admitted that, yes, maybe he was a trading-places sort of prince after all—— just this poor Prince looking for a pauper.

(Sid, we were on the same wavelengths. I felt returned to myself and so, to hear him tell it, did Larry.)

And it was still the montage the night Larry took me in his crestless, unmarked Jag on a remarkable drive around London.

We crossed the Thames near where the original London Bridge once stood.

"It must have been quite gorgeous, London Bridge."

"Hmn, yes," Larry said, "and profitable. Our family once had the rents from it."

"The rents? From London Bridge?"

"Many of the most fashionable homes in the city were built on it, some of the best shops, the smartest stalls. Well," he said, "location is everything."

"It's possible for people to own bridges?"

"It's possible for kings and queens to own bridges. Kings and queens may own anything, Louise. We could lay claim to the rents and rates on the entire London Underground if we wanted. On the Green, Blue, and Red Lines. On any of them. On the Number Thirty-nine and Seventy-four busses."

"Oh, lay *claim*," I said.

"There's the rub," he said.

We rode on in silence for a while. It was a beautiful evening. I let down my electric window. This time of night, the air was almost balmy. I relax in a car, and Larry was an excellent driver.

"Take Lord Nelson's monument there, for example," the Prince said.

We were in Trafalgar Square.

"What about it?"

"Well, it's ours, it belongs to us. Just imagine what would happen if we asserted our rights, though, tried pulling him down. The people wouldn't stand for it."

"Why would you want to pull down Admiral Nelson's monument?"

"I don't. I'm a sailorman myself, I admire Nelson. It's the principle."

We passed the National Portrait Gallery. Larry told me that belonged to them too.

"What, the National Portrait Gallery?"

"It's practically the family album, Louise."

"I suppose," I said, "looked at that way."

And went on, up Piccadilly to Piccadilly Circus and around the Statue of Eros—also in the family—and out to the British Museum—though they let others use it, also in the family, all, all in the family—and doubled back, past their parks and past their palaces, and on to where the Bank of England stood, and Larry stopped the car and turned off the engine and leaned across my knees and reached out to the polished-wood glove compartment where he kept a pack of cigarettes and took one cigarette from the pack and lit it before returning the pack to the glove compartment where it would stay for the week or so before he wanted another one.

"That's yours too, I suppose?" I pointed to the bank. "The Little Old Lady of Threadneedle Street?"

"The difficulty with theories about the divine right of kings," he said, "is that not many people are religious these days. We're holding on by the skin of our teeth. All that stands between us and the barbarians at the gates is the Archbishop of Canterbury, Louise."

"Is the Bank of England in your family?"

"My father's picture is on the notes," he said, "and his father's before that, and . . . Well."

And started to feel his queer financial heroism again, my own poor penniless place in the world—I swear to you, Sid, the fifty thousand pounds you gave for my story means nothing, nothing—and the great distances between us, our immense, light-years differences. It made a girl giddy. It gave me the galaxial shivers, a taste, I mean—can you understand what I'm trying to say?—of the spatial creeps—— all that power and certainty—— the astronomical fundament and absolute baseline depths from which the Prince, as much of an explorer as he was a Prince, was reaching toward me—— that, *that's* how I felt close to him, by dint of the sheer exponential, mathematical space between us. I never felt closer. He lowered the electric window on the driver's side and threw his cigarette into his street and started his engine. I began to move toward him. "Buckle your lap belt, please, Louise," said the Prince.

How Push Came to Shove

Because we hadn't made love since that time on the island. Not even on the yacht coming home. Not in the palace, not in the castle, not in any of the great houses we visited. For all their false walls and secret passageways, their concealed staircases and special, complicated hidey-hole arrangements, their ancient comic architecture of tryst and farce (Lawrence was a serious student of architecture and claimed that the first adulterers, at least those bold enough to commit their adulteries under the very roofs they shared with their spouses, must have been aristocrats, because only aristocrats could have absorbed the high structural costs of weekend affairs and one-night stands; he felt that rather than a mark against the highborn, all their hanky-pank had its plus side; discretion, he said, was essentially an aristocratic idea), for all the opportunity such places provided for assignation, he never once came to me in any of them. He never once came to me anywhere.

"It's because you're so high-profile, isn't it? We have to be careful."

We were in the unmarked, crestless Jag again.

"I'm not afraid of the people in this kingdom. These people are my people. Why should I fear them?"

"Look," I said, "if you're at all unsure, if you want to back out of this . . ."

"Don't be silly, Louise. I love you. Don't you know that?"

"I think you love me."

"I do love you. Almost from the time of our encounter in Cape Henry."

"You were all *over* me in Cape Henry."

I'd intended my remark as a rebuke. He hadn't understood me.

"Oh," he said, "taking the aloe plant from you, that was just chivalry. And when I saw the cuts on your hands, when you explained how you got them, that was just admiration for your bravery, the sympathy endurance earns one in a difficult world. But when you teased me"—here his voice dipped—"when we made love"—and here climbed back up again to higher ground—"and I saw how you handled yourself with the press when I sprung our engagement on you, and I realized how stunningly regal you so inherently are, that, my dear Louise, that was love!"

It was a pretty speech and, worthy or not of his noblesse oblige-obliged condescensions, brave or not, regal or not, like many women, I'm a sucker for pretty speeches, but that wasn't what stirred me. If he had me jumping—he did, he did—it was the old business of my simple human illiteracy again, the even bigger sucker I am for men I can't quite make out. (How brave or regal can I really be? There are gothic romance novels in my dumb-blond heart. I'm a throwback, Sid, a traitor to my liberated sisters.) For, even if I had not had the good evidence of his sexual aloofness, I would, a moment later, have had the even better evidence of his cloudy motives.

"Anyway, Louise what do you think this courtship is all about? This shouldn't be a factor, yet it is, and more on my part, I think, than on Father's or Mother's, but do you know how much money it's cost the Crown? Why in petrol alone! In nightclubs and restaurants and theater tickets!" (In our montage, like the cold chickens, salads, cheeses, caviars, and chilled champagnes laid out on a lawn on the splendid napery from those stocked, magnificent picnic hampers.) "But cost is the least of it; more important is the fact that I've given the world my word (let alone the nation) that we're engaged. And we're entering the final phases now. Guest lists are being prepared. *Our* appointment calendars are being synchronized with *their* appointment calendars. Heads of state have been notified. Such-and-such a president from so-and-so a superpower; such-and-so a chieftain from so-and-such a third- or fourth-world country. Contracts have been let out on bid for all those commemorative soup-spoons and keychains—— all that licensed Royal tchotchke and whatnot, which, cared for, or merely held onto long enough and passed from one generation to the next, might one day actually become the valuable museum-quality, self-appreciating marvels of historic artifact they're cracked up to be.

"You must trust me, Louise, this is a very delicate time. Hath not a prince eyes? Hath not a prince hands? I feel what you feel, but preparations for the Royal Wedding proceed apace and aplomb. We can't afford to place ourselves in compromising positions just now."

"Oh," I said, dismissively, "compromising positions. Fa la la, tra la la."

Just then the car phone sounded its rapid sets of twin, paired, ringing gutturals, a noise peculiar to the British telephone system that always startles me, reminds me, no matter how often I hear it, of the signal for emergencies in the engine rooms of ships.

"Yes?"

"Larry, Alec. I rang up your Bentley and tried you in the Land Rover, but no one was home. Where are you headed? Is Louise with you? Give me your coordinates, I bet I beat you there, vroom, vroom."

"What do you want, Alec? This phone isn't secure."

"Mary and Robin are with me, Cousin Anne is."

"How are you, darling?"

From the way he reddened each time her name was mentioned, I'd long ago realized Anne must have been one of the cousins my intended had fondled and whose frocks he'd looked up as a child.

"Hello, Anne," he said, "I should have thought you'd know better than to get into a car with my brother."

"Well, *you* never take me anywhere."

"She's teasing you, Prince," Alec said. "She's told me of just incredible places you've been together."

"Traffic is quite serious today," said Larry. "This phone is not *secure*," he hissed. "I'm ringing off."

"No no, wait," Alec said. "It's about your wedding. Hallo? Louise? It's about your wedding."

"Hello Alec."

"Hello Louise."

"Hello Mary."

"Are you still sore?"

"Hello Robin. No, no, I'm not at all actually."

"I didn't mean any harm. I was drunk." He paused. "I was drunk as a lord!" he said, and laughed heartily at his obscure little joke.

"What do you mean it's about the wedding?" Larry broke in.

"Why the Royal Wedding. *Your* wedding." Mary was my favorite among Larry's siblings. Indeed, she's the only one with whom I'm still in touch. I say this without much fear of jeopardizing her situation since she's always been pretty open about our friendship, treating me kindly in the press, the only one of them, in fact, to have stood up for me and gone on record that she never thought I was "working" the Prince. Mary certainly doesn't need my endorsement. Probably it would go better for her if I kept quiet about it, but in my view loyalty begets loyalty—though wasn't it, in fact, loyalty to my idea of the Crown that allowed all this to have gone so far in the first place?—and, for whatever it's worth, I think, though it's untrained, Mary has quite a nice voice and, except for the fact that rap might not be the material to which her sweet little instrument is best suited, I see no reason, though she's a Princess, she shouldn't make a perfectly decent career in show business.

"What about it?"

"Well, we were thinking."

"Alec and me."

"Me too. It was my idea."

"It was Robin's idea."

"But it's your wedding."

"We'd have to clear it with you first."

"Absolutely."

"Of course."

"No question about it."

"We'd never go behind *your* back."

"He'll never go for it."

"Oh, Anne, we don't know that."

"He'll never go for it. You'll see."

"This isn't a secure phone."

"Would it be all right, do you think, if we wore, well, jeans, to the wedding?"

"Jeans? To a Royal Wedding? In Westminster Abbey?"

"I told you he wouldn't go for it."

"Well, not jeans, or not jeans exactly. Regular morning coats and top hats for the boys, actually."

"And gorgeous gowns for the ladies. With these ravishing big hats and really swell veils."

"Just *cut* like jeans."

"From stone-washed denim."

"Oh, it would be such fun! The Sloane Rangers would just die!"

"Hello, Denise."

"Hi, Louise," she said, and I had this image of Britain's Royal Family stuffed into Alec's Quantra like so many circus clowns. If George and Charlotte, preparatory to standing down, had not been off on what they must surely have thought of—the Nöel Coward King, his Nöel Coward Queen—as their final farewell world tour—after our initial meeting, and with the exception of a few subsequent appearances with them at the house of this or that duke or marquess or earl, I seldom saw them—taking their last curtain calls in Tonga and Singapore, Belfast, New Zealand, and other Commonwealth ports of call, I could comfortably have thought of them back there with the rest of the zanies.

"You're wasting your time," Anne said, "he'll never go for it."

"Not so fast. Give him a chance. Let him think about it."

"No," Larry said. "I don't want to think about it. It's out of the question."

"You see? What did I tell you?"

"You never know, he could have said yes."

"The child is father to the man," his cousin said.

Larry rang off.

"What did she mean, Larry?"

"What did *he* mean?"

"What did who mean?"

"What did he mean are you still sore?"

"Robin?"

"What did he mean?"

I didn't want to quarrel with him. So I made something up. I don't even remember now what it was. Just some harmless white lie I passed off. To keep the peace. (Probably I picked up on the word "sore." Because that was mostly how we spoke to one another in those days—— in all love's thrust-and-parry, in all its stichomythic Ping-Pong tropes of engagement. Each hanging on the other's words as if love were some syntax of Germanic delay. Because this wasn't as it had always been with me, Sir Sid. Accustomed as I was to arias, soliloquies, lectures, speeches, promises.) Let's say I said, "I don't know, Larry, you know how Robin is. He probably thought he offended me."

"Did he?"

"Well, yes, I suppose he probably did."

"He drinks too much. He isn't kind when he's drunk. He forgets who he is."

"He forgets *what* he is."

"Hmn. Yes," Larry said, "he forgets what he is."

I always thought of Prince Robin as the pie-faced one, of his strange, vaguely rubbery features at once sullen and cheerful like the pressed pug nose and big puffed eyes on a victim of Down's syndrome. He reminded me rather of that actor Charles Laughton.

Two or so years ago, when I first saw California, I remember how very surprised I was that it looked exactly how I thought it would look, and seemed, it seemed, just how I thought it would seem. This wasn't déjà vu or any mystic sense of rightness; the sense, I mean, that California was some fate I'd been preparing for. Often it's nothing more than, oh, the availability of the world through all the telecommunication satellites that are constantly orbiting it, sucking up and spewing out geography across incredible distances so that nothing, not its poles, or rain forests, or the deepest trenches in its oceans, is unfamiliar to us. It is, I think, some salient hallmark stamped in perception and stuck in the blood. In the event, my years in America had largely cut me off from the hype from home, yet I knew before knowing him what Robin was like. He was a type, but we are all of us types. How could we be in the same rooms with each other if this weren't so? We should want bars between us, the protection of cages. Robin is Robin, neither mischievous like Alec nor playful like Denise, and of course he has none of Mary's sweetness or Larry's sense of responsibility. What can I say? I wanted bars between us, the protection of cages.

(What can they do to me? They don't go to court. A few years ago an intruder was caught in Charlotte's bedroom, sitting on her bed, watching her sleep. He was dragged off by bobbies. They searched him for weapons, asked him a few questions, and then released him. What can they do to me, Sid? I signed on to tell all and haven't told all. ——Not yet, and they know it, so what can they do? What can they do to me, I hold all the cards. What he is, our Robin, is evil.)

This was before any of that stuff found its way into the papers. So, playing on "sore," I made something up. The Prince hadn't a clue. No one had said a word about tattoos.

Prince Robin had taken me aside.

"Have you spoken," he whispered, "with the Royal Peerager?"

I mentioned the time I'd seen him in the King, his father's, palace.

"Yes," Robin said, "he told me about that. He'll be in touch with you. He has some things to impart. After you've seen him, I should very much like it if you would get back to me."

Well, I thought, this was a mystery, but it's often in the nature of people with whom one is uncomfortable that they say enigmatic, baffling things.

The Royal Peerager approached me at a charity ball and asked me to dance. I looked over at Larry, who was engaged in conversation with a fellow I recognized (without ever having met him) as one of his cohorts in earnest resolution. I turned back to Royal Peerager and shrugged my assent. Believe me when I tell you I'd quite forgotten Prince Robin's puzzling statement regarding any further encounter with, in Queen Charlotte's words, one of that "sweet assortment of jolly incumbents" who defined and so helped preserve many of the arcane rituals in our land (as one is first alarmed by, and then dismisses, the dark, abrupt remarks and elusive hints of certain—what can they do to me, their hands are tied—passive aggressives), so that I was all the more taken aback when, while we were still dancing, he began to recite, neither in conspiratorial tones nor stage whispers, in perfectly normal conversational accents, protected, I guess he would have thought, by the plain, preemptive music of the orchestra, *this* strange report:

"Though they may have seen its representation a thousand times, most of the people in this realm haven't the foggiest when it comes to the coat of arms of their own Royal Family. It could as well be Braille as heraldry for all they make of it. I say this not to disparage so much as to congratulate ourselves, for in the main it's as well that our subjects should not too much understand the devices and emblazonments, mottoes, bends, and color schemes of their genealogical betters. It's all right with us they haven't mastered leeks and lilies, fess and mantling; nor can parse achievement, hatchment, or do any of the revealing, reductive mathematicals—quartering, dimidiation—of descent. They can't tell crest from 'scutcheon, some of them, or tabard from surcoat. They've never learned the difference between five bears rampant and six lions crouching, nor can they decline the symbolism of twenty martlets perched on gold.

"On balance 'tis no detriment. Else let them loose to browse the privatest pages of our diaries or knock about in any castle's well-kept closets. Freedom's well and good for business, yet it's better than not the general have not the keys to this partic'l'r kingdom, or even inclination to dent

the knotty code of all our chesspiece, secret zoology, personnel, and architecture.

"Well *played,* Band Leader, well played indeed! Give us
another!"

All the time I'm looking at him, don't you know.

"Oh, listen," he said. "Please do me the honor, my dear.
This is one of my favorites."

In fact it may have been one of his favorites. Whereas before he'd held me in the most casual way, like a brother
dancing with his sister on Cabaret Night in the salon of a
cruise ship, say, now Peerager drew me tightly to him. I
think I was embarrassed. Larry and his friend were still in
deep discussion.

"What," I said, "what?"

He was at my ear. I needn't have worried. This old
smoothy was a smooth old smoothy. His voice laughed and
chuckled as it spoke as if it were telling me dirty stories or
giving me good gossip. Indeed, he even managed to shake
his head and do something almost imperceptible with his
eyes, closing them for a moment by way of a signal—No,
no, don't look now, but when you get a chance . . .—so
that people seeing us must have thought we were talking
about them and, offended, turned away.

Peerager said to me, "Hark! You're to be his bride. Quarterly one and four: Argent, three eagles conjoined in fess
gules. Quarterly two and three: Or, a King casting a knowing, sidelong glance displayed on a shamrock vert. Early in
the seventeenth century the knowing glance was changed to
a mask of tragedy. The tragic mask against the clover is a
heraldic pun. The Mayfairs are descended from the Lears—
née O'Leary—and are of Irish background."

"What did he tell you?" Robin asked the next time I saw
him.

"He thinks King Lear was a harp."

"I'll make an appointment for you with Royal Commoner!"

(Because what did I know, Sid? There are customs and
protocols for everything, everything. Some historic, buried

etiquettes of the anthropological—— stunning arcana, Grimm's laws, Great Vowel Shifts, the cryptic, hidden, hush-hush of a billion reasons. Why A precedes B, why zed follows Y; how it is condemned men get final cigarettes— and what they were offered before there was tobacco: fruit, a chance to hear their favorite song one last time, the opportunity to speak their last words. For *everything*. Why there's music at weddings and funerals. Hadn't I been there when that bevy of jolly incumbents came calling, that sweet assortment of royal intentioners and fashion engineers and selectors of ropes—— all those messengers of the traditionals and ceremonials with their inexplicable explanations of the improbable arrangements of kings?

(So why wouldn't I believe him when he told me I would have to see the Royal Commoner? I didn't even know there was such a thing, but I hadn't known there was a Royal Taster on the payroll either, had I? Then I saw him myself —— the thin, bony guy who managed to live on a spoonful of this and a single bite of that and a mere sip of the other, keeping his mouth clean for the flavors of poisons he'd not only never yet tasted but would probably only recognize after the fact, and then just by how they differed from the ordinary taste of meat and sweets and bread and vegetables. So why shouldn't there be a Royal Commoner, too? So far as I can see, there's at least one of everything anyway. So why shouldn't I believe that the office he held and the service he performed—to give instruction to commoners about to marry kings or queens or their immediate successors—maybe came up once, and never more than twice—and often never at all—during the entire course and tenure of one of these fellow's careers?)

So that when I went down with Robin to Greenwich that time, it was with a certain sense of sedate obligation and almost spiritual—at least historical—resolve.

Not for one moment was I under the impression that I was taking holy orders or anything, but I have to admit there was certainly something solemn about the business, and I approached Royal Commoner's dim figure in the dark old rooms in the ancient wooden chancery nervous as a convert coming for instruction to a priest. I couldn't quite make it out—it was bright outside, my eyes had not adjusted to the gloom—but through an open door I thought I saw a vague form—it might have been female—hunched over the shape of what could have been a doctor's fat black bag.

"Royal Commoner?" said the Prince.

"At your service, Prince Robin. And at yours, Miss Bristol."

"You shall be brought to blood by matrimony," Robin said quietly, "but you must do as he says."

(How would I know? How would I, Sir Sidney? Haven't I already said that there seems to be at least one of everything in this world? There are so many reasons and duties and traditions. For all I knew, maybe only the second brother of the future king could be the intermediary here. Maybe something of the sort was written into the tradition, as much a part of the customs and old deportments of humanity as the rule that brides and grooms aren't to see each other on the day of the wedding until the ceremony.

(So how would *I* know, how *would* I, Sir Sid?

(Because we're all of us anthropological. We are, we're *all* of us anthropological. I don't care how grounded a person may be, cosseted as a prince like Lawrence or Robin, made over like the only issue of oldest age, like Sarah's child, Isaac, or hopeless as kids in welfare hotels, the sun comes down every night and there are fearsome things in the dark: smells and hints and clues and sounds of death and worse things after, the horrible, stacked loneliness of men, the abominable godawful odds against anyone's not only ever managing to make it in the long run, but even so much as managing to just plain cope—— the insomniac's wakeful doubts and all the low blood sugar of the human race.

(So tell me, why wouldn't there be anthropology, why wouldn't there be ritual and faith and all the mumbo-jumbo of cultural reinforcement?)

"Of course she will, Prince Robin," Royal Commoner said pleasantly, "why wouldn't she? Do as I say?"

"Well," said Robin, "it isn't as if I actually spelled things out for her."

"Oh," he said. "Oh my."

"What?"

"Oh dear," he said. "This is awkward, this is very awkward."

"What?" I said again.

"For God's sake, Louise, don't make such a fuss. You too, Royal Commoner. It's not painful or anything. That's what you said, isn't it?"

"No, of course it isn't," he said. "It's not painful. There are topical anesthetics. Aren't there topical anesthetics, Mrs. Pfyfe-Philo?"

"Even without them," the woman said, for it was a woman I'd seen in the doorway, and she was carrying a doctor's bag. "Well, the tattoo needles barely break the skin. It's the powerful new dyes they have today that makes the marks."

"Tattoo needles?"

"You told her nothing?"

"You're the Royal Commoner, Royal Commoner."

"Is this what you're wanting then?" the woman asked me. She held up a cartoon with details from the coat of arms the Royal Peerager had described earlier—— a gold mask of tragedy superimposed on a green shamrock.

"Catherine the Great was tattooed," the Royal Commoner said.

"Catherine the Great already had noble blood."

"Cher's tattooed, some of the biggest stars."

"Cher isn't engaged to a prince. What is this? What are you handing me? You're not the Royal Commoner, are you? There's no such thing, is there?"

"Certainly I'm the Royal Commoner. I am and no other. What do you mean, anyway? You're not a queen yet, you're not even a princess. Not yet you're not. You've a lot to learn, Miss Bristol. You have to take my instructions. You think Royals *don't* get tattooed? It was a ransom thing. It was in case of Moors and Saracens. So they'd know what they had if princes and princesses, kings and queens, fell into the wrong hands. It was for their own protection. It's for *your* own protection, Miss Bristol. Tell her, Prince. Ain't I right? If I'm lying I'm dying."

I turned toward Robin. "Show me yours, then," I challenged.

"Oh, *I'm* not tattooed."

"Well, there you are," I said.

"*Where* am I? *I'm* not the King, *I'm* not his Successor!"

"*Please!*" said the one who was supposed to be the Royal Commoner impatiently. "The both of you!"

I must say I was more than a little surprised to hear him speak out so boldly to someone who, however far down the line of succession he may have been, was, after all, a prince. Perhaps that's why what he said next had some claim on me.

"Because it wasn't me who made the rules. I wasn't there whenever it was whoever it was said whatever it was had to be had to be. I've no say-so in the grand affairs that command history, the long by-and-large of incremental, ad hoc necessity, that piecemeal tinker and rising to social or biologic occasions that are all solutions, adaptations, and evolution ever are. *I* never seeded the oyster with sand. I was ever too small fry to cause an effect, I mean. What have *I* to do with the world? It's the curious meddle, stitch, and thick of things that gets things done. I'm just Royal Commoner, is all. My God, Prince, Miss Bristol, you don't even know my name. But when a living, breathing oxymoron of a man raised up to oral tradition and the learning of the law comes up and says to you that a tattoo isn't just, or even primarily, for the pomp and primp and privilege of sailormen in Southampton's or Marseille's or New York's low parlors, why maybe you ought to give him the benefit of the doubt.

"Catherine the Great was *too* tattooed! *Cher* is! And what is a tattoo, anyway? Semiotics, all those ultimate passwords of the flesh. Mother riffs, John-Loves-Mary ones, all those scratched affidavits, skin's deepest language. Flags, semaphore, and the body's loyalist bunting!"

Oh, how that man could talk!

I'm half hypnotized before he's done and don't even see him signal Mrs. Pfyfe-Philo to come forward. I don't see her open the bag she carries her tools in, don't see her dip the needle into the pot of green dye, or feel her wash me down with alcohol along the back of my left leg where the knee bends, or rub the topical anesthetic into my skin. I don't see the thin rubber gloves she's wearing to keep from catching a dose of AIDS off me in case a drop of my blood leaks into the pores of her skin. Royal Commoner's still talking away about a mile a minute. You'd think I was his troops at Agincourt and he was King Henry V rallying me, maybe jollying me along so I'd let Mrs. Pfyfe-Philo plant another one on the back of my right leg when she was done with the left. He was right, it is painless. I don't even feel the damn needle when it starts to go in and out, in and out, like she was some seamstress and the sensitive skin in the back of my knee was no more sentient than cloth.

No. What brought me out of it at last was what had put me into it. I'm listening to this smooth talker and suddenly it occurs that, oral tradition or no oral tradition, something would have had to slip through the cracks. This guy was improvising. He was giving too many reasons. Somewhere in the gloom Robin was smirking.

So, no matter I risked tearing the back of my leg to pieces, I pulled away. I examined myself. It was too dark to see, but later, in the light, I saw that all she'd managed to do was circumscribe the topmost arc in the highest leaf of the shamrock.

(I'd put him off with a quibble. Punning on "sore," admitting when Larry pressed me that, yes, Robin probably had offended me. Still, strictly speaking, I hadn't lied to him. I *wasn't* sore, just a little numb there where I'd taken the topical. And he had offended me. And, anyway, loophole and sophistry have ever been the mainstays of statesmen, providing them comfort and security, the sense they have to have of their own invulnerability, or they'd never get anything done. "None of woman born," the witches tell

Macbeth that other distant cousin of the Mayfair clan, and
". . . until great Birnam wood to high Dunsinane hill shall
come. . . ." And what about the stuff the Oracle fed Oedi-
pus? Softsoap about killing his father and getting it on with
his ma, so that all he thought he ever had to do to beat his
fate was just get out of town? That's in the tradition, too,
for people so sold on tradition. And, anyway, for all I know
maybe I was actually supposed to get that coat-of-arms tattoo. Wouldn't that be something? I mean wouldn't that
really be something, Sir Sid, if it weren't a hoax and all I
have to show—didn't I give back the clothes? didn't I give
back the jewels and Denise's fun furs?—for my brief encounter with the Royals was just this tiny bit of a circle
stitched to the back of my knee like a piece of green thread?)

"Hmn. Yes," Larry said, "he forgets what he is."

And lost in our individual thoughts—mine, now I'd
stopped thinking about what happened in Greenwich, were
of Larry, big and gorgeous in the driver's seat, larger than
life and more fit in his clothing (tweed now in the comfortable, abrupt autumn weather, tweed and cavalry twill and
the softest oxford) than a man in a catalogue—we drove on
in the crestless Jag to my parents' house in Cookham-upon-
Thames. Who knows what Lawrence was thinking of? The
money this whole business had cost the Crown, perhaps,
what a Prince's love drew down from a dynasty's treasure,
of positions even more compromising than any I—horny in
smoky fall's apple ambience, the polished leather promise
and poignant feel of its vaguely grainy fabrics—could ever
have hoped to put him in, now he'd given his word to the
world we were engaged.

I'm not being unfair to him, though none of this had occurred to me then, of course. How could it have done? I was
in love, I thought I was to be his Princess. I guess I was just
this romantic old silly. Tra la la, fa la la, hey nonny.

I had to hand it to Larry, I really did. With his Prince's
breeding and his almost cartographer's knowledge of the lay
of his lands, and his truly vast, dead-on sense of good hus-
bandry, he had a sort of perfect pitch for his holdings, for

all his rents and levies, and not only for his, but for the next lord's over, too, and the next lord's after that one, and for the next's and the next's and next's, ad infinitum, filling up the shires and counties and districts and ridings of the kingdom with some genius for property, some blood-driven instinct for the fixed boundaries, qualities, and intrinsics of possession till all England was drawn in on the fine map of his understanding.

He knew the annual rainfalls, the crops and industries and roads and forests, had a feel for its weathers, its wildlife, the fish in its rivers, the birds in its trees.

Cookham is a river village, almost a suburban wetlands. It is, in the best sense, unspoiled, quaint, almost precious. I cannot say how, but Lawrence even knew how to dress for the occasion of its suburban Sunday circumstances, his twills and tweeds, though he was Prince, perfectly, carefully, considerately matched—I found this touching; it made me more anxious than ever to bed him—to their own, the twills, tweeds, and oxfords of their aspiring squires' middle-class hearts. I hadn't seen it before, but when we stepped out of the car Lawrence was even wearing one of those soft wool visored caps that are part of the uniform, and that one sees everywhere in the country.

"Country," of course, is what Cookham so determinedly is. It was never large enough to be anything so grand as even the tiniest market town. It is what it must always have been—— a few hundred acres of lovely, ever so slightly remote real estate, its rich dirts vaguely hydrologic, geologic, strangely expropriate, as if they'd been thrown up like magic muds from the bottom of the river, or washed off the surrounding farms like some thick, complex, compact silt. (Nowhere in England is the earth so stocked with bait; nowhere is the soil so amenable, or crowded with the nutrients for flowers. The gardens of Cookham are its glory, its flowers' flaring pigments like wet primary colors.)

There is no school, no surgery, no library. There's no place where one may purchase film, postage, tobacco, a newspaper. There isn't even a shop to buy food. What there is is an old Norman church, two public houses, a BP station with a live-in mechanic, and an estate agent. The estate agent, with all the commisssions he's earned from the never-ending sale and resale of Cookham-upon-Thames's sixty-odd houses, must be a millionaire by now. The houses turn over so often not because of the damp—Cookham is damp—or because anything is so *very* structurally wrong with its housing stock, but because the village is such a marvelous place to live that people could never bring themselves to sell and live elsewhere were it not for the steadily, even incredibly, rising prices of the homes there. No matter what the rest of the economy is like, they double in price every half-dozen years. This is the rule of thumb.

We are, in a sense, a suburb of Richmond. A bedroom community where three out of four ratepayers have their income from antique shops, or the sale of estate cars, or are independent booking agents or the leaders of dance bands in fancy hotels. A queer aspect of society in a town so homogeneously employed is its conversation. People who book tours, for example, are, for some reason, reluctant to talk shop with others in the same trade. Instead, they'll pick up this or that bit of special information from people in professions different from their own and impart their newly acquired expertise to anyone (conventionally that fourth ratepayer or anyone else not engaged in the flogging of motors, tours, or the sale of fine furniture, or the leading of bands) who will listen.

Father sells estate cars in Richmond but is something of a connoisseur in the antique French-furniture field. Similarly, it isn't uncommon for antique dealers to know about palm-court orchestras or their conductors to be aficionados of world travel while professionals in this last enterprise will often tell you more than you'd ever want to know about estate cars. And so on and so forth in Cookham, a village of four idées fixes. Usually these conversations (monologues really) take place on weekends or in the evenings at one of the village's two pubs, though the venue can shift, rather like the tides of the sea-flowing river upon which

Cookham is located, inexplicably, mysteriously, almost whimsically, from one time to the next, so that a native whose rhythms are off, or who hasn't kept up, may discover himself in a pub that has "fallen silent" and find himself consoling (and suppressing) his gregarious spirits in lonely drink.

Do we sound quaint, picturesque? Do I, almost automatically falling in as I do with the eccentric, swollen tropes of my hometown every time I come anywhere near it? Who never even moved here until I was already twelve years old and who'd all but left it for good after I took my O-levels when I was fifteen, and who *did* leave it for good when I had taken my degree at university, do I sound quaint, picturesque? Maybe all home ever really is is wherever we happen to live whenever we reach puberty. This might account for the extra edge of horniness I felt as we approached the village, might account for the open, shameless way I bumped and rubbed against Larry when he parked the crestless Jag and we started up the path toward my parents' house, passing through the pretty obstacles of Cookham's frequent stiles. That's what *I* was thinking.

Lawrence was thinking something else.

"This place," he remarked almost scornfully, "this place is a refuge for Royalists."

"Have you been to Cookham then, Larry?"

"I know the type."

"Why do you sound so put out? It seems to me Royalists would be good for your business."

"Royalists," he said, "don't understand my business."

"That's dark," I said. (Larry *is* dark, and me this pushover for men in solar eclipse; small print, close-to-the-vest guys who won't give a girl the light of day. He had me jumping, he had me jumping and rubbing and bumping and grinding in my head.)

But, as I say, I had to hand it to Larry. My family is dead into that sort of thing. Like practically everyone else in Cookham's damp, moldy clime, they worship the Royal

Family. They take *Town and Country*, they've lifetime sub-
scriptions to *King and Queen*.

"I hope they won't make a fuss," he said.

"Old poo," I said, linking my arm through his, "you're
their daughter's fiancé, why *shouldn't* they make a fuss?"

"*I hope,*" he said so vehemently I almost couldn't stand
it, "*they don't treat me like some pop star dropping in on the
family as a favor to a character in a sitcom on the telly!*"

"You sound so mean. You haven't even met them. Or is
'your kind' just privy by birth to the type?"

Now I see I was only encouraging him, egging him on,
pulling strings.

"This place smells of bridles and neat's-foot oil," he said.
"It stinks of polished gun stocks and the ascot resins."

"Excuse us, Prince," I said, "if we're too caught up in the
English dream."

He glared and fell silent. We were but a hundred or so
yards from my parents' house now. (Larry had left the car
behind Cookham churchyard because he'd been reluctant to
bring the crestless Jag along the damp, unpaved ruts of the
wagon road.) Was it my imagination, or were those our
neighbors crouched down behind or slouched to the sides
of their French windows and peeking out at us like so many
posted hosts hushing each other and muffling their hilarity
at the approach of the guest of honor at a surprise party? I
couldn't actually distinguish anyone but had this sense of
urgent bustle at the periphery. The Prince, like some fast
feint artist who had perfected distraction, incorporated it
into his bag of tricks, a juggler, magician, or ventriloquist,
say, seemed never to lift his eyes from the road but directed
a steady stream of questions at me.

"Who's the tweedy type with the string of pearls? Do you
know the gent with the plate-glass monocle? What is *that*
creature? Are those really jodhpurs he's wearing?"

He meant Amanda Styles-Brody, he meant Winston
Moores-Wrightman, he meant Charley Narl. I hadn't seen
them, but it *could* have been they. They were my parents'
nearest neighbors, but how, from this distance, could he

possibly have known that Major Moores-Wrightman's monocle was ordinary window glass? Were we, indeed, types and phonies? Were all Englishmen, or all peoples really, viewed from the height of a throne, so categorical? And might not even the behaviors of princes, of kings and empresses, from God's point-of-view, seem at least a little ridiculous? Is He fond of a dirty joke, for example? "Look what we've here," would He say, "the empress is having her period!"? Is there, I mean, something petty about even our physical requirements, something inimical in Nature to nature, not just our renewable need to eat and sleep and move our foods along the degrading alchemical chambers of their digestion, converting not only red, gross meat into excrement but even grains and greens? If so, then I was a goner myself, a laughingstock of the universe, what with the itchings and urgings of my physical nature, my rut now (growing stronger as we came closer to the actual rooms where puberty had happened to me one afternoon between the time I'd been "Mother" to two or three friends at high tea, and the hour the last girl had been picked up by one of her parents and taken home) nothing more than blood in league with this intellectual masochism inexplicably programmed into my romantic, muddy, through-a-glass-darkly, sucker-punch imagination and glass-jaw heart.

(The gothic, girly inclinations, Sid, that do me *every* damn time!)

Not once feeling anger, no matter I'd teased and quibbled with him, at the Prince's disdain for our Cookham ways, so much as a heightened sexual desire. So that, despite Daddy's carryings-on and the fuss he made, his almost maniacal blather as he poured sherry into each of our glasses, giving in some exaggerated chivalric parody not just my mother the wine before he offered any to the Successor, the Prince, Duke of Wilshire, future King of all the Englands, but to me as well, probably saving the Prince till last not just out of manners but so he could pay him the steadiest attention. Meanwhile, as I say, keeping up this incredible monologue about French antique furniture, at one time actually raising his glass in a toast to the Royal Collection!

"To your rooms, Sir!" proclaimed my mad father. "To the seventy-three excellent fauteuils, forty-one vintage bergères, and thirty-five folding pliants in your family's palaces. To all the capital chaises in Wilshire House. To the master chairmakers: to each extraordinary Boulard, Cresson (I sat in one once!), and Gourdin. To your luxurious Jacobs, Senés, and Tilliards on the important Savonnerie carpets. To all the cylindrical, tabouret stools like so many upholstered drums, and all the beautiful banquettes along Balmoral's, Buckingham's, and Windsor's walls. A toast to all cunning, exquisite finishing touch—— your splendid accessories, the fire screens, gilt candlesticks, Imari bowls, Houdon marbles, and soft-paste porcelains. Your snuffboxes studded with gemstones like pimientos in olives. Clocks, chenets, bras-de-lumières, silver chandeliers, Kändler birds, girandole centerpieces."

" 'These are a few of my favorite things,' " the Prince remarked darkly, wryly, but if Father even heard him, let alone understood him, he gave no indication. Me, he had me jumping!

Meanwhile, Dad continued his absurd toast, rattling off names like Caffiéri, Duplessis, Saint-Germain, Gouthière, Meissonnier, Thomire. I was not his daughter for nothing. I hadn't heard him carry on in years, but the names of these classic metalworkers had been familiar to me since we'd first moved to Cookham when I was twelve and my father had taken up the eccentric conversation of the natives.

He was into the heavier pieces now, going on about commodes, chests of drawers, consoles, escritoires, Beneman's famous games table where Marie Antoinette lost so much money one night that Louis XVI abandoned his plans to add another wing on the palace at Versailles and thus, through inadvertence and his wife's bad luck at cards, put back the revolution and delayed his own beheading by perhaps three years.

He proposed toasts to the great cabinetmakers represented in the Collection—— to Carlin and Canabas and Cressent, to Dubois and Leleu and Riesener.

I don't know, maybe he was nervous. Maybe everyone in Cookham is nervous and they talk this way to cover it up.

He got round to the beds, the parquetry cradles in the nursery, the tall, sculpted, fabled four-posters in the King's chambers, the Queen's, the Princes' and Princesses', reeling off their inventory numbers in the *Journal du Garde-Meuble*. He toasted their dozen gorgeous canapés.

"How I should enjoy to spend a night in such a bed! A night? A nap! What dreams! I would exchange a year's reality for the visions that might visit me in such circumstances!"

"Really?" said Lawrence. "Me, I'm a seafaring prince, I sleep in me 'ammock."

Oh, he was wicked; oh, he was cruel!

Father looked as if he'd been slapped. Indeed, a red mark appeared to rise like a welt on his cheek just as if that were the place the Prince had stung him. Mother, who'd been quiet, who'd not once mentioned her garden or her work with Oxfam, who'd hardly moved, who'd hardly moved even as she curtsied when I introduced her to the son of a b-tch, and, in a way, whose silence and lockjaw paralysis of being was even more fawning than poor Father's helpless logorrhea, quite suddenly appeared to slouch, to crouch, to squeeze in upon herself almost as if she'd been that tweedy, string-of-pearls neighbor effaced behind the closed French windows, muffling not hilarity but a horror so complete it might have been its counterfeit.

Had the Prince been scornful I would have broken our engagement then and there, I swear I would. I would have demanded he leave our house, that he quit Cookham forever. But he reversed himself, was all charm and a noblesse oblige you could eat off of. He papered over his rudeness with a joke and a compliment to my father's astonishing knowledge of the holdings. "You certainly know your onions, sir," he told him, and promised to conduct them on a guided tour of the palaces any time Dad thought was convenient. He would send, he said, a car for them.

"An estate car," Father joked. "I'm in the trade."

"Of course," Lawrence said. "In Richmond. Louise told me."

I detected no scorn on the Prince's face, though I knew his heart.

Still, I could barely distinguish my anger from my pure let-fly lust. Indeed, they seemed to feed on each other. (Which just goes to show you, don't it, Sir Sid, that you can take the girl out of the country, send her to California, have her go for an au pair, or a housekeeper in a hotel, and even, when the really hard times come, for a sewer of houses, till her hands run with blisters, blood, and aloe; spring her, I mean, from all dependence and parasitical, female juniority; from all, I mean, the pretty, petty echelons of servitudinal, wide-eyed love, to the point where her arms and back run with muscle, but—WHOOSH! BAM! POWIE!—let one dark putdown or one sharp look be cast in her direction—provided, of course, it's the right direction—and she'll mewl like a lass in a story. As if California never happened, as if she never turned a mattress or ever swept sand.) What can I tell you, he had me jumping.

We were on the pretty upholstered bench in our large lounge. (Not even Father would have called it a bergère. Not even Cookham would have called it the library.) Mother explained it was Sheila's day off and went to prepare tea. I reached for the Prince's hands and took them in my own. I brought them down into my lap. I put this gentle pressure on them. I shifted position ever so slightly. And leaned my weight into the Prince. Pressing myself against his haunch. Imperceptibly, I parted my thighs and began swaying from side to side. I flexed my buttocks, I arched my back. Beneath my dress my body rose perhaps a fraction of a fraction of an inch above the bench. I relaxed and, settling my weight, started all over again. I shifted, I swayed, I flexed, I arched, I rose.

I came up against the Prince's hands. By displacements so

gradual they were almost infinitesimal, we exchanged momenta. He began to bounce my body like a ball.

As I've already told you, what can I tell you, he had me jumping. Push had come to shove. Aiee, aiee. I didn't care where I was. I didn't *know* where I was.

Poor Father.

I say "poor father," but I couldn't have said then, as I can't say with certainty now, whether he even knew what was going on. "Ever so slightly," I've said, "imperceptibly." I've said "displacements so gradual" and "almost infinitesimal," and implied that moment of inertia when we transferred momentum. So maybe he hadn't seen anything really. (It was moldly old damp Cookham, after all. It was a gray Sunday autumn afternoon in Cookham. The lights hadn't been turned on yet. It was dim in the lounge.) So maybe he *hadn't* seen anything. (And me hoping the water would never boil and get transformed into tea, wanting to spare at least one of them, you see. Look, we honor our fathers and our mothers. For a time, for a time we do. Then for a time, when the blood sings, while it rushes like wind through the terrible chambers and glands of our change and necessity, we don't. Or can't. Then, when we can again, we do again.)

So maybe it was just the awkward silence that launched Dad into speech.

"Do you know, Sir," he said, "something that's always bothered me, something I took the trouble to look up in the library but couldn't manage to pin down. Well, I'm a bit uncertain about a title is what it comes down to is all. If the living mother of a queen is referred to as the Queen Mother, well, once you and Louise are married, after the coronation I mean, well, would Mrs. Bristol be the King Mother-in-Law? Would one be the King Father-in-Law? It's only a point of order, of course. It isn't important. I'm only just asking."

"What? What?" said the Prince, who was breathing heavily now.

"Well," Father said, "it's simply a matter of—— "

"I don't know," said the Prince. "I don't know, I'm not sure, I shall have to find out. Look," Lawrence said, catching his breath, "we've had rather a long drive down from London. I find I'm suddenly quite tired. Perhaps it was all that talk of beds. I should so like to catch a nap. Is there a place one might lie down? Louise, you could show me. Please apologise to Mrs. Bristol for me, would you? I should quite like some tea, but after my nap."

Sunday, February 16, 1992
How Royals Found Me Unsuitable to
Marry Their Larry

We were in what despite the intervening years, and (from
the presence of the abandoned giraffes and tigers, monkeys
and bears, somehow come down in the world, reduced to
memento, simple stuffed souvenir) recognizably, too, was
still my room (which even without any fine antique French
furniture, could have been any schoolgirl's, even a French
one's, in any epoch, who, come fresh to her menses was
come fresh to virginity, too, since without their onset she
couldn't have known carnal desire, not *carnal* desire, that
queer, obsessive magnetism of the skin and heart and head
as much as of actual breasts or mysteriously furred-over
sexual organs) on what was (never mind it wasn't a rare
four-poster and boasted no gorgeous canopy) still (fourteen
or fifteen years after that alarming high tea with those two
or three childhood friends) my bed, though it was scarcely
longer or wider than a cot.

Because there must be something about the act of sex that
is indifferent to space. How otherwise explain how two full-
grown people—and one a prince with all that that suggests
of dimension and line—could manage not only to lie down
together on what the full-grown woman distinctly recalled
having outgrown all by herself fourteen or fifteen years earlier when she was four or five inches shorter and weighed
twenty or twenty-five pounds less, but thrash about on it
too? And something in the act of sex indifferent to time as
well. Or anyway oblivious of it, of anything but some overwhelming, all-inclusive Now. Because how else can one account for that seemingly magical obliteration or at least
smudge of each intervening sequence from how we met to
how we got engaged; through how I was received, and how
he courted me, and how push came to shove, until almost
the very day the Royals found me unsuitable to marry their
Larry (not to mention the half-dozen Sunday installments,

January 12, 1992, to February 16, 1992, inclusive, in which I not only tell all but apparently lay bare the soul of the entire Kingdom)? I mean how else can it be both the morning after one of those somehow issueless, drought-inspired, all-night Pacific blows in the two-a-penny wicky-ups when we—Jane and Marjorie and I—swept up sand and shook out mats and rewove walls in my good old beachcombing salad days before I was ever an all-but-crowned Princess rolling about on the floor of a wicky-up in mutual, amorous lock-leg and lusty, heartfelt grabflesh with your Heir Apparent, the two of us g--sing the he-l out of each other, spreading one another's but--cks, squeezing one another's p-rts (and the Prince singing out at the top of his voice, too, so that I actually had to cover his mouth in order to restrain him, lay hands on him, on a Prince, lest the guests, many of whom were our employers, recall—Jane's and Marjorie's and mine—in the adjoining huts hear him, those who hadn't already left for the Governor's Palace to see if they might not still get a chair near the reviewing stand where he was scheduled to appear that afternoon with Lord Mayor Miniver, Lord and Lady Lewes and Anthony Fitz-Sunday, muffling his "Road to Mandalay" exuberance—and the Prince l-cking the very palm over his mouth—sand in the high heels, aloe stains, patches of chlorophyll in the stockings and dresses on the frond-strewn floor of the unwinding wicky-up) one minute, and seven thousand something miles away and all that happened to us in between the next; push coming to shove, to pushing and pulling and thrusting and parrying, to all Love's earth defying sexual acrobacy on that same astonishing, flexible, accommodate cot where fourteen or fifteen years previous I first came to my virginity due to the simple human fact of the onset of my monthlies?

And he was singing now, too. Anthems, sea chanteys, tunes to hornpipes: "Rule Britannia," "Popeye the Sailorman." My astonished parents downstairs, staring up at the ceiling toward my room had to be; mother; my struck-dumb dad. Outraged, or humiliated, or even pleased as punch that Lawrence, Crown Prince of England, to whom, if all went well, he would one day be King Father-in-Law, might be up in her old room serenading and di--dl-ng his one-and-only daughter.

Which is when I opened my eyes. At the thought of my dad in the lounge. At the thought of me mum holding tea. I opened my eyes. Outraged, humiliated. But still into it (the sex act an annihilator of character, too, indifferent not only to time and space but also to circumstance), horny withal, I mean.

To see Lawrence watching me.

"Your eyes are open," he said.

"Yes."

It was his hang-up. All that old business about his inability to make even n-mber one in front of his mates at the Academy, his Prince's shame in having to -art and s-it and pi s like other men, the reason he nursed his own v--gin-t-, his Prince's aversion to ever having to show his throes. It was probably the reason he'd resisted making love to me since that day in the wicky-up.

I was suddenly fearful. Though I soon enough saw I needn't have been. Because maybe if you hide your throes long enough you forget you ever have them. Maybe all throes, even the most humble, lowly throes of the body, like having to cough, say, or sneeze, happen in what you think is a vacuum, in some almost unpopulated world of princes and kings. Because he never saw my outrage, didn't even notice my humiliation. Only—I was still horny, recall—the remains of my pleasure.

"What are you looking at?" he asked, not unkindly.

"I'm looking at my Prince," I said, Mother and Dad already forgotten.

"Why did you open your eyes?" he said.

"You opened yours first."

"I wanted to see if love disfigured you."

"Does it?"

He kissed me on my eyes. I loved him more than ever then. More than when I couldn't read him, all those times he merely had me jumping. More than the time in Llanelli, in Wales, when he did the bravest, noblest, most generous thing I'd ever seen done, and had not so much lost as traded however many thousands of pounds it was, to Macreed Dressel at the Springfield.

But he couldn't leave well enough alone. I guess no one can.

"You never opened them in Cape Henry," he said.

"Oh, la," I said with whatever modesty I have, "Cape Henry. I didn't know you very well in Cape Henry."

"What was it, Louise?" Prince Lawrence said. "You can tell me."

"*Lar*-ry," I said.

"No, really," he said, "we're to be married. Surely a princess may speak her mind to a prince. I supposed you were making the world go away. Please?" he said.

"The absolute truth?"

"Oh, absolutely."

"I'm not any ostrich," I said. "I don't shut my eyes and imagine the world anyplace else than it already is."

"I'm no more ostrich than you are, Louise," Lawrence said. "I know you weren't a virgin when I met you. You're a grown woman, for God's sake. You'd been to California. You'd worked as an au pair. You lived on a beach in a tourist attraction and had a great tan. You think it bothers me you weren't a virgin? It doesn't, it doesn't at all. You're a commoner, you're not to the manner born. You're not held to the same standards. One supposed you could have been fantasizing."

"What, making up a man, you mean?"

"Yes," Lawrence said.

"I had the Prince of England on top of me. Why would I make up a man?"

"Oh, Louise," he said, and kissed me on my eyes again.

But I saw that he had mistaken me, or that I had misled him. Like him, I couldn't leave well enough alone.

"It was another man, actually," I said.

"What, a man in the States? Not your employer?" he

said. "The one that engaged you, whose child was entrusted to you?"

"No," I said, "certainly not."

"Oh, Louise," he said, "*not* when you were in the hotel! Not for some man in the hotel where you worked turning mattresses and changing sheets? Like any common, comely chambermaid?"

He was grinning from ear to ear.

"I was perfectly faithful when I was in America," I told him evenly.

"Ah," said the Prince, "I was right. On that beach then."

"No," I said, "not on the beach. Not ever in exile."

"In exile," he said.

"For almost two years I had an affair with Kinmonth-Schaire, the newspaper publisher. I was never, in the conventional or continental sense of the term, his 'mistress.' He did not 'keep me,' he did not 'provide' for me. He did not even have a key to my flat. We were 'lovers' in the ordinary star-crossed ways of our times. He was twenty-seven years my senior, and married. At the time he was only penciled-in for his OBE. We knew that even the faintest *whiff* of scandal would have put the kibosh on that quick as you can say Jack Robinson. *Plus,* he had a daughter my age engaged to be married to a fellow a class-and-a-half up from her own, *and* a wife who was both delicate and busy with preparations for their daughter's wedding.

"What can I tell you; we were star-crossed; our timing was off, our cusps and zodiacal signs. Our houses were in the wrong neighborhoods.

"He gave me the money and asked me would I lie low in the States for six months. In three he'd have his OBE, he told me; in four his daughter would be safely married; in five he'd tell his wife about me and ask for a divorce, and in six it would be both safe and seemly for me to come back from America.

"And do you know something? He was right on the money, and as good as his word, he really was. He became Sir Sidney Kinmonth-Schaire, OBE. The daughter married,

Stanley Elkin

and he told his wife about us and asked for the divorce. And
do you know what? Do you know what she did? The delicate wife? Can you guess?"

Lawrence looked at me.

"She laughed at him. She laughed and petted him and
gave him a kiss on his eyes and said he was a fool, dear, and
supposed that she must be one, too, but she'd have to forgive him because when push came to shove she guessed that
that was the only choice left fools, because didn't one fool
deserve the other, and if he could just manage to let her
know next time he felt himself going off the deep end they
could put their fool heads together and come up with a way
out of their muddle that might just save everyone embarrassment. She didn't see any way round it, she said; he'd
probably just have to eat the few thousand pounds it had
cost him to put me up in America for those six months, she
said."

"OBE?" Larry said.

"Order of the British Empire."

"OBE?" Larry said.

"*Lar*-ry," I said.

"I never minded you weren't a virgin," he said. "It didn't
bother me to think of you sowing your wild oats with a
fellow your age on a blanket set out on a beach in Cape
Henry; nor even your doing it with some businessman type,
a commercial traveler, say, someone in town for a sales conference, the two of you making steamy love in the Los Angeles hotel where you served as a housekeeper, thrashing
about on the very bed in the very room you'd have to make
up yourself when the two of you had finished. I minded
none of this, Louise.

"But an OBE?

"I'm not small-minded, Louise. I could have overlooked
it if the fellow in question had merely been one of my subjects. It wouldn't have mattered to me he had seen you naked, had seen you in *your* throes!

"But an OBE? *An OBE?* An OBE is practically peerage,
the next best thing anyway. Never mind the title is honor-

ary, symbolic. An OBE has certain privileges. Ask Royal Peerager. An OBE? one might have to look him in the eye each year on the afternoon of the King's Birthday Party under the canvas tent, or out on the lawn at Buckingham Palace.

"I'm not small-minded. I'm not.

"*Oh, Louise,*" he cried out, "*what have you done, what have you done? Oh, Louise, what have you done? What you have done, Louise,*" he cried out, "*what you have done!*"

I hope I can explain this next part. I said "he cried out." He did. I mean it *was* a cry. It was fury and outrage and despair, the sound of a magnificent, powerful beast, new to pain, angered, stymied in a trap. A mortal noise so terribly affronted it was almost dignified!

Father, that soft, deferent, obeisant man, came running; Mother barely a step behind him. They burst into what— how can I put this?—now something historical had occurred there, had ceased to be my room.

"What," my father, confused, blind to my nudity, blinded by the Prince's, said, "what? What? What? What?"

"*Get out!*" Lawrence screamed. "*The both of you! Get out, get out!*"

"Don't you shout at my parents," I said, "don't you dare. Never mind what he says," I told my father, who had already begun to back out of the room. "His powers are only symbolic," I told him.

"Well, of course," Father shuddered, "all real power is," and closed the door behind them as they left.

People have only heard rumors. Up till now no one *really* knows what was in the message Larry wired the Noël Coward King and his Noël Coward Queen on board their Royal Yacht on what was supposed to have been their final world tour as reigning monarchs. Well, 'Sparks,' of course, I suppose he'd had to have known. There's always some 'Sparks' or other on duty when these important, eyes-only Ems telegrams go through, but apart from him, no one. I myself didn't understand how one minute I could be engaged to a prince in what was to have been, in light of King George's and Queen Charlotte's mutual, simultaneous abdications, perhaps the most colorful, elaborate ceremony in the history of the realm, and the next minute, bam, the clock had struck midnight, and, all sudden widdershins, Cinderella was just another pretty face.

Larry told me. I didn't ask. I don't even think I wanted to know as much as he wanted to tell me, as though he were dying for me to find out just how clever he was, throwing his cleverness around like a drunken sailor.

"Three little words," he said. "Three little words and you were done for, Louise. You know what they were? You know what I said in that telegram I sent?"

"What did you say in that telegram you sent, Larry?" I asked like his straight man.

"SHE'S HAD MISCARRIAGES!"

They said they'd take me to court if these installments appeared.

They're blowing smoke, of course. They don't go to law like regular people, these people.

So they threaten me. But I'll tell you something, Sid, I don't think they can touch me. After all, as I keep on saying, I promised to tell all but I haven't. Not all. Not yet. There's at least two column inches I'm holding back against a rainy day.

Meanwhile, I don't know, maybe next time they'll get it right, do it better, wheel-and-deal the way people like them are supposed to wheel-and-deal. Have the King, what do you call it, issue a proclamation maybe. Send out this call for the most beautiful virgins in the land. Set them tasks. Winner takes Prince, takes Crown, takes all.

That's about it, I guess. The only thing I don't get is why you offered me money for my story. I mean what could possibly have been in it for *you*, Sir Sid? I mean it isn't as if you come out smelling like a rose or something. For a time I put it down to your sweeps-week vision, your tabloid heart, but that can't be all of it, I think. Perhaps you hold a few column inches of your own in reserve.

What could they be, I wonder? Pride? The thrill of cuckolding a king? Even if it's only at some double remove, once for before Lawrence even knew me and the other for before he was ever a king.

Or those throes, perhaps, their veronican image, for the refractive, fun-house homeopathics of the thing, some hand-that-shook-the-hand-that-shook-the-hand apostolicity of love.

You men!

Van Gogh's Room at Arles

When the Foundation sent him there, Miller had absolutely no idea that he was to be put up in Van Gogh's room in the small yellow house at Arles. Indeed, he'd no idea that the room still existed, or the house, or, for that matter, even the hotel across the street that it was part of.

Madame Celli simply handed the key over to him on the morning of his arrival. No special fuss or flourish or ceremony. The key itself, which couldn't possibly have been the original, was attached to a short chain, itself attached to a heavy iron ball about the size of a plum. The number 22 was stamped both on the key and on the ball along with, in French (a language that Miller didn't have but whose vocabulary lists he'd memorized through the first few weeks of the second term of his freshman year in high school, *la plume de ma tante*), on the ball, a tiny metal legend (he made out "*boîte aux lettres*") to the effect, Miller supposed, that if whoever found it dropped it into a post box, the postage would be guaranteed.

It was this key, almost as much as the fact of the room itself, that afterwards was so stunning to Miller, the offhand way of it, the stolid fact of the ball and chain from which it depended like a key to a room in a second- or third-class railway hotel where travelers who were too weary, or too ill, or who could simply go no farther, might stop for the night.

This was a peculiarly apt description of his own condition the day he got there, exhausted as he was from the long series of flights and layovers. Indianapolis to Kennedy, Kennedy to Charles de Gaulle, Charles de Gaulle to Marseilles, and then the three-hour ride by motorcoach from Marseilles to Arles. Though this was the most spectacular leg of the journey (Indianapolis pals had specifically recommended the slower bus as opposed to the much faster train) because of the dramatic views it provided of Mediterranean fishing villages, the lavender vineyards of the Languedoc region, and the queer, boiling iridescence of the waters in the Gulf of Lions, from certain angles and in certain light like a great voile oil spill, Miller had registered almost none of it, only a few blunted impressions whenever the bus or the oppressive incrementality of his own soiled, staggered mileage jolted him awkwardly awake for a few moments.

So unceremonious, so unpropitious even, was Miller's reception, he was actually touched when Madame Celli agreed to allow him to leave his things—the big suitcase, his hanging garment bag, the plastic sack of duty-free liquor, film, and cigarettes purchased at Kennedy with almost the last of his American money—— another tip from the knowledgeable Indianapolis crowd: that he'd get a more favorable rate if he exchanged his dollars for francs at some one-or two-teller bank, or even at one of those cash vending machines, while he was still at the airport—in the lobby with her while he went off to find his lodgings at Number 2 Lamartine Place across the square from the old hotel that seemed to be the Foundation's main building in Arles. He'd come back for them after he freshened up, he assured her, an efficient enough, even agreeable-seeming woman, but one whom Miller had sized up as essentially uninterested in the various jet-lagged-out states of the Fellows the Foundation kept feeding her all the year round, one or two at a time, for month-long stays at twice-a-week intervals.

These perceptions had been established long before he'd ever actually laid eyes on her, for it was Madame Celli with whom he'd been in correspondence since he was first informed that his fellowship had been granted. Well, correspondence. On his part thoughtful, practical letters asking thoughtful, practical questions—— the weather one could expect in April, what forwarding address he should leave for his friends, the advisability of renting a car, if there was a dress code. And, on hers, in a charming, unexpected, quite witty English, only the salutation written in ink at the top, form letters, hospitable, boilerplate responses to inquiries he had no doubt she could reproduce in Spanish, or French, or Italian, or German, or in almost every EC language any of those one or two staggered, twice-weekly arriving birds of a month's passage might throw at her. Which only added insult to the injury of Miller's fatigue and took a little of the shine off his having been selected or, if not exactly selected, then at least approved by the Foundation. Which, too, was why he was so touched by Madame's routine boilerplate courtesy to his simple request that she permit him to leave his things in the lobby while he lumbered off without having to lug along the additional burden of thirty or so pounds of cumbersome luggage. It seemed a sort of relenting. She was, after all, mistress here, empowered, he didn't in the least doubt, by the Foundation with all the authority of a ship's captain, say, at once hostess, concierge, enforcer, and housemother. It was she, after all, who had assigned him to an outbuilding rather than to a room in what he had already come to think of as the administration building.

Scraping favor, he asked, in as close an approximation to French as he could muster, just where, exactly, he was headed.

"Vous voulez dire, monsieur?"

It wasn't the first time he had failed to make himself understood.

"I guess none of you people has had the benefit of the first term-and-a-half of freshman-year French," Miller said, and repeated his question in English.

Madame led him outside and pointed out the yellow house to him.

But if Monsieur was to freshen up wouldn't he be needing some of his toilet articles out of his valise?

"It's a done deal. I've got it covered," Monsieur said and,

feeling like a fool, but unwilling to go back into the lobby with her or to squat down over his suitcase rummaging through its contents while she watched, held up his laptop word processor.

There were only four rooms. Number 22 was to the left at the top of a flight of red brick steps at the rear of the small ground-floor hallway, and the key, it turned out, was just to his room, not to the house itself. The house could not be locked and, indeed, the other three rooms were either entirely or partially open to the gaze of anyone—Miller, for example—who cared to look in. In fact, it was only the door to Miller's room, warped, stuck shut in the Provençal heat, that was closed at all.

He saw that it had no toilet and would have called Madame but he saw that it had no phone either.

Some Foundation, Miller thought, some big fucking deal Foundation! Some big goddamned honor having them approve my project! Had to pay my own damn airfare! And some Madame Celli while we're at it! Big linguist! Some witty, charming command of the English fucking language *she* must have! Doesn't even know "freshen up" is the idiom for having to take a piss! Yeah, well. She even said that about needing my toilet articles out of my valise. Yeah, well, he thought, that's probably the idiom around here for go piss in your suitcase.

But really, he thought, a month? A month in Arles?

He shouldn't have listened to her, Miller thought, he should have rented a car.

And he was sore. Well, disappointed. No, he thought, sore. Sore *and* disappointed. If it had been beautiful. Or in important mountains instead of a sort of clearing among distant minor hills. Or on the sea instead of better than twenty-five miles away from it. What was it? From first impressions, and Miller was one who put a lot of stock in first impressions, it seemed to him to be a kind of gussied-up country market town with a faint suggestion—its long stone railroad trestle that traced one edge of the town like a sooty rampart, its several dubious hotels, bars, and work-

Van Gogh's Room at Arles

ingmen's restaurants, the gloomy bus station and cluster of
motorcycle agencies, bicycle-repair shops, and, everywhere, on the sides of buildings, on kiosks and hoardings,
on obsolete confetti of dated posters for departed circuses,
stock-car races, wrestling matches; even the small municipal
park with its benchloads of provocative, heavily made-up
teenagers in micros and minis, their clumsily leathered at-
tendants who looked more like their pimps than their boy-
friends—of light, vaguely compromised industry. What *was*
it? Well, frankly, at first blush, it might almost have been an
older, downsized, more rural sort of Indianapolis.

This was his impression anyway and, though he'd keep
an open mind (Miller hadn't many illusions about himself
and pretty much had his own number— a fellow of only
slightly better-than-average luck and intelligence, an over-
achiever actually, who had pretty much gone the distance
on what were, after all, rather thin gifts, even his famous
"selection" more a tribute to his connected Indianapolis pals
and colleagues who'd vouched for him, written him his letters of recommendation, than to the brilliance of his project), he knew it was going to be a long month. (Unless it
was to be one of those bonding deals—boy meets girl, or
fate, or somesuch under disagreeable circumstances and, by
degrees, through the thick and thin of stuff, ultimately
comes to embrace or understand what he'd hitherto
scorned).

Still, Miller, though he'd finally discovered the common
toilet and shower (a tiny room on the ground floor just to
the right of the stairway that he'd mistaken for a closet), felt
he'd every right to be uncomfortable. He was not a good
traveler, had no genius for its stresses, for dealing with the
money, the alien bath fixtures, the foreign menus that
turned meals into a kind of blindman's buff; all the obligations one was under in another country, to drink the local
wines, buy the local laces and silks and blown glass, honor-
bound not to miss anything, to feel what the travel guides
told him to feel, to see all the points of interest, but fearful
of being suckered in taxis and hotels and never understand-

ing how the natives managed. Missing nuance, sacrificing ease and the great comfort of knowing one's place.

This room, for example, which (though he'd seen and admired the painting at the Art Institute in Chicago perhaps a half-dozen times) he still didn't *really* recognize (and so, for that matter, didn't experience even the least sense of déjà vu) as Van Gogh's bedroom at Arles and which, even after the reality of where he was staying was confirmed, he still wouldn't entirely believe, attributing the undeniable correspondences between the room and its furnishings to some sort of knockoff, a trick on the tourists. (Which wasn't logical, Russell would argue, Miller being a guest of the Foundation. What could possibly be in it for them? Where was the profit?)

But (speaking of foreign travel, tourists, even Van Gogh would have been a tourist here, wouldn't he?) this room.

Miller's first impression of it was of a utilitarian, monastic-like setting. It reminded him of rooms in pensions, bed-and-breakfasts, no mod cons provided, not even a radio or simple windup alarm clock. He knew without sitting on them that the narrow bed would be much too soft, the stiff, rush-bottom chairs way too hard. (Nothing, he suspected, would be just right for this particular Goldilocks in the room's close quarters.) Though he felt—oddly—that one might spend one last fell binge of boyhood here in the narrow orange bed and rush chairs along these powder blue, shaving-mirror-hung walls of the utile. The basin and pitcher, majolica jug, military brush, drinking glass, and apothecary bottles clear as gin, a soft summer equipment lined up as if for inspection on the crowded washstand on the red-tiled, vaguely oilcloth-looking floor, poor Goodwill stuff, nitty-rubbed-gritty YMCA effects, weathered, faintly flyblown and pastoral, the narrow strips of pegged wood for towels, jeans, a T-shirt, a cap, all the plain, casual ready-to-wear of hard use. A few pictures were carelessly tacked to or dangled from the room's wash walls. A boy's room, indeed. A room, Miller saw, of a counselor at a summer camp, or of minor cadre, a corporal say, in an army barracks. Miller saw himself becalmed there, doing the doldrums in study's stock-still Sargasso seas.

He went to one of the room's big shuttered windows. Through a southern exposure, flattened against the town's low hill, Arles seemed to rise like an illusion of a much larger city. Out the window on the eastern wall he looked down on oleander bushes, shrub chestnuts, and yews, a lone cypress in the tiny courtyard of the small yellow house.

A boy's room. He could already picture himself noiselessly masturbating beneath the scarlet cover on the rumpled sheets and pillowslips yellow as lemons or margarine on the too-soft bed.

Someone knocked at the door. Miller's first thought was that Madame Celli had dispatched a servant to bring his things from the main building across the Place. When he opened the door, cracking it like a safe (it was still stuck from the heat, he had to pull up, give it a sharp twist and tug, applying, he didn't know how, the sort of "English" only a person accustomed to opening it this way might know, a leverage impossible to describe to a second party, a user's leverage, an owner's), he saw that the person across from him was no servant but a well-formed, immaculate little man (the word "chap" occurred), vaguely knickered, white-shirted, and argyled, like someone got up in old-time golfing garb.

"Hi there," said the man in Miller's doorway, "I'm Paul Hartshine. Kaska told me you'd be in. Saw you dribbling out of coach class in Marseilles this morning. *Tried* to catch your eye, but you were bottled up in *Douane* and I had to catch *le train grand vitesse.*"

Miller had never seen the man in his life but reasoned that Hartshine was a fellow Fellow scheduled to arrive in Arles the same day as himself. He'd evidently taken the fast train down while Miller had bumped along on the bus. And what was that about his dribbling out of coach class, a shot? And the remark about *Douane*. (*Douane* was the word for Customs. He recalled it from a vocabulary list.)

"Kaska?"

"Kaska Celli," Paul Hartshine said.

"Certain Indianapolis friends of mine especially warned me against the fast train," Miller said.

"Oh?" said Hartshine.

Miller didn't want to get into it. He felt like an asshole.

"Are you a downstairs neighbor then?"

"Me? No, no, I'm at Number 30 Lamartine." The man grinned at him, and it occurred to Miller that it may have been because Miller was quite literally blocking the doorway, filling it up—Miller was large, shaggily formed, almost a head taller than the fastidiously built little guy over whom he seemed to loom like a sort of ponderous weather—that Hartshine, sensing the absurdity of Miller's protective, defensive stance, found him amusing. (As he would, overheated, exhausted from his travels, burdened by his bulging garment bag, and clutching his ridiculous sack of duty-free prizes like flowers taken from a vase on a table at a wedding dinner, have been found amusing, as, he supposed, anyone in coach class might have seemed amusing to anyone in first, or anyone still hung up in Customs might appear at least a *little* silly to someone already waved through, or, when all else was stripped away and you were down to final things, the one on the bus was a laughingstock to the one on the train!)

Before Miller could move out of the way, however, Paul Hartshine was bobbing and weaving, impatiently trying to see around him and into the room as if, it could almost have been, Miller were some quasi-functionary, an observer of the technicalities, and Hartshine a reporter, say, there on behalf of the public.

The man had him pegged as one kind of asshole, so Miller stepped back and Hartshine poured through his defenses, talking away at a mile a minute.

"Look at *that*, will you?" he cried out to Miller. "I can't believe it. I'd never have guessed! *Would you?* Did you ever see anything like it? Well, this, this *is* a find! I'd *never* have guessed, I tell you! Well, one couldn't have, could one? The fourth wall! Just look. Just look there! *Everything that didn't get painted on the room's fourth wall!*

"Look at that chest of drawers! Well, you can see why he chose not to have painted that. It's entirely too grand for the room. I bet its proper place in the room was where that rush-bottom chair stands now. Next to the door. He must have rearranged it to make the room appear more rustic than it actually was."

"It's rustic," Miller said, thinking of his long, uncomfortable flight in coach, of the rough ride from Marseilles on the bus, of having actually to sit in one of those chairs, "it's plenty rustic." But if Hartshine heard him he gave no indication.

"Cunning," Hartshine said, "absolutely cunning! Wasn't *he* the old slyboots?

"And isn't that a piano bench? He must have had it from the bar. Doesn't he remark in a letter to Theo somewhere that there was a piano bench in the room, that sometimes, as an exercise for his back—it *is* damp in Arles—he sat on it to paint?"

He meant Van Gogh. It was Hartshine's reference to Theo that finally made him recognize where he was. In reality, without "rendering," the room could have *been* just another bed-and-breakfast. Now, Miller thought, what with Hartshine's relentless gushing, it was rather like living behind a velvet rope in a museum. He hoped he wasn't on the tour.

"Oh, I almost forgot! Kaska told me to tell you, if you're sufficiently freshened up by now, lunch is in fifteen minutes. There's no formal seating chart except at dinner but you'd better hurry if you expect to get a decent table. Sit with me, I'll introduce you round. I should think the other scholars will have already taken their drinks on the terrace, but if you're very quick perhaps Georges will make you one to take to your table with you. I'll ask him."

"I'll ask him myself," Miller said, determined to take his time and wondering at Hartshine's power to drive him ever deeper into asshole territory. When he was good and ready he'd cross the street by himself.

In the end, however, Miller hastily spit-combed his hair before the shaving mirror above Van Gogh's washstand, and hustled the lollygagging Hartshine, still examining the contents of the bedroom at Arles as if he were preparing an inventory, out the door.

Hartshine introduced Miller to Georges, who got him his drink even though the bar was already closed.

They entered what Miller was given to understand was the night café.

"You know the painting?" Hartshine said out of the side of his mouth.

"What did they do with the billiard table?" Miller said out of the side of his own.

Miller, in tow with Hartshine, was walked past all the green baize-covered tables set against the high red walls in the big square room. It felt rather like a promenade. The fop, pausing at each table, had a word with each pair, trio, or quartet of diners, and introduced Miller. He met, in turn, though little of this registered, Professor Roland de Schulte, Paul and Marilyn Ames, Farrell and June Jones, an Ivan someone, a chess master from the Kara-Kalpak Republic, a South African black man named John Samuels Peterboro, and a female composer from the University of Michigan named Myra Gynt. Hartshine introduced Miller to Lesley Getler and his wife, Patricia, married, chaired sociologists, one from the University of Leiden and the other from the University of Basle in Switzerland. There was Arthur Barber, a mathematician from the University of Chicago, and perhaps a dozen others whose names passed through Miller like a dose of salts. Well, everyone's did, really. Along with their disciplines, and the institutions where they held their chairs. He had never met so many high-powered academics in his life. The entire Ivy League must have been represented in that room. (Hartshine himself was from the University of Pennsylvania.) And even though he couldn't have told you a moment after he'd met them—it was exactly like arriving late at a party and being introduced to all the guests at once—who any of these people were, Miller was dazzled, filled with a sense of giddiness and elation. He recognized the names of people whose important, newsworthy op-ed columns he thought he had read in the *Times*. Certain faces were vaguely familiar to him from television news shows during times of national and international crises, think tankers with gossip and expertise whose opinions were sought. He was very close to calling on the sort of Dutch courage one feels in the first stages of drunkenness. Thus, when during his goofy circumambulation of the room the Oxfords, Harvards, Princetons, Cambridges, Columbias, and Berkeleys were introduced to him, along with the Göteborgs, Sorbonnes, Uppsalas, and Heidelbergs (where the Student Prince matriculated), he experienced divided, contrary impulses: to stand taller, this urge to stretch himself toward the full height of his respectability; and a mild outrage like a low-grade fever. A war between super ego and id. He was, for example, torn between asking someone he was almost certain he'd seen discussing the Arab-Israeli question during several segments on MacNeil-Lehrer whether one was paid for such appearances or, since it was public television, it was done pro bono. He was tempted, too, to nudge some Harvard shit in the ribs, wink, and tell him yeah, he thought he'd heard of the place.

Toed-in, all aww-shucks'd out, he'd let it ride, said nothing, stood unassumingly by as Paul Hartshine (who seemed to *know* all these people, who, according to his own testimony, like Miller himself, had only arrived that morning, a first-timer in Arles) introduced him to almost everyone gathered for lunch that afternoon in the night café.

"This is Miller. They have him in Van Gogh's bedroom at Arles. You ought to see the place. Miller's from Indianapolis. He teaches there at the Booth Tarkington Community College."

Everyone was very nice to him, they invited him to join them. They saw the drink Hartshine had talked Georges into giving him even though the bar was closed and suggested that he at least sit down with them while he finished it. They were very nice. They couldn't have been nicer. Miller wanted to kill them.

Hartshine, Miller suspecting that perhaps he knew this—why not, Miller thought, he seems to know everything else—hustled him off to the next table. They sat down at last with Kaska—— Madame Celli. Who, or so it seemed to Miller, flirted a bit with his peculiarly outfitted but well-tailored friend, and then, in what Miller could make out of her French, excused herself, having, she said, things to attend to in the birdhouse where smoke was falling off all the potatoes.

"Boy," Miller said to Hartshine when she'd left, "that fast train you took down?"

"Yes?"

"It really *must* have been fast! I mean you get around, don't you? You already know everyone here."

"Well, you do too. I introduced you."

"The only name I remember is Georges's," Miller said glumly.

"The servant's?"

"I'm in league with the servants."

Immediately he felt like an idiot. Well, he thought, *almost* immediately. It took time for his idiot synapses to be passed along their screwy connections. Cut that shit out, he warned himself. You've as much right to be here as any of the rest of these hotshots. Hadn't the Foundation put him up in Van Gogh's bedroom in Arles? Little Hartshine had practically pissed his plus fours when he'd seen it. *Look at that, will you? I can't believe it, I'd never have guessed! Pinch me, I'm dreaming, why don't you? Just look at that chest, just look at that chair! How rustically cunning, why don't you!* Prissy little faggot! In Indiana, in the old days, he might have taken a guy like that and committed, what did they call it, hate crimes, all *over* his faggoty little ass! And now look at him, breaking baguettes with the fella. Well, thought Miller, drowsy from his second glass of wine (on top of the drink, on top of his jet lag, which, if you'd asked him the day before yesterday or so, he'd have told you, as he might have told his widely traveled Indianapolis intimates, was nothing but a psychosomatic snow job; that time was time, an hour was an hour was an hour, what difference could it make to the body where you spent it? though he realized now, of course, there must be *something* to it, even if he'd yet to hear any explanation of the phenomenon—interesting, now it was happening to him; more interesting than anything, everything; than the historic bedroom in which they were putting him up, than the famous Provençal sun, or the countryside, or the vineyards, or all these chaired, op-ed, think-tanker, PBS media types put together—that made any sense), my my, feature that, Mme. Kaska + M. Hartshine. Why *him*? Why Paul? Why *that* little go-gettem go-gotcha? Miller overwhelmed, Miller drowning in his beer in his heart. (He could at that moment almost have been, Miller could, slumped in absinthe at lunchtime in the night café, one of the Old Master's stupored-out lowlifes.)

But time doesn't stand still in a flashback or in the stream-of-consciousness, and Miller, pulled up short, noticed that the little guy was grinning, amused in a way that could only have been at Miller's expense.

"What?" said Miller.

"Oh," said Hartshine, "I was just thinking."

"What?" Miller said.

"Well, it's just that you were coming *into* the country."

"I beg your pardon?"

"This morning. In Marseilles. You were coming *into* the country. You don't have to clear Customs when you come *into* the country. When you go *back* to America, that's when you have to clear Customs!"

"Yeah, well," Miller said, "I looked dangerous to them."

"Oh? Dangerous?"

"I fit their profile," Miller said.

"Please?" said Hartshine.

"Look, it's only my first trip, okay? I was in Montreal once, but I was never overseas before."

"Really?" Hartshine said. "Really? You're kidding!"

"No I'm not."

"Yes you are, you're pulling my leg."

Miller watched the outrageously dressed man, now staring back examining Miller with almost as much astonishment and wonder as he'd lavished on that unpainted fourth wall in Van Gogh's bedroom. Was he really such a freak? Hartshine continued to stare at him as if Miller were something between a sport of nature and an act of God. He would be thirty-seven his next birthday. (Which he'd celebrate in about three weeks and which just happened to coincide with his tenure in Arles.) Was it so surprising that someone his age should not have made a trip abroad before this? If pressed, he supposed he could tell them he'd had none of the advantages—— too old for Desert Storm, a hair too young for Nam. Then, too, when he was an undergraduate, there'd been no junior-year-abroad program at his university. (It had come up. The state legislature was unwilling to spring for its part of the liability insurance.) He hadn't back-packed through Europe, nor worked his way across on a cargo steamer. His parents couldn't afford to give him a summer abroad, and he'd never known the sort of people who might have set him up in some cushy job as intern in the overseas office. As a graduate student he'd had enough on his hands just trying to finish his doctoral dissertation. So, what with one thing and another, he'd slipped through the cracks of his generation, Miller had, and if it weren't for his cockamamy project he might still be, well, back home again in Indiana.

Still, it wasn't as if he were this wonder of the world or something, and if Hartshine didn't quit staring at him as if he were forty-two of the hundred neediest cases, with just that edge of sympathy, reassurance, and conspiracy curling around his expression like a wink (as if to say "My lips are sealed, your secret's safe with me."), Miller might just pop him one.

Jesus, Miller thought, what's with this violence crapola? I'm not a mean drunk. Hell no, I'm sweet. So cool it, he cautioned, behave yourself. No more anger. But where's the damn waiter? Those other guys are on their fourteenty course already. I'm hungry! (On *top* of the drink, on *top* of the jet lag, on *top* of the anger!) Just fucking calm down, will you? Just fucking make allowances, just fucking when-in-Arles.

"*Waiter!*" he exploded. "*You, garçon! A little service. A little service over here!*"

"Miller, please," Paul Hartshine said.

Had this occurred? Had he actually said these things? He looked around the room. No one appeared to be paying any attention to him. They seemed as caught up in their discussions, building their solemn, elaborate, intellectual arguments, scoring their various points, as when he'd first come into the night café. Much less disturbed than Hartshine when Miller had acknowledged it was his first trip to Europe. He took this as a sign that the outburst had not really happened, and for this he was truly grateful. (Boy, he thought, am *I* in trouble!)

"Miller, please," Hartshine said, "what's wrong? Is something wrong?"

"No. Why?"

"You seem uncomfortable. You're making these disagreeable faces."

"I'm hungry. I'm a bear when I'm hungry. I mean, how about you? Ain't you anxious to grab up your clubs and get back to the greens?"

"Hold on. Lunch is coming."

"I mean on top of the drink, on top of the jet lag, on top of the anger."

But now the waiter was shaking Miller's napkin out for him and, without so much as grazing him, cast it across his lap in a gesture like a sort of fly fisherman. Miller watched the linen settle gently on his trousers and, on top of the drink on top of the jet lag on top of the anger on top of the hunger on top of the hallucination (which he mustn't mention to Hartshine), was suddenly as content as he could remember ever having been in his life. The waiter's attentions wrapped him in a kind of cotton wool and he felt, well, like the privileged movers and shakers at the other tables. If things had been otherwise with him, he considered, if a few more balls had taken the right bounces, or a few more calls gone his way, why, he would have been as well served in self as the best of them. Life was a game of inches.

He heard the waiter tell them in French that but that because Madame Celli had become invisible in the laundry two horses must begin to be. Miller politely added his thanks four thousand times over to Hartshine's own and sat stiffly back as the man dealt out three plates of appetizers in front of the three place settings.

He wasn't born yesterday. He knew *calimari* meant squid. He had even watched with a certain queasy sort of fascination as a sophisticated pal ordered and ate them once in the dining room of the Indianapolis Sheraton. That he didn't choose to do more than introduce one of its ten purply, clawlike, little baby arms past his lips had less to do with its rubbery texture or its faintly, he suspected, forbidden taste, than with its jet black, gelatinous coating.

He removed the thing from his mouth and held it out by its small caudal beak. A few drops of dark fluid spilled on the toast point on which it was served.

"This would be what, its like ink then?" he remarked to his dinner companion.

"Oh, look," Hartshine said, "that one still has its suckers."

"I'm not big on the delicacies."

Though he quite liked his quenelles of pike, he had first to wipe off their thick, spiked whipped cream.

And didn't more than *sip* the bouillabaisse. Hartshine agreed, offering his opinion that while the stock was too bland, Miller really ought to try to spear up some of the lovely rascasse. He must be careful with the spines however, some were poisonous. Miller was. He laid down his soup spoon and fish fork. And was content to watch Hartshine spear great hunks of gray fish out of his soup. In their thick, piebald, mottled rinds they reminded him of the dark cancerous creatures behind aquarium glass. The sweetbreads smeared in anchovy sauce seemed sharp, foreign and, to

Miller's soured appetite, had the powdered, pasty, runny taste of eyes. Conscious of the waiter watching him, Miller didn't dare push them away. But burned his tongue on hard bits of spice and herbs laced into the bread like a kind of weed gravel. There were poached pears bloodstained by red wine. There was a sour *digestif*. There was bitter coffee.

Kaska (having evidently settled the problem of the two horses was no longer invisible in the laundry) had joined them again, rematerialized at their table. "Here," she said, "what's this? Is something wrong with your food? Clémence reports you have merely played with it, that you haven't touched a thing."

Now this got Miller's goat. (On top of the drink, on top of the jet lag, on top of the anger, on top of the hallucination and hunger.) He felt he had to defend himself, get things straight.

"Madame," he said, "it is true that I am only from Indianapolis. It is true that I teach at Booth Tarkington Community College. It is true this is my first trip to Europe. But I was born and raised in an Indiana town not more than an hour's drive from Chicago, that toddling town, city of the broad shoulders, hog butcher to the world, home to Al Capone and many another who with one cross look could scare the merde out of you. A place, I mean, of much seriousness and, for your information, my mother raised me better than that. She taught me that if I didn't like what was set on my plate I was to keep it to myself. Ask Hartshine if I made a fuss. Because I didn't. I never said a word, did I, Paul?"

She said he looked tired, she said it was probably the jet lag, the new country, the strange food. She suggested that perhaps he ought to lie down in the room for a few hours, that later she could prepare a tray for him and bring it over to the yellow house.

"Gosh," Miller said, "but my project."

She said he had five weeks, his project could wait, that no one really got any work done the first day.

His bed turned down, his yellow pillows fluffed, the shut-

ters on the windows angled to adjust the sun, he was installed in Van Gogh's room at Arles like a painting.

Madame Celli took away his water pitcher and returned
it full. She set it down beside him on the rush chair. "I'll put
your drinking glass where you'll be able to reach it. Will
you be all right?"

"Really," he said, "I'm fine. Much too much is being
made of my indisposition. It's probably the jet lag, the new
country, the strange food. All I need is to lie down for a few
hours."

Madame Celli looked at Hartshine. Hartshine looked at
Miller. "That's the ticket," Hartshine said.

"No harm done," said Miller, "no real damage. Unless—— "

"What?"

"Oh. Well. Nothing. Never Mind."

"No," coaxed Hatshine, "what?"

"What I asked before. I really never did say anything, did
I?"

"When? What? Complain about the food you mean?
No."

"*Did I make a scene? Did I shout out loud for the waiter?*"

"No," said Hartshine, "of course not."

"Well, all right then," Miller said, "then I was only hal-
lucinating. I thought I might be. No one seemed to be paying any attention. Of course, with that crowd, what would
you expect? They just carry on dum de dum, la de da, ooh
la la, with their usual business. Nothing gets to them, nothing. A fella from Indianapolis would have to have a Sherpa
and a Saint Bernard if he wanted to scale *their* ivory towers.
He couldn't just do it with a cry for the waiter! Those guys
don't hear the regular ranges. And who can blame them,
guys like them? No, they've their priorities. My *God*, they
do! Where to set the minute hand on the Doomsday clock,
or fix the borders in the New Geography. Handling the
headlines, worrying the world! It was a good thing it was
only a hallucination I had. God forbid I was starving, God
forbid I really needed a waiter in those conditions. Because

you want to know something? What I actually cried out in that hallucination was noise from the soul, the ordinary screeches and lub dubs of my Hoosier heart. Oh my."

"I like the way this man opens up with relative strangers," Paul Hartshine said. "I like how he gets up in your face."

Madame Celli said, "Let the poor man rest. I'm afraid we're exhausting him."

"No you're not," Miller said, "you're not exhausting me. I'm glad of the company. Truly."

He was. Madame Celli was earthy. Not, he supposed, his usual type, but a real babe. Older than him certainly—— forty, a year or so more maybe. Not matronly though. Anything but, as a matter of fact. How could he put it? Well, *European*. Probably she had hair under her arms. Probably her legs were not clean-shaven. (She wore dark stockings, he couldn't tell.) Possibly her teeth were bad. Possibly she wore no underwear. The broadness of her perfume might have covered certain feral odors, scents—— stirring messages from her glands and guts and organs. (Bidets would dissolve beneath her acids and grimes.) Hair plugged up her nipples. She was as foreign as the forbidden flavors and fluids of his calimari, the queer sweets and salts of all his difficult delicacies. (This odd, inexplicable concupiscence. On top of the drink on top of the jet lag on top of the anger on top of the hallucination on top of the hunger.) Sullenly, Miller recalled his pique at the memory of Madame's modest flirtation with Hartshine at lunch that afternoon. Would the fellow hang about all day? Reversing himself, Miller announced impatiently, "I'm better, I'm better. I'm tired is all. I need to get some sleep." Then, almost as if it were a threat, "I better get some sleep."

"The time!" the babe spoke up suddenly. "Monsieur Hartshine, have you forgotten the time? You will have missed your bus if we do not leave off. They will be going to the Alyscamps without you. Show me your ticket. Yes, that is just the one Rita sold you this morning. Run, you must hurry if you would catch your coach! Please, Paul," she warned, "under no circumstances should you go to your room for your camera! The camera is of no importance whatever, it is insignificant. There will be plenty of other opportunities for the camera. I vow you that. But for now entirely disregard it. And anyway Rita has many beautiful views of the Alyscamps, both wallet size and eight-by-ten, which you may purchase at the Fellows' official discount. *Run,* there is no time! Run and scamper! It would be too tragic if the coach should leave without you!"

Now I'm in for it, Miller thought. Now I am. What will this savage woman do to me? My condition, he thought. He wasn't up to any rough stuff. The jet lag, et cetera. On top of on top of. On top of Old Smoky. He closed his eyes and waited for the wild rumpus to begin.

When he opened them again in the strange country Hartshine and Madame Celli were nowhere to be seen of course.

Rita was the assistant in Madame Celli's office. She put through long-distance calls for the Fellows, she sold them stamps, exchanged money, cashed their checks. She took their wash to the launderette for them if they were desperate or particularly helpless, arranged for the odd emergency trip to the doctor or dentist and, through a brother-in-law who owned a bus, organized tours and day trips for the group. Speaking into a microphone in one of her several languages, she went along on these and provided a running commentary as their tour guide. Frequently, if the brother-in-law was unavailable, she drove the bus herself.

She was a bright, cheerful, pretty girl in her early twenties, supremely efficient, energetic, and, according to Russell, who knew about such things, was already regarded as one of the finest factotums in all of Europe. It was she, in fact, rather than Kaska, who prepared Miller's tray and brought it that evening to the yellow house.

He hadn't had anything acceptable in his stomach since before landing in Paris—could it have been only that morning?—and was beginning to feel hungry, though he was relieved to see that all the girl had brought him to eat was bread and butter, consommé, tea, and some fresh fruit. If she kept him company while he ate, he said, she could take the tray back, she wouldn't have to make two trips. It really hit the spot, he told her. After the rich, heavy meal of that afternoon, he told her, it was really delicious. Really. (It was Rita who informed him that the French took their big meal at lunch. If he wanted, she said, from now on he could have his consommé, bread and butter, fruit salad, and tea in the afternoons. Perhaps, she suggested, Monsieur might enjoy a nice cheese with that, a pleasant pâté, nothing too harsh. She would tell Chef. He could have omelettes for his suppers. Miller jumped at the chance. "You must think I'm a real wuss," he said, thinking perhaps she might not know the word. "Neither wuss nor wimp," she reassured him. "The taste bud is not a secondary sex characteristic.")

He asked about the afternoon tour, if he'd missed much, and was surprised when she replied that he had actually, yes. They had gone to Les Alyscamps, she said, and walked between the tall trees the length of L'Allée des Sarscophages beside the rows of limestone coffins where eighty generations were buried. What she told him did not seem delivered, a piece of her patter (though it occurred to Miller that of course it must be), but came out of her mouth almost conversationally. She described how Arlésienne wedding guests would leave the church directly after the ceremony, come out to L'Allée des Sarcophages and, sitting on the coffin lids, make a picnic of champagne and éclairs. Quite coincidentally, she said, such a picnic had occurred just that afternoon, he'd missed that.

"How extraordinary," Miller said. "Champagne and éclairs."

"Oh,"Rita said, "it's to do with the life cycle. The sweetness and sorrow newlyweds must expect."

"No," Miller said, "I meant the combination."

Had she flinched? It seemed to him, who had never really been able to read faces, who had seldom detected even a blush, or seen someone blanch, or understood the widely touted, famous signals of the eyes, that he saw *something* happen in her head, some faint temblor of hurt and shock.

(Miller too well guessed at its epicenter.) Because, he thought, earlier I'd been an asshole, and then (on top of on top of, etc.) went a little crazy, lay down for a few hours, woke up refreshed, managed to get something in my belly, and am now restored to being an asshole again. At least a fool. This is a nice girl, why should I cut myself off at the pass?

So he played it straight. Straighter. Got them back on the tour bus again, hurriedly asked her where else they had gone, what else they had seen. She answered mechanically at first, then (for she *was* a good sort or at the very least every bit the superb factotum she was cracked up to be) resumed the casual, conversational pace of her previous remarks.

From Les Alyscamps they'd climbed the hill to the Roman amphitheater. It was probably built in the first century, was a hundred thirty-six by one hundred seven meters, which was, let's see, maybe four hundred and twenty-eight, no, four hundred forty-*six* by three hundred fifty-one feet in Miller's money. It seated twenty thousand spectators. In the middle ages it had been turned into a fortress, which gradually became an actual town with around two hundred houses and a couple of chapels. The stones for its transformation had come from the amphitheater itself. Over the years the little village dissolved into a ruin, but excavation was undertaken in the nineteenth century—eighteen twenty-something, she thought—and the amphitheater was restored. It was really too bad he hadn't felt well enough to join the group today, she said. They'd climbed to the top of one of the three remaining watch towers to get an idea of the sheer massiveness of the arena. It had been very clear this afternoon. Their height had provided them with grand views. They'd been able to see all of Arles of course, but there'd been good views, too, of the Rhône, and of the Alpilles in the distance, and of Montmajour Abbey at the end of Arles Plain. Well perhaps another time. Yes, come to think of it, if they could get the bus, there were plans to go out to Montmajour Abbey tomorrow.

"When do they work?" asked Miller.

"Oh," Rita said, "everyone goes at their own pace here."

"It's a little like being on an ocean voyage."

"I have never been on an ocean voyage. I do not go at my own pace. I go at the pace of the others."

"Then that's your pace," Miller, landlocked in Indianapolis, who hadn't ever been on an ocean voyage either but who'd that very afternoon, beneath his napkin, momentarily felt himself benignly wrapped in the narcotic of his waiter's attentions and suspected the pleasures of deck chairs, of being held fast in tightly tucked blankets, and who now, this evening, tonight, in Van Gogh's room at Arles, contentedly surrendered himself to the barbery buzz of Rita's sweet voice, dreamily said. And who knew (Miller) that though he was rested now, restored to sanity, that his hallucination had been merely a hallucination, that the last thing in the world he wanted, the very *last* thing, was to get on a bus to go out with the others to Montmajour Abbey, whatever that was. That rested or not, restored or not, Miller could wait until it came out in an eight-by-ten. "Well, you know," he added, "perhaps I should stay in just a bit longer. I don't think I'm up quite yet for anything as rigorous as a tour. I may be coming down with something. I still feel a little funny. A little, I don't know, disoriented and strange. It could be the mistral."

"The mistral blows in the winter," Rita said. "I'll call a doctor if you don't feel better. But really," she said, "the best thing for your sort of malaise is not to give in to it. You should get up. You shouldn't lie about. You should try to make it down to breakfast. You must try to get out more. Make some friends while you're here. Monsieur Hartshine seems quite nice. He is very enthusiastic. He will get on nicely. Already, on the tour, I could see he is very popular with the other Fellows. He could introduce you, he could help you make your way. In any event, it is not a good thing to depend on trays and bland diets. I promised I would speak to Chef, and I will. That is no trouble. But it would be much better for you if you made some effort to adjust to the food. It isn't good for you to lie about all alone in the yellow house."

It was a lot to take in. Harder than the details and dimensions she'd been feeding him about Arles's historic buildings and monuments and parks, the grand tour as it might have been told to a blind man—— gently and patiently and with just enough consideration to make it appear as if she were rehearsing all this to him personally, even intimately. Now that it had *become* intimate—even personal—Miller was furious. He might have lashed out at any point in her lecture—— at her assumptions about what she called his malaise, about his social life, at any of her cheeky aspersions about his personality, even about her betrayal of his appetite. What he chose, however ludicrously (he was that furious), was what was nearest to hand.

"I am *not* alone in this house. There are three other rooms!"

"They are to be painted. No Fellows have been assigned to them. You are quite by yourself here." She turned to go.

"How many spectators did you say that amphitheater held?" he called after her as she went down the stairs "Thirty thousand? Twenty? Hah! *The Hoosier Dome in Indianapolis accommodates more than three times that many!*"

He thought he could hear his voice reverberating through what he supposed must have been the vacated, partially emptied-out, painter-prepared rooms. It sounded as hollow to him as his uncarpeted, unfurnished rage. But *God,* he was mad! Reason not the need and vice versa.

And was still going strong—to wit: why, the very idea! the nerve of that bitch! just who in hell—— *nobody* talks to—— if she thinks—— two can play at *that* game! if she thinks, if she thinks—— factotum, shmacktotum, *abada* figaro, *abada* figaro, figaro *la,* figoro *la!* because nobody can talk to me like that and still expect a good tip!—when suddenly the sound of his reproach just fell silent, just quit, fell dead away, every last damn reverberation collapsed in on itself like light down the toilet of a black hole, and he realized how far he was from back home again in Indiana and the glossy municipal comforts of Booth Tarkington Community College, where he not only had colleagues with whom he broke bread and ate lunch in the school cafeteria (to which not one of them had ever had to adjust), but his very own assigned space in the orderly, patrolled, tow-away-zoned faculty parking lot. His mood easing, eased through anger, melancholy, memory, and nostalgia, sloping away, declining downward like a grammatical form, and resolved at last to poor pure awareness.

Now am I alone, Miller thought, and sighed, and realized, appreciated, and for the first time since he'd been there recognized, not just where he'd come from, but where he had arrived. Miller in Van Gogh's room at Arles. Miller in Miller's room in Arles. And thought that whoever made the room assignments (Kaska Celli undoubtedly, Madame Low Down and Dirty) must certainly know her man. He not only meant himself, he meant Van Gogh, too.

Neither was in his element in Arles. They were about the same age. Both were bachelors. Both had been repudiated by the Establishment. Van Gogh never sold a painting while he lived and, what, you think Booth Tarkington Community College was the first place Miller applied or sent his curriculum vitae? He'd asked for a hundred jobs. It wasn't even the first place in Indiana. It wasn't even the first place in *Indianapolis!* Also, Vincent was a little nutsy too.

The day hadn't gone well for him, he'd been through a lot, he was tired, wrung out, tomorrow was another day. He made out the light. Though his fury had subsided he was still on edge. He got into their bed. He said his prayers. He pulled the drawstring of his pajamas. The secret of a long-lasting relationship, he told God, was never to go to bed angry. Rita was younger, and more beautiful, but her words had stung him. He was still too hurt. So he fixed on the older woman, on Kaska and, slowly bringing her into focus, the hair on her unshaved legs, beneath her arms, on the black, full bush that hung on the pantieless body under her skirt, and conjuring the stirring gale-force smells that rose off her flesh like all the molten perfumes of earth, Miller, coming, groaning, sighing, forgave the world and slept.

And woke next morning refreshed but somehow with no more urge to get up and take on the prospect of a new day than when he had first lain down.

"I'm not a malingerer," he told Hartshine, who had missed him at breakfast and had brought coffee, a brioche, a croissant, butter, some pony pots of jam, and a glass of juice over to Miller's room from the night café.

Today Hartshine had chosen a nautical costume—— white flared trousers and a wide-necked top of thick, alternating bands of black and white stripes. He looked vaguely like a gondolier.

"No, of course not," Paul Hartshine said. "We just haven't gotten our sea legs yet."

"What's this juice?"

"It's orange juice."

"Why's it red?"

"It's made from blood oranges."

"Figures," Miller said. Then, "I'm not, I'm *not* a malingerer."

"Are you really so very ill then? Kaska Celli is quite concerned."

"No," Miller said, "I'm not so *very* ill. I'm not ill at all."

"She's concerned."

"Now that makes me sore. It really does. She's the one that said I looked tired, that I ought to lie down. She diagnosed jet lag, the new country, the strange food. This isn't bad," he said, "though I prefer my orange juice yellow." He set down his glass. "She told me nobody gets much done the first day. I mean that really pisses me off. Ain't she the housemother here? I mean, my God, Hartshine, she must see malaise like mine two dozen times a year. Did she *say* I'm malingering?"

"No. This is a big opportunity. She thinks you should make the most of your time."

"I've got five weeks to make the most of my time. Nobody gets much done the first few days. Everyone goes at their own pace here. Like I suppose I'm the only one who didn't make it down to breakfast this morning. I suppose she takes attendance. I suppose she calls roll."

"Of course not."

"There you go then," Miller said.

"You *were* the only one who didn't make it down to breakfast. Well, Stanley Gassett wasn't there. Nan Hoffmann wasn't. Lesley Getler."

"Did I meet them?"

"You met Stanley. I believe you met Getler. Nan Hoffmann came in after we were already seated, I think."

"Well there you go then," Miller said again. "They don't sound any more reliable than I do."

"They didn't come down because they're making the most of their time. I heard Gassett banging away at his typewriter practically all night. Getler, too. Gassett's next door to me. Getler's working with him on the same project. They were still going at it when I went down to breakfast."

"They kept you up all night? That's terrible. Why didn't you say something? Or bang on the wall? No one should be allowed to interfere with another man's sleep."

"They didn't bother me. I was working myself."

"It was your first day," Miller said. "No one gets much done his first day."

"Oh," Hartshine said, "I didn't get *much* done. I knocked off after a few hours."

"Now what does that mean? That people will steal a march on me if I don't watch out? Are you assigned to me or something? Are you breaking me in? Is this the buddy system?"

"No," said Hartshine. "Nothing like that."

"Well," Miller said, "you can go back and tell her I'm settling in, getting the feel of things, getting the feel of Van Gogh's room. Because she's right. It is a big opportunity. Maybe, for me, even an historic one. God knows I'll probably never have anything like such an opportunity again. Hell, I don't know if I should even be flattered. Probably not. Maybe it's luck of the draw. Or maybe they pick the son of a bitch least likely to make it out of Indianapolis. I mean, *I* don't know. Maybe the Foundation matches up a Fellow's character and personality and prospects with where it decides to put him to bed. Maybe they debrief you when your five weeks are up, see if smothering you in the ambience of genius has any effect on the quality of your work. I'm in Van Gogh's room, man! I'm in Van Gogh's room in Van Gogh's house in Arles! You know the obligation that puts me under, the responsibility? You don't have to be an art historian. It's one of the world's best-known paintings.

"I'll tell you the truth," Miller said. "When I first saw this place it really didn't mean all that much to me. Well, I was tired. I didn't take it all in. As a matter of fact, I was a little steamed they hadn't put me up in the main building. That I was so far from the action. Not only that I didn't even have a toilet but that there wasn't even a toilet on my floor. That I had to go downstairs I wanted to use the facilities. You know what the place looked like to me? A bed-and-breakfast. I saw but didn't really take in the bottles on the nightstand, the cane-bottom chairs, the basin and pitcher. I mean I've known the painting it was based on for years, but when I saw the actual room there wasn't even this like shock of recognition.

"Only slowly, only gradually did it come over me. I'm using his things. I shave in his mirror, I drink from his jug. The miracle of that unpainted fourth wall that you pointed out? I sat on his piano bench against the fourth wall and contemplated his floor and bed and washstand and chairs and bottles and mirror and drinking glass and brown wooden pegs on the brown wooden strip on his blue walls. Who knew it was all so beautiful? I whacked off in his sheets."

"This is what you want me to go back and tell her?" Paul Hartshine said.

Miller, feeling heat (who couldn't detect a blush, who was effectively color-blind to the broad palette of the psychological hues in others), looked down in confusion. Was it possible Hartshine had guessed it was Kaska of whom he'd been thinking? Could he know that Miller (who wouldn't have vouched for the sailorman's romantic biases) had once considered him, and perhaps still did, a rival for the earth babe's attentions?

"No," Miller said. "Tell her, tell her I'll be coming down to the night café for supper."

And was as good as his word. (As was Rita as hers. Within moments of being seated—the night café reconfigured for the evening meal, the green baize-covered tables removed from along the walls and pushed together to make one grand table in the center of the room where the pool table stands in the painting, with what could have been the full company of all the Foundation's Fellowship surrounding him on the vaguely ice-cream-parlorish chairs— Georges presented Miller with a whopping gorgeous great omelette, cunningly folded in and over itself like a man's yellow pocket handkerchief. It was delicious.)

"There you are, Miller," Paul Hartshine said, sitting down beside him, having come in five or so minutes after Miller. "How do you like this? Isn't this grand?"

"What did they do with the billiard table?" he asked for the second time in two days, not so much as a wise guy this time around but as the interested scholar. And, when Paul Hartshine shrugged, he caught at the sleeve of a passing waiter, Clémence, the one he'd been rude to in his hallucination the previous day.

"Monsieur?"

"Didn't there used to be a billiard table in here?" he asked. From what Miller could make out from what the man told him, the table was cold eggs tonight but wouldn't be seen forever again until tomorrow.

Miller nodded, thanked him in French four thousand times over, and hoped it wouldn't rain.

It was amazing, he thought. Had the night café been restored or what? It was astonishing what a good job they had done. The big, bulbous, overhead gas lamps were electric now, of course, but somehow they had managed to replicate the precise illusion of waves of light that spin about the lamps in Van Gogh's painting like an aura. Unless, he thought, there was operative in Arles (or for those who came after him—like Miller, Miller thought—some mysterious persistence of vision, this optical trick of the Provençal light—even after the sun had gone down—that bent it and raised, even pushed, waves off solid objects like mirages burning in a desert), or operative for those who lived in his room anyway, or ate where he had eaten, this great participatory idea of things. Ain't I, he asked himself, seeing things through *his* eyes now? Ain't I beginning to, well, *render* the ordinary, even commonplace effects of the daily—— its beds and chairs and tables and towels?

It was a little scary, really. He wondered if he dare look up at the starry night for fear of discovering there flaring, burning balls in the sky, or ever fix his gaze again upon even the most innocent tree trunk lest it eerily bend and twist itself out of his glance. He'd accepted Georges's drinks, and even allowed him to refill his glass, but knew he wasn't drunk. Not on Georges's innocuous aperitifs.

He shook himself and concentrated his attentions on his eggs and toast and tea, on peeling his apple with his butter knife. Kaska Celli observing his performance from where she sat in regal charge at the head of the table. And capturing too, he felt, the wondering, even admiring glances of three or four of his fellow Fellows, guys, he shouldn't wonder, who'd thought, till they witnessed his display of the dessert carver's art, they had his number, had put him down as just another bimbo from down on the farm, alien to the sophisticated European skills of skinning fruit. Hah! Miller thought, basking. And took up a pear and proceeded to remove its pelt. And then a fruit—he supposed a fruit—he didn't recognize and wouldn't eat when he uncovered its black flesh. Still basking though. Fit to bust, as a matter of fact, if someone didn't ask him soon where he'd learned to handle fruit like that. Till seeing no one would he just up and volunteered.

"The truth is," he said forcefully into the crossfire of conversation, monologue, dialogue, discussion, and argument going on about him, "I never peeled a piece of fruit in

my life. I live in Indiana. How different can it be from whit-
tling?"

Even Miller had to admit that those who'd heard him—
though he'd barely made a dent in the din—looked at him
benignly enough, even benevolently, even, it seemed, inter-
estedly, expectantly, as though they waited for him to
expand on his theme. Miller was appalled, filled with snob-
bish, sudden disdain for his own boorishness. Still his little
audience looked to him for clarification.

"Oh, never mind," he said, frightened, realizing as soon
as he said it that it was true, "I'm drunk." (He'd been right
though. It hadn't been the aperitifs so much as the sack of
duty-free hootch at which he'd been sucking away—and
which was almost gone—in his room for close on two days
now.)

"But you make a good point," said a man several place
settings off. "I suspect the convention of taking a knife to
an apple or orange has less to do with dining etiquette than
with the hard practices of the old hunter/gatherers. Just the
residuals of some ancient exploratory hygienics. Slitting
open their prey with their flint to trim the diseased parts.
Then, by analogy, paring their fruits and vegetables as well.
A sort of stone-age quality control. Look before you eat,
that kind of thing. You make a good point. I agree with
you."

"Who *are* you?" Miller asked.

"I'm Russell," Russell said, a tall, cheery-looking man
with a rather large head who'd arrived in Arles just the day
after Hartshine and Miller.

Then, as Miller was about to respond, Madame Celli
tapped on her water glass with a spoon. All conversation,
monologue, dialogue, discussion, and argument dropped
off at once. It was, he thought, exactly as if a cease-fire, not
so much called for as demanded by an authority with whom
it would have been foolish to dispute, had gone into effect.
Miller felt this surge of immense, nutty pride that the very
woman whose image he'd invoked the night before when
he'd intimately handled himself should command such re-

spect and fear. It was as if his instinct and taste had been underwritten by all the moral and intellectual authority of the Foundation itself. It was as if he'd been seen with the belle of the ball.

"I rise," Kaska said, "ladies and gentlemen, to inform you that tonight, after supper, there is to be an entertainment in the music room. All are welcome. So as soon as you have finished your coffee please."

She did not resume her seat and, appearing to give a signal—it could have been the way she touched at her mouth with a corner of her napkin, it could have been the way, still standing, she laid her napkin alongside her cup, or her transitory smile—drew Clémence, Georges, and a waiter he didn't know yet in from the perimiters of the room to stand behind the Fellows' backs. Their presence seemed official, deputized, as if they had the power to enforce Kaska Celli's subtle coffee curfews and, indeed, most of the Fellows set their cups down without even bothering to finish them, and got up from the table.

Again, Miller felt a sense of pride in her powers, the sexual choice he'd made the previous night, a sort of ghostly, loony possessiveness.

Miller rose with the others as they moved off to the music room. He fell into step beside Russell.

"What do you suppose happened to the billiard table?" he asked for want of anything better to say.

"In all likelihood the felt must have torn," Russell said. "Or worn out. And the night café was a low bar, don't forget. There was probably a brawl. Someone must have been hit very hard, landed too heavily on the table, and broken the slate."

"Yeah," Miller said, "that's what I was thinking too."

What he was really thinking was, It's only five weeks. I'll live on croissants. I'll live on rich cheeses and pâtés and crackers. I'll live on fresh-baked bread that I'll cover with great heaping dollops of butter. I'll live on delicious omelettes. I'll live on delicious omelettes and pare my strawberries and raisins and apricots with a butter knife like a caveman. He has the largest head I've ever seen, he was thinking. He must wear a size nine-and-a-half hat.

The music room—there was a grand piano, there was a state-of-the-art CD player—was the single place in Arles Miller had seen that didn't look like an impressionist painting. It was a commodious, thoroughly modern, even modernistic, room with a pair of deep rectilinear sofas and big boxy chairs covered in light gray muslin. Great glass-topped tables in dark, matte-metal frames stood on matching brushed-metal legs in front of the sofas and, in smaller versions, beside each chair. Near the white bookshelves were two crushed—almost imploded—charcoal leather pillow chairs like soft fortresses or marshmallow thrones. Another chair, like a leather-and-steel cat's cradle, was positioned near the piano. There were cunning chrome lamps, museum-quality ashtrays, all appointments edge-of-the-field doodad and inspired house-dower, an ecology of lifestyle. It was as if the whole room has been designed by the art director of a major motion picture. Miller loved it.

Georges had wheeled in a portable bar cart and Miller, sunk deep in one of the big muslin chairs, was just getting comfortable with a large scotch-and-soda and enjoying the harsh, smoked-licorice taste of his duty-free Gaulois when a woman Miller hadn't noticed before stood up. Miller thought she was about to play the piano for them when, inexplicably, in his lap-robed, civilized circumstances, he suddenly started to cry. (Because if they could just see me now, he thought. Because just look at me, he thought, the kid from Indy. Because, he thought, this is the life. Listening to high-class lieder, art songs, words in languages he wouldn't understand set to melodies he probably wouldn't be able to follow. This *is*, this *is* the life, thought Miller in Arles, his stock-still ego laced with awe, no hero but a dilettante of idyll. Because if they could, if they only *could*. See him now.) And was about to snuff out his cigarette for the singer's sweet sake when abruptly, without even moving toward the piano, the woman began to speak.

She said her name was Anita Smynea and that she taught

theological psychiatry at the London School of Economics. (Miller figured it was an elective.) Her project in Arles, she said, would be to put together the raw data for a monograph she was preparing on a psychological profile of the saints and martyrs.

Miller listened fascinated as she reeled off evidence for her conclusion that the downside of their spirituality and devoutness was a zealotry even more off-putting and unpleasant than their self-rightousness.

"Oh, come now, really," one of the Fellows said, "off-putting? Unpleasant?"

"Are you serious?" Ms. Smynea said. "Those people couldn't get past the lowliest reservations clerk at Heathrow, let alone a metal detector!"

A man who identified himself as a political geographer spoke next, addressing the group in the music room from a wheelchair. He discussed his theories about why world-class cities were almost never found on mountaintops. From what Miller understood of his ideas it had less to do with the mechanical difficulties involved in hauling material up their steep, prerilous slopes than with some notion about "Man's innate fear of the sky and of exposure to most astronomical phenomena." Further arguing that the concept of shelter had as much to do with physical contact and sexual enterprise as it did with a need to protect oneself from the elements, he advanced the theory that from a child's security blanket on up the chain of architecture to the floor, the ceiling, the room, the apartment and neighborhood, one had before one the very type of the Platonic idea of "comfort." Thus, cities, mimicking lovemaking, were constitutionally "horizontal" rather than "vertical," and did not get built on the tops of mountains.

Miller, floundering, foundering, losing track, dropping behind, dropping out, was overcome with sadness. His interest, which was still high, availeth not. Unconsciously, he looked toward Russell for a sign of corroborative impatience. Russell was contemplative and serene inside his huge head.

It was someone else entirely who grew fitful, lost patience. "What is the point, please?" Paul Hartshine (now, for dinner, in a dinner jacket) demanded irritably.

"I'm a political geographer," said the cripple. "The point, of course, is that because of the synergy between the fear of sky-nakedness and sexual guilt there can be no such thing as a 'shining city on a hill.' "

"Denver!" Hartshine challenged.

"Denver is foothills."

A scholar from Hebrew University spoke about slang in the sacred texts.

Myra Gynt, a composer from the University of Michigan, explained how it was her intention to set the lyrics of various Broadway showstoppers to the more formal music of the twelve-tone scale—— serial composition, she called it. Miller watched closely as Ms. Gynt adjusted the piano bench and, inclining her neck first right, then left, repeatedly pressed certain keys at the high and low ends of the keyboard and played two chords to either side of its center. She was averaging, she said, testing to see if the piano was tuned. Her mouth turned sourly down at the corners, and though Miller could hear nothing wrong, she professed profound dissatisfaction with the instrument.

Miller sat back, luxuriating in the high-mindedness of his colleagues, taking pleasure in the word, the privileged, lofty fellowship of the communal it radiated, their joint fraternal, sororal mutuality of mission, dedicate, pledged to service history, as if there were something vaguely legislative about scholarship, the life of mind; at once neutral and senatorian in some wise old Roman way; there to learn, to sift, to consider, and then to choose. He'd been in the business maybe eleven years, but until that moment in France he had denied something noble and honorable in himself and hadn't realized what he should all along have taken for granted—— the collegiality of their enterprise, the professional courtesy one life owed another. He looked toward Russell, toward Hartshine, even toward the lame political geographer in the wheelchair, and smiled, certain that the look on his face

at that moment matched Russell's own almost godlike be-
nignity.

When Myra Gynt began to sing (he hadn't been wrong,
the lyric she'd chosen to transpose into her queer, discor-
dant, cryptic, rigorous new music was "My Heart Belongs
to Daddy" and was just as difficult for him to follow as he'd
anticipated the lieder would be), he felt a flush of pleasure.
If they could, he thought, bearing up under what he was
certain was good for him, ready at that moment, if a dish of
them had been passed round, to chew on the rubbery arms
of the squid, to lick from his fingers its black, bilelike ink,
if they only could. See him now.

And still luxuriated in his cozy aura of well-being and
pride when the famous Roland de Schulte of Harvard, modest and humble as the day was long ("Some of you may have
seen articles in a few of the scientific journals about work
being done in the pharmacological field to study a variety
of marine pathogens"), a shoo-in for the Nobel Prize in
chemistry if the FDA ever got off its ass and approved any
of a number of Professor de Schulte's promising homeo-
pathic preparations from sick sea creatures—— sharks that
were HIV positive, tubercular whales, cancerous eels, arte-
riosclerotic plaice. (Miller *knew* it sounded ridiculous, even
satiric. But *what* did he know? *What?* Any idiot could follow
the line of least resistance and laugh at what seemed far-
fetched to the touch and spirit. Any fool could send up what
he didn't love or understand. Myra Gynt's atonal music;
Professor Smynea's psychological profiles of the saints and
martyrs; Schiff's, the geographer's, wild analogies about
cities and making love. The Hebrew University guy's thesis
about Biblical slang, how the tetragrammaton itself was
merely coy, even facetious, coinage for all the not-to-be-
pronounced names of God.

And was still luxuriating, calm and at peace with himself
as a man in his tub, only less passive than that, beaming,
sending these messages of actual, active goodwill, this sort
of silly facial semaphore of the heartfelts and placables,
while Farrell Jones held forth regarding his conclusions

about the parallels between the mood swings of manic-depressives and babies, and Dr. Arthur Barber, Distinguished University Professor in Theoretical Mathematics at the University of Chicago, speaking in formulas, in signs and symbols, explained the implications of his research not only into the philosophic impossibility of the infinite number but of the high probability that a dozen could not exist in nature.

Miller was only gradually aware of this stamped rictus across his face, like a lingering sensation that he still wore a hat after he'd already removed it. The professor had lost him. Miller had lost his euphoria. And there was Miller, Miller thought, wooden, leaden, left behind, heavy as gravity and choking on a mouthful of his own stifled yawns as someone infectious conscientiously trying to hold in his germs. He tried to rekindle his attention but it had turned cold and gone out. If there'd been a mirror for him to look into he was certain he'd have appeared red-eyed, rumpled, in need of a shave.

Then the most peculiar thing.

Without meaning to, he caught Russell's eye.

Russell, watching Miller, even openly staring at him, distinctly mouthed, "He forgot to carry his two," and winked.

Miller, taken by surprise, embarrassed, shy as a schoolgirl, looked down at his feet. He felt himself redden, he felt himself grin. Fearful of looking up, he remained, head bent over the room's rich brown carpeting as if he were examining it for imperfections. His grin oddly fitting once the Getlers, the mutually chaired, married sociologists from Leiden and Basle, were into their turn. The term, Miller felt, not ill-considered since their area of expertise was the morphology of jokes and riddles. Miller was lost anyway. He understood them, those in English anyway, but had difficulty seeing the sociological implications the Getlers saw in them. Why does a chicken cross the road was, it seemed (despite slight variations in the answer), an almost universal riddle. Only in the most impenetrable New Guinea jungles and stone-age Amazonian rain forests where no roads existed, and arctic tundra and ice floes where no chickens did, was the riddle unknown. Frame of reference. Miller could dig that. What he couldn't understand was why so much depended on delivery.

What, he wondered, am I doing here?

Which, remarkably, was exactly what Russell asked him at that very moment. Tentatively, almost experimentally, Miller looked up from his post where he was inspecting the carpet. Russell, smiling, threw him and held a long, at least two-beat wink.

"What," Miller said, flustered, "are you talking to me?"

"Yes," Russell said, "why don't you tell the Fellows about *your* project?"

"You," Miller shot back almost hostilely.

"My project? Oh," said Russell, blowing it off, "just to think about things."

Miller's heart sank.

"What things?" he challenged. Because he was at a loss. Because he was cornered. Because he didn't know what else to say. Because he'd have given anything to be back safe in bed in Van Gogh's room at Arles at that moment. Because maybe he'd known even before he'd started to lose his phony well-being as he failed to keep pace with, or track of, the elevated star turns of the evening's show-and-tellers and had begun to expect to be called on himself (who even in Indianapolis in front of some of the better students at the community college had attacks of self-doubt, and sometimes couldn't help keeping the outright abject gratitude off his face during a night out on the town with his hometown betters—— reversing himself now, undoing his idle, informal invocation of their witness, his half-holy if-they-could-see-me-nows, suddenly suspecting that they could, that they actually could, the canny, cunning, knowing bastards, that they'd probably set him up!).

Russell talking now, breezily reeling off a list, possibly extempore, of various things he'd been thinking of the less than twenty-four hours he'd been in Arles, Miller only now tuning in, losing maybe two-thirds of what the huge-browed, immense-headed man had been saying.

". . . that if the holes in the ozone are real and the climates rearrange themselves, the temperate zone, pushing ever more northerly, sooner or later the prevailing culture will be the culture of the Laplanders, of the Inuits and Aleuts. How counterfeiting impacts upon inflation and, concomitantly, what the preponderant counterfeit currency—Deutsche marks, yen, francs, or dollars—along with its denominations can tell us about the true nature of the global economy at any given time. I mean to give some thought to how the endangerment and ultimate extinction of a particular species will affect fairy tales. How long will it be before *Goldilocks and the Three Bears, Little Red Riding Hood,* or *The Three Little Pigs* become obsolete? This would be a way of determining the half-life of the oral tradition.

"You?" Russell asked kindly.

The worst thing, Miller thought, isn't that the ball's in my court. No, he thought, not so much frightened as sick at heart (that same sick sinking heart of but moments before, which, as if it had fallen overboard, now felt itself to be turning over in some slow, twisting free-fall, snagged on the contrary currents of the thick, salted buoyancy in the death-dark sea, and thinking as he parsed all this: oh, *boy,* am I in trouble!), the *worst* thing is that Russell could probably have gone on. And *also* that the ball was in his court.

"Oh, *I* have a project," Miller said finally. "I had to have a project or the Foundation wouldn't have let me come. As a matter of fact, I'm depending on some of you to work with me on this. I was going to leave notes with Rita to put in your boxes. I simply haven't had time."

He thought he sounded reasonable. Not as razzle-dazzle as Russell certainly, nor as grand as the riddles, jokes, and infinity professors or some of those other guys, but reasonable. Clear. Talking like someone conducting a meeting, say. A sort of administrator, someone orienting the troops, telling them where they could get their letterhead, pencils, supplies. A kind of Rita himself actually, or even a Madame Kaska Celli. He even thought that so far, at least after all the dense, high-intensity talk they'd had to listen to this evening, his manner of speaking might actually come as a sort of relief, put folks at their ease. Why the hell not? It put him at his. He even felt his heart had stopped sinking.

"I," Miller said, "like you, am pleased and honored to be here. Certainly as pleased and clearly more honored. Well, I have no books, you see. Well, in community colleges, the sort of place *I* teach but scholars like yourselves wouldn't give the time of day and, quite frankly, don't have any reasons to think about much, where we consider ourselves lucky if our budgets can afford just to keep some of your seminal books amongst the library's holdings, and where we still manage to hold our heads up even if all we can work out is to connect up with some interlibrary-loan deal with a like-minded and similarly ground-down institution which might just possibly arrange to get one of your titles into the course instructor's hands sometime before the term is over, let alone the student's, it really isn't such a high priority to publish.

"Well," Miller said, "I don't mean to sound so negative. It isn't as if the community-college system doesn't serve its purpose in society. Admittedly, we're pretty much a bootstrap operation, but you'd be surprised how many of our kids graduate and then go on to earn real good degrees from our nation's most impressive four-year institutions, some of them. And even go on to apply to graduate school. I don't have the exact statistics in front of me right now, but I've read how almost half the nation's CPAs, tax accountants, franchisees, licensed real-estate brokers, and insurance salesmen have attended a community college sometime during the course of their academic careers."

He had their attention. They looked at him with that same aggressive kindness they'd shown when Hartshine had taken him right up to their tables to introduce him the day before. They looked at him, that is, almost hospitably, as if he were somehow their dubious guest. And Miller felt the same mild, useless, almost humble outrage. *Think tankers*, he thought, *fucking op-eders*. Holding his tongue at the same time that he wielded it. Like, say, Iago. And threw himself on their mercies as if he were daring them to drop him.

"Even so," said Miller, continuing, his heart no longer sinking he saw because it had already hit bottom, had come apart like any other settled, foundership, "I won't kid you, it ain't all roses and chocolates in our kind of operation. A considerable part of our student population is inner-city, and a whole lot more is, to put the kindest construction on it, well, vocational. Plus we get a host of boat people, and economic refugees, and English-as-a-second-language types. And a whole bunch of folks straight off the killing fields. And, well, a lot of what we do could be considered remedial—— glorified and not-so-glorified high school.

"So I guess you can see what a personal privilege it is for me to come in from the cold and be here among you for the next five weeks. I've listened tonight with great interest to many of your provocative, trailblazing insights and ideas, and let me tell you up front and just as frankly as I can that when I wasn't scratching my head I was catching my breath. I mean it. Who am I to butter *you* up? I mean it. Who am I to brownnose some of the greatest theoreticians and most famous hypothesists in their chosen fields? Where would *I* get off, a simple time server like me who's never been practically anywhere? I mean it."

He did. He really did. Who knew to the penny the exact amount of true awe and real viciousness he'd spent on them. He meant it, he meant it all. And knew, too, when enough was enough, that he better wind it up soon, was perhaps even now lecturing against the bell, but who had never appeared before a class like this before and, more than likely, never would again. But who *loved* his windiness. Who loved the sheer flourish, complicated as a monogram on a handkerchief, of his drawn-out speechifying, and who even at Booth Tarkington Community College, before the night school and boat people crowded in the two sections of the first, and pair of the second, and single section of the third course he taught—the five courses, the three preparations—loved above all the possibilities open to him in teaching, above love of learning, the possibility of doing good, of touching a life here, changing another there, the pure rock-bottom thrill, by sufferance here in Arles and the authority vested in him back at good old BTCC, of beating about the bush!

But who understood he was going too far, pushing against the envelope of even *their* compromised, condescendent patience. And who, in their shoes, would be shuffling his feet by now. (Though but twenty or so minutes before, in his own, he'd kept them still enough, his gaze locked in on the few square feet of scrutinized carpet, chased there by Russell's defiant wink.) Really, Miller thought, they were quite remarkable. For folks with so much on their minds, *quite* remarkable. They did even less shifting about in their seats than Miller's fender straighteners, hair stylists, data processors, communications majors, Central Americans, Cambodians, other assorted third worlders and drug dealers back home. Then again, according to Rita's testimony, these Fellows walked the paths beneath tall trees, climbed the hills, were sightseers by nature, viewfinders. Perhaps, to them, he was just another pretty sight, quaint as those champagne-and-éclair picnickers, a piece of the life cycle, the sweetness and sorrow. Well, he thought, I'll show *them*! I'll knock off the humility, sacrifice the sweet windiness, close down the tap dance, and just bring it on home!

But just couldn't quite. Since he'd failed to let them in on something, a matter of some delicacy.

He cleared his throat. (This, it occurred, was rather like a singer vocalizing, a pianist's tuneless scales.)

"Well," he said, "you can imagine. You can just imagine. I don't have to draw you any pictures or put too fine a point on it. Everything boils down to self-esteem. Those poor kids. I can't tell you how my heart goes out to them. I just can't tell you. Because the fact of the matter is they've no illusions. I have statistics. I bet two-thirds of you are on your second or third marriages. It's not my place to pry and I won't ask for a show of hands but I wouldn't be surprised if there weren't at least two people within the sound of my voice who've been married four times. At *least* four times. And that a lot of your romances were with students, and that they began, innocently enough, with some really sensational insight you dropped on them in one of your lectures, or in class discussion, or when they came around during office hours to discuss their term papers. Sure, you have the insights, they have the legs.

"Well that doesn't happen in a community college. There's no hanky-panky. If they run into us at the library they know it's not the Bodleian or the Widener, or see us climb into our cars in the parking lot they know full well it ain't Harvard Yard. What I'm saying, there's no stars in their eyes. To this day I'm single and not one of my students ever came on to me. They've no self-esteem," Miller said. "Or maybe that's backwards. The point is you don't get points for anything that comes out of *Cliff's Notes* or *Masterplots.*"

Someone raised his hand.

Uh oh, he thought, worried, recalling Hartshine's challenge to the crippled political geographer, the hard time Anita Smynea had been given by one of the Fellows, even Russell's private mockery of Arthur Barber, the infinity maven who'd forgotten to carry his two. "Yes," Miller said, "is there a question?"

"What's your project?" he asked politely.

"I'm trying," he said, "to get some idea of the image of the community college in the eyes of establishment academia." Then he fell out of his deep muslin chair and fainted.

When, moments later, he came to on the carpet (his tie had been loosened, his collar undone; establishment academia, giving him air, had moved back a floor lamp, his chair, cleared a broad avenue for him, and now stood patiently on either side of the room exactly like people quietly observing an accident from the curb), Russell, Miller's wrist in his hand, was on one knee beside him. He was grinning so widely someone might just have brought him good news and holding a wink so steadily Miller thought for a moment he looked like someone engaged in an odd athletic event, like seeing how long he could go before taking a breath, say.

Miller, embarrassed, said "Where am I, where am I?
Wherever in the world am I?" just to get Russell to open his
eye.

"Dr. Rey is on call," a girl said. "I sent for him."

"Rita? Is that you, Rita?"

They put Miller to bed in Van Gogh's room in Arles, and
though he heard them go down the stairs and leave the yellow house he had the impression that they'd left someone
behind to stand guard in the hall. Perhaps Russell, perhaps
Hartshine or Rita, or even the one who'd asked him the
question in the music room. Fear and anxiety—he'd never
passed out before—had left him half conscious during the
press of their urgent rush with him across the square to
Number 2 Lamartine Place. It seemed important to Miller
to learn who'd been chosen to stay with him, but he
thought it better to discover the identity of whoever it was
posted outside his door by listening to the nature of the silence, or whatever was done to disturb it, made by the person keeping the vigil, than to demand it outright. He closed
his eyes so he might better concentrate on the problem.
Never had his senses been sharper. He tried to judge his
guardian's sex and size by the creak of the weight made on
the flooring, to see if he could reconstruct the nature of the
clothing—its fabric, even its color—by the quality of the
sound—its rustle or rub—made when it was brushed by a
hand. And opened his eyes. To see could he detect some clue
in the breathing or make out in the darkness some gloomy
giveaway thickness or layer of shadow that might reveal the
character of its source. There was nothing. He received no
impressions, heard nothing, felt no pulsations shaken loose
from the brusque agitations and invisible jitters and shivers
of whatever body rested against the wall outside his room.
He *saw* nothing. And so he closed them again and went to
sleep.

Only to look when he waked, not so much refreshed or
even rested as startlingly wakeful, directly into the very odd
face of someone gazing down at him. The face was somehow as disturbingly familiar as it was strange.

"Oh," said the man, "I am penitent to startle you. You must are the ill American monsieur, Mr. Miller."

"Am I ill?" Miller asked, for he realized even before he took in the man's old-fashioned black bag he must be the doctor.

"This is something we will shall be deciding together. Dr. Félix Rey, Mister Monsieur."

"Do we know each other?" Miller said. "You seem familiar to me."

"Oh," laughed the doctor, "This is a common mistake I have so the likeness of my great-great-grandfather, Dr. Félix Rey, the médecin of Vincent Van Gogh, whom he attended for the amputate of his ear." He took a card from the breast pocket of his suit coat and handed it to Miller. It was a postcard from a museum gift shop with a reproduction of Van Gogh's "Portrait of Dr. Félix Rey."

"You *do*," Miller said, "you're his spitting image!"

"Not a handsome man," said Dr. Rey.

It was true. Both grand-grand-grandpère and grandfils had thin, vaguely Oriental faces like inverted equilateral triangles that were made to seem even more triangular by both the long, dependent Vandykes at the bottom of their chins and their flat, dark, brushcut hair. Astonishingly, like points of interest, the prominent left ears of the two young men (for they *were* young; both Miller's physician and Van Gogh's could not have been more than twenty-five or -six years old) seemed to flare out from the sides of their heads red as shame and exactly matched the shade of their full, pouty, Kewpie doll lips. (As they stood out against the general jaundice of their complexions.) Both men wore handlebar mustaches. Both evidently plucked their eyebrows.

Miller kept shifting his glance from the picture postcard to the great-great-grandson. For all the flawlessness of their unquestioned resemblance it seemed a bit stagy, as though one of them were cross-dressing, say, or as if some feature on one of their faces—the beard, the plucked eyebrows— had been cultivated for a specific effect, accented as a nose or a hairline in a caricature.

"It is very remarkable, is it not, Mister Monsieur? Do I state the case amiss? One might summarize that Vincent was so geniused that he fixed the gene pool forever with his picture brush. But you will see from your eyes. There live in Arles to this day descendants from the peasant Patience Escalier; the postesman Joseph Roulin and his femme, Berceuse, their sons, Armand and Camille; and of Madame Ginoux and of even the fierce Zouave."

Handing back the "Portrait of Dr. Félix Rey," Miller wondered if the physician had picked up his English in much the same sort of way Miller had picked up his French, studying rubrics on the backs of postcards as he had memorized vocabulary lists. Yet there was something about Dr. Rey's speech Miller, admittedly no student of languages, didn't quite buy. His accent, measured against the accents of Frenchmen in films, seemed wrong. It wasn't so much uncultivated as uncluttered by their smoky, theatrical rumble and heavy breathiness. It seemed to Miller that even the man's syntax was off by four or five hundred miles, as though it belonged at least that much further up the Mediterranean coast.

Now Rey listened to Miller's heart, tuned in on his lungs, took the measures of his pressure and pulse and temperature. He examined Miller's ears, ran light into Miller's eyes, palpated Miller's belly, dug his fingers painfully deep into Miller's groin. He had Miller gag three strained *ahh*s under a rough wooden tongue depressor. He had him sit along the side of the bed and tested his reflexes with a little hammer. He took his pressure a second time, removed the stethoscope again from where he had stuffed it into a jacket pocket and asked Miller if he minded submitting to a second examination of his chest. He breathed on the little black disc at the bottom of the stethoscope, warming it the way one might move breath across one's lenses before rubbing them clean with a tissue. Nothing the doctor had yet done so alarmed Miller as this little gesture of solicitude. Then he had Miller cough. Hard. Harder please, s'il vous plaît. Press, Miller interpreted freely, the pedal to the metal.

And Miller, accommodating, coughed with such force that he brought up the reduced, soured biles of the gorgeous great omelette, toast, tea, peeled fruit, and apéritifs of his delicious dinner. Félix Rey gave him a handful of toilet paper, which he removed from his doctor's satchel.

It had been a thorough, even arduous, examination. "Is something wrong with me? What's wrong with me?" Miller asked nervously. "I'm no hypochondriac, doc, but I have to admit, ever since my arrival I've been a bit off my feed." It was so. Whatever else, appearances to the contrary notwithstanding, Miller generally enjoyed good health. Almost thirty-seven, he was still active in sports, still played a good, hard-driving pickup basketball game with the students in the BTCC gym, or handball at the Indianapolis Y. Unlike many others younger than himself he detected no loss of spring in his step under the boards, and was, despite his liquor and cigarettes, still a strong jumper, and an aggressive, even combative, player. He usually drew more fouls than any other player on his team. (Indeed, he had a small reputation as something of a bad sport, and had always vaguely equated this as a sign of stamina and good physical health.) And on the lively YMCA handball courts he was as quick as ever, his aces and killers as devastating as they had ever been. "What's wrong with me," he asked again, "am I ill?" And felt, who'd been unable to pick up any of the steams and busted light waves pouring off the solid objects in his darkened room, his alarmed features anxiously arrange themselves on his face.

"Mais not, Mister Monsieur. I am just remarking what strange fabulousness is it that the physical qualities of so differents citizenships should such often present liberté, égalité, fraternité, the European as well as the Berber, the Berber as much as the Japanese, the man as the woman, a Mexican like an American like a Jewish gentleman like a Turk. Palpation and respiration and the rate of the heart are demonstrations. The Zulu and Eskimo are both at normal at centigrade thirty-six degrees.

"There is nothing needed for further testing, Monsieur

Sir. Of wounds to your body there are none presenting.
Nor pathologies neither. I have not need to take your blood,
I have not need to collect your urines. If there are damages
it is in your spirit you are weakly."

"My spirit?"

"Oui."

"My spirit?"

"Non non. Do not alarm. It will see you out the night."

"The night. Terrific. That gives me, what, seven hours?"

"And more. How long is your arrangement at Arles?"

"Five weeks. This is my second day."

"Mister Monsieur is an artist?"

"I teach at a junior college in Indiana."

"But Mister Monsieur's soul suffers?"

Miller stared at the odd-looking physician with his queer,
Oriental, triangular face. He fixed on the man's fiery left
ear, his dagger's-point beard, the sprawling flourish of his
mustache like elaborate handwriting above his almost fem-
inine lips. It was almost all he could do to keep himself from
laughing at its foolish excesses. "Yes," he admitted quietly,
"it sure does."

Then Dr. Félix Rey looked about the room, taking in his
surroundings for apparently the first time.

"This is where *he* live."

"Yes," Miller said.

"Yes," said Dr. Rey, "I have been here. Oh, many years
since. But not much since the Foundation have kept it for
Fellows. Well," he said shyly, "for a group photograph
once. Of the Club of the Portraits of Descendants of People
Painted by Vincent Van Gogh. Here, may I present? My
pleasure, my pleasure."

He produced a second postcard from somewhere in his
suit and extended it toward terminally cracked-spirit, soul-
weakened Miller, a blurry black-and-white photograph of
people as vaguely familiar to Miller as Dr. Félix Rey had
been. In it, ranged about Van Gogh's room at Arles, which
somehow disappeared, was absorbed, swallowed up by their
relentless, insistent, novelty presence as some historical

place (where a famous general had died of his wounds, say, or the room where an important document had been signed or great book written) might be by the presence of tourists, were the peasant Patience Escalier, Joseph, Berceuse, Armand and Camille Roulin, Madame Ginoux (who herself bore a striking resemblance—they could have been sisters— to Kaska Celli), Rey himself, and the fierce Zouave. Six of the eight were crowded onto the room's two chairs and along the side of Van Gogh's bed. The other two, the postman Roulin with his salt-and-pepper, broad shaggy beard so layered with hair it was impossible to make out his neck or determine whether he wore a tie, or even if his shirt was buttoned, and the dashing soldier boy, surprisingly slight but with a large head and a powerful neck, posed for their picture in what was left of the room, in a small clearing on the tiled floor. It reminded Miller of some remarkable class photograph. (Good heavens, he thought, this might have been taken at one of the English-as-a-second-language courses back at Booth Tarkington.)

"We have not changed a day. It is as if the time stood still."

"Indeed," said Miller.

"I am a physician, Roulin is a postesman. Even the young lad is demob'd from the Foreign Legion."

"And the peasant, Patience Escalier, is he still a peasant?"

"He *is*! It is a thing wondrous how that man wizardized us with his masterpieces left and right. It is beyond *my* poor proofs and scientifics. Art has its mysteriousness, eh, sir mister? We eat its dusts."

Miller, though it struck him as an odd observation even at the moment he made it to himself, noticed that he was totally without appetite. Not even the burning, sour, transformed taste of his supper, still in his mouth from the bile he'd brought up when Dr. Rey had him cough, left him with even the most remote urge to clear it, neutralize it with a sip of water, the relief of gum. He guessed, too, that he'd had enough of Dr. Félix Rey.

Though he had complete, almost surprising, faith in Rey

as a doctor, he understood that there'd been no reason to draw his blood, he understood that a sample of his pee would have revealed nothing of interest, and though Miller was as taken with his peculiar distinction (his residency in Van Gogh's room at Arles) as the physician's mad notion that in painting his great-great-grandfather, Van Gogh had somehow laid a spell on the great-great-grandson and fixed his fate forever. This, Miller realized, was probably *not* good medicine and he would have been content to bid the doctor goodnight and been permitted to turn the young man's diagnosis (that he was weakly in spirit) and prognosis (that it would likely see him out his sojourn in Arles) over in his mind.

Then he noticed the muzzy class photo Félix Rey had given him and which he'd briefly examined and set down on the washstand. "You'll want this," he said and made to return it to the physician.

"Non non non. I insist not, Mr. Miller. It is yours to keep it. It is but a cheap trinket. The club makes them up."

"Well," he said, shifting, "thank you." Miller, whose health, until Arles, had been so good he'd not had enough contact with doctors to understand that it was they rather than their patients who sent such signals, nevertheless hoped Rey had picked up enough English from the rubrics on his postcards—on this one, too, everything was in four languages—to guess by such shifts that their meeting was over.

As it happens he had.

Félix Rey rose from the rush-bottom chair beside Miller's bed. "I shall see in on you again, Sir Mister Monsieur."

"You don't think you'd better leave me something to help me sleep?"

"What, pills?"

"Well sure, pills if you think that's what I need."

"An injection? Powders and sedatives?"

"You're the doctor," Miller said.

Félix Rey looked at him. "Did you know, Monsieur Mister, that it was to this chamber your neighbor called my great-great-grandfather on the night of the blood from the knife on his ear?"

"What," Miller said, "because I asked you for something to help me sleep?"

"Does Mister have a gun?"

"If I had a gun do you think they'd have let me through airport security?"

"Knifes?"

"Please."

"Ropes and poisons?"

"If I had any of that stuff what would I need with a sleeping pill?" Miller asked reasonably.

"Please," said the doctor, "raise no hand against yourself. I know your position. You've nothing to fear from your position."

"My position?"

"Your position, your bloom, your hale and your hardy. Your soul is a little sprained. It's nothing. We see it all the time. If you like, I can ask them to alter your accommodations. It would be nothing."

"My room? You mean my room? I *like* my accommodations, my accommodations suit me right down to the ground!" Miller shot back angrily, furiously really.

"Please? Suit you right down to the ground? Rest. Please Mister. I will see in on you."

He was a country doctor, Miller reminded himself after Félix Rey had left. He was nothing but a country doctor. And a self-proclaimed curiosity. (Miller put him down as probably the president of that Sons of Van Gogh's Subjects, or whatever it was, that he so liked going on about.) The Foundation probably called on him more for his language skills than for his medical ones.

What, Miller's soul was sprained? He needed a doctor to tell him this? Ask the man who owns one! was all Miller had to say about it. And then the silly sod wouldn't even leave him with a lousy sleeping pill to take a little of the edge off his god-awful wakefulness. What had he told him? Raise no hand against himself? This was his considered medical opinion? Well, thought Miller, we'll just see about that! And then, to ease a little of that soul sprain and lift a little of the edge off that god-awful wakefulness, Miller, calling up images of Kaska Celli, got a wrong number, got Madame Ginoux instead (but who looked so like her) and, imagining the round, competent arms beneath the heavy sleeves of her thick black dress, raised a hand against himself and whacked off.

Gradually he lost track of the days, of the time he had been in Arles. On some days (though he couldn't and wouldn't have said whether the condition of his spirit and soul—how did hospitals put it?—was satisfactory or serious or critical) he went down to breakfast or even had the kitchen make up a box lunch for him to take with him on his ambles through Arles. One afternoon he walked by himself out to the olive orchard that Van Gogh had once painted and had his bread and cheese and bottle of wine and then settled down to sleep under the pale pink blossoms of its slender trees. (Where he dreamed of a wedding couple making a picnic of champagne and éclairs on the limestone coffins alongside the tall trees in Les Alyscamps where Rita had taken the Fellows on his first day in Arles. The groom was the peasant Patience Escalier, and his bride was Berceuse Roulin. They fed and toasted each other while Miller wept for the sweetness and sorrows of life. He wept into their champagne and wept over their éclairs, and when he woke up in the olive orchard he had a salty taste in his mouth, which even the last of his wine would not loosen.) Another time, without in the least knowing where he was headed, he found himself at the Arles-Bouc Canal where he came upon the Dutch-looking drawbridge of Van Gogh's famous painting, vaguely resembling one of da Vinci's sketches of a military device, some water catapult, say. Other times, however, he slept in, and couldn't, at the end of the day, have said whether his spirit and soul were the better or worse for their lack of wear.

What he'd told his doctor (this is how he thought of Félix Rey, though it had been more than a week since he'd seen him) was true. His room at Arles suited him right down to the ground. He did no work on his project and his laptop PC remained unopened even to write the letters he had promised his pals back in Indianapolis. If he'd been able to bring himself to write any letters at all in that room they would have been to Theo, but Miller had no brother, let alone any Theo, and the idea of spilling the beans about himself to anyone else struck him, even after his performance in the music room, as an absurdity, even an act of hubris. (The one time he *did* turn on the laptop all he did was doodle, making odd designs and even faces out of the period, exclamation point, pound, asterisk, paragraph, section symbol, ampersand, dollar, slash, percentage, left and right bracket, single and double quote, plus, minus, cedilla, diacritical, tilde, hyphen, underscore, and other signs he did not know the name for on his keyboard. Alas, Miller thought as he turned off his PC, I'm no Van Gogh.)

On the whole, however, if only to avoid the Fellows' questions, he usually chose to be away from Number 2 Lamartine Place more often than he chose to be in it.

So he would find himself—the weather had been amazing—outdoors, sometimes taking a bus to the edge of town and then striking off on his own. Or, if the bus went to some small village nearby, getting off there and then striking off. Once he rode all the way out to Saintes-Maries-de-la-Mer, about twenty-five miles from the city. When he stepped down from the bus and out into the dusty street (more a lane than a street) he had the sense of having been there before. Perhaps he had passed through on the coach during the long ride from Marseilles to Arles his first day in France. This might have been one of those places he'd been momentarily jolted awake and that had left him with his few rough impressions of that journey. But the name of the village was familiar, too. Surely he wouldn't have retained that as well. While he was looking at the row of peculiar but quite beautiful cottages with their layers of tiered, dyed thatch like actual crops of roofs contoured into the architecture, and their whitewashed sides like thick stucco brushstrokes, it occurred to Miller that he *had* seen this street before. Not on the bus but in one of Vincent's paintings. Then a wind blew up, filling his nose with the strong smell of brine. Of course! thought Miller, cuffing his head, suddenly recalling one of those first weeks of the second term of his freshman year in high school. *La plume de ma tante!* It's like riding a fucking bicycle! *Saintes-Maries-de-la-Mer!* Nothing was wasted in life. Those vocabulary lists! He knew his French would come in handy one day. "Mer" *means* sea! Then, facing the wind, tracing the source of that brine, turning this way and that, going up one lane and down another, he came at last to a clearing from which he could see the Mediterranean and where there, on the beach, lined up it seemed to Miller almost exactly as they had been lined up in Van Gogh's painting of the scene, were four pretty little fishing boats, one red, one green, and two blue, their anchors struck into the sand. Their owners were nowhere about. Indeed, except for one shining white gull, the only other signs of life were four other boats diminished in the distance in the Gulf of Lions.

He was not, Miller understood, a man given to epiphanies. Who, him? With *his* soured soul and sick spirit? Him, *Miller,* the man from Indy who—get his dumb aria and parlor-game melodramatics in the damn music room out of your head—had not once during all the times this or that had been "familiar" to him in this queer foreign country, not—count 'em—once ever put down to déjà vu or anything faintly psychological any of his creepy encounters and strange doings. Yet he had his epiphany now. It was this. All his rambles and maunderings of the last few days, all of them, why it was like being on a scavenger hunt! That's it, that's right, thought Miller, a scavenger hunt for Van Gogh's sketches and watercolors and oils, this was what his half-ass project came to, this was what the meaning of his off-again, on-again raids into Arles and its countryside had turned out to be!

He was in Arles at the entrance to the public garden. A man stood with his legs planted so far apart that they might almost have been kicked into position by police. The man was reading a newspaper with the upper half of his body while darkly clothed men and women sat isolated on benches in the attitude of mourners taking time out from their grief along the sidelines of a community nature in the community air. Van Gogh had painted just such a scene. Miller turned away and would not look.

He was approaching at street level the broad, bluish stone steps of the Trinquetaille Bridge, an iron pedestrian bridge across the Rhône. He recognized the bridge as the subject of one of Van Gogh's paintings. He would not look.

On another occasion he found himself walking south along the Avenue de Montmajour. At almost the last moment he looked up to see that he was about to step under the railroad-bridge underpass a few blocks up from Van Gogh's room at Arles in the yellow house at Lamartine Place. Van Gogh had done two views—an oil and a sketch—of the underpass. Rather than go past the site, he turned about and went the long way round to his room.

He would not look, he would not look. He would not look at the Provence farmhouse the color of mustard with its haystacks high as a house, or at its low pink stone walls and gateposts. Nor glance at the isolated cypresses rising in the distance behind it like high green flames.

He would not look at the wheat fields set out before him like so many landscapes. He would not look at the sheaves, at the clouds, at the low outbuildings.

He saw a sower, a youth of seventeen or eighteen wearing a hat like a cloth pith helmet, a great bag of seeds attached to him like a paperboy's sack, and striding forthrightly through the fields like someone on a brisk walk. Crows hovered above the seeds and a little way back of the sower. He wouldn't look.

There were immense, brilliant sunflowers. He would not look at the sunflowers. He avoided gazing at them as he would have avoided staring into the sun itself.

And so, in this way, Miller was at last driven back to Van Gogh's room at Arles. Which, unless the bed were unmade—he rumpled it in the morning after a housekeeper had made it up—or he had rearranged the washstand and chairs, he would not look at and could not stay in.

He spent time in the music room, seeking it out because it was one of the few places around Lamartine Place Van Gogh had not painted.

People came by—the music room was a public space, open to all the Fellows—and always saw him there. He listened to CDs. He read *The International Herald Tribune*. He browsed American magazines as out of date as the copies in barbershops and dentists' waiting rooms back home. After a while he just sat, changing every once in a while from this chair to that or switching to one or another of the room's sofas to create at least the illusion that he was not simply vegetating.

People respected his privacy even more than he did, but because he was too shy (or too much at a loss for something to say to them) to initiate conversation, he waited for someone to speak to him first, waited for a signal. A simple gesture of the hand, a nod in his direction would have done, just some preemptive eye contact would have, but no one, perhaps because their memory of his behavior in this room was still too fresh, ever offered it.

His feelings for his situation, that he was outgunned in this country, outsmarted, outmanned, overwhelmed, overcome, did not make him anxious to return to his room, however. Yet there was no question of his quitting Arles, or even France, and returning early to America. For one thing, he had neither the funds for gallivanting about Europe (and even if he had, what guarantees were there that there would not be sights in any of those other places that wouldn't pull him up just as short as they had done here?) nor the nerve to admit to his Indianapolis pals that he couldn't go the distance. And, frankly, there was an even more practical reason he could not quit Arles. His job, at least the possibility of his being promoted to Full Professor, may very well have been on the line. Miller had no reputation as a scholar. He hadn't published so much as a textbook. He wasn't, he thought, a *bad* teacher, but the fact was that his classes didn't always make and when that happened and (always at the last minute) he was pulled out of a section and assigned to teach a different course altogether, there wasn't always enough time for him to bring himself up to speed and, well, naturally the teaching suffered. His fellowship in Arles had been a feather not only in his cap but in Booth Tarkington's, too, and if he were to throw up his hands and go back to Indianapolis now, his tail between his legs, before the full five weeks were up, he could kiss his advancement goodbye. (Because there actually was a record. And there was actually a place on it where black marks could be set down against you on it.) Admittedly, there were many people his age who weren't full professors. *Most*, probably. He wasn't necessarily even in competition with them. (Community colleges weren't bad places to teach. It was pretty laidback, really. So it wasn't as if Miller were in any particular rush or something. The idea of a thirty-six-year-old—thirty-seven by the time he'd be in Indianapolis again—Associate Professor—or even a forty- or forty-one-year-old one—wasn't particularly bothersome.) It was the thought of still being locked into his present rank when he was in his fifties that got to him, of becoming this school crossing guard of a professor. So it was out of the question that he abandon Arles. He didn't even have to produce the monograph. All he really had to do was just give them some evidence—it really was laidback, it really was—that he was still working on it, that it was in the works.

It may have been all this thinking about time (the weeks left to him in Arles, the years ahead of him when he would pull himself up hand over hand from one rank to achieve another) that led him to notice that there sometimes appeared in the music room persons he hadn't seen there before. Only then did it occur to him that for some of the Fellows at least rotation had already happened. (He hadn't seen that crippled political geographer around lately, he hadn't seen Myra Gynt, the composer from the University of Michigan.) Rather than panic at the thought that he'd lost track of time—he *knew* he'd lost track of time—or let it bother him much that possibly weeks had gone by without his doing any work on his project, he took a sort of encouragement from the idea that these might be people who hadn't witnessed his debacle in the music room, who may not, in fact, even have heard of it.

So he climbed down from his high horse, broke radio silence, and greeted these strangers before waiting for them to make the first move. He asked what they thought about the place, he asked how they were adapting, it was *some* place wasn't it, he asked where they were from, he asked about the projects they were working on.

And they, in turn, asked where *he* was from, and he told them Indiana (which was true enough), and asked about *his* project, and he said (which was true enough) that, oh, he was trying to put a study together about the image of the American community college among academics from the more prestigious think tanks and universities.

"Hmn," said Lou Rangerer, a trade-union historian from Cornell, "don't they do rather a lot with closed-circuit TV? And language labs? It seems to me they have all these language labs. They set students up in dozens of little cubicles in front of interactive computers where they let them work at their own pace."

"Language labs, yes, that's good. Language labs. Work at their own pace," Miller said, making a note, and checking the spelling with him of Rangerer's last name.

"I don't know," said Barbara Neil-Cheshi from the Wharton School, "aren't they open all hours? Don't they make a fetish of utilizing their plant around the clock all year long?"

Miller thanked her and made a note.

"You know what this sounds like?" Ms. Neil-Cheshi said. "Market research."

"No no," said Miller, "this is more open-ended than market research. In market research they always ask specific questions. I'm here in Arles looking for impressions. I particularly stipulated that when I filed my grant application.

No no. Nothing like this has ever been done." He folded the scrap of paper on which he had recorded their remarks and stuffed it into his pants pocket. He gave back her pencil. "It's almost time for lunch," he said, and left the music room.

Entering the night café a little before the others he sat down at one of the small, vacant, green baize-covered tables along a red wall. He finished his drink and held up his empty glass until one of the waiters took it from him and returned with a full one. He spotted Paul Hartshine but looked away quickly. He came over anyway.

"May I?" Hartshine said.

"Sure," Miller said. "Long time no see."

"Now, Miller," Hartshine said, "you know that's not true. We've seen one another in the music room practically every day. You've cut me quite dead. I take no offense because you treat everyone in this manner."

Hartshine, dapper as ever, was wearing a huge bow tie. His silk suit pants were almost like tights and his jacket flared up in back as if he were mooning the room. Miller had an urge to beat him up, at least to pick a fight. (He was drinking too much. Two or three of these apéritifs put him away these days. On top of on top of on top of on top of.) He considered what he might tell Hartshine. It was a toss-up between a remark about the way he dressed and the way he spoke. He was about to go with the clothes thing when suddenly he changed his mind and pulled out all the stops.

"Hartshine," he said as if it were some problematic wine he rolled about in his mouth experimentally. "Hartshine, Hartshine. What is that, Jewish?"

Hartshine was shocked, stunned. He looked as if Miller had pulled a knife on him. He seemed terrified. This passed and a murderous anger moved across his face like weather. As Miller watched, Hartshine slowly lifted his right hand away from his lap, brought it level with the table and, raising it further, reached out and brought it to rest on the lapel of Miller's jacket.

Miller leaned far back in his chair. "Hey," he said. "What? What?"

Then Hartshine did an amazing thing. Removing his hand from the lapel he jerked it back toward his own throat and, rooting with his fingers under his big bow tie seized one end of the tie and tugged at it until the big floppy affair came undone. He pulled it through the collar of his shirt like a magic trick and set it down on his empty plate. Hartshine got up from the table wordlessly and crossed the night café to another table. Before anyone saw, Miller tried to cover the tie with his hand. Then, almost as if he were scratching the plate, he proceeded to palm Hartshine's bow tie. He watched its elaborate print disappear into his fist, then, first looking about nonchalantly, stuffed it deep into the pocket of his pants.

After his lunch (which he ate even less of than usual) Miller had no desire to return to the music room and he went back to Number 2 Lamartine. Dr. Félix Rey was standing to the side of the stairs in the tiny ground-floor hallway addressing a small, rough-looking fellow in rapid French, one of the painters perhaps, who, his back to Miller, stooped down over the stairs, tying his shoe. Rey seemed angry, even quarrelsome, but spotting Miller abruptly broke off. "Ah," said the doctor, "the Mister Monsieur. My friend plus myself have been waiting on you. Show him, Maurice!" Almost militarily the man removed his foot from the step and snapped to a kind of attention. "Eh?" said the doctor. "Eh, eh?" He was talking to Miller. "Eh?" he said again. "Hmn?" It was as if he were offering the Hoosier a piece of merchandise he'd been at some lengths to procure and now sought, as though Miller were a connoisseur or (he suddenly recalled the phrase of an unlikely Indianapolis pal, a broker) "made a market" in the commodity, corroboration of its worth or of the doctor's judgment.

Miller neutrally shrugged.

"Well," Dr. Rey said, "let's have a look at you, will we?" and abruptly came toward him. Miller, momentarily flashing on Paul Hartshine's strange, bold movement in the night café and conscious of the bow tie, undone in his pocket, instinctively backed away. The doctor reached out for his wrist, which, at a loss, Miller reluctantly surrendered. "Pulse normal," he said, turning it over, examining his hands. "Tch tch tch. Monsieur tastes his nails. Color superb," he said and touched the edge of his hand to Miller's face. "Skin quite dry." Miller looked at him. "Non non non non non. Skin quite dry is an excellent circumstance. I should say you are out of the woods," Rey said. Then he turned to the mean-looking guy and seemed to relate in French (his tone calmer than when Miller had entered the house) everything he had just been telling his patient. (Miller caught "Tch tch tch." He caught "Non non non non non.")

"Please," Félix Rey said. He indicated the stairs with a gesture, at once proprietary and deferential. "I promised the Zouave he could see the room" he whispered.

Of course, Miller thought. Maurice. The fierce Zouave. I didn't recognize him out of uniform. And wondered, and not for first time, Why me? What am I doing here? Are you really out of the woods if the doctor has to examine you in a hallway? What is the meaning of life?

Leading the way, followed by the good doctor and with the fierce Zouave bringing up the rear, Miller climbed the steps to Van Gogh's room at Arles and muscled open its stuck, Provençal-warped door. (Where he saw that the maids—they came in pairs now—had put the furniture back in its original position.)

Félix Rey looked at the ex-legionnaire and waited with the same air of deferent appraisal (and muttering some of the same sounds) with which he'd appealed to Miller some few minutes earlier. Both looked toward the scowling young tough, Miller surprised to find himself as expectant as the doctor, as anxious to have the room's authenticity acknowledged as Rey (apparently) had been eager to have Miller vouch for the kid's uncanny resemblance to Van Gogh's untamed original.

The Zouave nodded and went to the rush-bottom chair closest to the bed, unceremoniously tore it from its place, set it down against a wall, and planted himself in it, his legs spread wide, one hand resting in his lap and the other along a thigh as unselfconsciously as if he were sitting on a toilet.

"Hey!" Miller said. "Hey you!"

Without moving his face, the Zouave's eyes seemed to follow Miller, to find and fix him, exactly as they would in a portrait, so that, in a way, it was almost as if Miller were the sitter, the subject, and the Zouave the one free and loose in the gallery. Maurice, in place, stolid, narrowed his eyes, oddly red, almost phosphorent, like something dangerous and defiant and shining in a jungle.

Miller wanted the intruders out of there. What the hell? The way the wiseguy had just marched in and taken over the place? Who the hell? Félix Rey had promised him? Promised him? Examines me in the fucking hall and *promised* him? Who the hell, what the hell? He wanted these Scrooge's ghosts the hell out of there.

Miller started toward the demob'd legionnaire.

"Monsieur Miller Mister!" Félix Rey cried out suddenly. Miller, startled, pulled up short, his first thought not Watch it, he has a gun, but Careful, he has a knife! "Si'l vous plaît, Miller, please," the doctor said, and Miller, turning, saw that Rey was holding a camera, that he was taking a picture, aiming the camera at the fierce, posing Zouave.

Breathing heavily, sweating profusely, his heart hammering at him in ways familiar to him only from his heavy, bad-blooded performances in the pickup handball and basketball games in the Indianapolis gyms, Miller felt a kind of fury that Rey and Maurice seemed not only indifferent to but totally unaware of his presence, that he had become irrelevant not merely as a man but—his flushed skin, his racing pulse, his pounding heart—as a patient. And, what was even more important, as the proper tenant of this room as they made their fanatical snapshots of each other.

They left only when they were out of film.

He woke the next day remembering that there was something he had to do. When he saw them he asked the maids—neither spoke English—for *un packette, la petite packette*—he did not know the French for "box"—and made clipped, angular gestures with his hands. He gestured wrapping paper, he gestured string. To Miller's total surprise the box, paper, and string, in *precisely* the proportions he'd stipulated, were waiting for him on his bed when he returned after lunch to Van Gogh's room at Arles. Miller went to the drawer in which he had been keeping it and, carefully folding Hartshine's big bow tie, placed it in the box, wrapped it in the paper, and tied it with the string. He printed Paul Hartshine's name neatly across the front of the discrete little package and took it to the desk at the inn.

"Please see that Mr. Hartshine gets this," he told Rita (with whom he was still so miffed he was absolutely unable to invent a convincing enough scenario to which he could jerk off). "I think it's his ear."

Having completed his errand, he felt a curious, off-center, but unsatisfactory and incomplete sense of relief.

In the days following he wanted to try to explain his feelings about Arles. Surely among all these infinity specialists, why-the-chicken-crossed-the-road investigators, and big-bad-wolf revisionists, along with all the other heavy hitters (one of the Fellows was writing a psychological biography of God), there must be *someone* who could explain why Miller was having such a heavy time of it here, why he was experiencing all this complicated shit, a big, raw-boned, straw-in-the-mouth, normally merry-go-lucky like himself.

Then, as sometimes occurs in the short range *for* the short range, an opportunity arose as he was leaving the night café one evening. Russell had fallen into step beside him.

"How are you?" Russell said. "I've been meaning to speak to you, but whenever I had my chances you were either in the music room apparently locked up in your thoughts or I've been too busy with my own. Would *this* be a good time?"

"Oh yes," Miller said, and he and Russell walked out of the inn, crossed the square together, and entered the small yellow house. Russell followed him up the stairs to the room.

He invited Russell to sit and went to the chest of drawers where he kept the not inconsiderable stash of booze that he had put together from the time of his day trips around Arles. "There's some gin left," he said, "and a little scotch and vodka, and here's a bottle of one of those poofy apéritifs that Georges serves us. What's your pleasure?"

"Well, I don't really drink," Russell said, "but I see that you do, so I'll have whatever you're having."

Miller looked at him to see if this was a shot. Russell gazed benignly back at him and winked.

"I'm having," Miller said, "I'm having all of it, this sort of alcohol cassoulet." He poured off about four inches of gin, scotch, vodka, and liqueur into the pitcher in the basin on the washstand, swirled it around, and filled first Russell's water tumbler and then his own. He held out his glass. "To *him!*" Miller offered.

"To him," said Russell mildly, and raised his glass too.

"It's not because this is my first trip to Europe or anything," Miller said. "I mean what's that? That's just geography. Geography's no big deal."

"No," Russell said, "it isn't."

"I don't even think it's because I'm in over my head. I mean over my head's geography too," he giggled. So I *ain't* the fastest gun in western civilization. Who cares about that? I don't care about that."

"You shouldn't."

"I don't." He lowered his voice confidentially. "There's plenty around who aren't a whole bunch faster than me if you want to know. Because the last *I* heard a taste for squid ink over your noodles isn't necessarily a sign of a state of grace. That's all right, Russell," he said, "you're a good sport. You don't have to finish it if it tastes too much like piss. Set it down, I don't mind."

"I told you," Russell said, "I'll have what you're having."

"That's good," Miller admitted, "that's a good thing. You cultivate your palate. You educate your taste. You live and you learn. That's good. Because between you me and the lamppost my palate was cultivated years back. Shit, Russell, after chocolate, strawberry, and vanilla, it's *all* wog food to me. Wait a minute, let me get rid of this." He poured the rest of his drink into the basin in which the pitcher was standing. "It's pretty foul," Miller said, "I have to admit it. Who am I trying to impress? Can I give you something else?"

"I'm fine," Russell said. He'd already finished over half his glass. He seemed unaffected.

While Miller, the drinker in the outfit, who'd barely managed to get down more than a few sips, was unable to stop talking. It wasn't, he thought, a matter of in vino veritas (or scotcho or vodko) so much as the fact of company. "I had this visit," he blurted. "I think something's up between Rey and the fierce Zouave."

The really astonishing thing as far as Miller was concerned was that he didn't have to explain his terms. No more than he'd had to elucidate whom he'd meant when he'd raised his glass to *him*. It was one thing to come on all abnegant modesty and disclaimer, boasting (as it were) his ignorance and submissive second fiddlehood, but another altogether to get up into the very face of genius. It didn't make one humble (and wasn't Russell, right here and right now, showing him—albeit merely by Russell being Russell, by forsaking agenda, by what he did with poor Miller's gag drink—what it was like in actual real time to educate one's taste, to live and to learn?), it quite made one breathless with despair. It was rather like watching synapses spark and blossom in a visible brain. It was all right, as he'd said, not to be the fastest gun in western civilization, but for only so long as no legitimate claimant to the title was around. It was something like that, he wanted to tell Russell, that put him off about this whole Van Gogh's-room-at-Arles thing, but, when he tried, it came out snarled, garbled, artlessly done. It came out—— gossip.

"I mean," Miller went on helplessly, "they were taking each other's *pictures*, for Christ's sake. Snap. Snap snap. Setting the goddamn thingumabob on the camera and dashing across the room so they could be together for the photograph. They'd have posed on the bed if I wasn't here. Their forebears and great-greats sat for their fucking portraits for him! Some fierce Zouave *that* guy must be," Miller said. "I bet they kicked his old ass out of the Foreign Legion!"

"Don't get so upset. It interferes with your work."

"Oh yeah," Miller said, "my work."

"The whole deal is only five weeks," Russell said sweetly, "it will all be over soon."

"You should have seen them," Miller said. "Compared to something like that, diddling myself is small potatoes."

He'd shocked Russell but was sober enough to see that it wasn't propriety or fastidiousness he had sinned against, it was decorum. And felt such a thrill of rage that he lashed out at his guest. "So what's all this winking then? What's *that* all about?"

"I'm sorry," Russell said softly, "I have a tic."

Oh my, thought Miller in his cups, now I've hurt his feelings. Russell, he saw, for all his credentials and lustrous, curricula-vitae'd life (this year, for example, he was not only Distinguished University Professor at the University of Bologna, they'd made him Chair of their philosophy department), would be unused to the aggressive, bluff roughneckery of someone like Miller. Why, to someone like Russell, Miller, Miller thought, probably represented the racketeer class, or, a step or so up or down, maybe the life force. My God, he thought, *me*? Ain't that a kick in the ass? When it was the life force, or something so like it he didn't even know a name for it—geography? squid ink on the noodles?—that gave him the heebie-jeebies in the first place.

But give the devil his due. He owed Russell an apology. He'd try to be more specific.

"You don't want to get too near the light," Miller told him. "You get too near the light you burn up. Rey and Maurice are examples. They never got over light proximity, they never got over the presumed heroism and idiosyncrasy of their circumstances. You should've seen them. Maurice is this little guy. He could have been a preemie. You don't get a neck and arms like that unless you work at it. The son of a bitch must have bench-pressed a million pounds in his time. He had to have spent half his life in gyms. And Dr. Rey? You think mustaches like that grow on trees? And you can't tell me determinism made him go for a doctor. It was determination. They started out, or rather somebody started out for them, as simple flukes of art. They bought into all that. They ain't mountebanks. Hell, Russell, they're not even clowns. Clowns on velvet, that's another story, but chiefly they came too near the light is all." He was breathing heavily now. He was in a damn state. He was in such a sweating, breathless, stupid damn state he almost felt someone ought to take *his* stupid damn picture.

Is *that* specific enough for you? he wondered. Is *that* enough of an apology?

Miller didn't notice until it had already passed that he'd had his birthday. One morning he woke up and realized he'd been thirty-seven years old for about a week. A person who'd always been as conscious of his age as others of their weight or appearance, it struck him as extraordinary, strange, and fantastic that he'd failed to observe the occasion. The word wasn't casually chosen. Birthdays for Miller were, quite literally, red-letter days, occasions. Nor did it matter if others made no fuss over him. He wasn't looking for a fuss. He wasn't looking for cards or telegrams or presents or special treats. He didn't hang around waiting for long-distance phone calls. He didn't take the day off. He didn't *celebrate* his birthdays so much as pay attention to them, sit up and take notice, all eyes and all ears. Turning thirty-seven after being thirty-six was as qualitatively different to Miller as turning ten after being nine. Only now, having missed turning thirty-seven, he'd never really know, would he, and that was just one more mark Miller could set down next to Arles. It was as if he'd failed to take note of the change of season, like finding oneself in winter without passing through summer.

He'd begun to work on his project after his meeting with

Russell but that had little to do with the reason he'd missed his birthday. Indeed, rather than its giving him pleasure to be at last engaged on the work that had been the ostensible reason for his presence at Arles, he found his labors as dispiriting as he had found the burden of sharing Van Gogh's environment and sleeping in Van Gogh's bed and going about his business in Van Gogh's room at Arles. He wasn't inspired, he'd made no resolutions, turned over no new leaf. Simply, one morning he came across the piece of paper he'd slipped into the pocket of his pants that day in the music room when he'd voluntarily come out of Coventry and written down the union-movement guy's remark about the high priority community colleges gave to language labs, and Ms. Neil-Cheshi's not inaccurate observation that of all educational institutions, junior colleges seemed determined to make the most efficient use of their physical plants. He punched these thoughts into the laptop PC and turned them over and over in his mind.

Time didn't pass in the blink of an eye. He didn't fall into a rapture. This was his research. The comments became the basic building blocks of his paper, not its inspiration so much as the sandy irritant slipped into an oyster that might, over time, accrue into a pearl. Joylessly he developed an outline, joylessly he revised and expanded it. Tediously he pushed his thin thesis, padding it almost to the breaking point. Listlessly he began to write, affectlessly to realize that he might actually produce enough material in the days he had left in Van Gogh's room at Arles to make it back to Indianapolis undisgraced. Distractedly he invented sources, quotes, footnotes, taking no pleasure in the fact of the fraud he was perpetrating, or in his certainty it was all so very bloodless that it would probably go undetected—if it ever was—for years after he'd been made Full Professor, and that since he had no intention to publish, by the time he was discovered—if he was—they'd do nothing about it.

And this was the way Miller stuck it out, getting through almost his last days in Arles until almost the time he had to do his final laundry, return the unused portion of his round-trip ticket to the bus company, and buy a ride to Marseilles on *le train grand vitesse* (he'd learned *something* in Europe, it hadn't been a *total* loss), get ready, that is, to do those last things people do when they're ready to break camp. (And with just that increment of sadness and regret that descends like a curtain whenever one experience, no matter how negative or disagreeable it may have been, is about to pass over into another—— the woe of endings, the death of death.) So that, in a way, he was too busy or just too anxious to work on his project and he abandoned it as abruptly as it was begun.

Which left him, after the day's small chores (settling accounts with Rita at the inn's front desk—— the astonishing hundred-twenty-seven-dollar phone bill she said he owed because of the three relatively brief calls she'd put through to Indianapolis to his pals in lieu of the promised postcards he'd failed to send, the letters he'd been unable to write; the thirty-five due for a group photograph of the Fellows she'd taken and said she'd send on to America after it was developed; the forty-four she told him was still outstanding for odds and ends—— the two hundred-and-six-buck grand total, which once he paid would square him with France with just enough left over to tip Georges, the waiters and housekeepers, and leave him with a few dollars for some cheap souvenirs and maybe a carton of duty-free Gaulois to take with him back on the airplane), with a little time to actually socialize.

Rita stood up one night at the end of the evening meal, lightly tapped her water glass with a knife, and made an announcement. Madame Celli had left Arles to be with her son and his family who would be arriving in Paris the following morning from Canada. It was her son's holidays and Madame was going to travel with him, his wife, and their two young children to Ngozitnlabad where they were to join a tour that would take them to islands all along the East Coast of Africa. Miller, who hadn't known of Madame Celli's son, or of the son's wife, or that they had children, or that Madame C. was a grandmother, was shocked. Birthday or no birthday he was still a young man and he felt a little betrayed, a little done in, worked over, roughed up. All that passion and reverie, he thought wincing, spent on a grand-mère.

Rita, who'd evidently been left to mind the Foundation, went on to say that since there were so many new Fellows in the group (it was true; until she mentioned it Miller hadn't noticed how many faces were unfamiliar to him) this might be a good time for the new people to familiarize themselves with the region. For their touring comfort her brother-in-law had put new seats and installed a brand-new air-conditioning unit in his bus. She said she would be post-ing sign-up sheets on the bulletin board near the front desk for a trip to Les Alyscamps, L'Allée des Sarcophages and the Roman amphitheater. Miller would pass. (Brooding, he was saddened that one of Europe's finest factotum's could make such a bold-faced pitch, sent into deep mourning by the cycles that kept on coming and kept on coming, and thought, This is where I came in, and wondered where one was supposed to go and what one was supposed to do to meet the suitable girls.) For those who were interested, she said, they would be running a special trip out to the asylum at Saint-Rémy where Vincent Van Gogh had been commit-ted, along with a side trip to Auvers where he shot himself not long after he was discharged. Miller, minding his pen-nies, minding his mind, decided to pass on that one too. And on the boat trip down the Rhône delta, and the outdoor market near the medieval church (with its crypt and painted, arranged skulls like so many heads of lettuce in a produce bin) where one might occasionally pick up genuine Roman artifacts at bargain prices. They should keep their eyes on her, she said. If an authentic piece of real value should turn up in the stalls she would pick it up, handle it, and pretend to dicker with the seller before replacing it. That would be their signal, she said, that they weren't being gulled. Just don't, she warned, tell anyone about their little arrangement or she and her brother-in-law could get into real trouble.

I came *that* close to spilling my seed over this one! Miller thought ruefully.

But despite himself felt a sudden stirring, some attraction he felt to the rough leather of the woman's character, and lo and behold he was nursing an extraordinary tight hard-on right there in the night café.

He signed up for Les Alyscamps and L'Alleé des Sarcophages and the Roman amphitheater. He signed up for Saint-Rémy and the side trip to Auvers. (He sat as close to her as he could in the newly seated, newly air-conditioned bus and pressed tips into her hands for her splendidly educational commentaries.) He signed up for the boat trip down the Rhône delta and returned to Arles that evening exhausted from the air and the heavy Provençal sun (and from getting out of the little launch with Rita and the others and stooping most of the day examining the murky waters as they tramped barefoot along the river's muddy bank searching out the rare reeds that grew there and which Rita cleaned and filed down and then sold in individual packets of a dozen to professional oboists all over the world, asking her again and again, "Is this one, is this?" and managing to bump against her, or even pretend to lose his footing in the insignificant current). He even signed up for the tour of the outdoor market where Rita was a shill, dutifully browsing the stalls for the faux relics (thrice faux: first when they were manufactured, twice when they were wholesaled to the trade and, finally, when Rita, the beautiful factotum–cum–desk clerk, cum–tour guide, cum–this and cum–that, performed her vicious gypsy triage over the toy SPQRs stamped into the hilts, helmets, and masonry of the little sections of viaduct manqué) but (still minding his pennies though he had lost his mind) making no purchases.

He was her best customer. And wooed her as an old-timey, love-struck young mooncalf might once have sent unsigned flowers or been in attendance at every performance his heart's ingenue ever gave, lost whole-hog for the run of the show. He was, this Miller was, some tied-tongue, stage-door Johnny of an admirer.

But, at night, back in Van Gogh's room at Arles, he still could not manage to put her into any of his imagination's beds. It would have been like trying to bring himself off to some image of Leda, say, or Venus, or any other superstar of myth. (Because he couldn't stop thinking of her as of some woman actually *painted* by Van Gogh, but something turned and awful in her beauty, hardened, slumped and stupored as a strumpet in the night café, thickened and stupid and mean as a peasant in the landscapes he always shared with her now on their outings. Though why this should have bothered him he couldn't have said, and perhaps even Russell couldn't have told him.)

There were only four days left.

Some of the Fellows—all the scholars who'd been in Arles when he and Paul Hartshine arrived had packed up and gone; piecemeal, or in little clumps of two or three, they had dropped off; Miller was part of the establishment now; no one but Rita, Russell, and Hartshine were left who had witnessed the disaster in the music room—decided to take a day trip to Cannes.

They brought their idea to Rita, proposing to engage the brother-in-law's bus. Well, but Cannes was not really her territory, she told them. She wasn't that familiar with Cannes, Cannes was for tourists, not academics. Cannes was crowded this time of year, she couldn't guarantee them special deals in the better restaurants. She was sure her brother-in-law was not licensed for Cannes, that there'd be special fees for parking his big, upgraded bus with its brand-new seats and special air-conditioning unit.

She's a genius, Miller thought. She's more than a great European factotum, she's a world-class piece of work. And wanted to rip out her heart and, simultaneously, devour her with kisses. But, with the others, dutifully ponied up all the vigorish, add-ons, and excise taxes she extorted, Miller thinking, There go the tips for the maids, there go the ones for the waiters, there goes Georges's tip, there go the duty-free Gaulois.

When the brother-in-law pulled up in front of the inn at

Number 30 Lamartine on the morning of the day trip to Cannes, in addition to Miller, Russell, and Paul Hartshine (who hadn't spoken to him since the afternoon he'd passed his remark in the music room), some of the Fellows who boarded the bus were Sir Ehrnst Riglin, a history historian at Uppsala University, Jesus Hans, the revolutionary political statistician for third-world countries, Samuels Kleist, a vernacular architect in his late sixties, Yalom and Inga Basset, pop psychiatrists, and Robert and Heidi Lear.

With the exception of Russell and Hartshine, who averted his eyes whenever Miller looked his way, he knew none of them very well. For all that they'd spent entire days together on the recent flurry of excursions since Kaska Celli had run off to be with her grandchildren, and for all his decision to kick back and socialize, and for all their apparent friendliness, their reputations got in his way. (It *was* their reputations, only that. He'd seen photographs of Kleist's queer structures, the strange, almost pueblo-like tiers of caves built into the sides of New Mexico's red cliffs, and was convinced that the buildings were silly, uninhabitable, virtually inaccessible to mailmen, milkmen, the man who reads the meter. Only their reputations. For though he'd no clear notion of what someone in the history of history field did, it was the fact that Sir Ehrnst had been knighted for it that scared him off. Nor had he read the Bassets' books. He'd heard them on their morning call-in talk show mediating the lunacies, counseling the killers, abusers, swingers, cheaters and incestors, sometimes homing at least a little in on even his own small shames. It was the fact of their famous voices, however, that held him at arm's length.)

Of Robert and Heidi Lear he knew nothing at all, not even their disciplines (or whether they worked in tandem). What he had against *them* was that of all the people with whom he'd come into contact at Arles, Robert Lear was the only Fellow he actively disliked. This went back to an incident he'd observed in the music room. There'd been a bridge game one evening. Miller didn't play bridge, of course, hadn't enough knowledge of its rules even to kibitz. One of the other players—he couldn't remember his name, the man was gone now—had asked Robert, aside from Miller the room's only other smoker, if he might borrow one of his cigarettes. Robert had visibly hesitated.

"It's not your brand," Robert said.

"Oh," said the guy, "that's all right. I've run out. I've just had dinner. I'd smoke anything."

Robert hesitated again, frowned, and then finally, reluctantly, retrieved a cigarette from what seemed to Miller like a full pack and pushed it a little way across the table toward the bridge player. In about an hour the man asked if he could borrow a second cigarette. Robert frowned, scowled, openly sighed, and shook one from what now looked to be a considerably diminished pack.

What Miller held against Heidi was that she was married to Robert.

On the night before he was to leave, the bridge player appeared in the music room. He was holding a carton of cigarettes. They were Robert Lear's brand. He brought it to the chair in which Lear was sitting and handed the carton to him. "Smoke them all in one place, why don't you?" he said and left the room.

Miller was scandalized. As much as he disliked Lear, he was astonished that anyone could be rude to someone who'd received the Foundation's blessing and been invited to Arles. Indeed, though he was still shy, reserved, and even guarded with everyone else, he made at least a little effort, in spite of the fact that the Lears didn't seem to welcome or even notice it, to be forthcoming with them.

It was Heidi Lear, in fact, who seemed to have invented the scheme for their trip to Cannes. Miller learned of this only on the bus that morning.

The trip was designed, at least in part, to be a sort of shopping expedition. Although Miller, Russell, and Hartshine would miss it, the Fellows were going to do a play reading the following week—in French—of The Misanthrope. Heidi had approached Rita to see if it was possible to procure the amphitheater one afternoon for their little production. Rita thought the idea of a play reading a good one and came up almost immediately with an even more ambitious proposal. Why not, she suggested, have the reading at night in the amphitheater? Why not invite the townspeople of Arles, why not take advantage of the stadium's lights and sound system? She thought she could arrange it so the entire evening wouldn't cost them more than, oh, fifty dollars a person.

They jumped at it. They jumped, too, at Heidi Lear's additional embellishments. She thought the actors should be in costume. Oh, nothing elaborate of course. It was too late for anything *fine*, but Heidi had been associated for just years and years with socio-theatrics. That was her field, socio-theatrics—— theatrical therapies for prisoners, old people in homes, the dying in hospices, as well as individuals who found themselves temporarily thrown together in groups like the one the Foundation had assembled in Arles. It was how she'd met Robert (whose field it turned out was the inventorying of eighteenth-century houses). She was, at least according to Robert Lear (whose testimony in his wife's behalf was the first indication of generosity Miller had seen in him), this genius of the make-do and at-hand. A wizard of odds and ends.

Thus the shopping expedition to Cannes. For props and stuffs and materials. For the building blocks of all impromptu improvisation and inspired, makeshift arrangement. They would hit up the hotels, the special booths and shops a town like Cannes with its annual film festival and concomitant obligations to make the sets and adjust to the needs of some eleventh-hour show business would be sure to have.

On the trip out that morning the coach was abuzz with plans for the upcoming show. Even Rita was excited, and Paul Hartshine (who was wearing his big print bow tie) had practically made up his mind to change his reservations and stay on at a hotel in Arles until after the performance. Russell said he would have stayed on too but that Bologna was paying him $200,000 for the year, and he was, at least pu-

tatively, Departmental Chair. Also, he'd already been away
five weeks from a sinecure essentially carved out for him.
They were nice people. He oughtn't, he thought, take advantage, he mustn't, he felt, hurt their feelings. Much as he
might want to hang around and take in their *Misanthrope*
leaving was the honorable thing to do.

"Two hundred thousand?" Miller said.

Russell looked at the scenery.

Miller was astonished at how excited they were. Him too.
It seemed odd that he, of all of them the most frivolous, the
one with probably the least good reason to be there, should
be the one under the greatest obligation to leave, to go home
to what was only Booth Tarkington Community College in
what was only Indianapolis in what was merely the State of
Indiana, to get down to work at last on what was plainly the
flimsiest of projects.

It astonished him too how all this (about the real purpose
of the trip to Cannes; about the Lears, Heidi's talents, Robert's devotion; about Hartshine's decision to stay on; Rita's
genuine enthusiasm; Russell's salary) came out on the bus.
Other things too. Something ad hoc and original and abandoned in all of them, their lives made suddenly available,
opened up like responses to the sunshine laws or the rules of
discovery. Sir Ehrnst, for example, the history of history
man from Uppsala, admitted that he never read his students'
papers. He distributed grades solely on the basis of his first
impressions of how they dressed, if they wore glasses,
whether they *looked* scholarly, how he expected they would
strike a class of their own graduate students, sometimes on
nothing more than how they smelled—— their colognes,
their aftershaves and toilet waters, whether they seemed
cloying. And old Samuels Kleist, whose wife was feeling
too ill to make the trip with them to Cannes (and who,
though he knew of her existence, Miller had never seen because she remained, to hear Kleist tell it, who, indeed,
fetched her her breakfasts—bran muffins, an orange, tea—
her lunches and suppers), was in love, had not one but two
mistresses installed in a pair of his cliff dwellings back in

New Mexico, and was on his way to Cannes to buy presents for both ladies. Though he had no idea, he gushed, what either of them wanted from France, no notion, God help him, of their sizes. Both drank wine, *loved* wine. If he could find a specially designed label with a pretty view of the beach at Cannes, the great architect said, a half-dozen bottles like that might be the very thing. He never touched the stuff himself, he said. Neither did his wife. Where could he hide them so they wouldn't be discovered? He asked for suggestions.

"Ship them," Inga Basset suggested, "have them shipped."

"That's so impersonal," Samuels Kleist said.

"Get them head scarves," Sir Ehrnst Riglin said. "You can line a head scarf inside your trouser cuff or stuff it up the sleeve of your jacket."

"That's not a bad idea," Kleist said.

And Yalom and Inga Basset, the drive-time psychiatrists, were openly contemptuous of the creatures who called them for help, contemptuous, even scurrilous, about psychiatry itself.

"It's a crock," Yalom Basset said.

"It's gas in your pants," said Inga, a slim, fit-looking woman in her forties, handsome and rakish in a Borsalino hat, a cigarillo in her lips, one eye squint shut against its smoke like the face of an experienced card player.

"It leaves wind," her husband put in.

"It clouds men's minds," Inga said.

Committing voluntary truth against themselves like people turning state's evidence. All of them, all, all abandoned and vulnerable as so many summer houses in the winter.

Jesus Hans, statistics advisor to the third world, running his mouth at the back of the bus.

"I'm from Cali. They know you're Colombian they want to dance you, they want love songs and good moves, that you give them dips. Famine girls from the horn of Africa.

"I give old Kleist due. Hey, two mistresses? He worries

about gifts because he's an ancient, sentimental guy from the old school.

"I have two sweet daughters, a wonderful wife who fucks like a mink. Better than my girlfriends even. She holds no candles to that Rita though."

Not Miller, Miller thought. Count Miller out, Miller thought. Keep your mystery, thought stunned Miller. Hold on tight to your famous poker-puss heart. Don't give them a thing, not a thing. I gave at the office, Miller thought. I gave and gave out in the music room. Don't, Miller thought. Don't tell them you jerk off to ghosts and grandmas.

And held his tongue all the way to Cannes.

Which was still France, still Europe, only no longer Van Gogh's Europe.

The brother-in-law drove the big bus right up to what must have been one of the newest, grandest hotels in town. He opened the doors, waited until his passengers descended, then descended himself and casually tossed his bus keys to a broad, magnificent doorman, splendidly attired in what vaguely reminded Miller of the Zouave's uniform in Van Gogh's painting. The doorman handed the keys to a young man who was actually going to valet-park the damn bus, for God's sake. Somehow this seemed the strangest, most extravagant thing Miller had ever seen.

"We'll cross the boulevard," Rita said. "There's the most marvelous café right on the beach. We'll have a coffee there, freshen up in their facilities, and decide what we must do."

The air was ferociously bright. Hot and clear and bright. Miller felt the lack of sunglasses. As palpably as he might have felt the absence of an umbrella in a rainstorm.

White yachts rode at anchor. Barebreasted, girls swam out from the beach and climbed rope ladders hanging down over the sides like a kind of nautical laundry. They boarded the yachts like dream pirates. A hundred feet off, women lay supine, topless in the powdery sand, their breasts sexlessly flattened against their chests.

Salads, fruits, parfaits of bright ice creams. Careful clusters of color on black wrought-iron tables in the beach café. Miller greedily studied his menu. He demanded that Russell translate everything for him. He loved being in an outdoor café on a beach in Cannes. He didn't want to ruin it by choosing the wrong food. At last he made his decision.

The waiter brought him long cold spears of kelly-green asparagus topped with two perfectly fried eggs. There was the best iced coffee he had ever tasted. For dessert he had a peeled pear that had been sliced and reassembled into a sort of fruit fan. it was spread out on a plate buttered with a dark chocolate sauce.

"That was wonderful," Miller said.

"It looked wonderful," Inga Basset said.

"I'm sorry I didn't order it," Samuels Kleist said.

Her brother-in-law lazily hung an arm across Rita's shoulders. Jesus winked at the bus driver.

While they waited for each other to finish their lunches, the members of the *Misanthrope* cast gossiped about some of the absent actors. They agreed that Derek Philips was much too serious and that Meyers Herman tended to mumble his words. They wondered how he'd ever manage to be heard in the huge amphitheater.

"He's musch too shy," Sir Ehrnst Riglin said.

"Yet he has the best accent," said Yalom Basset. "Don't you think so, Rita?"

"He has a good accent," Rita said.

"But if he can't be heard?" Sir Ehrnst said.

"You're forgetting about the sound system Rita's organizing for us," Heidi Lear said.

Miller wasn't sorry he'd be missing their performance though he was upset that Hartshine might be staying behind to see it. Meanwhile, while they carried on about Meyers Herman's accent (he hadn't met the man, he didn't even recognize the name), Miller listened to someone at the next table who spoke a sort of agitated, gossip-column English in which people planed about the globe, trained from one country to the next, and cabbed through its cities. Idly, he wondered what happened to such people in accidents, whether they were ambulanced to hospitals down whose halls they were gurneyed to operating rooms. The fellow to whom the first man was speaking said "ecomony" for economy and pronounced the *b* in debt.

Such people were comic and, however idiosyncratic, types. Miller wasn't amused by them. He was, he thought, a type himself. So, for all their honors and dramatic three-quarter and full-column entries in Who's Who, were the Fellows. And momentarily flashed on Van Gogh's vacant, heartbreaking room at Arles.

They had finished lunch and were parsing the bill. Miller owed the most, and, after he paid, saw that he was down to his last twenty dollars in francs. He had forty dollars more in traveler's checks. Even if he watched his money carefully he realized he probably wouldn't have enough left over to rent headphones to watch the movie on the flight back.

And now they discussed the groups into which they would break up so as to make the most of their time. Heidi, Robert, and the Bassets would do the rounds of shops, booths, and hotels to see what they could find for the costumes. Jesus Hans invited Rita to a hotel he knew of that gave, he said, a splendid late-afternoon tea dance, but Heidi wanted her with her on the shopping expedition. Jesus shrugged and said no problem-o, he'd go by himself. Despite Samuels Kleist's surprising confessions to them on the bus, he told the group—how this worked wasn't clear to Miller—it would be both a betrayal of his wife and his mistresses should he permit them to be in on the actual purchase of the mistresses' gifts. Sir Ehrnst Riglin had made arrangements to meet with three members of the Swedish Royal Family who happened to be in town that week. Russell and Hartshine decided to take in the flick that was touted to win the *palme d'or* at the festival that year. Russell invited Miller to come with, but Miller, doling francs, said it was too nice a day to spend inside a theater and told them to go on, he thought he'd just take in the sights. Everyone agreed to meet back at the hotel by seven. That gave them just over four hours.

Miller watched as Rita and the nine Fellows struck out in their various directions, watched until they disappeared, and then, wordlessly started to walk alongside the brother-in-law.

They strolled for a bit on the wide white sidewalk that ran parallel to the beach. Everywhere around them, on towels and blankets, on flimsy canvas beach chairs or sitting in the sand, men and women gave themselves up to the sun, offering, venturing, compromising, accommodating, and finally surrendering almost their entire bodies to the forces of this charged place, only, it seemed to Miller, reserving to themselves a sort of ultimate modesty of wall-like indifference, somehow bolder—certainly more heartless—than Miller's or the brother-in-law's prurient but furtive sightseeing. It was like a contest of wills for which neither Miller nor the brother-in-law either (no matter he'd so ostentatiously draped his arm about his sister-in-law's shoulders) had much stomach. They were humiliated by the seminude bodies of the women and embarrassed by the lewd assertion of the men's genitalia inside their bikinis, and Miller was not surprised when his companion abruptly broke off and crossed the boulevard at an oblique angle to the gawking, slow-moving traffic.

Miller continued beside the man as he moved at a brisk pace through important districts of the city.

They came to the port and stared at the great yachts, little smaller than small cruise ships some of them. The brother-in-law pointed to individual yachts and called the names of their globally rich owners, powerful fortune celebrities. Sometimes he would repeat the name. Miller nodded appreciatively with a look of great understanding, as though Rita's kinsman had delivered himself of some sober, clever gloss. He seemed to wait until he was certain Miller had taken it all in and then coughed his readiness to resume their tour. Miller smiled agreeably and they renewed their inspection of the city.

They made their way to the flower market, which now, in the late afternoon, was apparently experiencing a second wind as proprietors of the various stalls—each putting forward a featured variety—began to grant heavy discounts on great bunches of flowers.

The brother-in-law pushed roses on Miller, tulips and mums and daisies and carnations. He handed him dahlias and sprays of orchids.

"No no," Miller said, returning them, doling francs but protesting, "what would I do with them? I go back in three days."

His guide told Miller but my God, man, flowers of without the sun march in only fourteen years, this is certainly truly isn't it? and pressed another bouquet on him. Miller handed the new bouquet back to the brother-in-law, who then gave him another new bouquet which Miller again returned. They looked like jugglers.

The fellow shrugged and (Miller had lost track by now of where they were in relation to their starting point) they continued walking.

This is the arrondissement of tomatoes and apples, said Rita's relative.

They seemed to be in the heart of the produce district. As in the flower market, business had pretty much wound down for the day. The few people still picking over the somewhat faded fruits and declining vegetables were older, less chic than anyone Miller had yet seen in Cannes, and seemed to deal with the merchants from a position of strength, beggars who could afford to be choosers, hard bargainers who openly scoffed at the men who, even as their trucks backed up to haul off the unsold produce, countered all offers with proposals of their own, as indiscriminately, almost high-handedly, they continued to sweep their unsold merchandise into crates and cardboard boxes probably intended to hold distinct varieties (let alone classes) of produce. It was apples and oranges, thought Miller. Potatoes and cauliflowers. And smelled this faint mash of garden liquor, fermented earth chowder.

Just as one of the merchants was about to load a last carton of mixed fruits and vegetables onto the tailgate of his truck the brother-in-law spoke up.

Make halt! he declared. Please! he implored. If the mister demanded to steal the fruits of without the sun march, he thought he, but a poor miserable, could give for the most grand strawberries and others, say, many many thousands of francs.

It's good, the merchant agreed, and gave over the carton to Rita's bus-driving relation. Who, in turn, handed the fellow maybe four dollars American.

For the soups of my spouse, the brother-in-law said, and they were out of there.

They saw the district where chefs came for their meats in the early morning before the sun had risen, and a place near the docks where fishermen brought their catch to market. They even went into a church, not an old church but a large modern one, built after the war, no earlier than the late sixties probably, but by this time the bus driver was beginning to tire from carrying the not inconsiderable carton of day-old fruits and vegetables and he suggested that they arrest for a whiskey.

They stepped into a hotel.

They were looking for the bar when they heard music, a romantic, companionable melody of the easy-listening variety, and they made for its source.

They found a table in the almost empty bar and sat down. On a narrow stage in back an orchestra was playing and, beneath it, three couples moved across a polished, circular dance floor, which might comfortably have accommodated perhaps five or six times that number. Somehow, there being so few dancers gave the place an air (like so much of Cannes: the flower stalls and produce kiosks where commerce was winding down for the day, the moored, empty fishing boats by the docks and shutdown meat and fish markets, even the big and graceless church) of having been used up, some vaguely off-season sense of things, the dancing couples clutching each other out there on the floor not so much licentious—beyond licentious—as anachronistic, caught between day and night, in desperate, now-or-never, off-joint time.

Miller thinking as he drank his drink: How mysterious, something mysterious here.

Which is just when the brother-in-law nudged him, laying into him conspiratorially, even intimately (which Miller was certain he wouldn't have tried with any of the other Fellows) with his elbow.

Attention beyond, he said. Attention beyond, attention beyond.

Miller looked at the bus driver, noticing for the first time that Rita's relation bore, though he was at least thirty years younger, a striking resemblance to Van Gogh's portrait of the peasant Patience Escalier. Both looked more Mexican than French.

"*Non non, Monsieur,*" he hissed, "*la-bas, la-bas,*" pointed toward the dance floor.

Miller looked where he pointed.

Jesus Hans, wearing her Borsalino, was dancing with Inga Basset, his hands loosely cupping the psychiatrist's rear end as though he held it in a kind of sling.

Inga's thigh was planted in Jesus's crotch and he rocked in place, slowly rising against it to the beat of the easy listening.

The scene was stunning to Miller, incredible, immense. Even the logistics were stunning. How had Hans gotten her away from Basset? How, if the idea to hook up with Jesus had been Inga's, had she known where the tea dance would be?

The band finished its set. There wasn't time to ponder the big questions. Neither Miller nor the driver wished to be discovered in their discovery and, without a sign passing between them, both rose at once to quit the bar and get the hell out of the hotel. Miller even picked up the brother-in-law's carton for him, handing it over only after the man had found his bearings and Miller knew that they were well on their way back to the rendezvous at the hotel where Rita's brother-in-law had given the keys to the bus (*Rita's bus!* Miller suddenly realized) to the doorman.

They were about forty minutes early.

Miller spotted Russell and Hartshine at a table in the outdoor café. Indicating he was going over to meet them he gestured that the driver was welcome to join him, but the fellow declined, pointing from his watch to the carton.

The fruit is getting late, he explained to Miller. The apples of the ground were falling fast and it was necessary for some of the vegetables to make the bus.

Miller nodded and crossed the boulevard.

"How was your show?" he asked Hartshine and Russell. "What about it, boys? Was it worthwhile?" What he wanted most was to tell his colleagues what he and Rita's brother-in-law had seen in the hotel.

Hartshine, without even looking at him, touched the points of his shirt collar. He appeared to straighten his bow tie.

Miller repeated what he'd said when he'd told Russell it was too nice to spend the day cooped up in a movie. He said that he and the driver had decided to go on this walking tour of Cannes.

"That guy," Miller said. "He knows this town like the back of his hand that guy." He told them about the stalls in the flower and produce markets. He told them about the yachts and the district where the chefs came to inspect the fish and meats they would be preparing for their restaurants. What he was dying to tell them was about Jesus Hans and Inga Basset. He wanted to tell them about the thigh Inga had thrust between Jesus Hans's legs and the way Jesus held Inga's ass as he dry-humped her to the accompaniment of some soft show tune. What stopped him, he realized, was that he'd be going back to Indiana soon and he understood how very complicated it was to speak one's mind or make overtures into mysteries at the last minute.

Russell wanted to know if he could buy Miller a farewell drink.

"What? No. Of course not," Miller objected, openly resentful but helpless, and realizing even as he spoke to them how his protests must have sounded, how transparent his franc doling must seem to them.

"Gosh," Russell said, "they've brought the bus round. I think I'll go to the gents before we have to board. You, Hartshine? No, you went just before Miller showed up, didn't you? Miller? No? Be right with you then."

When Russell left, Miller sat awkwardly before Hartshine. He had no idea what to say to him. However difficult it was to keep from spilling the magic beans he'd picked up that afternoon at the tea dance (and which would have served to patch over not only the terrible silence between them but their awful breach as well), he was determined to say nothing about it. It wasn't his honor that was at stake. Miller didn't care a damn for his honor. It wasn't even that his silence now could do anything to abate the devastating disclosures—and the cloud he'd since lived under—he'd made in the music room. Nor had Miller any illusions he was protecting anyone. This particular cat would be out of the bag before the evening was out. The brother-in-law would see to that. He'd tell Rita what they'd seen as soon as it was convenient.

No, what Miller did now (or did not do) he did for Van Gogh, for Van Gogh and the privilege of Arles. He did it, he meant (or did not do it), because he could not do it justice, because in his mouth the immense, incredible, stunning thing he'd seen would have been reduced to mere gossip.

He stared at Hartshine.

"You think Bologna really pays him two hundred grand?" he said at last.

"Why do you ask me this?" Harshine said. "You think because I'm Jewish I have an interest in such questions? I'm a scholar!"

"Go fuck yourself, Hartshine," Miller said. "Go fuck yourself and kiss my Hoosier ass," he said.

He got up from the table and went to board the bus. He passed the brother-in-law without a glance, picked up the carton of fruits and vegetables the man had set down on an aisle seat, moved it to the window seat, and sat in the aisle seat himself. With his eyes almost shut and pretending to sleep, with his eyes almost shut so all he could see shoot past his window were objects drained of definition and color in an illusion of speed, he managed to ride all the way back to Arles without saying a word to anyone.

Late on the night before Miller left Arles, someone rapped on his door. He straightened up and looked from where he was stooped over his things, packing the last of them into the suitcase open on the bed in Van Gogh's room at Arles. He thought twice before answering the uncivilized knock, a sound so persistent it didn't seem to have had any beginning. He looked toward the noise and wondered who could be making it. Russell had already left town and was almost certainly in Bologna by now. He didn't think it could be Hartshine, seeking some rough reconciliation.

"Yes?" he said finally. "Yes?"

"Ah," said Félix Rey on the other side of the door, "the good professor is in. We have not lost him."

"I'm packing," Miller said. "My train leaves first thing in the morning. It's very late, I haven't finished packing."

"We will help you, Professor Monsieur. With three of us it will go by in a dream."

"It's awfully late," Miller said. "I'm dog-tired."

He hadn't actually identified himself yet, Miller was thinking. If I can just hang tough until the man goes away and pretend not to know who it is, Miller was thinking, it can't, on some technical level at least, be considered rudeness.

But at that point the physician not only resumed his knocking, he also formally announced himself.

"It's your médecin, Monsieur Professor American. It's Dr. Félix Rey and a friend."

"All right," Miller said at last, giving in. He opened the door.

"What?" Miller said. "What?"

The physician was drunk, his prominent ears, redder

even than he remembered, were flush, filled with blood. His clothes were disheveled, and even his brushcut hair and handlebar mustache seemed mussed, his plucked eyebrows. His full, fat Kewpie doll lips were slack. He was giggling.

Coming into the room Félix Rey extended his hand in greeting, but when Miller put out his own to shake it the doctor brushed it away and took Miller's wrist as if feeling for a pulse. He mimed shining an imaginary penlight into Miller's eyes and ears. He leaned into Miller's chest and, cupping his ear, pretended to listen to his heart. Miller, who had the private drinker's disdain for acts of public drunkenness, twisted away from him, causing Rey to stumble. It wasn't until she laughed that Miller was aware that there was a woman in the room.

"May I," said the doctor, "have the honor to represent to the American Mister Monsieur my very good friend, L'Arlésienne—— the incomparable and very beautiful Madame Ginoux."

She was the woman in the black-and-white photograph on the postcard Félix Rey had given him (the one who so resembled Kaska Celli), the woman whose image he had once called upon in one of his masturbatory flights. Almost as if she might have been conscious of this, Miller looked down.

"I am so very happy, sir," Madame Ginoux said. "The doctor has spoke."

"It's good to meet you," Miller said.

Then the woman did an odd thing. Bending her left arm at the elbow she lightly pressed the knuckles of her pale hand alongside her face in a sort of pensive salute. Miller identified the gesture at once. It was exactly as Van Gogh has posed her antecedent in his portrait more than a hundred years earlier. Madame Ginoux had the same long, wide nose as the woman in the portrait, the same blue eyes and black, black hair (so black, thought Miller, she had to have worked thick dark dyes into it) as Vincent's model, and had gone so far as to affect her nineteenth-century costume right down to an almost identical white tulle jabot that she'd attached down the front of her full Prussian-blue dress. She had painted in almost punk-red eyelids and etched sharply defined lips above her wide, flat mouth.

Madame Ginoux, L'Arlésienne, was a hooker or his name wasn't Miller, Miller thought.

"It was good of you to stop by," he told the doctor. "Gee," he said, "my time here's passed by so quickly. I hadn't realized. You think you've all the time in the world. That's always a mistake. First thing you know you're trying to pack so you can get some sleep and still get up and make an early train that will get you to Marseilles in time to check your bags through to America and clear Douane and get to the duty-free before your plane takes off without you and leaves you all high and dry in a foreign country with nothing to do but hang around the airport for another twenty-four hours looking at the newspapers and trying to figure out from the photograph what the story is about. So thanks for helping me out when I passed out that time, and for the postcard, and for introducing me to your friends. Goodnight, Dr. Rey. Goodnight and goodbye. It was a pleasure to meet you, Madame Ginoux. The doctor has spoke."

He had practically pushed them out of the room. He didn't know what this was all about. He didn't at all understand Félix Rey's motives or the meaning of all their disguises, the complicated costume party and tableaux vivants of their shutdown lives, but whatever it was he knew it could not be wholesome. Yet whose life is, Miller wondered, and where do *I* get off? And without knowing what he was up to quite suddenly relented. He would hear the man out. He would promise nothing but he would hear him out. That was the least he could do.

"What?" Miller asked. "What do you want?"

"To have the lend of your key," Félix Rey said.

"My key? What key?"

"To here," said Rey, "the key to here." He waved his arm about.

"But it isn't my key," Miller said. "It belongs to the Foundation. I have to return it."

"The *lend*," Rey said, "the *lend*. I will have it duplicated. Before the sun has arose I will bring it back. You shall have it in your hand before you start back for Indy. I will guarantee for this, Monsieur Sir." He looked closely at Miller. "I shall leave—ooh la la—L'Arlésienne behind as my pledge. Is this agreeable, Madame Ginoux?"

"*Très* agreeable."

"But *why*?" Miller asked.

"Have I not said you of our little group? Have I not very here speak of the Club of the Portraits of the Descendants of the People Painted by Vincent Van Gogh? You have seen for your eyes on the group photograph. On there is the peasant, Patience Escalier. On there are the Roulins—— Joseph, Berceuse, Armand, and Camille. On there is the Zouave whom you have know. And the incomparable Madame Ginoux. As well as your humble servant, myself, Felix Rey. Here is the venue of the portraitees. For this is the key needed."

"Nonsense," Miller said, "go to the public garden, why don't you?"

"In winter in the public garden the mistral blows through. It could kill the peasant, old Patience Escalier."

"Go in summer to Les Alyscamps," Miller said. "Meet by the Trinquetaille Bridge."

"Monsieur, here is only the proper venue. You know it, I know it," the doctor said with some dignity. And then, with none at all, he said once again that he'd leave Madame Ginoux as his pledge.

"I'm sorry," said Miller and, to his surprise, he genuinely was. "Come," he said, "I'll go downstairs with you."

That night he couldn't sleep. He laid out his clothes for the morning, stripped down, and got into the bed, but within minutes, realizing that he didn't even desire sleep, he got out of bed again and put on the clothes in which he'd be traveling back to America. It wasn't that he was not drowsy—— nor so very wide awake. It was rather a question of how interesting it had all been, how very interesting it still was. It wasn't a question of happiness. Happiness (or unhappiness either) was not part of the equation. A lot of it had to do with being abroad, but he still didn't mean geography. He'd been abroad in the sense of some surrounding or enveloping substance, abroad, he meant, in *conditions*. The way men were abroad, say, in airplanes, or in submarines fathoms, leagues, beneath the surface of the sea. On this last night in Arles he was just too interested to sleep.

He made the bed he had so briefly untidied. He fluffed the yellow pillow slips, turned down the yellow top sheet over the red blanket, and then tucked the blanket tight about the mattress. He brought his parcels and PC, suitcase and garment bag over by the piano bench in front of the fourth wall and sat down to study the room from the very place where Van Gogh must have been when he painted it. He'd done this before, of course. He remembered telling Hartshine about it. But he'd never studied it at night before, in the light given off by the room's puny overhead bulb. The color values were so very different. It was not at all like looking at a bad reproduction. It was more like looking at an entirely different painting, a work of genius, and immensely interesting.

Then, toward dawn, but while it was still dark out—if anything he was more wide awake than ever—Miller decided to turn off the light. Low as the light had been, his eyes still had to adjust to this new black dark. What he saw now, the almost colorless configuration of shapes and masses, made a different and still stranger picture and, as dawn came and the light turned milky, and then, as the sun rose higher and the room experienced its gradual yellowing, it seemed almost to go through a process of queer simultaneity, of aging and renewal at once.

It was time to go. He had to cross the square to Number 30, drop off his key (without, he hoped, having to see Rita, or Hartshine, or, for that matter, anyone he knew), and then wait out in front of the inn for the taxi he'd arranged to pick him up to take him to the train station. He looked around Van Gogh's room at Arles one last time and took up his things to bring them down with him.

There, in the hallway, he was able to see the still unpainted rooms and, just for a second, rendering them with
his own poor unrendering eyes, Miller imagined he could
see paintings on all the blank, colorless walls of Van Gogh's
yellow house—— the gorgeous asparagus he'd eaten in
Cannes topped with their two, perfectly made eggs, his
marvelous iced coffee the brown-black color of roots and
bears. But rendering, too, the canceled flowers and the unsold fruit; the men and women dancing in the hotel, Inga
Basset's thigh insinuated between Jesus Hans's legs; the
brother-in-law with his carton of spoiling produce. Rendering everything unrendered, all the still lifes and unpainted
masterpieces of Cannes—— what shot by his all-but-shut
eyelids on the bus and, spilling over onto the unpainted
fourth wall of Van Gogh's room at Arles, the ghost Rey,
and the ghost Zouave, and the ghost Ginoux, and all the
other ghosts, the beautiful ruin of the world he couldn't
quite catch, like everything else he couldn't quite catch,
everything untranslated and left unsyntaxed in his inade-
quate French, the guts, the soul, the brains and eyes, all
the inner extremities and other moving parts of vision, of
vision.